The
Thousand
Eyes

Books by A. K. Larkwood

The Unspoken Name

The Thousand Eyes

The
Thousand
Eyes

A. K. Larkwood

TOR

A TOM DOHERTY ASSOCIATES BOOK · NEW YORK

THE THOUSAND EYES

Copyright © 2022 by A. K. Larkwood

A Tor Book
Published by Tom Doherty Associates
120 Broadway
New York, NY 10271

www.tor-forge.com

Tor® is a registered trademark of Macmillan Publishing Group, LLC.

The Library of Congress Cataloging-in-Publication Data is available upon request.

ISBN 978-1-250-23894-8 (hardcover)
ISBN 978-1-250-23893-1(ebook)

Our books may be purchased in bulk for promotional, educational, or business use. Please contact your local bookseller or the Macmillan Corporate and Premium Sales Department at 1-800-221-7945, extension 5442, or by email at MacmillanSpecialMarkets@macmillan.com.

First Edition: 2022

Printed in the United States of America

0 9 8 7 6 5 4 3 2 1

to Daphne and Juno

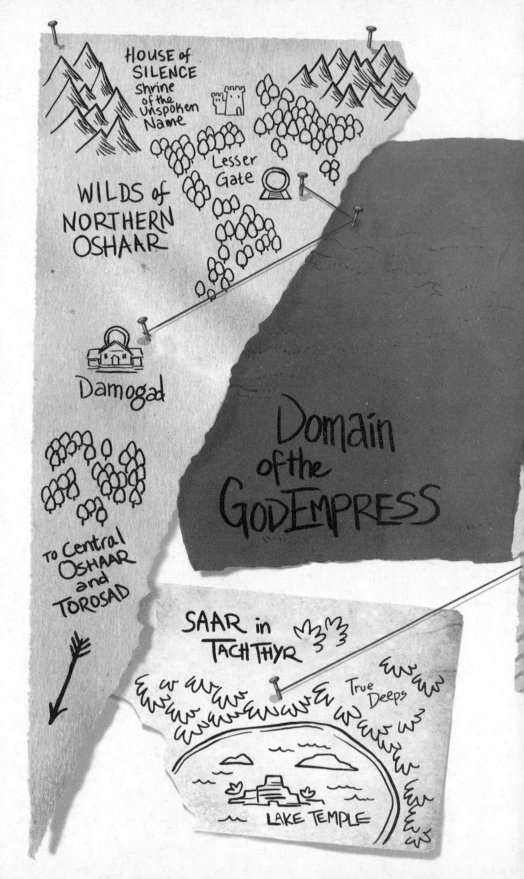

IMPERIAL QARSAZH

to NORTHERN PROVINCES

QARADOUN

Bay of Qaradoun

Cricket Station

the TRAITOR'S GRAVE

RELIC WORLD

PEACOCK GATE

ECHENTYR

THOUSAND EYES HATCHERY

THE WITHERED CITY

Those Persons Involved

Csorwe

A swordswoman of Oshaar, who grew up among the cult of the Unspoken One at the House of Silence. After escaping her fate as the Chosen Bride, she trained as the right hand of the wizard Belthandros Sethennai, but left his service two years ago to find a new life with Shuthmili.

Qanwa Shuthmili

A renegade scholar-mage from the Empire of Qarsazh. Shuthmili was brought up in the School of Aptitude, and was ordered to surrender herself to one of the military hive-minds of the Imperial Quincuriate. Instead, she fled her homeland with Csorwe at her side.

Talasseres Charossa

Csorwe's ex-colleague and rival, a young nobleman from the city of Tlaanthothe, where he is best known as a family disappointment and writer of unpleasant notes. He broke off a brief affair with Belthandros Sethennai two years ago, and truly believes he is over it.

Oranna

The former librarian of the House of Silence. Once romantically involved with Belthandros Sethennai, now single-minded in religious fervour, she has abandoned the cult to follow her devotion to the Unspoken wherever it may lead. An unreliable friend to some and an inconstant enemy to most.

Belthandros Sethennai, also known as Pentravesse

Chancellor of Tlaanthothe. Csorwe and Tal's former employer. An immortal wizard of exceeding power and, as it turned out, a living incarnation of the serpent goddess Iriskavaal. He carved out his own heart and now keeps it in an ornate reliquary as part of his bargain with her.

Atharaisse

A giant serpent who befriended Csorwe during their imprisonment by the warlord General Psamag. A scion of the fallen serpent empire of Echentyr.

ZINANDOUR, *Dragon of Qarsazh, the Traitor*

goddess of things hidden and things decaying, the flame that devours

Shuthmili's patron divinity, imprisoned in the void for millennia as punishment for ancient atrocities. It is said that she seeks a mortal vessel through whom she can return.

THE UNSPOKEN ONE

who knows all that is dead, and all that is dust, and all that is to come

Oranna's patron divinity, sleeping within its shrine in the mountains above the House of Silence. Reputed to demand the sacrifice of a Chosen Bride every fourteen years.

IRISKAVAAL, *Lady of the Thousand Eyes*

sovereign of all space and time, she who withered Echentyr

Sethennai's patron divinity, who once ruled over the serpent empire of Echentyr as God-Empress. Her being was splintered into many fragments when her own people rose against her. She laid waste to her entire territory, surviving the carnage through her incarnation as Belthandros Sethennai.

ALSO

DR. ILVER TVELUJAN, a Historian

CHERENTHISSE, an officer of the Thousand Eyes

NIRANTHOS CHAROSSA, Tal's older brother

NIRANTHE CHAROSSA, Tal's mother

CWEREN, Prioress of the House of Silence

KELEIROS LENARAI, a secretary and intelligencer

TSEREG, a fugitive

Pronunciation Guide

Oshaarun

CSORWE: *ksor-way*

CWEREN: *cweh-ren*

ORANNA: *o-ran-uh*

TSEREG: *tseh-reg*

Echentyri

IRISKAVAAL: *ih-riss-kuh-vahl*

ATHARAISSE: *ath-uh-rai-seh*

CHERENTHISSE: *chen-ren-tiss-eh*

THALARISSE: *tha-la-riss-eh*

PENTRAVESSE: *pen-tra-vess-eh*

Tlaanthothei

TALASSERES CHAROSSA: *tal-uh-seh-rez cha-ross-uh*

NIRANTHOS: *nee-ran-thos*

NIRANTHE: *nee-ran-thee*

BELTHANDROS SETHENNAI: *bel-than-dros seh-then-ai*

KELEIROS LENARAI: *kel-ey-ros leh-nar-ai*

Qarsazhi

QANWA SHUTHMILI: *kan-wuh shuth-mee-lee*

THURYA MISHARI: *thur-yuh mee-shah-ree*

ZINANDOUR: *zin-and-or*

I

The Mantle of Divinity

The forest is dust, the river is dust,
      for their ruination has come.
The gardens are dust, the orchards are dust,
      for the day of ruination has come.
In the shining city the weepers fall silent,
      for ruination is upon us.

"Lament for the Fall of Echentyr," from *The Record of Isjesse*

1

The Hatchery

IN ANCIENT DAYS, all this world was veiled by a green wood. Now tree trunks scatter the land like bones and dead cities fall to ruin beneath a dull unseeing sky.

Someday even they will be gone. But dust is not the only thing that lingers here. Along a certain mountain ridge, the stumps of forgotten beacons trace a path for ships to follow, up to the belly of a volcanic crater which rests among the mountains like a kettle among coals. Resting in that crater is the last bright thing that remains in this world, a shining mineral eye among the debris: the great tiled dome of an Echentyri hatchery complex.

The serpent conquerors built this place long ago, to incubate their successors. Now, amid the desolation of their empire, the hatchery tiles still gleam, scattering the sun's glare into a thousand dancing points.

The hatchery is still and quiet but not altogether empty. The past sleeps soundly in these halls, and may yet wake.

The first person to set eyes upon the hatchery in three thousand years was one Qanwa Shuthmili, sitting in the cockpit of a little hired ship as it soared above the ridge.

The corpse of a world should have been a sad and terrible thing to see, but Shuthmili clung to the rail of the cutter and laughed in triumph. Her unbraided hair streamed behind her like a black pennant, and she bared her teeth against the wind as if she might take a bite of it.

She hugged her knees in triumph and turned to Csorwe, beside her in the pilot's seat.

"There!" she said. "My goodness, it's really all still there, the dome and everything, the whole complex!"

"You've got a whole complex," said Tal, who had his feet propped up on the back of Csorwe's seat despite her regular objections. Even he sounded pleased, and so he should, because their business depended on success, and even if you didn't care about ancient history, the fact that the hatchery complex really *was* here meant they were probably going to get paid.

Csorwe took them in, landing the cutter with a bump. The crater was every bit as deserted as it seemed, a shallow bowl of dull stone sheltering the complex. The hatchery was even bigger than it had looked from the air, a cathedral of white marble and blue tile. The blue dome looked more like the sky than the actual sky overhead, which was a streaky yellow-grey.

The people of lost Echentyr had been giant serpents, and their buildings were all on a scale to match. The arch in the wall of the complex was fifty feet high. Beyond its cool shadow, sunlight pooled in a courtyard just as enormous.

"Even the Survey Office didn't know this place existed," said Shuthmili. "We might be the first people to walk here since the fall of Echentyr."

"That never gets old for you, does it?" said Csorwe with affection, as she shouldered her backpack.

"I can't believe nobody's looted this place," said Tal, running his fingertips over the tiled wall. The tiles were a brilliant sea-blue, minutely patterned with a design of interlocking spirals. "Even these would sell," he added, tapping one. "People would love it. Do up your dining room with some genuine snake rubbish."

Tal was Csorwe's oldest friend and oldest enemy. Next to each other they made a perfect contrast: Csorwe was only just taller than Shuthmili, square and compact; Tal was a tall, stringy Tlaanthothei with twitchy petal-shaped ears.

"We aren't looters, we're surveyors," said Shuthmili. She had shed a lot of scruples, but some of them really stuck. "We sell maps."

"To looters," said Tal. "It's not our fault looting is all we know."

"It's not—they're *scholars*—oh, put a lid on it, Talasseres," she said, seeing that Tal was grinning at her. "It's not *my* fault you have a lack of transferrable skills."

She consoled herself that the ruined Echentyri colony worlds were famously sparse pickings for looters anyway: acres of dust and damage, with usually nothing to show for it but a few clay cylinders and a scattering of serpent bones.

"People don't like stealing from Echentyri worlds, anyway," said Csorwe, flicking Tal in the shoulder as she passed him. "You heard them back on Cricket Station. We're courting a horrible snake curse just visiting here."

"Don't let the professor hear you," said Tal.

"I am fairly certain Professor Tvelujan would think a horrible snake curse was the most exciting thing that had ever happened to her," said Shuthmili.

"Speak of the devil," muttered Tal, as Professor Tvelujan's minuscule cutter landed beside theirs. The engine puttered out, engulfed by the immense, encompassing silence of the dead world.

Tvelujan was their client, an elderly historian from a university in distant Tarasen. She wore a hat with a translucent veil to shield her bone-white hair and skin from the sun. As she approached them, she walked with the slow swimming gait of one enchanted, and the veil billowed behind her like the mantle of a jellyfish.

"All right, Professor? Need a hand?" said Csorwe, who generally treated Tvelujan with the patient, resigned cheerfulness one might use on a fragile relative.

"No assistance needed," said Tvelujan, in her small quiet voice. It was odd for a client to want to join them—their job was to chart the place and squash any obvious threats, to make way for the researchers who would follow—but Tvelujan's devotion to her subject came before all else. "The most wonderful. An intact hatchery. Never have I imagined it." Her Tarasene accent became more marked when she was emotional, though she still spoke in little more than a whisper.

Shuthmili checked through her notebooks, while Tal and Csorwe counted off their provisions. They always carried more than they needed, since there was nothing growing and no running water in the dead world.

Tvelujan, meanwhile, had her own rituals to conduct. Before they entered the hatchery proper, she knelt on the stones of the courtyard and poured out an offering of scented oil, murmuring prayers in the sibilant language of Echentyr.

Shuthmili knew the serpent language well enough to understand most of it: *Blessed Lady Iriskavaal, forgive us our boldness, we come to you as supplicants.*

"Wouldn't want to miss an opportunity to suck up to our old friend the snake goddess," muttered Tal.

They were all somewhat superstitious about saying the name of Iriskavaal out loud. By now they had visited countless Echentyri relic worlds. They had even found their way back to the homeworld, where the dry bones of innumerable serpents lay curled in dust. They had searched in the dead city, in the Royal Library and the ancient palaces. All the same, you never forgot who had ruled in these places, and who had laid them waste.

Three thousand years ago, the serpent goddess had destroyed her own territories in vengeance for a grand betrayal, and died. It was her curse which had blighted this world and dozens of others.

For most of her life, Shuthmili had believed that was the whole story. Iriskavaal was an extinct goddess. Her throne had been shattered, and she had faded from history along with the whole empire of Echentyr.

Two years ago, all three of them had learned better. Iriskavaal had cheated death, and taken a mortal vessel. Belthandros Sethennai still ruled over his city, far from here. As far as they had heard, he was still perfectly contented playing at being Chancellor of Tlaanthothe. If any of the Tlaanthothei had figured out what he really was, nobody was talking about it.

Shuthmili put it out of her mind. In every way that mattered, he had no part in their lives now. It had been two years since the others had left his employment. The past—Csorwe's and Tal's lives as Belthandros' sword-hands, Shuthmili's service to the Church of Qarsazh—felt less real day by day.

Tvelujan finished her prayers and drifted on across the courtyard to the door of the main hatchery building. It was circular, almost as big as a maze-gate, and composed of many interlocking metal plates, shining like a second sun. It was almost hard to look at directly, not that that stopped Tvelujan, who gazed up at it with dizzy reverence in her large grey eyes.

Shuthmili rolled up her sleeves. She could almost see the power that flowed within the door, the great sigils and countersigils which formed its mechanism. She had taught herself to read the Echentyri language as well as almost anyone, but their magic was still alien, always more of a challenge than it needed to be. Working on their devices made her feel like an ant exploring the interior of a clock. The trouble was that there were no Echentyri mages left—except Sethennai, maybe, and she could hardly ask him.

She retrieved her gauntlets from inside her jacket and pulled them on, reflecting, not for the first time, that they fit her better than ever. Csorwe had taken the gauntlets from Belthandros Sethennai, as a layer of protection to shield her from magic's corrosive effects. When she had first put them on, they had been too big, uncomfortably reminiscent of the man who made them. Now, two years later, they were a second skin.

She positioned herself opposite the door, too careful to actually touch the surface. It was never the obvious trap that got you, after all. By now they had encountered enough doors which belched fire or seeped poison that it would be tremendously embarrassing to be caught out in front of Tal.

She closed her eyes and let her perception sink into the mechanism of the door. She floated through it, watching how one part of the great lock fit with the next.

People are like locks, her aunt had used to say. But locks were also like people. Sometimes they just needed a little coaxing.

As she rummaged around looking for the control sigil, she felt the familiar creeping shadow, and her goddess spoke to her.

THERE YOU ARE, SHUTHMILI, said the lady Zinandour. Her voice was as soft and intrusive as someone lightly touching the back of Shuthmili's head.

Not now, said Shuthmili, swallowing her unease, *I'm busy.* Now was not the time. This was going to be a good day. There was a moment of reluctance, then Shuthmili gathered her focus and Zinandour's presence dispersed like petals on the wind.

There was the sigil she'd been looking for, the axle holding the rest together. She erased it, and the echoes of its dissolution rippled out through the rest of the mechanism. The door opened as sweetly as if it were welcoming them inside, without even a wisp of smoke.

"All good?" said Csorwe, unable to hide the faint shadow of concern. Csorwe knew the risks of magic almost as well as Shuthmili did herself. Channelling the power of a divinity damaged the mortal mind and body in infinite small ways—usually minor, but occasionally not—and Shuthmili's goddess was not a gentle one.

"I think I'll live," said Shuthmili. "And it worked, didn't it?"

The metal plates of the door had slid away into the frame, revealing an immense chamber beyond. Much of it was occupied by a tiled pool the size of a small lake, now dry, with raw pitted stone at the bottom. The apex of the dome overhead had been glass-paned once, and now it was a lattice open to the sky, casting a fishnet shadow across the empty pool. Colonnades ran along the edges of the chamber, with more corridors branching off from them. It all reminded Shuthmili a little of a bathhouse.

"Extraordinary," breathed Tvelujan, clasping her pale hands in front of her. "Never was there another empire like it. Not even your people."

Shuthmili slightly resented this—she was no part of Qarsazh's imperial ambitions these days—but it would have been unkind to squash Tvelujan in her state of rapture.

The four of them approached the edge of the pool. Tvelujan moved slowly, as though this was a sacred place. Tal slouched along behind them, although Shuthmili knew him well enough by now to recognise that all that indifference was to cover up the fact he was watching their backs. Tal had run into Csorwe and Shuthmili the year before last, when all three of them were on Cricket Station looking for work. The decision to go into business together had been an idea born of one too many algae beers in the canteen, and Shuthmili was amazed that the partnership had held together as well as it did.

"A hot spring, here," said Tvelujan, gesturing at the bottom of the pool. "To keep eggs warm. Before rank allocation."

Csorwe raised an eyebrow.

"The Echentyri sorted their eggs by caste and rank before they hatched. They would have loved it back in Qarsazh," said Shuthmili, feeling she should apologise either for Echentyr or for her homeland. How would it have been, to hatch from an egg and have your whole destiny unroll before you, written out before you ever opened your eyes? Actually, Shuthmili thought she could imagine it very well.

"Very efficient system," said Tvelujan softly. "Never were their warriors matched in all the Maze of Echoes. In seven days only, the Lady of the Thousand Eyes subdued Oshaar. Some things in this world you have to respect."

Csorwe, clearly marked as Oshaaru by her grey skin and her tusks, rolled her eyes.

"I thought that was a myth," said Tal, all innocence. "I mean, how would a big snake even hold a sword? Makes you think."

Tvelujan did not deign to answer, but Csorwe grinned behind her back. It was one of the continued marvels of Shuthmili's life that Csorwe and Tal got along all right these days, at least when they were out on a job. When they got back to the apartment, it would be right back to whether it was Tal's turn to wash the dishes and whether Csorwe had been poaching from Tal's liquor cabinet, but when they were working, a fragile ceasefire held.

They left the main chamber and began charting the smaller corridors. The place was a labyrinth, coiled in on itself. The sunlight lay like bolts of white silk across the tiles, and a soft breeze blew in through open windows. Tvelujan was in her element, drifting from one inscription to another and occasionally murmuring about old Echentyri victories.

Most of the furniture and equipment in the hatchery had long ago turned to dust, and what was left didn't mean much: metal and ceramic vessels, inscribed tablets and cylinders which would take several days to decipher. Shuthmili glanced over them, trying to figure out which might be worth translating. Later on, Tvelujan's team would return to gather up any that looked promising, but Shuthmili suspected they would just be accounts and inventories.

The only unexpected thing was the decoration. Most of the Echentyri ruins Shuthmili had seen were covered with friezes, ancient triumphs and ceremonies in fresco or bas-relief. The hatchery was no different, except in its subject matter. Instead of serpent queens and heroes, the walls of the hatchery were blazoned with curious hybrids: women with the heads or tails of snakes, crowned snakes with five-fingered hands grasping weapons. Which answered Tal's question, but raised several in its place.

"Have you seen anything like this before? Do you know who they are?" said Shuthmili to Tvelujan. It struck her as odd, eerie even. Back in the day, the Echentyri had not really believed in other worlds or foreign peoples—there were only Echentyri worlds which had not yet been conquered and vassals awaiting subjugation. Most of the friezes depicted the serpents' two-legged vassals as tiny stick figures, anonymous background swarms at work on the latest royal mausoleum. The halfway creatures in the friezes would surely have been a strange blasphemy—and yet some of them wore the mantles and garlands of Echentyri nobility.

Tvelujan frowned. "The Thousand Eyes, perhaps."

"You mean—er, Iriskavaal?" said Shuthmili, not wanting to wound Tvelujan's religious sensibilities but unsure how else to put it. She had always assumed Iriskavaal's title was just a reference to the way she was always sculpted, with eyes running down her body like gems.

"No," said Tvelujan, brushing her fingertips over one of the friezes, "though they were named for her, I believe. The splendid honour guard of the Lady of the Thousand Eyes. But this is strange, to show them like this. Yes, certainly it is curious."

"You know what else is strange?" said Tal, kicking at a heap of potsherds in a way that made Shuthmili's archaeological training cry out for justice. "The weird lack of skeletons in here. Normally you can't move for old snake bones."

"Maybe this place was out of commission," said Csorwe.

"We're pretty far from Echentyr and the central worlds," said Shuthmili, putting aside the friezes for the moment. "The curse spread outwards from the capitol world. If they had some warning here, they could have evacuated."

She could imagine the scene. Hundreds of Echentyri rushing for their ships, trying to outrun the end of their world. Surely they would have made sure the eggs were loaded first. And how would it have felt, to know that their goddess had turned on them? She almost preferred to think they had been vaporised without realising it.

At the end of one corridor, they found a small staircase descending, which was unusual, both because the Echentyri had favoured smooth inclines and because it was so narrow that the three of them had to go in single file. The corridor at the bottom was similarly small, and lined with small doors.

"What is this, some kind of maintenance duct?" said Csorwe.

"Ah . . ." said Shuthmili. "No. I don't think so." She peered round the nearest door, confirming her suspicions. The room beyond was long and low-ceilinged, windowless, with walls of bare stone. Most of the furniture had collapsed, but they could make out the rough outline of what was probably a line of cots.

"The servants' quarters," said Tvelujan, with undiminished excitement. "Many hatchlings. Many servants."

Not much light filtered down from above, so it was hard to see detail, but there were curled shadows on some of the cots.

"If they evacuated, I guess they didn't take the staff," said Tal, with a grimace.

Shuthmili shivered and drew back. The Echentyri had conquered countless worlds in their ascendancy, and made vassals of their people. And now these crescents of pale residue were all that was left of them. Her earlier buoyant mood faded, and she reminded herself why she did this work: not only to know the past but to memorialise it. Nobody else had borne witness to these dead.

Csorwe was very quiet. Head down, shoulders squared.

"Tvelujan?" Shuthmili said, hanging back with her.

Csorwe laughed, trying to play it off. "Always gives me a look when she talks about the conquest of Oshaar. I haven't lived in Oshaar since I was fourteen. It's weird."

Shuthmili reached for her hand and squeezed it, knowing how rare it was that Csorwe would admit to anything upsetting her.

"There are people like that in Qarsazh," said Shuthmili. "Glorious Precursor heritage and so on. All the kind of people who make me glad that you and Tal have taught me the useful vocabulary word *shitlord*."

"Tvelujan's not that bad. It's just . . . *some things in this world you have to respect?*" said Csorwe, curling her lip.

"Yes, well, I can tell you about some of them later, if you like," said Shuthmili, raising an eyebrow. It suddenly felt imperative to make Csorwe laugh, and flirting usually worked.

"Wow," said Csorwe, but she grinned.

"Do you not respect me, Csorwe?" said Shuthmili, lifting her chin and schooling her features. "That's very disappointing—"

Csorwe was clearly trying hard not to laugh. "Shh, you are *asking* for a horrible snake curse—"

Csorwe broke off as Tal came up the stairs. Shuthmili wondered whether Tvelujan had been getting to him too, although Tal was practically immune to insult. He certainly looked tense, but it was a vigilant tension. His ears had pricked up like those of a cat that hears something behind the wainscot.

"You hear that?" he said—to Csorwe, not to Shuthmili, one of those occasional reminders that these two had been working together, or at least in proximity, for years before Shuthmili had ever come onto the scene.

Csorwe nodded, looking past Shuthmili to a round archway that opened onto another corridor. She had gone tense in a different way, tightly coiled as the spring of a bolt-thrower.

Now Shuthmili heard it too. In the distance was the sound of water. A pleasant gurgling sound, like a stream or a spring, rippling through the halls. It took Shuthmili a moment to realise what was worrying about that. There shouldn't have been running water left anywhere on the surface of this world.

They fetched Tvelujan, who listened with her head cocked for half a minute, frowning.

"Perhaps the oracle pool," she said suddenly. Her eyes widened, and she strode briskly off toward the direction of the sound.

Csorwe made a choked noise and ran after her. Tal and Shuthmili followed.

The archway that led to the chapel was ornately carved with a pattern of interlocking coils. The room beyond was immense but windowless, as dim as the rest of the hatchery was airy and bright. As they stepped inside, there was a moment when Shuthmili was convinced there was someone else inside, as though she felt the breath of some huge creature on her bare skin—and then there was a kind of release, and the room lit up.

Wardlights gleamed into life, like rivers seen from the air on a clear night, silvery-pale and meandering. They coiled around columns which reached from floor to high ceiling up and down the length of the chapel. On the wall was a frieze of Iriskavaal herself, depicted in light: a hooded snake with many eyes, crowned in stars. Even here the goddess was surrounded by the strange snake-tailed people. They were carved with the same delicacy as the goddess herself, plaited hair and finely muscled shoulders, smooth scales and forked tongues all as one.

Tal muttered uneasily. The misty light turned his dark skin to a ghostly opal as he stalked into the room, hand on the hilt of his sword.

Shuthmili tried to get Tvelujan's attention to ask her about the friezes, but she—along with Csorwe—was staring at the platform in the centre of the chapel.

It was surrounded by a deep channel. The channel ran with clear water that glowed from within, illuminated by wardlights set into its base. On the platform itself was a great pale coiled object, white and translucent as fine parchment.

Even if Shuthmili hadn't been to the ruins of Echentyr, she would have known what she was seeing: the shed skin of a snake the size of a cart-horse.

Lying among the coils of dry skin was a naked woman.

"I was right. One of the Thousand Eyes," said Tvelujan, breaking their silence. She took off her sun hat and clasped it respectfully before her. Shuthmili could have laughed if not for the strangeness of the moment.

The woman in the circle was sparely muscled and tall, curled into a tight crescent, with long pale hair hiding her face. She was covered in a layer of dust that made her look as though she might have been carved from stone. She must have been here for years. Hundreds of years, perhaps.

Despite all this, Shuthmili could see her ribs rise and fall slightly. She was alive.

Shuthmili reached out with her magic, trying to figure out how this had happened.

There was a binding circle in the water, wrought with the usual complicated Echentyri logic. It was maddeningly readable, like a page of text seen through steamed glass. It itched at her. She wanted to wipe it clean, to properly understand how it worked.

She channelled a spark of power, and there was Zinandour, as usual—

SHUTHMILI, LISTEN TO ME—

Not now, she thought, in irritation more than alarm.

The circle described an area of stillness. A holding place. It was astonishing that it had lasted so long. It was featherlight, no more substantial than a ring of dust on a window ledge.

Careful, she told herself, and then Tal's voice shattered the silence:

"What the *fuck,* Professor!"

Tvelujan had stepped onto the platform. She knelt beside the sleeping woman and touched her shoulder.

"Wait, no!" said Shuthmili, understanding too late. The binding circle trembled and collapsed, dispersing in the water with a fading glimmer of light.

The strange woman was awake and on her feet before any of them could blink. In another instant, she had Tvelujan by the throat.

"Wait—" said Shuthmili, but there was a horrible crack of bone snapping and Tvelujan slid limply to the ground.

Csorwe and Tal drew their swords.

The stranger stood up very straight, trembling and wild-eyed. Her skin was a faded gold, a shade lighter than Shuthmili's own olive-brown complexion. Her eyes were pale grey, and a red spark burnt within them, like an ember half buried in ash.

Her hands clawed, clenched, loosened in front of her face, and she looked down at them with her head to one side as if they were alien things. When she spoke, it was in a voice like the hiss of wind on sand.

"Prey-servants," she said. "You are not of the hatchery. What are you doing here? Where are your uniforms? Is the evacuation complete? I must make contact with my superiors."

Shuthmili's breath caught. She must be imagining it. It couldn't be—but then, Csorwe had once met a serpent who said she had come from Echentyr. Perhaps it was possible. Echentyr had possessed many strange magics which had been forgotten. If another living Echentyri citizen had been preserved, somehow—

Shuthmili had sometimes wondered what she might say if it ever happened that she encountered some ancient being from the former world. She had not imagined that it would be "Pardon me?"

"You killed Tvelujan," said Csorwe, who understood what was happening just as quickly, albeit from a different angle. "Why shouldn't we kill you?"

The stranger's jaw worked. "I believed she meant to attack me."

The softness of her voice was willed, not natural. "I require assistance. One of you, go now and fetch your master. Whose servants *are* you?"

"Nobody's," Tal started to say.

"By the grace of the Empress, if none of you can talk sense, where is the nearest of my own kind?"

"What are you talking about?" said Tal.

But Shuthmili thought she was starting to understand. "Those friezes . . ." she said. Tal and Csorwe didn't take their eyes off the stranger, but she could sense Tal rolling his eyes. "They must have been meant to show some kind of transformation . . ."

The stranger blinked and blinked again, her mouth opening and closing as if in unconscious imitation of a serpent's flickering tongue. "You," she said. "Practitioner. Of what school are you?"

Oh, Mother of Cities, she thought. *Of course. If she is from Echentyr, she doesn't know what's happened.*

"Ma'am, I am an Adept of Qarsazh," said Shuthmili, and stalled. This would mean nothing to an Echentyri, and it wasn't even true anymore.

The serpent-stranger shook her head, as if she should have known this was a futile line of enquiry. "Very well. I am Cherenthisse of the Thousand Eyes. I require your immediate assistance, in the name of the blessed God-Empress."

Cherenthisse stepped down from the platform, a little unsteady on her feet. Csorwe and Tal moved to block her path.

"Wait—" said Shuthmili. "We should talk to her."

"Don't see why," said Tal, very indignant for someone who hadn't liked Tvelujan all that much.

Cherenthisse looked down at the crumpled body on the platform. Tvelujan's veiled sun hat had fallen into the channel, and the water turned the light straw the colour of earth.

"A mistake," said Cherenthisse. "She ought not to have touched me."

"Does she look like she's about to attack us?" said Shuthmili. Csorwe lowered her sword a fraction, and after a pause, Tal did the same.

Cherenthisse nodded and strode past them before Shuthmili could stop her.

She emerged from the chamber into the huge empty corridor, where cracked pottery lay in pieces and a vacant window looked out on the wounded sky.

Cherenthisse stopped abruptly, staring at the ruin of the hatchery. "Explain," she said.

In the silence they could hear the wind blowing outside. Despite the bright sunlight, it was a desolate sound.

"Answer me!" said Cherenthisse. "What became of the evacuation ship? How long was I held in the circle?"

Shuthmili swallowed, and said:

"More than three thousand years."

Cherenthisse bore Shuthmili's explanation in unbending silence. When Shuthmili finished speaking, she bowed her head, and the silence went on for several excruciating seconds.

"I see," said Cherenthisse at last. "All is lost, then. We have been punished for our ingratitude." Her voice was strained, crackling and snapping like burning twigs. She fell to her knees, as if she had reached the limit of her endurance, and then listed to one side and lay on the floor, curled up like a weeping child.

"I suppose we should give her a moment," said Shuthmili, drawing Csorwe and Tal aside into an alcove.

"I don't like this," said Csorwe. Which was an understatement if you asked Shuthmili, but coming from Csorwe it meant *I think this is dangerous and we should get out of here.*

"What, you mean just leave her?" said Shuthmili. "We can't!"

"I don't think she's a friend," said Csorwe.

"I'm pretty sure she's one of them—an Echentyri, I mean—" said Shuthmili. "Some kind of shape-changer. I didn't know that was even possible."

"Oh, great, that makes me feel a lot better," said Tal. "You know, I was worried about how she just snapped Tvelujan's neck like it was nothing, but if she's an *ancient shape-changing serpent,* let's let bygones be bygones—"

"Hate to say it, but I think I'm with Tal on this one," said Csorwe.

"I thought Atharaisse was friendly to you, back in Psamag's fortress," said Shuthmili.

"Yeah, but—" said Csorwe.

"I was there too, you know, and she definitely also ate people," said Tal. His expression twisted. Shuthmili still didn't know exactly what had happened to either of them in the fortress. They didn't talk about it; it seemed to be one of the few topics that was considered off-limits.

"But think of what she could tell us! Time does nothing but take from us," said Shuthmili, struggling to explain how it had been, working on endless Precursor ruins, how ancient things flowed through your hands like water. "I thought it was all lost—so much of it is lost—and it's never going to come again, but if one of the Echentyri has survived all this time—it is a gift."

If this Cherenthisse had lived out the dust of her world and the ruin of her cities, it would be more than a gift. It would be an instant of unmerited and unimagined grace.

"What about the university?" said Tal. "Could we just send her back instead of Tvelujan?"

"What, you think they won't notice?" said Csorwe, her lip curling.

"No, you dolt, I was thinking they might be into it," said Tal. "If they're big snake fans like Tvelujan was."

"I'll think of something to do with her," said Shuthmili. She really didn't look forward to telling the university department what had happened to their professor, right under Shuthmili's nose. She would be lucky if all it did was wreck her professional reputation. If she was really unlucky, they might tip off the Qarsazhi Inquisitorate that their rogue Adept was apparently out and about in company with an ancient shape-changing serpent. "Maybe there's a way to help her."

"You want to just . . . take her back to Cricket Station?" said Csorwe.

"I tell you what, she's not staying in *my* room—" said Tal.

"I don't see what else we can do," said Shuthmili. "If we leave her here, she'll die. She's completely alone. I think we have a responsibility."

This swayed Csorwe as nothing else had. She nodded.

"Well, shit," said Tal. "I guess this means we're not going to get paid."

2

Midsummer's Eve

THE EVE OF the Feast of Midsummer was shaping up as one of the worst parties of Tal Charossa's life, even before the School of Transcendence exploded.

A week had passed since their doomed hatchery trip, and Tal was back in Tlaanthothe for one reason only, which was that Professor Tvelujan's university had refused to pay them, and they badly needed money.

The enormous roof garden of his mother's mansion was rammed with crowds of Charossai, cousins and second cousins all talking over one another. You could tell who was a blood relation because all Tal's family were alike, thin and sharp like an especially self-satisfied box of pencils. The ones who were there by marriage looked bleak and puzzled.

From the garden you could see out over the whole city of Tlaanthothe. All the marble townhouses overflowed with flowers, and between them the wide streets were already crowded with festival stalls. In the squares, the priesthood of the Siren were arranging the city's offerings for tomorrow's festivities. On all sides there was no getting away from it.

Before he found his mother, he almost tripped over someone he recognised as the particularly horrible cousin Essanthi.

"Well, well, Talasseres," said Essanthi, trampling through the awkward silence with relish. "Very rare to see you these days," they added, with the suggestion that Tal was an unusual infectious disease, a puzzle to medicine.

"Yeah, it's been a while," he said. Tal would have had no intention of attending, but his mother had written to invite him to her Midsummer's Eve party, and his brother Niranthos had followed up with a more strongly worded letter to the effect that Tal had better attend if he ever hoped to draw his allowance from the Charossa treasury again.

"Still working for Chancellor Sethennai?" said Essanthi.

Tal had known someone would ask him at some point, but he hadn't thought it would come up immediately. Three years ago he had spent the festival working security up at the Chancellor's Palace, in his former life as Chancellor Sethennai's bodyguard. Two years ago he'd missed the festival because he'd spent several months dead drunk on a beach after quitting Sethennai's employment.

"Not so much," he said.

"That's the trouble with the city these days," said Essanthi, who always sounded as though they were about one hundred years old despite being the same age as Tal. "All our promising young people, wasting their talents. So what are you doing with yourself?"

Tal had some ideas of what Essanthi could do with themselves, but he was trying to behave, so he bit his tongue and managed, "Travelling a bit."

"Ha," said Essanthi. Their ears gave a brisk little flick of disdain. "Is that what they're calling it these days? My brothers travelled after university too. A year drinking themselves silly in foreign wineshops, I don't doubt. But you didn't go to university, did you?"

"No," said Tal, with a flare of temper, because of course everyone knew he'd been expelled from school at sixteen and was famously the family dud. "Didn't bother applying. Prefer wasting my talents."

Essanthi gave a slow blink, like a tortoise, and turned to their neighbour as if Tal had made an embarrassing scene, although really on his usual scale of embarrassing scenes, this didn't even register. Tal rolled his eyes and went on to look for his mother.

The skyline of Tlaanthothe skewered all the humiliating events of Tal's existence like bits of steak awaiting the grill. There were the turrets of the Tlaanthothei Academy for Boys. There, crouching in the wall, was the Gate-fortress where he had spent seven months as a hostage. Here, quite close by, was the spire of the Chancellor's Palace, of which the less said the better.

In the far distance, beyond the city wall, was the fading expanse of the desert known as the Speechless Sea, black sand bleached to rust under the unforgiving sun of his homeworld. Tal fixed his eyes on that dead margin and reflected that he would soon be out of here.

He supposed he ought to make conversation to show willing, or something, but he could hear the cousins' talk bubbling away on all sides, and from what he could catch, it sounded like you had a choice between art or politics. Tal would rather jam a cake fork into the back of his hand than try to have an opinion on either, especially in front of his family.

"... heard he might not even appear tomorrow," someone was saying.

"Well, that's almost an implied abdication, don't you think? By default . . ."

Tal slunk along behind them, his ears twitching. *Abdication* could only refer to one person. But the conversation had moved on, and he found himself trapped between a group of dull uncles and the fountain dais where the Charossa family offering had been made ready.

Tlaanthothe's tutelary goddess, the Siren of the Speechless Sea, was honoured with honey and salt water. The salt-water fountain was a permanent fixture, large and deep enough for Tal to swim lengths without touching the bottom. For the festival it was garlanded with grapevines, artfully arranged to leave space for golden dishes of honeycomb. Something broke the surface of the water, and Tal glimpsed the pale edge of a fin.

Before he had time to work out what *that* was about, someone tapped him on the shoulder. Tal swung round, fists clenched and shoulders squared, and realised with a start that he'd been ready to punch someone in the face.

It was his older brother, Niranthos, who was a shipping lawyer, or something else equally depressing. Tal could still picture Niranthos as a schoolboy, smilingly saying something like *oh, Talasseres, do you really think the word* equilibrium *has a K in it?* He wasn't smiling now. Niranthos' hair was tied back in neat braids and he was wearing shiny white formal robes. He looked afflicted by Tal's presence, by his clipped curls and the creases in his shitty old party clothes.

"What's that thing in the fountain?" said Tal, by way of greeting. It wasn't exactly a fish, despite the fronded tail which occasionally flicked up over the water's surface. Tal had caught sight of a long horse-like muzzle. Perhaps it was a dolphin.

Niranthos' expression lapsed from aggravation to disgust. "Someone thought it would be cute to import a real life hippocamp as part of the offering." The sea-horse was part of the city's crest, supposedly dating from ancient days when the Speechless Sea was a true ocean. Tal had never seen one before. It explained the strong seaweedy smell rising from the fountain.

"Those things kick like real horses. I assume it must be heavily sedated," Niranthos added.

"Yeah?" said Tal. "Lucky for some."

The look on Niranthos' face didn't change. Tal thought, *Hey, you wanted me here, fucker, now you have to make conversation with me.*

"So how's it going?" said Tal. "How are boats?"

Niranthos only got stonier. He might actually be hating this more than Tal was, which was one bright spot.

"Why am I here, then?" said Tal. "You were pretty clear I didn't have a choice. Where's Mother?"

Niranthos gave a kind of snort of displeasure and dragged Tal to one side of the fountain dais, behind a potted lemon tree.

Their mother, Niranthe Charossa, was sitting there under a trellis of flowering jasmine. She too was in full formal dress, and her braids were wound up to support a cup-shaped headdress full of summer flowers. Her deep brown skin had been burnished to a high gloss and her eyes were delicately outlined in gold. She looked—of course—like the model Tlaanthothei hostess, except that she was hiding in a dark corner. Her face had gained new lines of anxiety since Tal had last seen her. Niranthos', too.

There was something going on here. Some Charossa bullshit manoeuvre. That was the problem with his family. Get enough of them in one room at one time, and someone would start nudging and winking about whether this could be the *dynastic moment*. Always poised for the main chance, that was the family trait.

It's fine, he told himself. *Calm down*. He only had to make it through today, and somehow find a way to bring his mother round to the question of hard cash, and then he was going home to Cricket Station. Whatever it was they were up to, he wasn't going to get drawn in.

"Ah. You came," said his mother.

He wouldn't have said her eyes lit up at the sight of him or anything, but she seemed reasonably pleased to see him at first. Then she fell silent, apparently at a loss what to say to him after that. Tal didn't know what to say either. He realised with a squirm of shame that she hadn't at all expected him to turn up. He swallowed, sticking his hands in the pockets of the robe he had dug out for the occasion in a halfhearted attempt to look smart.

"Yeah," said Tal, inadequately. He and Niranthos sat at the table.

From here, beyond the trellis, the dome of the School of Transcendence was visible—green dome and white marble colonnade, floating above the noise and ornament of the city like a cloud. The Siren's earthly mansion and most sacred temple was garlanded with olive branches for the Feast of Midsummer. It was empty now, but Sethennai would go there tomorrow for the ceremony and would enter the Inner Chapel alone to receive the goddess' blessing on the city.

Tal had seen the inside of the Inner Chapel himself, and seen the true form of the Siren: she was a broken stone obelisk, just one of the many scattered pieces of Sethennai's stupid snake goddess. Presumably that made her just another one of his lackeys.

"When was the last time you heard from the Chancellor?" said Niranthos. For once there was no condescension, no attempt to cloak the fact that Tal might know something Niranthos did not. This was such a surprise that it took Tal a second to understand what he was being asked.

"I don't know, never?" said Tal. He felt the warning flash, the sense that the ground was unsteady beneath his feet.

"Exalted Sages, Tal," said Niranthos. "You don't have to be stupid on purpose."

"We only wondered—" said his mother. "You've really heard nothing from Chancellor Sethennai?"

"Er—no," said Tal.

"What on earth *have* you been doing, all this time, anyway?" said Niranthos. He was angry with Tal, still, for some reason, as though Tal had done all this specifically to spite him, and it was drawing him away from the point.

"He's taking some time to find himself," said his mother smoothly. Tal wondered how she knew this, since they'd certainly never discussed it. Her letter had been polite, but both she and Niranthos had made it clear how the family felt about his current *lifestyle,* the fact that Talasseres had given up a position on the Chancellor's staff for the worst possible company a backwater like Cricket Station had to offer. Tal couldn't tell if she was defending him or just trying to put a more palatable gloss on his situation.

"No letters? Nothing?" said Niranthos.

"Why would he write to me? I quit," said Tal.

To be fair to them, there were some facts they didn't know about Tal's relationship with his old boss. Tal had done a really good job so far that day of not thinking about the fact that it had been on the Feast of Midsummer that Sethennai had kissed him the first time, five years ago.

A possibility dropped into his hands, sharp and bright as a shard of glass. "What, did he mention me?"

The public festivities had been a struggle, a punishingly hot day with a dust storm threatening beyond the city walls. Sethennai had looked so tired. Tal had ended up in the study after Csorwe and the others had all gone, and the night had been full of almost unbearable possibility, and—

Tal thought again, hard, about stabbing himself with a fork. It was over.

"No," said Niranthos. If he noticed the break in Tal's composure, he didn't say anything. His ears were drawn up close against his skull, and Tal thought he must be making an effort to stop them twitching. "No, he didn't mention anything, because he hasn't been seen in public for over a month."

Tal shook this off. None of his business. "I don't see what that has to do with me."

"You knew him better than anyone," said Niranthos. He managed to put a nasty shine on it that made Tal worry for a second that his brother had figured it out, but on balance it was probably just Niranthos being Niranthos. "And you're still in contact with that girl."

"Do you mean Csorwe?" said Tal, who was still coming to terms with the fact that he and Csorwe were apparently stuck with each other, as if she was some kind of disfiguring freckle he'd been born with. She and Shuthmili were still on Cricket Station, looking after Cherenthisse, who was taking things hard. At the point Tal had left, Cherenthisse had divided her time between sleeping, refusing to wear clothes, and demanding that somebody duel her to the death.

"Doubt Csorwe's heard anything. She . . . *left* him, same as me." Tal couldn't quite make himself form the word *betrayed.*

"Yes, and the only reason she isn't being pursued for theft and treason is that Sethennai declined to open a prosecution," said Niranthos.

"He's changed in the past two years, since the two of you left," said Tal's mother.

"Oh, and you two know him so well?" said Tal. They had to be wrong. Tal had never even let himself fantasise about the idea that Sethennai might be really sad and different now. Sethennai's indifference was one of those constants you had to remember, or you could really take a wrong turn.

"Not well," said his mother. "But I've known him for many years, and well enough to see a difference."

"Changed how?" said Tal.

"Colder. More distant," said his mother.

"Very distant," said Niranthos, as if wanting to prove that he *also* knew the Chancellor quite well. "Doesn't seem to hear anything you say. I'm on the Logistics Committee now, and he hasn't attended a meeting for two months. We've tried contacting his staff at the Palace, but they're stonewalling me."

"Wow," said Tal in his flattest drawl. "If he's missing *meetings of the Lo-*

gistics Committee, something really must be wrong. Everyone loves those meetings."

"My god, Talasseres, you really are incapable of behaving like an adult," said Niranthos. "Would you listen to what I'm saying? The Chancellor is *missing,* he's been behaving strangely for months, his staff won't admit there's a problem, but I don't think they know anything more than we do—"

"Yeah! Great! Sounds bad!" said Tal. "This shit is why I left. I have my own life."

"On Cricket Station, Tal? With your *friends?* Do you know what it's doing to—" Niranthos shut his mouth, lips tightly pressed, and glanced at their mother with a significance so clunky it was almost audible. "Half of Tlaanthothe says you've become a drug runner or something," he added.

Tal snorted. "Hey, tell me the name of one drug you know—"

"This is not the point," said their mother sharply. "Tal, you are needed here. If something is about to *happen*—for instance, if Belthandros Sethennai fails to show up for the Feast tomorrow and pay his respects to the Siren—then we need every Charossa."

Elsewhere in the garden, the conversation simmered on. There was a *glop* as the hippocamp turned drearily over in the fountain.

"Right," said Tal, as the whole grim tableau fell into place. "You think someone's going to challenge for the city. Or—no—you think it's going to be a big free-for-all."

"Look, it only takes one idiot," said Niranthos. "One Lenarai or Kathoira to decide it's their chance to make a play for Chancellor before anyone else does."

"Yeah, it's almost like duelling is stupid," said Tal. "As if you want some random dickhead with a sword in charge."

"Well, actually, in former ages, martial prowess was considered an essential part of—"

"It's cleaner than civil war," said their mother, before Tal could tell Niranthos what he thought of his martial prowess. "And in any case, the people accept it, so it hardly matters whether it's sensible or not."

"And I'm not a sword-fighter," said Niranthos, "and Mother's duelling days are obviously behind her, so . . ."

"Oh, my god," said Tal, suppressing the urge to pour scorn on *sword-fighter.* "You want me to do it."

"My concern is that if someone does not take control early on, there will be a bloodbath," said his mother.

"Ha ha, bullshit," said Tal. "You two want to get a Charossa in first, that's all. Sethennai wouldn't give up the city, I was there when he fought Olthaaros for it. You think he's just going to let it go? It's not going to happen."

"Sometimes one needs to plan for a contingency," said his mother. "In any case, Sethennai could be unwell, or—"

This tweaked at Tal's heartstrings for a moment. He'd only ever known Sethennai to catch a mild cold, which meant nothing worse than wearing a dressing gown and sipping ginger tea. Anyway, Tal didn't think Sethennai *could* get seriously ill, given that he was immortal, and—

Oh, of course. If they were right that there had been some change in Sethennai, it was nothing to do with Tal. Not even anything to do with Csorwe, except that both of them had been involved in retrieving the Reliquary. Two years ago, Belthandros Sethennai had opened the Reliquary of Pentravesse and learned what he truly was. No wonder he was different now.

Tal hadn't told anyone about it. He hadn't known how to express it, and he didn't have the energy to persuade anyone of something they wouldn't want to believe. Well, it made things simpler. It was just as he'd always known, really. Sethennai had never cared for him. And he would never get anything from his family without getting himself dragged into some scheme against his will.

He could leave now. Wait for a quiet moment and slip out. He could be on a ship back toward Cricket Station before next morning. He'd just have to tell the others there'd been no luck getting money from his family. They had another month's rent saved on their apartment, so they wouldn't be kicked out right away, and maybe the others would come up with something good. There would have to be another way. He wasn't signing up for this.

Niranthos took his distraction for contempt. "Dear gods, Tal, you could at least think of your duty to Tlaanthothe—"

"Fuck Tlaanthothe, and fuck you," said Tal. "I'm not getting involved."

Niranthos began to growl some response. Their mother just looked at Tal, her brow creased. She looked tired and unhappy, not angry.

"Tal—" she said, and then the School of Transcendence blew up.

Or at least, that was how Tal tried to describe it, later on. In fact there was no explosion. An explosion would have left a crater in the centre of Tlaanthothe, flung chunks of ancient marble through the walls of nearby palaces, opened up the dome like a seedpod popping. None of this happened.

What happened was a burst of concussive force centred on the School, a shudder so violent that Tal's teeth rattled in their sockets. It felt as though someone had ripped the stitches from the fabric of reality.

Tal's mortal brain didn't understand it as it happened. All he could do was reconstruct it later. There was a flash of darkness, an annihilation. When his vision returned, he smelled hot metal and a wave of ozone, like the end of a thunderstorm, and tasted blood on the roof of his mouth. Something hot was running down his face.

At first he couldn't hear anything at all, only a slow, echoing boom. When he remembered he had hands, he reached automatically for his sword—which wasn't there, because he'd left it with his luggage—and he realised he'd been thrown backward out of his chair and flung into the trellis.

Gradually his vision cleared. His mother was clinging to the lemon tree, upright somehow, mopping at her face with her sleeve. Niranthos was still on the ground. Everyone in view was bleeding from the nose or mouth or both, clinging to each other, wailing.

"The School must have been struck by lightning!" someone was saying, although the sky was a cloudless blue and the School of Transcendence was, somehow, intact, shimmering and whole. Someone else was screaming about how the city was under attack.

"Everyone be careful, there may be aftershocks," said Niranthos, on his feet and ready for the people to listen to him again. He and some of the other cousins began shepherding people inside. Perhaps it seemed safer under cover, but Tal knew, somehow, that there was no safety from this, that everyone in the city must have felt it, down to the deepest cellars.

"Mother?" he said, picking himself up.

"No bones broken yet," she said. She began to follow Niranthos and the others toward the stairs. "Tch. My mistake for thinking we had another day." She rubbed her face, loose petals cascading from her headdress. "It will start now, you understand. You are too young to remember the beginning of Olthaaros' usurpation—the chaos, the uncertainty, the stupid violence—the wretched *scrabbling* . . ."

"What do you mean?" said Tal, then followed her gaze.

Above the School of Transcendence, the blue sky swirled and darkened, writhing with knots and ribbons of cloud. Within the clouds a green light flashed—sometimes like lightning, sometimes like eyes gliding in the deep sea.

"Belthandros has done something he cannot take back," said Niranthe. "Get downstairs, Talasseres. We need to consider our next move."

Tal was still collecting his wits, about to say that he wanted no part of the next move, whatever it was, that he hadn't changed his mind just because Sethennai had done something awful. Then, out of the general noise of Charossai retreating, there came a piercing scream, rising and falling with abject horror. A child, Tal thought. He stumbled in the direction of the noise. It was coming from the fountain dais.

The fountain was now dry, thickly encrusted with white drifts of salt. Lying among the soft, spiky crystals was the dead body of the hippocamp, withered almost to mummification. The creature's strange skeleton was visible through the dry skin, already sloughing away. One of the little cousins was staring down at it, her mouth open in an unending wail.

"Yeah, you and me both," Tal muttered.

Dragging his eyes from the grisly corpse of the hippocamp, Tal saw that the wreaths of grapes had withered black. The golden dishes were flecked with patches of grey-green encrustation as though infected. The wedges of honeycomb were dark and crumbling.

His mother seemed not to have noticed. She scooped the little girl up over her shoulder and followed the others inside. Reluctantly, Tal went after her.

Perhaps to Niranthos' disappointment, there were no aftershocks. Dozens of Charossai gathered in the grand parlour of the mansion and talked loudly at each other, their panic already filming over with theories. Tal loitered at the edge, thinking about how to slip away and get to the docks without being harassed.

For a second his treacherous brain started trying to imagine what Sethennai could have done, but as soon as he caught himself, he banished the thought. Not his problem anymore.

"Some of us ought to go up to the School and find out what we can about what's happened," said Tal's mother. She had a way of making herself heard in a crowded room without raising her voice.

"Agreed," said Niranthos. "In these circumstances the city looks to the great families to show leadership. Talasseres and I will be happy to go."

The crowd parted, encircling Tal, and they all peered at him, most only just registering that he was here. Tal saw exactly what Niranthos was doing, and it made him furious. Even an emergency could be made to serve the grand plan. This was just another step toward the ultimate goal of forcing Tal to fight a duel.

If Niranthos had smirked at him, it would almost have been bearable, but his expression was bland. He hadn't even considered the idea that, when it came to it, Tal might do something other than exactly what he was told.

"Actually, nah," said Tal.

"Sorry?" said Niranthos. The crowd started up talking again, and Tal raised his voice, making sure they all heard.

"No, thanks," said Tal. "Sure, you'll have a great time playing Niranthos Charossa Shows Leadership, maybe they'll put up a fucking statue of you with your head up your arse, but this is not my problem. Maybe you weren't listening before. *I'm not getting involved.*"

He didn't wait to see his mother's face or hear his brother's response. He turned and elbowed his way out of the room as the noise rose around him.

It had been a mistake to come back, Tal thought, throwing his bag over his shoulder. He should have left earlier. God, and if his mother was right and Sethennai was at the School of Transcendence, Tal would rather die. He never wanted to see him again.

He strapped his sword belt back on and strode out of the mansion. The streets were empty, but they hummed with a restless silence, the sudden absence of hundreds of people. Abandoned festival stalls listed, shedding their canopies. The swags of flowers hanging from facade to facade had sagged and given way. A heavy fall of rotten petals had splattered on the paving stones. The plant matter left clinging to the twine was slimy and unrecognisable.

The wind dried the sweat on the back of Tal's neck. He shivered, but pressed on. He didn't look back at the School of Transcendence, at the angry swirl of cloud massing above the dome.

He kept his head down, not wanting to be recognised. For so long he'd been the knife in the Chancellor's hand. There were plenty of people who would know his face. He needn't have worried. All the way down to the docklands, the city was quiet. Those he passed hurried on without looking at him.

Halfway there he passed a priest of the Siren wandering in the opposite direction. The man's face was buried in his hands, the breeze whipping his robe of office around his ankles. Tal thought he might have been sobbing, but it could have been the wind.

At last he saw the quays from above. Cutters waited like pigeons on a wire, and great ships rested in their mooring cradles. Beyond them, the city wall and the Gate-fortress and the Gate itself, looming like the memory of a bad dream. The fortress in particular was a reminder of what happened to you if you let yourself get drawn into your family's stupid infighting. Locked away with two hundred mercenaries and General Psamag.

He dragged his eyes away. He'd got himself out of the fortress, and he'd learned his lesson since.

The quays were closed, and so were the city gates. A cluster of soldiers and port administrators were directing a crowd of would-be passengers, and a barrier had been constructed to block their way. Tal could see the great round-bellied ships in their cradles, but nobody was getting on or off. Overhead, beyond the mailship quay and above the bulk of the fortress, the Gate gleamed, bright and still and undisturbed as a green glass coin, and patrolled by a military vessel. Nobody would be leaving Tlaanthothe until they had sorted out the disturbance at the School of Transcendence.

Tal cursed. He couldn't stay. He had almost no money left—only his return ticket for the mailship. If his mother was right and things were about to go bad, soon everyone would be trying to get out of Tlaanthothe, and Tal intended to be gone before that happened.

There were no good options. Go back into the city and hide, try to get over the wall without being noticed by the soldiers . . .

The Gate-fortress loomed over his shoulder again, reminding him that there was at least one other way out of Tlaanthothe. Long ago he'd escaped from the Gate-fortress through the tunnels under the city, and he remembered how to find the entrance, hidden in a park at the bottom of Broad Street.

The park had been decorated for the festival, with huge cheaply printed banners depicting the Siren as a shapely mermaid riding a hippocamp. Most people did not know what it was that stood alone in the windowless dark of the Inner Chapel, and the mermaids were a Midsummer tradition. The banners flapped in the breeze, discoloured as though eaten up with mildew. A few trestle tables had blown over, their tablecloths looking just as filthy. Another priest was crouched under a tree, his head buried in his arms. This time Tal was sure of what he heard. The man was openly weeping.

Well, no use wondering about that. Tal made his way down an avenue of cypresses toward the hidden stairway. Csorwe and Sethennai certainly knew about the tunnels, but Tal had never told anyone else. It was his own secret knowledge, won through a series of indignities, to be kept to himself. Inside it was cool and damp, a flight of steps descending through darkness to the catacombs below. Only now it occurred to him that Sethennai might have had the place walled up or filled in, but when he reached the bottom, it was just as it had been, an ancient underground boulevard built through a natural cave system. Maybe it suited Sethennai to have a secret escape route.

He retrieved his alchemical torch from his bag and let out a long breath. He'd done it. He was almost out. The tunnel let out into the desert. Not ideal but better than being trapped in here with Niranthos and Sethennai and thousands of other people he hated, and he might have better luck finding a cutter. He could go north through the desert to Grey Hook, or to one of the lesser Gates in the south. It would be several days' journey, but each day would at least take him further from Tlaanthothe and everything that lurked inside it.

He turned a corner, and the beam of his torch fell on a cloaked figure, inspecting something on the ground.

It was a woman, wrapped up against the chill of the caves. She leant on her staff as she stood up to face him, and he thought she must be very old. Then she pulled back her hood and Tal recognised her. She couldn't yet be forty, but her dark hair was shot with grey. There was a malevolent gleam in her pale yellow eyes, and her expression dangled at the exact midpoint between amusement and exasperation.

"*You,*" he said. "Aren't you dead yet?"

Oranna's silver-capped tusks glinted. "The grave calls, but it does not yet demand."

Oh, fuck off, Tal thought, but all he said was "What are you doing here?"

"The same thing you are, I imagine. Leaving a sinking ship."

Oranna was the former librarian of the House of Silence. She had been Csorwe's teacher and Belthandros Sethennai's lover, and she remained Tal's least favourite person in the world. She always reminded him of his teachers at the Academy, poised ready to spring when he said something stupid. He ignored her and took a step forward, and she raised a hand.

"I wouldn't. The path is sealed."

He couldn't see what she meant at first. Then he spotted the thin silvery line of marks inscribed from wall to wall across the tiled floor. Tal had stumbled blindly into a curse-ward before, and he didn't care to repeat the experience.

"For a generally careless man, Belthandros is always so diligent when it's least convenient," said Oranna. She knelt again, lowering herself carefully to the ground, and poked at the markings with a small metal pointer. "*Nasty piece of work.*"

After a couple of years living next door to Shuthmili, Tal knew what someone sounded like when they were doing a bad job hiding their anxiety. Something had Oranna ruffled. Normally Tal would have enjoyed this, but he didn't want to imagine what it might be.

Oranna picked and scratched at the curse-ward on the ground, and after a few minutes straightened up. The curse-ward fizzled away, and she rubbed out the remnants with her foot. "Right. Time to get going."

Tal didn't know what to say to this. Even looking at Oranna filled him with a mute loathing, and the fact that she didn't seem to hold it against him made it worse. He wanted to come up with something really devastating to say. Tell her to slither back to whatever hole she'd crawled out of.

"God, piss off," was all he managed.

Great.

Oranna raised an eyebrow at him, and set off down the tunnel ahead of him, moving surprisingly fast. "Things in Tlaanthothe are about to get very bad indeed," she called back to him. "The Siren is dead, and Belthandros is gone, and I do not like the implications of that. But don't let me stop you if you really want to stay."

"That's dumb," said Tal, catching up to her. "Gods can't die." He felt very sure as he said it, and then he remembered the shrivelled hippocamp in the fountain, the priests weeping in the streets. "The Siren was a big rock! What happened, did someone break in with a pickaxe?"

"The obelisk is still in the chamber, an inert chunk of mineral matter," said Oranna grimly. "But the divinity who dwelt within it is extinguished. As the Unspoken teaches us, all things have their end."

"Sethennai wouldn't leave Tlaanthothe," said Tal.

"There is nothing Belthandros Sethennai would not leave behind if it served him. He has a sentimental attachment to the city, but nothing weighs with him more than his own safety," said Oranna. For once there was no twist of amusement at the corner of her mouth. Whenever she wasn't smiling there were lines of pain on her face. Under her cloak, her dress was dusty and much mended, and her hands were rough with exposure. Tal noticed without pity that she was missing the little finger of her left hand. "There was no sign of him at the Chancellor's palace this morning, nor anywhere else in the city," she went on.

"What are you doing in Tlaanthothe, anyway?" said Tal.

"Visiting Belthandros for the Midsummer Festival," said Oranna.

"What, did he invite you?" said Tal. He'd only ever worked security. He'd never been a guest.

"Regardless of who was or was not 'invited,' he wasn't there. I missed him. He's gone. Probably gone this way, in fact, given the curse-ward here."

"His own *safety*? You think he's in danger?" said Tal, recalling too late that he didn't care about Sethennai or the Siren or anything that happened in Tlaanthothe. The idea of Sethennai in trouble, suffering somewhere, out of control, was both unpleasant and interesting, like the itch of a bandaged wound.

"I do," said Oranna. "And anything that can threaten him is a problem for all of us." She shuffled on down the tunnel, her staff tapping on the ancient tiles. Tal thought she relied on staff more than she would admit.

"What's wrong with you?" he said.

She grinned at him. "You're not the first to ask. Where to begin? My old friend Cweren once told me I have *an offensively instrumental attitude towards others—*"

"I mean—"

"Yes, I know perfectly well what you mean, and I must say you take rudeness beyond what is charming. I have the mage-blight, and I am dying of it. I watched my teachers at the House of Silence succumb, one after another. Joint and muscle pain, chills, fatigue, fragile bones, incoherence, and death. Much to look forward to."

Tal, as usual, recoiled from discussion of mortality. He was twenty-five years old and did not need this. Nor did he know what to say. Even to someone you justifiably loathed, there was probably some way you were supposed to respond to *I'm dying* that wasn't *good thing you like tombs so much*. Luckily for him, Oranna wasn't finished.

"If one were a weak talent—someone like my old friend Cweren, for instance—perhaps one could tolerate having the power and not using it. One might live most of a normal span. But whatever else might be wrong with me, I am not mediocre. I have perhaps two years left. Three if I restrain myself, but I do not plan to restrain myself. Nor do I plan to get myself killed by whatever is after Belthandros. There is too much to do."

The passage had begun to curve up, and sunlight was filtering down ahead, picking out the striations in the stone in bands of gold.

"You *are* still in touch with Qanwa Shuthmili?" said Oranna. "You'd better take me to her."

"What?" said Tal. He liked Shuthmili, which was odd since she was exactly the kind of wispy supercilious pedant he'd always hated, but he couldn't imagine she would be pleased to have Oranna turn up on their doorstep. On the other hand, it might be worth it for the look on Csorwe's face . . . "Why? Why should I?"

"*Why*: when I tell her what happened here, she will help me find Belthandros. *Why should you*: if I am right, and some ancient power has arisen to rampage in Tlaanthothe, then you would do well to find a powerful mage and stand behind her."

"So you *are* going to find him?" said Tal, trying to ignore that last part. "To help him?"

He'd meant to sound scornful—Sethennai was beyond *helping*, and running around after him was pathetic—but it came out plaintive.

Oranna stepped out of the tunnel and into the afternoon sun. "Find him? Yes. I have business with him," she said. "Help him? That depends."

3

The Hope of the Empire

WHEN THE DAY of ruination came, Cherenthisse had been on her way to address the graduating class at the Thousand Eyes hatchery.

She had been aboard her war-dart, resting in her true aspect, her proper serpentine body. Her vassal pilot hadn't needed much direction, leaving her free to try and remember her speech and think about how much she was looking forward to getting this over with.

Like the other Thousand Eyes, she had spent her infancy and early training at the hatchery. Her memories of it were distant, and not warm. More than half of her hatchmates had died before graduation. There was honour in being hatched for the Thousand, but few of them remembered the place or its discipline with pleasure. Cherenthisse was one hundred and twenty years old, and she had not returned to the hatchery since her own graduation, and she hadn't seen a Thousand Eye hatchling in years. She was always startled by how tiny they were, how bright and glossy, and tinier still when they began to shed their skins and learn to take on a prey aspect.

The first Cherenthisse heard of the cataclysm was the pilot's scream. Then she saw it, a wave of darkness which rippled out through the Gate, burning and draining everything it touched.

She assumed it was the rebels. The civil war was in full flood, and there were rumours that the revolutionary faction had got hold of a void-weapon, that they might attack the Gates.

The hatchlings! she had thought, before anything else.

The pilot was dead. Cherenthisse assumed her prey aspect, took the controls, and accelerated toward the hatchery, the war-dart flying before the devastation like a bird before the storm.

She meant to supervise the evacuation, to play her part in safeguarding the future of the Thousand Eyes. She had not known the nature of the catastrophe.

The goddess had punished them all.

I could have died not knowing that, she thought, and although it was beneath her to feel hatred for prey, she could not help hating the prey creatures who had woken her.

There were none of her own kind left. Not a single Echentyri infant in existence. Not a single Echentyri but her, and she was trapped in the weak fronded shape of her prey aspect.

And still the speech she had meant to give kept going through her head. She had written it herself, though oratory was not her strong suit and she hardly remembered who had spoken at her own graduation. *In this time of upheaval,* it had begun, *it is you who must carry forward the hope of the Empire.*

She laughed. It made a dry sound in her throat, and hurt her chest. Three thousand years, and all that was left of Echentyr was her alone.

The prey who had woken her had brought her to a place called Cricket Station, to quarters so small and cramped she would have been ashamed to provide them to the prey-servants on her own estate in Echentyr.

Once she was alone, she had tried to return to her true aspect, thinking it might bring some comfort to feel her own strength, something wholesome and familiar amidst this degradation. She couldn't do it. The unfurling which had once come so naturally refused to take hold, as though something in her had dried up and withered away as the years slipped by. Her useless body shuddered, twitching within its dead wrappers as though trying to shed its skin. This struck Cherenthisse as such a cruel parody that she threw herself against the wall of the cabin, slamming bodily into the timber in rage. It hurt, and the maddening newness of the pain made her angry enough to do it again.

One of the prey creatures came in. Shuthmili, that was her name. Cherenthisse had known the names of all her own servants. She had taken pride in it. The estate would be ruined now. The park where Cherenthisse had hunted. The temple to the God-Empress where she had made her vows of dedication. The banqueting hall where she and her squadmates had celebrated their victories. There was no safe or comforting place for her thoughts to rest. Everything was gone.

Cherenthisse bared her blunt and useless teeth, trying to make Shuthmili leave. Shuthmili put her head on one side.

"I've brought you something to eat," she said.

There was a deep pit of sickness and anguish in Cherenthisse's belly. She never wanted to eat again.

"There is nothing left for me," said Cherenthisse. "No purpose in nourishing this useless body."

"Well," said Shuthmili. "You killed Professor Tvelujan—may she rest at the Hearth of the Mara. So I'm sorry if I don't feel particularly sympathetic. She was a strange person, but she did not deserve that."

"She ought not to have intruded."

Shuthmili's face crinkled in disgust.

"You are aggrieved by it. It was an insult to you," said Cherenthisse, guessing a little. She took Shuthmili for the leader of the group, insofar as prey had leaders. "She was a servant of yours? If so, I apologise for any disrespect."

"No," said Shuthmili.

Cherenthisse felt a flare of anger. This creature clearly did not realise what an immense concession it was for Cherenthisse to apologise to her.

"You cannot think it brings me pleasure to be here. To be trapped in this form," she said coldly.

Shuthmili did not seem moved by this.

"Eat. You'll feel better."

"My people are gone," said Cherenthisse. "My order are all dead. My duty is obsolete. Better to submit to the just punishment of my goddess and die."

"There may be another," said Shuthmili, hesitant. "Csorwe once met a great serpent who said she had come from Echentyr."

The moment of hope hurt like someone pulling a knife out of her flesh. "And where is she now? She lives?"

"We don't know," said Shuthmili. "She disappeared. Csorwe tried to find her a few times, but we never got anywhere."

Shuthmili went on for a while about the worlds they had searched, but Cherenthisse was overwhelmed by memory. The Thousand Eyes assembled for parade in a courtyard of the God-Empress' palace. The scent of lily and tuberose, the sound of cool water, the opaline brilliance of Echentyr's sun gleaming on marble. The others around her, the rest of the Thousand, the knowledge that she was part of something far greater. She would have died for any one of the Thousand Eyes, and how she wished she had been given that opportunity.

"I'll leave this here. It's just porridge," said Shuthmili. She put a bowl down on the floor beside Cherenthisse's bunk and left. *Cooked* food, such as a servant would eat.

The smell of the cooked grains filled her with a mixture of disdain and wretched hunger. Cherenthisse had always tried to avoid eating in her prey aspect. Its senses were still so alien, and it always wanted to understand things by touching them.

There was a metal implement for eating with, but Cherenthisse ignored it. She took the bowl in both hands and lowered her face to it for a mouthful of porridge. It tasted so good that she lost herself for a moment in slurping up as much of it as she could.

She did feel better. She *had* been hungry; that had been a part of the lurching emptiness. That made her angry all over again. Her world was dead, and with it everyone she had ever known. All her Thousand Eyes were dead. The Maze was overrun with prey, and she had no idea what she was supposed to do now, and yet somehow her prey aspect was so hungry for servants' gruel that it was enough to blunt the edge of her suffering.

There is a reason for this, she told herself. *The will of Iriskavaal is just. My goddess would not have spared me for nothing. There is no cruelty and no degradation I cannot tolerate if my suffering serves her ends.*

Cricket Station was a little teardrop of timber suspended in the deep Maze, a stopping place for merchant ships and travellers, wanderers and pirates, and people like Csorwe, Shuthmili, and Tal, who were none of the above but had no other home to go to. For the past year they had run their business out of a rented apartment on the station's upper tier, and while the apartment itself was small, poky, and airless, the place had its compensations.

The station was far from any world with viable agriculture, so permanent inhabitants could claim gardens on the upmost tier. There weren't many crop plants which flourished in the dry air and unearthly light of the Maze. Everyone's gardens were full of small grey potatoes, huge pallid squash, and an unfamiliar vegetable with a pink snappable stalk, which Csorwe called *rhubarb*. At least fresh vegetables made a change from the algae and mealworms which were the station's staple foods.

The gardens were designed for utility rather than beauty, but Shuthmili liked them all the same, especially compared to the cramped interior of the station. Here were dark earth and crisp leaves below, and the ever-shifting Maze above, pieces of sky shimmering from blue to green to purple between the great stone arches. If you sailed through one such arch, and then on, deep into the curlicues of the Maze, you might come eventually to a Gate that would spit you out somewhere else. Travel far enough, and you could reach any corner of the known worlds. One day she and Csorwe would see them all. They'd save enough money to buy their own ship, not the rickety thing they'd been hiring for expeditions, and they'd go. They would walk in the light of foreign suns, and maybe one day they would find a world where they wanted to settle down.

Until then, the gardens of Cricket Station weren't bad at all. Now that Cherenthisse seemed resigned to behaving herself, they took her along with them. Back in the apartment, her formless grief filled the three small rooms like a miasma. Shuthmili was trying not to think too hard about what they were going to do with Cherenthisse, long term. They did owe her a responsibility. Csorwe was the one who felt that kind of thing most deeply. Shuthmili wasn't sure how far their obligation extended: Was it enough to let Cherenthisse stay with them for a week or two? Did they need to teach her how to feed herself and how to get a job?

After Shuthmili's flight from the Inquisitorate, Csorwe had patiently taught her about money and laundry and groceries and all the other exciting things which had formed no part of her education in Qarsazh. Cherenthisse was even worse off than she had been, because her knowledge of geography was three thousand years out of date.

One thing they had discovered was that Cherenthisse liked to have a task and would set to anything you asked her with bitter determination. That was soldiers for you, Shuthmili supposed. Just now she was pulling weeds with Csorwe.

"Couldn't you blast all these dandelions and speed this up a bit?" said Csorwe, wrenching out a handful by the roots and tossing them into the bucket of weeds. Shuthmili was wearing her gauntlets already, pouring warmth and encouragement into the roots of their crop plants.

"If you want the soil and all its produce cursed for a couple of decades," said Shuthmili dryly, pausing the fertiliser spell to admire how Csorwe looked in a sleeveless jacket.

"See why they were so scared of you back in Qarsazh, if you're always cursing vegetables," said Csorwe.

"Mm. Squash that bleed. Potatoes with teeth. Botany is really hard."

Csorwe murmured something—from experience, Shuthmili thought it was probably "*your* botany is really hard"—and sauntered off to the compost heap, taking the bucket with her. Shuthmili busied herself with weeding.

Some kind of wild geranium had sprung up at the edge of the bed. It seemed a shame to throw it in the bucket with the other weeds—maybe she could put it in a pot in the apartment? They could do with something to cheer the place up.

She laid her gauntleted hands flat on the soil, feeling for the seed tubers sleeping in the earth. She tried to relax into it. You were meant to let the power seep gently from your fingertips and settle into the ground like rainwater. It was frustrating when every fibre of her being wanted to burn hot, to pour everything she had into the soil and raise a canopy of rhubarb leaves that would soar over Cricket Station like a sail.

Her eyes settled on the geraniums again, and the nodding pink flowers disquieted her. Pink flowers . . . Something in the back of her mind associated pink flowers with the metallic taste of blood. Cherry blossoms and the taste of iron in her mouth.

SHUTHMILI. I WOULD SPEAK WITH YOU.

Leave me alone, my lady.

REMEMBER ME. REMEMBER ME.

I would prefer not to, thought Shuthmili, trying to wrench her focus back to the garden.

Shuthmili had not yet told Csorwe about the voice. That faint murmur in the back of her head whenever she used magic. It was not at all a threatening voice—it was quiet, and it came from somewhere very far away, but her teachers at the School of Aptitude had warned her well enough about what it meant to hear the voice of the goddess. Zinandour was not called the Corruptor for nothing.

Not to mention that the first time she had heard it was when she had killed her aunt. She had come close to losing herself in that bloody scramble to escape from the clutches of the Inquisitorate. She did not regret killing Aunt Zhiyouri, but she did not want to return to that state, every nerve in her body singing with the lust for atrocity.

She needed to talk to Csorwe about it. She would do, soon, unless she could find a way to fix it—and she did have one idea about that. The gauntlets kept her safe from some of the everyday risks of magic. Without them, every time she called upon Zinandour's power, it would damage her body in minute but unfixable ways, a constant slow erosion, until the mage-blight eventually took her. The gauntlets shielded her from the blight; perhaps there was some way she could alter them so that they also blocked out the voice of the goddess?

She'd need to figure out how they actually worked first. There was some fiendishly complicated magic embedded in their fabric, etched into the lining at a microscopic level. Deep Echentyri craft, difficult to understand at the best of times. She couldn't even tell what kind of creature the leather had come from. If only she could find some Echentyri spellbook or at least a proper dictionary of arcana . . . She had looked, covertly, in every ruin they had surveyed, but the snake empire's magicians had kept their secrets well.

"What is wrong?" said Cherenthisse abruptly. Shuthmili realised she had been staring into space.

"Nothing," said Shuthmili, hoping the presence of the goddess did not show in her face.

"I see," said Cherenthisse, and there was a long, uncomfortable pause, until at last the serpent said, "There is something you wish from me. I can see it in you."

What a question. Shuthmili had not been lying, back in the hatchery. Cherenthisse's survival itself was a miracle and a wonder, and you could not treat such things lightly. And of course, there was the mystery of the gauntlets, as Shuthmili had been so recently reminded.

"Well . . . I'm a scholar," said Shuthmili. "And you're a primary source."

"I am a soldier," said Cherenthisse. "You will have to speak more plainly."

"I suppose I want to know about Echentyr," said Shuthmili.

"My homeland is now the subject of ancient histories. I understand this. I am becoming accustomed to novel griefs."

"Yes. I thought it would be insensitive to bother you, while you're recovering," said Shuthmili.

"I do not think there will be recovery from this," said Cherenthisse. "What is it? There is something in particular."

Shuthmili wondered how on earth the serpent knew this. Cherenthisse's eyes were fixed steadily on her, the red point glittering in each pupil.

It was at least worth a try. She pulled off the gauntlets and held them out. Unremarkable dark leather, shiny in places with wear. There were faded sigils stamped into the leather, only visible when they caught the light.

"They are garments," said Cherenthisse, doubtfully, after peering at them for some time. "Hand garments. This is why you keep me alive?"

"They're Echentyri," said Shuthmili. "An artefact. I'm trying to understand—"

Cherenthisse's face twisted up in confusion and disgust. "Why should my people produce such an object?"

"I believe they were made by or for a . . . I suppose you'd call him a vassal mage," said Shuthmili. "You've never seen anything similar?"

"No," said Cherenthisse. "I am no practitioner."

"Even so," said Shuthmili. "Anything you could tell me about their construction, or the magic used? I am reaching in the dark, here, so *anything*—"

"The priests of Iriskavaal are hatched at their own sanctuary in the deepwood of Tachthyr. They are our mages. But you tell me they are all dead, and all their sanctuaries turned to dust." Cherenthisse hunched her shoulders, sorrow battling frustration. "I cannot tell you anything you wish to know."

"But you aren't exactly mundane," said Shuthmili, not prepared to give up hope. Anything was worth knowing, and might bring her closer to understanding. "Your transformation—I'm right about that, aren't I? You can take a serpent form?"

Cherenthisse hissed, drawing back. "I am a serpent," she said. "Every part of me that exists is a serpent. This body is a mockery."

Shuthmili watched her expectantly.

"There are things that everyone should know, and things which none but the Thousand are to learn, and you are so ignorant—" said Cherenthisse. "The goddess granted the Thousand Eyes our double aspect. We may walk among prey for a time, to better serve her ends, but *this* is not all that I am."

"I see," said Shuthmili. "And you can't change back?"

Cherenthisse's face hardened, as though she regretted having admitted it. "I do not doubt that the Lady Iriskavaal has spared my life for a reason," she said. "But it is hard, what she asks of me. To serve is an honour, but how it hurts."

Shuthmili was struck again by the inadequacy of any comfort she could offer.

"I could have a look at you," she said. "I might be a prey creature—which is a fascinatingly horrible choice of words, by the way, I must ask you about it at some point—but I am also quite a powerful magician, and I've worked as a medic before. If you'd let me examine you . . . ?"

Cherenthisse hissed. "You would use me to pry into that blasphemous artefact," she said. "No. I do not trust you."

Shuthmili blushed. She hadn't entirely meant it that way, but Cheren-thisse wasn't entirely wrong either.

Before she could think what to say, boots crunched on the gravel path behind her. She turned, expecting it to be Csorwe.

It was not.

Tal was back, looking—as usual—like a grasshopper that would spring a foot in the air at the least provocation. And next to him was an Oshaaru woman, wrapped up in a thick scarf and hood so that it took Shuthmili a moment to recognise her.

"Tal?" said Shuthmili, and then, "*Oranna?*"

"Oh, great," said Csorwe, returning with the bucket. "Nobody told me the circus was coming to town."

"So what do you want?" said Csorwe.

"You people always want so many explanations," said Oranna. "Surely you recall that the Unspoken teaches us to embrace obscurity and surrender to unknowing. *All voices sound in silence, and silence relieves them at last,* hmm?"

Oranna settled in the booth, in the attitude of a large grey cat stretching itself in the sun. It really was embarrassing how good she always looked, even with her dark hair streaked silver. Shuthmili had mentioned it to Csorwe once, and they had stared at one another for five full seconds in horrified agreement.

"But since you're good enough to ask," Oranna went on, "I would like a pot of tea, thank you, and some biscuits if this place has such a thing on offer."

The station canteen was still full of late breakfasters, for there were people on Cricket Station who were prepared to linger over a bowl of porridge or sour rhubarb soup. The five of them had crammed into a booth meant for four. In the far corner, Cherenthisse hunched up on her seat, her long arms wrapped around her knees and her cheek resting on the pitted surface of the canteen table.

"You must be Cherenthisse," said Oranna. "Talasseres has told me about you. The last of your kind. How interesting."

Cherenthisse did not respond. Csorwe set a pot of tea on the table and settled opposite Oranna in a manner that emphasised the breadth of her shoulders. You might describe Csorwe as wiry but only in the sense that a steel cable is technically a wire, Shuthmili thought, and could not help smiling secretly to herself.

"Well, isn't this friendly," said Oranna, sipping her tea with apparent enjoyment, though, in Shuthmili's experience, the tea on Cricket Station was an oversteeped broth the colour of tar, and the coffee was worse. "It's sweet that you all come as a matched set these days. Csorwe, must you really *loom* like that?" she added. "I don't see why you must be so distrustful. Last time we met, I helped you."

Csorwe gave her a long look. "And the time before that, you kidnapped Shuthmili, murdered at least twelve acolytes, nearly got us all killed in a rockfall—"

"Poisoned me," added Tal.

"The Unspoken contains multitudes, and so do I," said Oranna, dipping a biscuit in her tea. "I am here to help you, and to ask your help in return. The Siren of the Speechless Sea is dead, and I believe that whoever killed her is hunting Belthandros. He has many enemies. Disgruntled mercenaries, hostile foreign agents, Tlaanthothei political rivals—take your pick. If one of them somehow has the capacity to kill a god all of a sudden . . . I doubt they will stop at Belthandros. Which means we're all in trouble."

She told them what had happened in Tlaanthothe. Shuthmili and the others listened in growing unease. She wasn't entirely convinced of Oranna's theory, but maybe that was just because she couldn't imagine Belthandros Sethennai being hunted. It was uncomfortable to imagine that there might be a bigger fish out there than the man who had shaped half of Csorwe's life.

"Doesn't it seem most likely that *he* killed the Siren?" said Shuthmili. "Belthandros, I mean? And then fled the scene of the crime?"

"I considered that theory," said Oranna. She peered down at the dregs of her teacup, where the black leaves swirled like seaweed, and ran a fingertip thoughtfully round the rim before continuing. "But he would gain nothing by killing the Siren. He and she are both remnants of the same old god. Survivors from the wreck of Iriskavaal's being. You could almost think of them as siblings."

Cherenthisse raised her head from the table, red sparks flashing in her eyes. "These matters are not for you to speak of," she said. "It is a desecration to take the name of the goddess so lightly."

Oranna ignored her and went on explaining. After the fall of Echentyr, some of the shards of Iriskavaal's shattered body had grown into smaller divinities in their own right. The Siren was one of them, and they had encountered at least one other, back in the Precursor world where Shuthmili had first met Csorwe: a stone pillar that sang endlessly of oblivion.

"The Siren was a goddess in her own right, but a very minor one," said Oranna. "She served Belthandros without complaint. Why would he turn on her?"

"If she turned on *him*, maybe—" said Csorwe.

"Well, possibly," said Oranna. "I think it more likely that a third party is involved."

"Another one of Iriskavaal's remnants?" said Shuthmili. There were probably hundreds of them scattered through the Maze, shards of stone lying undiscovered in caves or at the bottom of the sea. "The only one we know that walks and talks is Belthandros, though."

"Belthandros is a special case," said Oranna. "He was a mortal man, once upon a time. As Pentravesse of Ormary, he willingly accepted the snake goddess into himself. But there could have been others. Belthandros kept his identity so well hidden that he himself forgot what he was, for a time. Who's to say for sure that there were no others? You or I or even Talasseres might be secretly divine—"

Shuthmili shook her head, thinking uneasily of the voice in her head.

"Joking aside," said Oranna, "the Siren is dead, and so is every other remnant of Iriskavaal I have managed to trace. There is trouble ahead—"

"Right," said Csorwe. "And it sounds like you expect us to do something about it. Seems to me like Sethennai deserves what's coming to him."

"That may be so," said Oranna. "But do you have any idea what a god on the rampage can do? Zinandour's reign of terror in Qarsazh razed cities. Isn't that right, Shuthmili?"

From far away Zinandour murmured appreciatively, and black flames flickered across Shuthmili's vision. She shook her head hard to banish them.

"Yes," she said, feeling dizzy. "Thousands of years ago. These things don't—"

"These things don't happen? If that's the case, why does the Qarsazhi Inquisitorate keep its mages so tightly bound? Why does the House of Silence appease the Unspoken One with sacrifice? A volcano may lie dormant for millennia, you know. Our gods lie sleeping, and I think it all too likely that—"

"Yeah, yeah," said Csorwe, much to Shuthmili's relief, "there's probably some kind of secret monster out there, I get it, and you want someone to deal with it."

"Someone surely must," said Oranna.

"I can tell you it's not going to be us," said Csorwe, and before Oranna could respond, there was a cough from outside the booth. A nervous young man in the uniform of station security stood there, flanked by two stolid colleagues.

"Er, ah—" he said, and cleared his throat. "Is one of you a Professor Ilver Tvelujan?"

"Tvelujan's sick," said Csorwe, not missing a beat. "We work with her. What's the matter?"

"There's a cutter registered to her name moored in the shuttle bay—it might be easier if you come and see. Something is *growing* in it . . ."

4

The Water Lily

THEY HAD BROUGHT Tvelujan's cutter back to Cricket Station from the hatchery world, moored it, and more or less forgotten about it. Tvelujan had liked her privacy, so Shuthmili had only been aboard the tiny ship a few times.

That was enough to tell her it was changed utterly.

There had been a curious resistance as they'd opened the hatch, and now she saw why. The inside face of the panel was patched with some kind of—moss, was it, or lichen? Something dense and damp and so brilliantly green it was almost luminous. The same stuff had grown over the windows, leaving the cabin in a living darkness which was all one with the smell: medicinal, thick with decay.

"How unpleasant," said Oranna, and conjured a magelight to see by.

The last time Shuthmili had been in here, every surface of the cabin had been stacked with books and papers, the maze-oak timbers covered with tacked-up maps and lists. The vague shapes of these were still visible, but they had been overrun with strange fungal life, furred over with something that could have been moss or could have been patches of colourful mould.

Huge flowering plants had run wild inside the ship. Blossoms the size of babies' heads lolled on withered stalks. The edges of the petals were already brown and crumpled.

Csorwe and Tal were silent and ready. This frightened Shuthmili far more than anything else, because it meant they thought there was a real threat here. She pulled her gauntlets on, determined she would not be taken by surprise.

"Where is this coming from?" said Shuthmili. All this plant life obviously had some kind of arcane source, something that had swelled and maddened in Tvelujan's absence. She could sense magic in the air like the smell of fire.

Oranna coughed into her sleeve, her lungs sounding like sheets of metal flapping in the wind. "I haven't the faintest," she managed. "*Vegetation* is not really my strong suit—"

"Tvelujan wasn't a mage," said Shuthmili. "Er, may she rest at the Hearth of the Mara," she added, because some habits died hard and she had been a very well-behaved Qarsazhi young lady for many years.

"Then it must be some artefact," said Oranna. That made sense. If Tvelujan had found something on one of her earlier expeditions, it was all too likely she would have concealed it from them.

Cherenthisse shrank back against the wall, holding her head. "Saar-in-Tachthyr," she said, but Shuthmili couldn't at that moment remember where she'd heard the name before.

Csorwe cut a path for them through the undergrowth. In among the plants there were still sad traces of Tvelujan's existence: a pile of unwashed clothes, a stack of tea-stained mugs.

"Found something," said Tal, hauling something out of a huge crate full of rags: an ornate statue, dull with lichen. "Fuck me, this is heavy."

Csorwe leant over him critically. "It's solid stone, and it's the size of your whole chest, you moron."

"Get bent, Csorwe, at least I *have* a chest—"

Oranna scrambled up from the bed and elbowed Csorwe out of the way. "My," she said, "look at that. Cherenthisse, this must be one of your people."

She brushed off the lichen. The statue was one of the hybrids Shuthmili remembered from the hatchery friezes: a woman's head and torso tapering into a coiled snakelike body.

"The dual aspect of the Thousand Eyes," said Cherenthisse tonelessly. "What of it?"

"Holy shit," said Tal, scraping away at the statue with his nails. "It's *not* solid stone. Some of this is gold."

He was right. The statue's scales were detailed with inlaid gold, and her hair had a gleaming sheen under the moss: the same gold as Cherenthisse's hair.

"How gaudy," said Oranna. "But it isn't magical, I'm afraid. We'll have to keep searching."

For almost an hour the five of them cut back vegetation and sorted through what remained of Tvelujan's belongings. Chipped crockery, crumpled linen, and a bottle of some dark poison which Csorwe said was anchovy sauce. Oranna settled on a crate, directing them in acid tones. Doing her best to disguise how tired she was, Shuthmili thought. She recognised the signs of blight well enough: she'd always been a bit of a hypochondriac, and had first diagnosed herself with early-onset mage-blight when she was twelve. Oranna undoubtedly had the real thing.

Shuthmili wondered, not for the first time, how things would have panned out for her if she'd ended up running with Oranna instead of Csorwe. Nothing good—most likely she would have ended up facedown in a sacrificial pool—but she couldn't help having a certain sympathy for a fellow mage on the run.

At last they cut through to Tvelujan's bunk. The pillow had a dent in the middle. Csorwe shook it out and straightened the sheets, automatically, without thinking about it, and for a moment Shuthmili was overcome by the kind of soft foolishness which still always took her by surprise whenever Csorwe did something that was so characteristically herself.

Pull yourself together, Shuthmili told herself. *This is why Tal says you're unbearable.*

Puddles of mould in bright rings spilled out from under the bunk, vilely beautiful, like cut agate. Shuthmili knelt and peered, trying not to inhale anything. Under the bed were what must have been stacked books and journals, now damp slabs of wet pulp—Shuthmili's heart bled at this more than anything else in the little ship—and a box, thick with flaking patches of mould but recognisable as a leather-bound travelling case. Was it her imagination that the rings of mould were spreading from the box, like ripples in a pond?

She dragged it out, leaving streaks in the mould. It was in better condition than most of Tvelujan's belongings, but the clasps were rusted with age, and it took a little effort to pry them open. She managed it eventually and lifted the lid, and—

"Mother of Cities," said Shuthmili. "I *knew* she was hiding something from us."

Inside the case, nestled in drifts of nameless rot, was a sphere of faceted glass. It was so clean and fine and delicate compared to the rest of Tvelujan's possessions that it took Shuthmili a moment to process what was inside it. The bud of an immense water lily, as big as her head. It looked very fresh, glossy and waxy, as though it had been plucked only moments before.

There must be wards of preservation in the sphere, she thought, dazedly. *Like they use to keep food fresh aboard an Imperial frigate. But it's so elegantly done . . .*

Despite her best efforts, she must have breathed in some of the spores. They smelled overwhelmingly sweet and strange: flowers and rot, cool water and dead things, burning paper and decaying wood. She swayed, suddenly woozy, and realised that along with the smell a curious yearning had crept up on her, a thirst. Her gauntleted fingertips brushed the surface of the sphere, and it drank up power from her like cool water.

BE WARNED! said Lady Zinandour, and at the same time, she heard Csorwe shout her name.

"Ah," said Shuthmili. "I'm sorry. Yes. I think we'd better leave this here."

"Are you—"

"I'm fine," said Shuthmili, shivering a little, and started rattling through the checklist before Csorwe could prompt her.

"My name is Qanwa Shuthmili, I am twenty-five years old—is this really necessary?"

"Go on," said Csorwe.

Any dark power which chose to invade Shuthmili's body would be able to pluck this knowledge from inside her skull as if choosing olives from a bowl, but the ritual clearly made Csorwe feel better, and it was, in a way, nice to know that she hadn't lost anything obvious.

"My father was Qanwa Adhara, I was born in Qarsazh in the Year of the Peach, I feel a terrible lust for blood upon me, the abyss yawns, alas, my Corruptor summons me—"

"Yeah, yeah, all right, you're fine," said Csorwe, rolling her eyes.

"If you two are quite done," said Oranna, tapping the surface of the sphere with one fingernail. "Look at this. It's made to open."

The panes of the sphere were curved like petals, with gold joints between them, and Oranna was right. The thing was made to open up like a flower. One of the panes had opened a crack, and a thin pale tendril that grew from the lily's stem had worked its way out. Barely thicker than a hair, and yet it had made its way out of its prison and crept out into the box . . .

Oranna withdrew her hand sharply, and brushed a lock of hair behind her ear as if to cover for it.

"Saar-in-Tachthyr," said Cherenthisse. "It is. It *is*."

"Pardon me?" said Shuthmili.

"The priests' sanctuary at Saar-in-Tachthyr," said Cherenthisse. "The temple complex—the shrine of Iriskavaal. Those flowers. They grow there. Only there. I've been there," she added.

"Really?" said Shuthmili.

"It still exists?" said Oranna, her yellow eyes gleaming.

"The priests' closed library, vaults, laboratories. Their hatchery," said Cherenthisse. "I do not know—but if this flower survives, then perhaps—"

Shuthmili felt excitement bubble up unbidden. "Cherenthisse, I wonder, do you remember how to get there?"

"Yes," said Oranna, "I very much wonder that too."

"I must return there," said Cherenthisse. "If it survives, there is no other choice for me." She was holding her head high for once, a flash of brilliance in her eyes which looked very much like hope.

"And I think we will come with you," said Oranna.

Csorwe and Tal stared blankly.

"No, she's right," said Shuthmili, addressing the others. "If even a fraction of the complex has survived, it would be the most important Echentyri site still in existence. And we could be the first to survey it. We'd be *in demand*. It wouldn't matter if Tvelujan's people *do* blacklist us. We could get a permanent job at some other university if we ever wanted to settle down, or we could make our names as freelancers—or maybe there will be other artefacts—"

Shuthmili did not mention the gauntlets, but if Saar-in-Tachthyr really had been the stronghold of Iriskavaal's mages, she might never have a better chance to learn about Echentyri magic.

"Why do you even want us?" said Csorwe to Oranna. "What's in it for you?"

"Well, as you can see," said Oranna, "I'm not as nimble as I once was, and I need the help of those I can trust."

"What makes you think you can trust us?" said Csorwe.

"You know exactly what," said Oranna, with a little smile. *"May the abyss consume the breaker of promises."*

It was rare to see Csorwe flinch. Shuthmili might have missed it if she hadn't been watching so closely.

"You mean the pledge," said Csorwe.

There was a scar that snaked across the back of Csorwe's left hand, the remnant of a long-ago bargain. Shuthmili had got used to the scar—just another part of Csorwe's history—and forgotten what it meant. Almost, but not quite. Two years ago Csorwe had made a deal with Oranna, and sealed it with a pledge in blood, and Oranna had not yet called in what she was owed.

"Of course," said Oranna. "I am not interested in compelling anyone to do anything that they do not wish to do."

"Sure, that definitely sounds like something you would say if it was true," said Tal.

Csorwe rolled up her sleeve, revealing the scar: a pale wriggling curlicue. In an ancient Oshaarun script, it was the character signifying *obligation*.

"I promised Oranna three days' service. So she could force me to do this if she wanted to."

"Yes," said Oranna, "Csorwe is bound to me by blood. I could call in the pledge, if I needed to. But I do not yet need to, and if you are *truly* opposed to working with me, I will leave. If you agree—and I hope you will—we can talk terms."

"Good job bringing her here, Talasseres, one of your top choices of all time—"

"Oh, screw you, Csorwe, what else was I going to do?" said Tal. "I didn't know you'd signed some kind of insane blood pact with her—"

Oranna was back in the canteen talking to Cherenthisse, and as much as Shuthmili would have preferred to keep an eye on them, someone needed to make sure Csorwe and Tal didn't come to blows.

"Anyway, didn't you hear everything she told you?" said Tal.

"Yeah, Sethennai is missing, and some dangerous wizard or fragment or whatever wants him dead? They can join the club," said Csorwe. Shuthmili sometimes suspected the two of them just sniped at each other when they didn't want to think about something else, such as what exactly Belthandros Sethennai might be up to. "Why do you care?" Csorwe went on. "Why are you helping her?"

"Because I love to hear constantly all about what an idiot I am, and then get stabbed in the back," said Tal. "Or the front, probably, all standing around like, *I dunno, maybe she's changed, wow what a big knife that is.*"

"You just can't let go of Sethennai, that's what's going on," said Csorwe. "Do you really think that if you help him he'll say, *Come back Talasseres, all is forgiven?*"

"Fuck off, obviously not! Either she's right and something's after him—and look, I know he's an asshole, but I don't want him to fucking die, all right?—or she's wrong and he's *up to something.*"

"And if he is?" said Csorwe, although Shuthmili could see very well that this was a facade. After all this time—after devoting the better part of her life to Belthandros Sethennai, and after two years free of him—there was a part of Csorwe which still wanted to drop everything and come running at the mention of his name.

"If he's up to something, I want to know what it is. So I can stay away from it," said Tal, which was a certain kind of logic, to be sure. "And stop Oranna getting her nasty hands all over it. And if there are loads of gold statues in this place, you never know, we might be able to come away from this with bags of cash—"

"Tal's right," said Shuthmili. "Not about the bags of cash, I've made my position on looting quite clear, but . . . I'd prefer to know what's happening. Better to find out it's nothing and feel stupid than to sit here and then get taken by surprise when it turns out it's *not* nothing."

"I did give Sethennai back the Reliquary," said Csorwe, with reluctance. She gave Shuthmili a rueful smile. "And before you say he's not my responsibility, I know. But nobody knows him as well as we do. And Cherenthisse wants to go," she added.

"I do think she might try to get there on her own if we don't help her," said Shuthmili. "And I can't blame her. It's all that's left of her home."

"Uh-huh," said Csorwe, "and I saw how *you* looked when she was talking about the place."

Shuthmili felt her cheeks redden. She hadn't been conscious of looking any particular way.

"It's not just about Cherenthisse. It's more than making our names," said Csorwe. She reached out and clasped Shuthmili's hand in hers. "This is what you've always wanted to do. You said *time does nothing but take from us.* I don't want to stop you from taking something back just because I can't face him."

At last Shuthmili thought she understood. While Belthandros Sethennai had remained in Tlaanthothe, he had been a known quantity, a spider hiding out in his web, visible but far out of reach. Now that he was out in the world, he could be anywhere, and Csorwe would rather know for certain than be taken unawares.

"We've faced up to him before," said Csorwe. She looked terribly brave. What must it be like, to have that kind of courage? Once Csorwe saw what needed to be done, she never turned away from it.

"You too, Tal," said Csorwe. "He's just a person. I think we should go."

5

The Whale-Road

THE SHADOW OF the whale looked small from above, skimming like an arrowhead over the billowing canopy of the deepwood. The shadow of the *Meat Cleaver* was even smaller, flitting along after her. Tal watched uneasily, keeping a firm hold on the rope he had been told to grip.

"Nothing like a whale close by, eh, Charossa?" said Cujug, the first mate. "Nothing like it to make you realise what a rickety old hulk this is."

Cujug wasn't wrong. The *Meat Cleaver* was an old whaling ship, rusty and greasy with decades of whale oil, and the whale was a great sleek monstrosity that flew as if it was a knife making fillets of the sky. If the *Cleaver* hadn't been the only ship that would take them within reach of Saar-in-Tachthyr, none of them would have gone near it. Tal was pretty certain it would take just one good shove for the whole thing to come apart.

They had agreed to Oranna's proposal. Of course they had. Shuthmili couldn't leave an old ruin alone. Csorwe couldn't help running after Shuthmili. And Tal—well, they all knew how badly they needed money after the way the last job had gone, and if there was one thing Tal knew about ancient temples, it was that they were bound to be packed with treasure. Csorwe had made her little speech and set her jaw in the way that meant she'd made up her mind, and it was a done deal. Cherenthisse had spent several days piecing together old maps to plan their route. And now here was Tal, working for his fare aboard the *Meat Cleaver*. At least all he had to do was hang on to this rope. That was his whole thing, hanging on.

"Poor old sow still doesn't know she's being chased," said Cujug, indicating the whale. Cujug was a stout Oshaaru woman whose tusks were engraved with tiny ships. "They hardly ever know until you prick them, ha ha."

Up ahead, a flock of red starlings hung above the canopy. The whale slowed to feed, opening the sieves of her jaw like a lady's fan and mowing birds from the sky.

"Head down, Charossa!" said Cujug. Tal doubled up, shielding his face, and the ship hit the cloud of birds. Claws, beaks, stench, feathers, screaming. The bodies of birds beat against Tal's stomach and shoulders like hailstones.

When the ship emerged from the flock, the whale was gone, dipped beneath the surface of the forest, and Tal's cheek was sliced open from the corner of his eye to his jaw.

Tal swore and clapped a hand to his wound. It was deep enough that it wasn't hurting yet. The sting would start to set in soon.

"Go and see the medic, you lummox, that'll fester," said Cujug.

Unfortunately, the medic on duty was not Shuthmili but Oranna, who grinned at him even as he presented his cheek to be fixed. Oranna didn't use magic to heal, which was fine with Tal, but it did mean he had to sit there and clench his teeth while she dabbed at him with an alcohol-soaked rag.

"Yeah, laugh it up," said Tal, "I got feathers in my *mouth*, when I see Sethennai I'm going to kick his arse—"

Oranna clapped her hands as though promised a high treat, and began to prepare a dressing.

"Sit forward and take your medicine, Talasseres, unless you think it will be a good revenge to appear to Belthandros with advanced sepsis," she said, and slapped the dressing across his face, pressing it carefully in place.

"Yeah, and what about you?" said Tal. The dressing stung as if it were full of nettles, and he resisted the urge to pick at it. "What do you want with him, anyway? I thought you just really wanted to bone down with *the one whom must not be named*."

"My goal, as it has ever been, is true communion with the Unspoken—"

"Oh, *cackle cackle, I know something you don't know*, sounds a lot like a fancy way of saying *bone down* to me."

She laughed. "Talasseres, you must have had a very alarming sex life. Normally, when a god possesses somebody, it is the end of them. Divine power gnaws up the living body like a dog with an old sock. But supposing a mortal vessel and a divine patron could nourish one another? Could grow together as one?"

Tal had spent more of his life than he cared to countenance listening to long discourses about wizard stuff that he didn't understand, but unlike Sethennai, Oranna seemed to expect a certain amount of input.

"Yeah, what then?" he offered. She smiled, horribly pleased. He was just hoping he could forget he'd ever heard her say *sex life*.

"There would be a fusion of identity, both halves mingled in one body.

That is true communion. True incarnation. Immortality. And that is what Belthandros Sethennai has achieved."

"This is why I don't like magic, you know," said Tal. "You're all *such* freaks."

"It must get tiring, being so normative," said Oranna. Tal didn't know what this meant, so score one to him. "I'm sure Belthandros spun you a line about what a ruinous thing it would be for the world if someone else achieved what he himself has been doing for years. But Iriskavaal was a tremendously destructive goddess, and yet Belthandros has used her power to—remind me?—amass a substantial wine cellar, indulge his corporeal appetites, and brainwash a couple of orphans. Spare me your concern on that front."

"I'm not an orphan," said Talasseres. "My mother's alive."

"Thank you, I welcome education on this point," said Oranna. "In any case—"

"The Unspoken sounds a bit shit, to be honest. Don't get why you would want it."

"It's not for myself that I want it," said Oranna. "There is such thing as a higher purpose. I intend to become the Unspoken One's living emissary on earth."

"But what would you even get to do? Just hang out in a cave and eat a bunch of kids?" said Tal.

"I would live," said Oranna. "Can you really blame me?" She flexed her hands, cracking the knuckles. "I hadn't anticipated how *tired* the blight would make me. I can bear very well with pain, and I have no fear of death per se, but I do resent the days when I am good for nothing."

Tal, in fact, could blame her, and was about to say something about how it would be doing everyone a favour if she would succumb to mage-blight as soon as convenient, but she smiled ruefully.

"Complaints are so gauche," she murmured. "If I had longed to spend my last years sitting by the fire and groaning, I could have stayed at the House of Silence. I have not been in the business of making life easy for myself, and it is no use getting self-pitying about that now."

Before Tal could formulate an answer to this, there was a scream from one of the foretopmen. The crew were paid in a share of whale oil, and there were bonuses for the sailor who spotted the whale. He rushed back to the deck.

The canopy rustled—an enormous noise, like wind sweeping down a hillside—and the whale breached, coming up from the treetops in a perfect evasive arc.

There was a storm of activity as the deckhands swarmed to their stations. Cherenthisse was among them, bare-armed, hauling on a rope as they towed the struggling whale aboard and clamped it.

Cherenthisse had adapted surprisingly well to life aboard the *Meat Cleaver*. Tal didn't quite know what to make of her. She mostly wanted to be left alone, and Tal could respect that.

The chase began in earnest. As usual, Tal's only job was to hang on to the rope, but he couldn't look away from the whale. The urge to stop and gawk at something nasty was a powerful one.

"Here we fucking go!" yelled Cujug, and the harpoon crews deployed into their dart-shaped cutters.

When the chase was on—when they were close enough to smell the leaf-mould reek of the whale—the crew of the *Meat Cleaver* moved together like the limbs of a single terrible beast. A single hunter, compound of iron and flesh, stretching its claws across the open sky. The death of whales, thought Tal, and felt a weird pang of sympathy for the huge stupid monster.

The harpoon crews arced and threw in array. One long volley and another, piercing hide and muscle. The harpoon cutters were tethered to the *Meat Cleaver* itself, and there was only a half second of slack before the whole ship shuddered and the whale began to pull. For less than a minute they had the sensation—mostly terror, partly exhilaration—of being dragged along under the power of something stronger.

Then the whale's resolve faltered, and it slowed. It was over. They had it.

This time, it was Shuthmili's job to deal with the whale. Although they were supposed to divide the work equally, Oranna had an ingenious way of vanishing at the critical moment.

So be it. Shuthmili was, as Oranna said, the better butcher. She pulled on her gauntlets in readiness.

Three steel clamps held the wood-whale in place, locked helpless to the deck of the *Meat Cleaver*. It was not yet dead. The tail still beat against the stern, like an arrhythmic hand on a skin drum. The rank and panicked breath poured from the slits in its flank.

The fore-clamp was set with a ladder of rungs, and Cujug lifted Shuthmili up to the crown. This was what they paid her for. At the crown of the steel collar was an opening, exposing the nape of the whale's neck. Shuthmili knelt down, clinging to the rail with one hand. The whale was not aware of her. She wondered whether it knew the crew of the *Meat Cleaver* were living things like itself, or whether it thought the ship itself was the enemy.

It was suffering. Anyone could tell that from the way it moved, but Shuthmili could see its pain in pale, jagged flashes. Its flesh heaved, rising up to brush her bare hand, and now she saw the lines of agony so vividly that she recoiled, as if they could burn: jets of pain where the harpoons had punctured its skin, and where the piles of the clamps were driven down through hide and fat.

Still, if the whale got away now, it would live, and it would probably destroy the ship. There were stories of such things happening. It was possible that some grand predator hunted wood-whales, down in the depths of the forest beneath, but the whales had no fear of anything in the sky, and they were known to be vengeful. The wood-whale ate nothing but birds, but its jaws were wide enough to crush the ship whole.

This was why whalers were prepared to hire mages. If you didn't have Shuthmili, you needed a specialised blade, shaped like a trefoil, which you drove down through the opening in the clamp, and severed the spine of the whale. Cujug had told her that it usually took them two or three tries to kill the thing, and every attempt maddened it. With each desperate moment, it was more likely that the whale would shatter the clamps and thrash the ship to pieces. Shuthmili did not need the blade.

The stretch and snap of the ship's canopies faded, and then the endless rush and sigh of the trees below. Her vision darkened.

The body is a palace of many rooms. A whale is no different from anybody else in this respect. A thousand thousand subdivided rooms, all flooded with rage and terror. Shuthmili drifted from one to another, following the current of the pulse to the whale's heart. She watched the chambers contract and release like a closing fist. In here, she could kill with a thought. The whale wouldn't feel anything. It was almost easier to do it than not. It was dizzying.

Every chamber of the wood-whale's heart could have held Shuthmili's own body easily, squeezed and released it without crushing her, if she had been there in the flesh and not just in thought. She positioned herself at the wall of the greatest chamber, shaped her will into an executioner's blade, and brought it down.

Silence. Stillness. Cease.

The whale's heart stopped, the blood stilled, the great brain went quiet. Shuthmili clung to the top of the fore-clamp. Her skin was sticky with sweat, and for a moment she thought she was coated in whale's blood. Ichor bubbled at her lips and spilled from the corner of her mouth. The salt-bitter taste of it was grounding for a moment, and then it was gone.

—she was nowhere, there was nothing left of her, her consciousness floated in darkness like a single mote of dust. Before her, above her, an immense shape, a grand dark brilliance, a single regarding gaze which would have incinerated her flesh if she had still possessed any—

QANWA SHUTHMILI. I SEE YOU AS YOU SEE ME. YOU KNOW WHO I AM. WE MUST TALK.

The Queen of Decay. The Fire That Devours. The Dragon of Qarsazh.

Lady Zinandour, said Shuthmili. *Where are we?*

THIS IS THE VOID, said Zinandour. THE VOID'S IMAGE, MADE VISIBLE.

Floating, as if immersed in black water, but without substance. Above her, the goddess glowed. Zinandour's form coiled and twisted on itself, larger than the cathedral of Qaradoun, scales and claws and many exquisitely feathered wings. She had taken the form of a dragon, of the kind which had ruled the skies of Qarsazh thousands of years ago. The feathers were blue-black, like a magpie's wing, but with an iridescence a thousand times deeper, every colour reflected in on itself, magnified in darkness.

I HAVE SOMETHING TO OFFER YOU.

In one sense this was all very strange and new. In another sense, not. Shuthmili had been a child when she had first realised that the shadow watching over her was something much bigger and much worse than a person.

No. Let me go back, she said.

IN TIME. YOU SEE AND COMPREHEND ME. YOU KNOW WHAT I AM.

I always knew what you were. Children don't have imaginary friends in Qarsazh. If your daughter tells you about something you can't see, you call the Inquisitorate. Let me go!

Shuthmili noticed only now that the goddess' immense body was bound all over by golden shackles, great hoops of engraved metal that pinched at her scales and contorted her clawed limbs. She did not believe physical bounds could hold a divinity, so this must be some kind of metaphor. Long ago, in punishment for an immense betrayal, Zinandour had been severed from her vessel and banished into the void beyond worlds.

At the School of Aptitude, Shuthmili had learned of the Traitor-Dragon and her due punishment, and accepted it as truth, and had never until now imagined what it might be like to live through it—

No. I do not want what you are offering, she said, shutting herself off as hard as she could, pushing away any pity she might feel for the goddess.

The vision dissolved, and she opened her eyes. Csorwe was shaking her, eyes wide with concern.

"I'm all right," she said. "I'm fine."

To distract herself, she hooked her arm round the back of Csorwe's neck and pulled her down to kiss her. This was good, this felt right, and real, and as if she belonged in her own body.

Behind them they were already flensing the whale. Shuthmili had watched them do this in the past, and she hadn't seen a corpse dealt with so summarily since her medical training. Well, not so neatly, anyway. Even once they were belowdecks she could see it in her mind's eye: a living thing reduced to lamp oil and corsetage, stripped to gristle and arches of ribs, like a mechanism laid bare for cleaning.

"Tell Oranna she can do the next whale," she said, and for the first time in a very long while, she offered up a prayer to the Nine Gods of Qarsazh that they might find something at Saar-in-Tachthyr to help her understand the gauntlets, something that could help break Zinandour's hold on her. She had no wish to face her goddess again.

"Think that was the last one," said Csorwe. "Apparently we're almost there."

The *Meat Cleaver* put in to resupply at Shallow Point, and the five of them disembarked. Shallow Point was a small town built on timber platforms, anchored in the crown of a single tree. On their outward journey over the great forest that covered this world, the *Meat Cleaver* had passed over settlements from time to time: villages nestled in clearings or swaying in the branches of the trees. Shuthmili had sometimes seen bird-fishers trawling the treetops with nets suspended between two cutters. They were now going beyond mortal habitation. Shallow Point stood at the edge of the true deeps, the last settlement for thousands of miles. The true deeps were the forest proper: an ocean of great trees, fathoms high and thousands of years old, blanketing the continent and cosseting away all manner of strange secrets in the darkness of their roots. The ruined Echentyri temple complex of Saar-in-Tachthyr was one such secret.

Now, as the *Meat Cleaver* shrank toward the horizon, the five of them stood on the quay with their baggage and took stock. Tal in particular looked as if he'd be glad never to see the *Meat Cleaver* again. Shuthmili hadn't seen much of him on the journey, although at one point Cujug had asked Csorwe if he was single and she had laughed until she choked on a biscuit. Once upon a time Shuthmili would have worried that he might bow out. Since then she'd learned that one of the things he shared with Csorwe was a complete inability to quit.

Csorwe hired a cutter with the last of their cash, and they loaded themselves and their baggage on board. It was half a day's easy sailing above the canopy, and then Cherenthisse indicated that it was time to descend.

The treetops rose toward them, a slow explosion of green. Then they hit the canopy: an assault on the senses like dropping into the plunge pool of a waterfall. Leaves foamed and branches whipped in the wind. All around them was noise and confusion.

Then, almost at once, they pierced the canopy. The branches closed overhead. The noise ended as if they had stepped out of a crowded room, and they were in a green darkness. Shuthmili felt as if she'd put her face underwater, with the same sense that this place could not be survived for long. Above, the sunlight came through the leaves in mottled patches.

"Enjoy the light while you can," said Oranna. A light breeze blew her hair in shining waves around her head.

"Do you have any idea what we should expect, on the forest floor?" said Shuthmili. "I remember reading a little about the true deeps, but—"

Oranna grinned. "Did it take you a real effort not to raise your hand?"

"Yes, I was a pleasure to have in class," said Shuthmili. "Well?"

"I have never been here," said Oranna. "But by all accounts, it is alien, intractable, and dangerous. I am looking forward to it."

By now, the daylight had given out altogether. Shuthmili pulled a blanket round herself and tried to rest. The cutter moved in a sphere of bluewhite light from the lanterns, one near to where Shuthmili was sitting and one nodding at the bow like the gleam of an angler-fish.

All around them, the trees were visible only as shadow on shadow, a shifting and unfamiliar architecture. Shuthmili felt like a spider clinging to a pillar in the cathedral of Qaradoun. Then she made the mistake of looking down.

The trunk of the nearest tree plunged away—impossibly far, dizzyingly far, like a road stretching into the distance—until it found its vanishing point or lost the light. The ground was no more visible than the bottom of a well.

She closed her eyes against the fear. *The light is not for me, anyway,* she said to herself. Her goddess was a creature of the deep earth, the darkness under the world. *Zinandour, Queen of Decay, Paragon of Rot, Devouring Fire, keep me from my enemies—*

A sudden flash of pink blossom. A smell of iron, rotting fruit, smoke on the air. The cherry tree in the courtyard of the Qanwa townhouse.

I AM WITH YOU ALWAYS, said Zinandour. *REMEMBER—*

Oh, I remember well enough, said Shuthmili.

The five-year-old Shuthmili had loved that tree in the way any small girl loves a floating palace of blossom. In a rare moment of interest, her father had told her that the tree would never bear flowers and leaves at the same time. The flowers fall to make room for the leaves. This had not made sense to her: why *shouldn't* the tree have leaves and flowers at once? Why not fruit, now she was thinking about it? The leaves were sleeping in their beds inside the twigs, and every blossom was the future ghost of a cherry. The tree knew how to make them.

She had curled up at the bottom of the tree and poured herself into it. It had taken a little work, but once started, it was easy. The tree rustled, and shimmering waves of green poured out along the branches. The flowers swelled and burst like raindrops. Blood and ichor dripped from her nose.

I lost four teeth, you know, said Shuthmili. She had to imagine how they had found her: slumped in the grass, surrounded by piles and piles of already-rotten cherries. *And they sent me to the School of Aptitude.*

MORTAL CHAINS ARE COBWEBS, QANWA SHUTHMILI. I WILL MAKE YOU FREE. FREE OF ALL WHO WOULD PERSECUTE YOU.

I see. And I return the favour. Is that it?

I OFFER YOU AN ALLIANCE THAT HAS NOT BEEN KNOWN FOR MILLENNIA. AN HONOUR BEYOND PRICE.

To be the gate through which you return? I don't think so.

Zinandour growled, a rumble which would have rattled Shuthmili's bones if she'd had any.

MY BEING IS INFINITE. MY PATIENCE IS NOT.

I know the terms of your imprisonment, said Shuthmili. *You can escape the void if you can convince a mortal vessel to accept you in true incarnation. I am hard to convince.*

AND YET, IN FOUR THOUSAND YEARS' IMPRISONMENT, YOU ARE THE FIRST TO HEAR ME CLEARLY—

What do you mean? said Shuthmili.

CONSIDER WHAT WE MIGHT ACHIEVE TOGETHER. THAT IS ALL I ASK.

Of course it is, said Shuthmili. *You know, they spent years in the School preparing me to resist this very temptation. It's almost a bit embarrassing that you're exactly like they said you would be.*

I AM AS I HAVE EVER BEEN. ARE YOU? YOU FREED YOURSELF FROM THEM. WHY SHOULD YOU BE THEIR CREATURE STILL?

The vision was broken by the sound—the wonderful, perfect, familiar sound—of Csorwe nearby, trying to light the alchemical stove and swearing.

"Why won't this piece of shit ever work when you want it to?"

One of the others must have taken the wheel. Csorwe had set out the teakettle and the caddy of ironwort and the tin cups on a bench in the cabin, all with the same eternal unassuming neatness. Shuthmili could almost have wept. Instead, she rose from her bench and kissed Csorwe on the top of her head.

The portable stove was an ancient enemy. They'd got it secondhand, and it was probably older than Shuthmili. She snapped her fingers, and the stove crackled to life.

"Wow, you're so cool," said Csorwe, in only half mockery. She gave Shuthmili a lopsided grin that made her gold tusk glitter. Shuthmili thought she had never seen a more beautiful sight. What a thing it was to have met someone so remarkable. What a strange cast of the dice that all space and time should have conspired for her to love like this, what an undeserved and impossible blessing to be so loved in return. She wrapped her arms round Csorwe's waist and pulled her close, pressing her face to her neck. Her shirt was unbuttoned, and Shuthmili could feel her heartbeat in her throat, a tenderness that almost hurt her.

All the while, the goddess was still waiting for her answer, a dark pressure behind her eyes.

I am not anybody's creature, said Shuthmili, with finality. *I am not anybody's but hers.*

6

The True Deeps

Dust and stillness lay on the forest floor in drifts, thick and stifling, smothering noise and slowing their progress. The very bottom of the true deeps was a labyrinth of rocks and stumps and pillarlike tree trunks, endlessly dark and half buried in spongy, vegetal dust, knee-deep where it wasn't waist-deep. The air was still and thick with spores, smelling richly of mould.

The cutter engine coughed and choked, and all of them but Oranna had to get out and walk to spare the engine for the return journey. Cherenthisse assured them that they were no more than a few miles from the temple.

The muffling quality of the dusty air made it difficult to talk much, but Shuthmili had enough to occupy her in their surroundings. Alien, intractable, and dangerous, as Oranna had said, the true deeps were more than anything *beautiful*.

Overhead—unimaginably high above—was the colossal vault of the canopy, the moving sea of life and growth and noise, and they were down here, small and slow-moving, crawling across the jagged face of a warm and living darkness. Every surface was draped and layered with moss and lichen, as heavy and as intricate as the blood vessels of the gut wall. Shoals of fungi gleamed like coins at the bottom of a well. Spores glittered. Fruiting bodies shivered. Swarms of silvery beetles scuttled away from the light. Shuthmili had to school herself to keep walking, to focus on only what fell within the scope of her lantern. After a while it was futile to try and identify what kind of life she was seeing: worms and tendrils, sacs and tubers, florescent moulds and sloughed petals.

"Well, it's official," said Tal. "This is the most disgusting shit I've ever seen, so you're probably like, *Will anyone notice if I lick it?*"

Shuthmili jumped. She'd been so absorbed in watching that she hadn't even noticed him approaching. "Surprise, I've been licking everything since we got down here. What's the matter?"

"When was the last time you saw the cutter?" he said.

"What?" she said. "It's just—" She looked up, expecting to see the blue-white bubble of the lantern just ahead. No sign. She looked round, fear rushing back up to clench round her heart, and there it was—three hundred yards away, far to the left.

"Right," said Tal, and grimaced.

"I suppose I'm lucky you're not the lecturing type," she said. Her heart was still racing. A few more minutes, and the cutter would have passed out of sight altogether. If Tal hadn't noticed she was gone . . . "There's something distracting about this place."

"Yeah, it looks like god threw up on it," said Tal. "Had to round up Csorwe and Cherenthisse earlier too, wandered off like a couple of bloody toddlers." Cherenthisse had been very quiet for most of the journey, focused entirely on the route. Shuthmili's best guess was that she was past the first shock of loss and was deliberately losing herself in the task.

"Her and Csorwe are such a fucking pair," said Tal.

"Pardon?" said Shuthmili.

"You don't see it?" said Tal. "They're both like, 'I *could* pull this stick out of my arse, but it would take time out of my packed frowning schedule.' Next time I look away, you're gonna be married to both of them."

"They'll both have to present a compelling matrimonial petition to my family's solicitor," said Shuthmili. "Which will come as a surprise to my father, because the last he heard of me, I was convicted of murdering my aunt."

"Qarsazh is weird," said Tal.

"Everywhere is weird," said Shuthmili. "Do people even get married in Tlaanthothe?" It was nice how much easier she found it to talk to Tal now than when they'd first moved to Cricket Station, she thought, now that they each knew they could let their guards down a little.

Tal shrugged. "You don't have to. My mother never did. It's not a big deal."

"Do you think you ever will?" said Shuthmili. She knew immediately that it hadn't been a good question to ask. The guard went right back up. Romance was a touchy subject with Tal, as was anything in the nature of long-term plans for the future. Shuthmili had lived with Tal for two years, on and off, and she was pretty certain that he hadn't met anyone else in all that time. He never brought anyone back to the apartment, and whenever they went to meet him in a bar, he was sitting alone. Her plans with

Csorwe were sparse but solid: their own ship, and all the worlds ahead of them. Csorwe sometimes talked about maybe opening a restaurant. Shuthmili daydreamed about having her own library. As far as she knew, Tal had no such dreams, and nobody to share them with. It really must have been pretty intolerable for him, at times, living with them.

"You can wander forever," said Tal, absently. Clearly not an answer to her question. Just something that had occurred to him.

"Pardon?"

"You can wonder forever," he said, striding on through the undergrowth. "You never get an answer."

He sounded awfully distant. Shuthmili raised the lantern to try and see his expression. It was dreamily unfocused, at odds with how fast he was walking. Much faster than she could easily go.

"Tal," she said, scrambling to keep up with him. "Stop. Look at me."

"We're nothing to them," he said. "Nothing."

"I know," she said, reaching for his hand.

"Small things," he said, to nobody in particular. "Just little earwigs that die all the time. That's all we are."

He didn't sound upset or angry about it, but reflective, almost amazed, as though it had all become clear at that moment.

"We don't matter," he said, reaching out and turning his hand in the dust that sparkled in the air. "None of it matters. Look at all this. This is real, this is really real, everything here is dying, but it'll never die. And after we're gone, it'll still be all the same. I'm going to put out the lantern."

"*No*," she said, grabbing for his hand and clutching tighter to her own lantern, just in case he went through with it. "Talasseres, where is the *fucking* cutter?"

He stopped, and she managed to catch hold of his hand, and clung to it as if he were hanging from a high window.

"I didn't know you could swear," he said, and gave her a smile of such genuinely maddening blitheness that she understood why Csorwe talked all the time about murdering him.

"Look around!" she said. "It's gone! I have no idea where we are!"

"It's got to be something wrong with the forest," said Shuthmili. They had walked in circles for what felt like hours, and had finally set themselves up at the bottom of a tree to wait. "Perhaps because it was once the place of Iriskavaal . . . Even if she's long gone, the shadow of a divinity can be very persistent. There are cursed objects from the reign of Zinandour which still have to be kept under seawater in the Inquisitorial Treasury, and her half-life is probably much shorter than Iriskavaal's because she's a younger deity, so—"

"Just imagine me nodding and smiling," said Tal. "Back in Tlaanthothe, our goddess was just a big mean rock that muttered at you."

"It's all right," said Shuthmili. "It *will* be all right. Once Csorwe realises we're missing, she'll come back in the cutter and search."

She wished she could be sure of that. They were lost in a maze of endless night, and even if Csorwe hadn't been led astray as they had, she could search forever without finding them. All their supplies were aboard the cutter. They had no food, no water, and that was without knowing what else might lurk out in the forest.

Tal seemed less worried. Maybe it helped not to know anything about magic. That way you didn't know what might happen to you, lost in the dying domain of a goddess. A quick death, or a slow death, but a certain death all the same.

Then again, Shuthmili had a divinity of her own. Iriskavaal mouldered, slow and ancient; Zinandour burnt hot and vicious. Perhaps what this forest needed was the fire that devoured.

She pulled on her gauntlets. The surge of possessive intent was vivid and immediate but not, this time, distracting. Cherry blossoms fluttered across the surface of her mind and then cleared, leaving her perfectly lucid.

YOU WILL DEAL WITH ME, THEN?

Not yet, she said. *But you are still my patron, if I may still call upon your power.*

Shuthmili scrambled down from her perch and knelt on the ground, sinking an inch or two into the seething dirt. Hands flat on the ground, she sent a pulse of enquiry directly into the earth. A moment of vertigo as she felt the edge of the root system, almost as big as the tree itself, extending far in every direction—much further than she'd expected. A net that extended for miles, a web of astonishing beauty and complexity, precision and elegance. She could fall into this forever and never hold it all in her head. She could sink down and become one with the pattern, and—

No! MINE!

"Shuthmili!" She felt a pressure which she identified at length as a hand gripping her shoulder. "Your eyes rolled back in your head, try and fucking focus for one *second*—"

"They're all one tree," she murmured. "All the same organism. Like the Quincuriate . . ."

"Can you even hear me?"

She murmured assent, reaching further. The root system seemed to have no centre point. It *was* like the Quincuriate, a distributed intelligence. Which made her life harder because, unlike the whale, it had no heart to stop. But perhaps a self-replicating curse—something which could multiply itself along the roots, branch and adapt and poison as it went—it would take an extraordinary amount of power, but she *had* that power, if only she'd reach for it.

YES. IT WOULD NOT EVEN BE SO FAR TO REACH.

Tal was saying something, but she couldn't understand what he was saying over the roaring in her head, the awful formula unfurling itself. She knew exactly how she would do it. It would be the best magic she'd ever done. She had been the best in the School of Aptitude, and this would make her the best in the world, perhaps the best of all history—

"What is a forest, anyway? Worlds die all the time," she said.

Tal grabbed her by both shoulders and shook her. She could feel the useless panic in him like a trapped animal, beating against the bounds, and it would be so easy just to quiet him, and then she could concentrate, but—

"What the fuck are you doing? How is this helping? I thought we were going after Csorwe—"

DEAL WITH HIM. THERE ARE THINGS FOR US TO DO.

"No!" she said.

There was a horrific struggle in the dark. Tal tried to hold her still, and her limbs fought back, clawing and slapping at him, but at last her hands were free again and she was on all fours on the ground, choking on the dust and ichor in her throat. The two of them struggled back upright and leant back against a tree root, breathing hard.

"I'm fine," said Shuthmili, her voice shaking as much as her hands.

"You threw up a whole lot of slime!" said Tal. "On my shoes!"

"Yes, well," she said. "If I start doing it again, I'm fairly certain you know where to hit someone to knock them unconscious."

"It's not as easy as it looks," said Tal.

"I'm sure you can manage," she said. "But perhaps it's best if I don't use magic for a while. I don't like this place, and—"

She broke off. Over Tal's shoulder, glowing like the first light of dawn, was a lantern, and from the way it was moving, it was attached to a cutter, fast approaching.

She should have felt relief. Instead, anxiety knotted in her stomach. This was not the blue-white light of an alchemical lantern, but the sunny yellowish glow of a freshly cast magelight.

The cutter came gliding into view and slowed. A tall, broad figure leant over the side, silhouetted in the light, but evidently considering them.

"You two look lost," said a voice.

Tal's eyes widened. Shuthmili would have known from the unbridled horror on his face if she hadn't already recognised the voice.

"Maybe I can help," said Belthandros Sethennai.

Not even Tal thought it was a better idea to die in the woods than to go with Belthandros. They got into the cutter.

"You know, upon running into old friends in the woods, one might experience a moment of awkwardness," said Belthandros, seated in the cockpit. He looked exactly as Shuthmili remembered: deep brown skin, curly hair doing its best to escape from an expansive topknot, an expression of veiled and watchful amusement. From the sharp flicks of kohl at the corners of his eyes to the gold rings in his leaf-shaped ears, the impression he gave was calculatedly that of a pirate king who still found time to visit the barber. "But luckily I never feel awkward."

Tal clenched his fingers in the fabric of his trousers. His ears were low and flat against his skull. "*Old friends,*" he said, with a visible effort.

"What would you prefer?" said Belthandros, without looking round at them. "You're here with Oranna, are you? Looking for me?"

"Yes," said Shuthmili, at the same time Tal tried to deny it.

Belthandros gave an odd laugh, one part genuine amusement to one part resigned exasperation. He and Oranna really were a good fit for each other.

"Typical of her. Another flock of ducklings," he said.

Shuthmili was still reeling. She had come close to something irrevocable. She might have vomited if not for the indignity of throwing up on the fresh varnish of Belthandros Sethennai's immaculate cutter. But however weary and however shaken she was, this was going to be her conversation to handle. Tal had gone as silent and surly as she had ever seen him.

"We're here with Oranna, but she's looking for Saar-in-Tachthyr. I expect you are too."

"You're Csorwe's friend," he said, thoughtfully.

"Yes," said Shuthmili, raising her chin, daring him to make something of it. In the end, though, all he said was:

"What does Oranna think she's going to find there, I wonder? I would not have imagined that the lost temple of Iriskavaal would interest her."

Belthandros' cutter was sharp-nosed, glossy, and compact, as if designed specifically to navigate the true deeps. Perhaps it had been: the engine purred, apparently having no trouble at all with the dust, and the passenger area was covered by a sleek canopy that protected them from the worst of the spores. Speaking of which—

"We ought to take some precautions," she said. "The forest is affecting our minds in some way—I think it must be the shadow of Iriskavaal, since—"

"Possibly," said Belthandros, and she felt an unexpected flush of embarrassment to realise that she had been trying to show off. "I'll see what I can do to shield us."

Belthandros looked back at her and grinned. It was objectively a charming smile, unguarded but conspiratorial. You were meant to feel that you were being welcomed into a joke, whether you liked it or not.

"Well," said Shuthmili. "This explains what they tell you about getting into boats with strangers. You never know who'll turn out to be a living serpent god."

Shuthmili sank back into her seat. Something about Belthandros' presence made her very aware that she was covered in dust, that a trail of prickly spores had worked their way down the back of her neck, and that she smelled of sweat and rotting plant matter. Next to her, Tal had folded his spindly legs into his seat and wrapped his arms around them, a tight defensive kernel.

The yellow magelight cut a path through the forest, illuminating the immense curvature of the tree trunks in bright segments, gilding the intricacy of the undergrowth. It was almost like a library, she thought. The colossal uprights, the dust falling in beams of golden light, the sweet mild smell of decay. Like being a single mote floating between bookshelves.

Csorwe had tried to explain to her, in the past, how pleasant it had sometimes been to work for Belthandros. How safe and familiar you felt, knowing that everything was under control, that someone else was doing the thinking for once. Shuthmili hadn't understood it until now. Her thoughts drifted, and she didn't realise for some time that Belthandros and Tal were talking quietly.

"There's nothing to stop you coming home, you know," Belthandros was saying. "Once everything's washed up here."

"No?" said Tal.

"Csorwe seemed very determined to burn that bridge," said Belthandros. "But I did wonder . . ."

A long moment of silence. The ship swept smoothly over a fallen trunk, where a cluster of mushrooms glowed like pearls.

Was this why Tal had never met anyone? Because he was waiting for something like *this*?

Shuthmili shifted in her seat, torn between her desire to know and her sense that she was intruding on something private.

"What did you wonder?" said Tal, very quiet. His voice sounded constricted, and as Shuthmili's eyes adjusted, she saw that the points of his ears were fluttering. This made her miserable. The whole appeal of Tal was that he was rude and lacked contrition, so what was the point of making him crawl?

"You can wonder forever," said Shuthmili, sleepily but loudly. She yawned and blinked as if only just waking. "Where are we?"

Tal jolted upright and gave her a look. She couldn't tell if he was furious or relieved.

"As it happens," said Belthandros, "we are approaching the compound of Saar-in-Tachthyr."

The cutter darted out between two trees as if emerging from a canyon, and suddenly they were in open space: a glade so vast that the foliage must have thinned out overhead at its centre. A faint dappling of light reached down from above, gleaming jade and gold on the surface of an enormous lake. It was perfectly flat and perfectly round, and the surface was thick with flat floating leaves, each one big enough to wrap the cutter twice over, overlapping each other so that the water seemed to be covered with smooth green scales. They bore flowers like white water lilies—exactly like the specimen they had found in Tvelujan's cutter, except that each petal was as large as a sail. The scent of water rose in the air, sharp and beguiling.

Belthandros steered the cutter down to dart between lilies, apparently for no reason but the joy of it, something Shuthmili could not bring herself to resent. She leant back in her seat and let out a slow breath, relieved to experience fresh air and natural light for the first time in a while. Skimming over the lake felt, she imagined, how it would feel to be a dragonfly on the ponds of the Botanic Gardens in Qaradoun.

"Once upon a time, this was the inner domain of Iriskavaal's priesthood," said Belthandros. "This was a sacrificial basin. The bones are probably still down in the water."

"Goodness, really?" said Shuthmili. "Oranna would love that."

"Probably best not to mention it. Most of the sacrifices were Oshaaru prisoners from the cult of the Unspoken."

Shuthmili had almost forgotten about the conquest of Oshaar, though Professor Tvelujan had never shut up about it.

"One of Iriskavaal's first annexations," said Belthandros, with neither pride nor regret. "Long before the House of Silence was built, long before I assumed my incarnation, the Lady of the Thousand Eyes and her honour guard subdued the Unspoken and subjugated its people. I remember parts of it, in fact."

"How?" said Shuthmili.

"My goddess split off a part of herself to join with me in the incarnation. In becoming the person I am now, I inherited some of her memories," he said.

Shuthmili thought, with a bizarre pang, of Dr. Lagri Aritsa, her old supervisor at the Survey Office, a mild and gentle fusspot who would have knifed his colleagues to be first to talk to Belthandros. Here was an eyewitness account to confirm or disprove centuries of conjecture. He couldn't be trusted, of course, but if only you could sit him down and get it on the record, what a source you'd have . . .

"But as I said, the conquest of Oshaar was many thousands of years ago," said Belthandros, "and I have enough difficulty retaining even the memories of this body."

"It must be strange," she said. "So you do still remember being a mortal? Being Pentravesse? Do you remember having a mortal childhood?"

Tal scowled as if this was an impolite question, but on the one hand she didn't care whether Belthandros thought she was polite, and on the other hand he didn't seem to mind talking about himself.

Belthandros smiled thoughtfully. "Perhaps it would help to think of Iriskavaal and Pentravesse as two streams flowing into one river. At the beginning of the incarnation, there were two of us, goddess and man, together in one form. But now . . . I am who I am."

He wasn't just a source, then, but a living artefact, an unprecedented magical phenomenon. Shuthmili wondered with a sudden yawing of the stomach what it might mean for her, given how often she'd been hearing Zinandour in her head these days.

"Are we nearly *there* yet?" said Tal, with more spirit than she'd heard from him in a while. She turned to smile at him encouragingly, but he returned a sour look that she couldn't interpret, looking almost like a flash of actual hatred.

"What's wrong?" she mouthed at him, but he shook his head, dull-eyed with resignation once more, as if wishing he was a hundred miles away or dead.

Shuthmili realised, horrified, that it had been a look of jealousy, that he must have assumed she was somehow trying to get Belthandros' attention. She blinked, feeling as if the cutter had suddenly dropped a few feet.

I was only making conversation! she thought, staring at Tal. *What on earth?*

He didn't meet her eyes. Csorwe had talked sometimes about the way they had squabbled for attention. Years of fighting for the notice of this man who clearly thought of no one but himself. After that, no wonder anyone could look like a threat.

The cutter swooped close to the surface of the lake again, the keel almost brushing the water, and now Shuthmili saw there were islands in the lake. The nearest was a small crescent-shaped spit of land, half overgrown with weeds and mottled with patches of light from above.

There was still no sign of the others. The glade was very quiet: water whispered, but there was no wind, no hum of insect life. Despite the humid warmth, Shuthmili shivered.

"Something is here," said Tal. "In the water." His hand had gone to his sword hilt.

"Yes," said Belthandros, and now Shuthmili heard it too: a shifting in the water, an almost undetectable rippling. Before she could pinpoint the source of the noise, there was an almighty roar, a great detonation of water, and something burst up from the surface of the lake. A wave broke over the edge of the cutter, slapping the timbers with enough force to send them spinning off course.

"Get down!" called Belthandros.

Shuthmili flinched and ducked, shielding her face with her arm. When she looked again, she saw it, overwhelming and inescapable as a solar eclipse. Soaring up out of the depths, cascading sheets of weed and water, there came a gigantic serpent.

7

The Most High Atharaisse

T HE SERPENT MOVED with terrible precision and terrible speed, a single arc of muscular power driving directly toward the cutter. As they spun out of control, Shuthmili saw only brief flashes: the ivory scales of the snout, the cavernous mouth opening, the red tongue flickering, and then Belthandros wrestled back the steering and swooped up out of reach. The serpent's mouth snapped shut with a hiss like water on gravel, and she reared back. The serpent's coils were pale in the green water, the great tail stirring up waves as it whipped back and forth.

"Pentravesse," she said, without speaking. Her voice tore across the surface of the mind like a scalpel slicing paper.

"Really, Atharaisse?" he called. He was out of breath but otherwise sounded as if this was no more than a mildly complicated social call. "Won't you pay me the compliment of asking questions first?"

Atharaisse regarded him through a red and gleaming eye.

"We know the reason for thy coming, 'Belthandros Sethennai,'" she said. "Ambitious as ever. We are disappointed in thee."

"Oh, *spare* me," said Belthandros, taking the cutter up and back, out of reach of those great teeth. "How long have you known what you are, Your Highness?"

"We awoke with thee," she said. "We are Iriskavaal's loyal handmaid, and thou art a pretender to an incarnation that thou didst not deserve."

Not just words now but images, scrawling themselves viciously across Shuthmili's brain, burning as they went.

—*In a room high above the city, Belthandros opened a rosewood box—in a cave far beneath the desert, Atharaisse opened her mouth to scream—in the lost and distant reaches of the worlds, after the sleep of centuries, many eyes opened in darkness, and all the scattered fragments of Iriskavaal saw the world anew—*

"We know of thy dealings with the Siren, and not only with her," said Atharaisse.

Distantly, Shuthmili heard Tal screaming. She clutched her temples, trying to defend herself from the onslaught, but it was impossible to shut them out.

—*In a room lit by a single suspended lantern, Belthandros stood before an obelisk of polished stone.*

—*Deep beneath the glassy surface of a dead world, he searched the wreckage of a fallen monument.*

—*In other worlds, in sea caves and marshes and barrows, he sought, and found what he was seeking. And he raised his hand to destroy.*

"The two of us are not Iriskavaal's only inheritors, Atharaisse. There are countless other godlings, countless shattered pieces, and all of them are waking. And yes. I have destroyed as many as I could find. I do the world a service. A mercy."

"So you *did* kill the Siren," said Tal.

"Yes," said Belthandros. "I regret it, as I regret any loss of friendship."

"Thou needst not lie," said Atharaisse. "There is no mercy in thee. Thou wishest to complete thy usurpation of my God-Empress' dominion. Thou wouldst not share power with any other."

"My dear, the God-Empress is gone. Iriskavaal is dead. You and I are the last embers of a glory that has left the world."

"Pretender! Scavenger! Desecrator of the dead!" hissed Atharaisse, and launched herself at the cutter again. She had been hanging back deliberately, letting them drift closer, now she struck the gunwale with an impact that overturned the vessel, spinning it end over end like a flipped coin.

Shuthmili saw none of this. Her bones rattled in her sockets with the concussion and the world turned in on itself as she was flung into midair. A flash of sunlight overhead, then green-dark-green as she fell. She hit the surface of the lake and went under.

The water was shockingly cold after hours in the thick warmth of the true deeps. The impact drove the breath from her lungs in a jangling cascade of bubbles, and she took a panicked gulp of lake water before clamping her mouth shut.

She could swim, but not with confidence, and the more she struggled, the heavier her clothes seemed to become. It was too dark to find the surface. Then she felt a strong grip close around her, and she was sure it was the serpent, meaning to crush her or drown her. She kicked and flailed as best she could, but she was so cold and her boots were like weights dragging her down.

Then whatever it was lifted her above the surface, and she took a huge involuntary gasp of breath.

"Shuthmili, stop—it's *me*," said Csorwe. "Hold on—"

The world turned over again, and she had the sensation of being hauled roughly up out of the water, and the next solid thing she knew, she was on the deck of Csorwe's cutter, coughing her lungs up.

Oranna was standing on the stern, one hand on her hips and one on her staff. "One of you get to the wheel!" she called. Shuthmili felt Csorwe press a kiss to her forehead and saw her throw herself into the cockpit.

Ah. That's right, thought Shuthmili, spitting out a strand of waterweed. *Some kind of fight going on.* The others must have arrived on the scene just as Atharaisse struck. But where were Tal and Belthandros?

Cherenthisse crouched beside her, frozen behind a bench. Her eyes were very wide, the red spark in them burning vividly in the half-light.

"Another lives," she muttered. "No—no . . ."

That was going to be a problem, but it would have to be a problem for later. There was Belthandros: still at the wheel of his cutter, darting around the serpent's head as if trying to disorient her. The steering was partly blown. His cutter drifted choppily in the air, and every time it stalled, Atharaisse made another attempt to bite.

"Oh, we should let him die," murmured Oranna, nearby. She was working up to something. Shuthmili could sense the power building around her like a cloud massing. "How deeply he would deserve it."

"No!" said Csorwe, but Shuthmili didn't think she meant Belthandros. Tal was there too, on the stern of the other cutter, the blade of his sword flashing silver in the twilight, as though he himself had become part of the lake. Shuthmili still didn't know anything about sword fighting, but seeing Tal in action, you realised why he had been born so long and thin and flexible. When he had the blade in his hand, everyday gawkiness was suddenly translated to an unexpected speed and grace. Csorwe fought with brutal precision and efficiency. Tal was a calligrapher.

But even Tal could only do so much in the air, against a monster ten times his size, and Shuthmili could see he was getting desperate.

"Don't be *stupid*—" hissed Csorwe. She brought her cutter round at speed, swooping in toward the fight. Cherenthisse yelped and ducked, Shuthmili gripped the bench with both hands, Oranna merely adjusted her footing. They were too late to stop him. Tal sprang from Belthandros' cutter and landed squarely on the serpent's head, driving the point of the blade down into her neck.

The serpent shrieked, a crackle of psychic rage that threatened to black out Shuthmili's vision all over again. The wound didn't seem to have harmed her—Tal clung to the hilt of his sword as she thrashed from side to side, and then he and the blade were flung wide, arcing up through the air, limbs flailing.

He fell to earth on the shore of the crescent-shaped island, driving up a white blade of spray as he skidded through the shallows and lay still on the sand. He didn't move.

"Tal!" said Shuthmili. They could reach him in a few moments, but the serpent's whole body roiled in the water between them.

"The loss of thy friendship I regret also, Pentravesse," said Atharaisse, in a soft rasp that fizzed like seafoam settling, and she dived toward Belthandros' cutter with her fangs parted. He gave up on trying to steer away and leapt free of the cutter.

Belthandros hit the surface of the water just before her jaws could close around him, narrowly dodging her bite. She reared back to strike again, raw power in the curve of her neck like a drawn bow, but at the moment of release, something stuck. Knotted coils of mud and weed closed around the serpent's body, pulling her back and down.

Nearby, Oranna was standing upright, her eyes closed in concentration, her hand braced on her staff. She had done this, but Shuthmili couldn't see how—

It wasn't just mud. Swarming up from the lake, thick with silt, draped in pelts of weed, came hundreds of revenants. Intact through long ages, the devotees of the Unspoken who had died in the sacrificial basin returned to serve.

Shuthmili glanced up at Oranna. Her eyes were open now, and bright with glee, her whole expression suffused with exhilaration.

"*Nothing is to be forgotten that belongs to me,*" she said.

The revenants continued to rise, finding their footing on each other's ribs and skulls, scrambling up to clutch at Atharaisse in their dozens, making chains of mud and bone to drag her down into the water.

"Such blasphemy," muttered Cherenthisse, pale with disgust.

There was no sign of Belthandros. In the confusion of the moment, Shuthmili had no idea where he had gone—was he still in the water?

Atharaisse hissed, recoiling. Every thrash of her tail threw off a few bodies, sending them sloshing back into the lake, but there were always more to come, and they were fearless. She lunged toward Csorwe's cutter, trying to break her focus, but Csorwe dodged easily, and with a mouthful of sludge and fragments of bone, the serpent could not bite.

"Indignity!" howled Atharaisse. "All shall suffer!"

The serpent sank back into the water, dislodging wet skeletons as she went. She darted a single red glare of hatred at Oranna before disappearing beneath the surface. The water closed over her and settled.

Oranna lowered herself carefully back onto the bench, leaning on her staff for balance. The revenants turned to face her, hundreds of them standing up out of the water like reeds.

"Go—" she murmured. "Go, rest . . ."

As she flopped sideways onto the bench, the revenants dispersed in the water like so much stirred mud.

As soon as it was clear that Atharaisse was gone, at least for now, Csorwe landed the cutter on the shore of the little island and leapt out. Shuthmili and Cherenthisse followed. Tal was still lying facedown on the sand.

"What the fuck was that, Talasseres?" said Csorwe, kneeling beside him and touching his shoulder. "What was the *point*?"

Shuthmili scrambled down out of the cutter—she would see to Oranna later—and took her place at Tal's side, pressing a hand lightly between his shoulder blades.

"He's alive," she said, "still breathing. Heart beating—I think it's just a bruised rib."

"Yeah, no shit I'm alive," he said, and rolled over onto his back with a groan. "You don't hurt like this if you're dead."

"Nice going," said Csorwe. "Next time just gut yourself and get it over quicker."

"Bet I looked cool."

You looked like a pigeon flying into a window, you dick."

"Do you need me to look at your rib?" said Shuthmili.

"No, I've got loads," said Tal. "Just let me lie on the ground for a few years, I'll be fine."

Shuthmili, Csorwe, and Cherenthisse between them helped Oranna out of the cutter and onto the island. She sat propped against a rock, uncharacteristically limp and silent. By now the water had settled back to stillness, lapping softly against the gravel beach. Everything was very quiet.

"Where's, uh—what happened?" said Tal.

"Where's Belthandros, you mean?" said Oranna. The last they had seen of him, he had dived into the lake to escape Atharaisse's jaws. She withdrew a tin of resin lozenges from her pocket and popped several into her mouth at once. "I'm sure he's fine."

Tal's ears twitched. If not for his rib, Shuthmili was sure he would have been pacing. Csorwe's nervous tics were less obvious, but unmistakeable if you knew what you were looking for. Her elbows were drawn in tight at her sides to make herself a smaller target, her head bowed slightly as if in fear of falling rocks. Cherenthisse loped up and down behind them, her thoughts clearly turned inward.

"I guess we know who's been trying to kill him now," said Csorwe.

"Perhaps," said Oranna. She shut her eyes and sat back in what was clearly meant to be an attitude of repose, belied by the taut line of her mouth.

"I think we've been wrong about that," said Shuthmili. She explained what she and Tal had witnessed of the conversation between Belthandros and Atharaisse.

"Wait—" said Csorwe. "That was Atharaisse? The snake?"

"No, some other fucking snake," muttered Tal.

Cherenthisse's head snapped up. "Atharaisse? The Most High Atharaisse?" she said. "They were all dead—everything was gone—and yet she lives?"

"Apparently so," said Oranna.

"You would have made a traitor of me," said Cherenthisse, her eyes widening.

"No—" said Shuthmili. "Listen, who is she? The Most High Atharaisse? You knew her?"

"She is the chosen favourite of Iriskavaal, our princess, the blessed heir to the God-Empress—I cannot explain. You know so little. Your words are inadequate."

Oranna nodded, a slow smile creeping across her face. "This confirms a great deal. Shuthmili, you will have seen references to the *God-Empress* in Echentyri literature, I do not doubt?"

Shuthmili nodded. "It's a title of Iriskavaal."

"Yes. But I have long suspected that *God-Empress* is a reference to a specific manifestation of a specific aspect of Iriskavaal. The Throne was her wellspring, but it is difficult to rule an empire as an inanimate object. I think this confirms my theory. We know that one divided part of the goddess became Pentravesse. But I think he was not the first. She also routinely chose one of her subjects as a vessel. A princess, to succeed when the former God-Empress inevitably necrotised under the strain of divinity. Cherenthisse, is that correct?"

Cherenthisse looked as though she had been casually asked to identify the corpse of a loved one. Reluctantly, she nodded.

"So!" said Oranna, delighted. "If I surmise correctly, our friend the Most High Atharaisse was hatched and raised to become a vehicle for the goddess. Perhaps became incarnate around the same time as Belthandros, since they clearly know one another. Does that sound about right?"

Cherenthisse's lips were drawn back from her teeth in disgust. "These are sacred mysteries."

"It's all right, dear, I'm a priestess," said Oranna.

"I do not have to listen to this," said Cherenthisse. "You will have no more answers from me."

She turned her back and strode down to the water's edge, her shoulders high and tight, moving even more jerkily than usual. Shuthmili would have to talk to her later and smooth things over.

"Perhaps I should not be surprised to find Belthandros and Atharaisse so much at odds," said Oranna. "My sister was ever my greatest ally—but I suppose not everyone is so lucky."

"I knew her, too. Atharaisse, I mean," said Csorwe. As usual, her expression didn't give much away, but there was something in her eyes which perhaps only Shuthmili recognised, a distant, wounded expression. Csorwe had a special sympathy for those who were born for sacrifice.

"We should talk to her," said Csorwe. "She saved my life."

"She can get in line, we've all saved your life," said Tal. "And she's not interested in saving it anymore. Her and Sethennai were like, you know when a bird sees itself in a mirror?"

"No," said Csorwe.

"You know what he used to be like, when he was really focused on something," said Tal. "Like nothing else even existed."

Csorwe grunted in what Shuthmili took to be assent.

"Like that, but two of them," said Tal.

"I suppose that explains why she wants Belthandros dead," said Shuthmili. "But she hasn't been destroying the other fragments of Iriskavaal. That was him."

"I *told* you he was up to something," said Tal.

"And Atharaisse is here to try and stop him?" said Csorwe, hopefully. "We might be on the same side."

Shuthmili suppressed the urge to gather Csorwe up in her arms. There was nobody in the world who felt the smallest kindness the way Csorwe did. This Atharaisse had been slightly nice to her ten years ago, and won a friend for all time.

"Possibly," said Oranna. "Or else they're both here looking for something else, and she doesn't want him to get there first." She popped another lozenge and chewed it thoughtfully. The smell of the resin was penetrating and surprisingly familiar. Shuthmili only now recognised it as black lotus, a hallucinogen employed by the cult of the Unspoken. "I don't think I like that idea very much."

"Well," said Shuthmili. "We came here to find Belthandros. We've found him. What now?"

Nobody responded. Shuthmili looked from one to another, finding Csorwe startled, Tal stricken, Oranna feigning amusement. This seemed disproportionate to what she'd actually said.

"My ears are burning," said Belthandros. She spun round to find him standing ankle deep in the shallows, looking exactly as a person might look had they walked out of a lake: soaked to the skin, trailing waterweed, and not very amused by the situation.

"You're bleeding," said Csorwe, sharp with alarm, as if the years had fallen away all at once. Shuthmili reached out to take her arm, but she'd taken a step toward Belthandros.

He looked down, frowning, as if she'd told him his waistcoat had come undone. His shirt was dark red, and the stain was spreading.

"Careless of you, dear," said Oranna. Her expression was a carefully composed blank, empty and unblinking as a clean dinner plate.

"Ah. Just as well I can't die," he said, and fainted.

8

Something Very Difficult

THERE WAS A still moment, as fragile as an eggshell, in which it seemed as though the four of them might just stand there and watch as Belthandros Sethennai drowned in three inches of water.

Then Oranna said, "Well? Must I do everything?" and the stillness broke with a snap.

Csorwe and Shuthmili dragged him out of the water, hard work because he probably weighed as much as the two of them put together. Unconscious, their greatest enemy, the thing they had feared for so long, was just a bulk like a sack of onions, which left a furrow in the sand as they hauled him up the beach.

Csorwe stood back, examining him from a safe distance. Her expression shifted uneasily between cynical grimness and a blinking horror. She had always been so bad at trying to be cynical. Belthandros was leaking blood into the gravel.

"Is it true he can't die?" said Tal. He'd clearly meant to scoff, but his voice was strained, as if the pain of his bruised rib had only just caught up with him. It wasn't the first time Shuthmili had wondered what supernatural quality Belthandros possessed that made smart and sensible people lose their minds.

She knelt on the gravel, pulled on her gauntlets, and peeled away the shredded flaps of Belthandros' shirt. She noted clinically that his entire torso was tattooed, fresh designs overlapping faded ones like graffiti on a wall. The wound was wide and deep, slicing into his belly just below the rib cage. He'd be lucky if it hadn't punctured a lung. Much easier if she could think of this man as a squashy machine of tissue and bone, rather than the person who had, for better or worse, meddled with the psyche of everyone she cared for.

"Bad but fixable," she concluded, and set to work.

Zinandour returned to her, immediately and urgently. The power flooded through her at once, knitting Belthandros' flesh and skin effortlessly: no pain, no inflammation, the whole system sluiced with clean blood—no scar, in fact, the skin fused so exactly that there was scarcely a shivering in the lines of his tattoo.

Shuthmili felt a wave of satisfaction at a job neatly done, though she couldn't have said whether this was the goddess or herself. It felt so very right, so safe, so pleasant. She couldn't remember now why she'd been worried about trying to stop this connection. This was *her* thing: reading the body, untangling its syntax, amending and resolving. It had always been her thing, and Zinandour had always been with her. Shuthmili had spent her whole life in the palm of her goddess' hand. Surely it was not such a terrifying thing to take that hand in her own. It would mean letting go of herself, but then she'd never enjoyed being herself very much, had she? Fussy and fretful and inhibited, frightened of herself, fundamentally limited, probably lacking something other people had—

I WOULD MAKE YOU WHOLE BEYOND WHOLENESS, said Zinandour. *BEYOND FEAR AND BEYOND LIMITATION.*

"Shuthmili!"

Csorwe stood over her. She reached out and touched Shuthmili's face with her sleeve. Shuthmili puzzled over this odd, careful tenderness, and then realised she must have had blood on her cheek.

"I'm all right," said Shuthmili, but she leant in and buried her face in Csorwe's chest all the same, breathing in her scent. She felt as if she was falling, tumbling over and over into a bottomless well.

"What's your full name?" said Csorwe, stroking her hair.

"Qanwa Shuthmili," said Shuthmili. The seal of the Qanwa house was a blue iris, it had been painted on all the doors of her childhood home, the townhouse where she had killed the cherry tree—

"Where did we meet?" said Csorwe.

"Precursor World Alpha-Twenty-Something—I don't remember the whole designation, but I was very distracted by you—you looked like a wild creature, so watchful—"

I do not want it, she said, and hoped the goddess could hear her. *I do not want the incarnation. I only want to be here with her. And if I am limited, so be it. She loves me like this.* She took off the gauntlets and tucked them into the pocket of Csorwe's coat.

By now it was almost night, and the patches of murky sunlight were dwindling to nothing on the water. Soon it would be just as dark on the shore as it had been in the woods. Only the faintest flicker of reflected emerald light was visible on the deeper green of the lake.

Tal and Belthandros were recovering from their injuries, Oranna and Shuthmili were both drained, and Cherenthisse showed no sign of moving from where she had sat herself down, huddled at the water's edge with her arms wrapped round her knees. After a minimum of argument, they decided to stop and rest here on the island.

Oranna and Shuthmili used the last of their energy to ward off a rough perimeter, so they would at least have warning if Atharaisse returned, or if anything else came up out of the dark to attack them. Csorwe fetched poles and oilskins from the cutter and set up the tents. Tal lit a sorry sort of campfire and sat staring into it, wilfully ignoring Belthandros' prone form beside him.

Belthandros regained consciousness gradually, with Oranna hunched over him like a particularly territorial vulture. Once he was leaning upright against a rock, Csorwe sat down opposite him, crossed her legs, and squared her shoulders. Shuthmili recognised her way of making herself an immovable obstacle.

"All right," she said. "Time for some answers."

Tal rolled his eyes, but after a moment's hesitation, sat down beside her. Shuthmili took up her station on the other side.

Belthandros gave Oranna a sidelong look—sharing a joke, rather than looking for assistance.

"No, actually, I rather agree with them," said Oranna. "Do I understand correctly that *you* destroyed the Siren of the Speechless Sea?"

"The Siren served me faithfully," said Belthandros, folding his arms behind his head. "I don't see that it's any of your business to be outraged."

"Don't misunderstand me, dear heart, in fact I'm moderately impressed that you had the necessary follow-through to carry it off," said Oranna.

"Would you believe me if I told you that she begged for an end?" said Belthandros.

"Not really," Tal muttered.

Oranna's lip twitched, but she went on smoothly. "And you are the one responsible for eradicating the other remnants of Iriskavaal."

"Yes," said Belthandros. "I cannot regret doing so. You saw what was left of the Sleeper yourself. They were sad, broken, half-formed things, hungry for power and carelessly destructive."

"How very sad for them," said Oranna, with all the gentleness of a razor's edge.

"Why are you doing this?" said Csorwe.

"That's what I want to know," said Tal. "You used to do all the Siren's festivals—"

Belthandros gave them both a look of mingled curiosity and irritation, as if a piece of furniture had spoken up for itself.

"You two have become very inquisitive," he said.

Shuthmili doubted he would give away anything of his reasons unless he was forced to. She pinched the bridge of her nose, remembering what Atharaisse had shown them.

"He's been killing the other fragments—and he's been *eating* them, I think," she said. "Like tadpoles. We had them in the pond at the School one year." She had always liked watching them. "Eventually there was just one big, round, self-satisfied one left. It turned into an even worse frog."

Belthandros raised an eyebrow at her. Oranna gave a wry smile.

"An apt metaphor is always so troubling," said Oranna. "It explains why Atharaisse is so eager to get in your way. Such blasphemy against the goddess! You really must be trying to impress someone."

He laughed. "As a matter of fact, you have it the wrong way round. I have been labouring this past year to get in Atharaisse's way. Another reason to destroy the fragments is that if I do not, they may fall into her hands. As quickly as I can neutralise one, she hunts down another. It has all been rather exhausting."

"I see," said Oranna. "Nobody else can have what you want. Such jealousy is not attractive, I must say."

He laughed again, without mirth. "Perhaps you do not know what remains in this world. Alone of all the territories of Echentyr, Saar-in-Tachthyr was preserved to serve as a monument. The surviving priests stored up the most treasured remains of their civilisation and closed the temple before swallowing poison."

Oranna nodded at this proper priestly behaviour. Shuthmili could not help experiencing a small thrill at the idea of treasured remains—what might that mean?—before looking around for Cherenthisse, wondering how she might have reacted to any of this. She was still down at the shoreline, however, sitting with her back to them, staring out at the dark water.

"So let me guess," said Tal, in a sleepy drawl which did absolutely nothing to mask the bright spark of panic in his eyes, "there's some heinous snake bullshit here and you want your hands on it."

"How I've missed your way with words, Talasseres," said Belthandros.

Tal looked as if he'd been slapped. Csorwe looked as if she might slap someone.

"The Mantle of Divinity was brought here to be buried," Belthandros went on. "It is one of Iriskavaal's most sacred relics. The last and greatest reservoir of her power, sewn from the shed skins of her incarnations."

"And I assume Atharaisse wants to take it for herself," said Oranna.

"Or maybe she assumes *he* wants to take it for himself," said Tal.

"Also a strong possibility," said Oranna.

"She did call him a desecrator of the dead," said Shuthmili.

Belthandros gave them all a hard look.

"As a matter of fact, neither Atharaisse nor I could take the Mantle for ourselves. Like most objects of power, it is surpassingly dangerous. It cannot be taken. It can only take from others."

"You expect us to believe that?" said Tal, still bristling.

Belthandros shrugged. "I cannot prove anything to you. But that was the original purpose of the Mantle. To provide a mouthpiece for the goddess, a speaker of prophecy, entirely under Iriskavaal's control. Rather like Csorwe's original situation with the Unspoken One, breathing lotus and speaking with the voice of the god. Not something in which I have any need or desire to participate."

"If that's true, why have you both come here?" said Shuthmili, trying to ignore her aggravation at the casual way he brought up Csorwe's past.

"Oh, I think I've got that," said Oranna. "Neither of them can tolerate the idea that the other one might have found some way to exploit the Mantle without risking themselves."

"It's not possible. The Mantle consumes and controls the wearer," said Belthandros. "Back in Echentyr, it devoured the bodies of innumerable sacrifices. I very much doubt that Atharaisse wants to be consumed any more than I do."

"You're still here, though," said Csorwe. "Just in case there's something you missed?"

"None of you are inclined to give me very much credit, are you?" said Belthandros. Shuthmili had expected him to bite back at them, but he only smiled sleepily and ran a hand back through his hair. "I believe the Mantle is dangerous and ought to be destroyed before some fool gets themselves possessed. That's why I'm here. Atharaisse thinks it should stay locked away here as a memorial to the blessed memory of our patron goddess. That's why *she's* here."

"You're sure about that?" said Csorwe.

It was the first time Shuthmili had seen even a twinkle of hesitation on Belthandros Sethennai's face. Oranna was right: he might be almost entirely certain that he was cleverer than Atharaisse, but the remaining sliver of doubt would eat him up.

"Well, tomorrow I mean to enter the temple and find out," he said. "And I suggest you all think hard about whether you plan to get in my way."

The priests of Saar-in-Tachthyr had once had a handsome bathing house on one of the islands, an enclosed portion of the holy lake covered by a dome of white marble. It was now overgrown with weed and water lilies, so that only the faintest outline of the elegant columns remained. The smooth incline down to the surface of the water was thick with moss. Cherenthisse dragged herself up onto it by her fingernails, gasping. Working out how to swim in her prey aspect had been three parts drowning and one part thrashing. Only the memory of her true aspect, the feeling of her own muscular strength cutting through cool water, had kept her going.

Still, for a long time all she could do was lie there. She was alone, surrounded by the sound of the water lapping at stone. She could just stay here, listening and remembering, and let her broken body give itself up to the moss.

The others had not seen her go. They had no respect for her, nor for her goddess. To them, Echentyr was at best a mystery to be unravelled, and at worst, a corpse to tear apart. But there was another alive, and not just any other, but the Most High Atharaisse, the last true serpent, a surviving remnant of the goddess to whose service and protection Cherenthisse had devoted the greater part of her life. The hope that surged in her was painful, like a rush of bile, but it was enough to raise her to her feet.

She made her way unsteadily into the bathing house. A frieze of painted tiles recalled the Thousand Eyes' ancient conquest of Oshaar: there was the fleet rising above the mountains, there was the *Blessed Awakening*, sunbright, raining fire. There was the God-Empress descending in splendour.

There was the triumph in the streets of Echentyr, the parade of Oshaaru captives, every one of them rendered in detail with individual tusks.

They would have been painted by some prey creature, of course—that was the kind of manual work suitable for them. Cherenthisse had never much reflected on this, and did not like to dwell on the fact that she was now stuck with hands that could hold a paintbrush. She looked up at the painted skyline of Echentyr, almost as she remembered it. That was home. They would make it home again, and even if she never found her way back to her true aspect, she would be where she was meant to be.

Water rippled in the channel beside her. Cherenthisse did not move. She had been waiting for this—hoping for it, in fact, with a desperation she would not let herself feel in full.

The Most High Atharaisse rose up from the water in a white arc, hardly disturbing the surface, and looked consideringly down at her.

"What art thou?" said Atharaisse.

For a moment Cherenthisse knew shame and terror. Presenting herself to the Most High in this degraded form was an insult. But what else did she have?

"My Princess," said Cherenthisse. She kept her head bowed, feeling her cheeks grow hot with mammalian blood. "I am Cherenthisse. I am the last of the Thousand Eyes. And I am here to offer you my service."

Shuthmili slept like the dead, and, like the dead, she was woken in total darkness by Oranna's voice.

She sat up, rubbing her eyes. Csorwe and Tal were both fast asleep, though each of them was curled tightly against opposite sides of the tent to avoid touching the other.

"Shuthmili," came the voice again, whispering from outside the tent. "We need to talk."

Shuthmili wriggled upright, without disturbing the others, and peered out of the tent-flap. Oranna was wearing only her shift, and her hair fell loose to her waist.

"I don't think we do," said Shuthmili. "I'm sure this can wait until morning."

"I need your help," said Oranna. Her jaw was clenched, and Shuthmili realised she was holding her hand tight against her side, and saw that what she had taken for a shadow was a splash of blood all down the side of the shift, running in streams down the skirt and muddied at the hem as if Oranna had mopped at something with it.

"Can't you ask Belthandros?" said Shuthmili. Oranna and Belthandros had taken the other tent, and even at this distance Shuthmili had been able to hear them laughing. Cherenthisse had said she preferred to sleep on the ground outside, and Shuthmili did not blame her.

The blood on Oranna's shift was ink-black, so probably Oranna's own, since Shuthmili now knew that Belthandros bled red.

"*No*," said Oranna, with startling force. "If you won't help, I'll do it myself." She clamped her left hand around her right, pressing it tight to her ribs, and Shuthmili saw another rivulet of blood escape.

"I don't know if I can heal you," she said. She didn't want to do too much magic until she'd figured out how to block out Zinandour's voice.

"I don't want healing," said Oranna. "If you're holding out in the hope that I'll say *please*, stop hoping."

Shuthmili had to admit she was curious. She glanced back at the others. The faint glow of the alchemical lantern picked out the sharp lines of Csorwe's profile, softened only a little by sleep. She would be all right by herself for a moment.

"Fine," said Shuthmili, and slipped out of the tent.

Oranna stumbled down to the beach. Her staff stood upright in the sand, with a silvery magelight burning at the top like a beacon. By its illumination, Oranna's face was pale and lined, and her lip was bloody too, where she had bitten it.

"What's wrong with your hand?" said Shuthmili, gesturing her to sit down.

Oranna uncurled her right hand on her thigh with a hiss, and renewed gouts of blood. The black blood and silver light looked unreal, unreadable, and it took Shuthmili a moment to understand what had happened. The little finger on Oranna's right hand was missing, matching the long-healed stump on her right. The amputation was clean and neatly done, but there was no getting over the essential brutality of it.

"I don't think I can reattach this, even if you still have the finger," said Shuthmili, regretting again that she had wasted so much power on Belthandros.

"Tch," said Oranna, through gritted teeth. It obviously hurt to hold the hand outstretched like this. "Defeats the point. No magic. I don't want magic. Just stitch it up. I'd do it myself, but my damned hands keep shaking." She gestured with her good hand to a bag that lay on the sand, beside a pile of notebooks and papers. "Needle and things in there. Have you done this before?"

Shuthmili nodded. She had been trained at the School of Aptitude in minor medicine, on the grounds that it wasn't worth squandering your power on small injuries, never mind that every mage she knew would rather waste a little spark than fiddle around with bandages.

She found the needle case in the bag, and Oranna directed her to a reel of thread.

"Csorwe could probably do this better than I can," said Shuthmili, holding the hand flat and squeezing the edges of the wound together. Oranna took a sharp breath, her whole body twitching.

"Yes—maybe—but you *understand*," she said.

"Mutilation?" said Shuthmili. "Nice girls don't."

It had been a forbidden topic at the School of Aptitude, something distantly understood, that there was power in maiming the body, that Zinandour might accept flesh and bone as fair exchange, and that this would send you slithering rapidly down the bloody slope to corruption. No doubt the Followers of the Unspoken were more relaxed about these things.

Oranna gave a breathy laugh and tensed preemptively as Shuthmili prepared to make the first stitch. It had been a long time since she had done this, but she made neat enough work of it, and Oranna was very stoic, only gasping when Shuthmili poked the needle in. She tied it off and snipped the thread, suddenly aware of the soft weight of Oranna's hand in hers, uncomfortably corporeal. To distract herself from this, she hunted through the bag for bandages, binding them carefully around the palm.

"Pass me my wretched lozenges," said Oranna, once it was done. Shuthmili did so, and she tipped two of them into her mouth at once, directly from the tin. "Ah. Filthy stuff."

"You'll need to keep it clean yourself," said Shuthmili. Keeping out infection was one of the easier healing techniques, surely not beyond Oranna's abilities. "I don't see why you couldn't have gone to Belthandros," Shuthmili added. "The two of you clearly work well together."

"He's asleep," said Oranna.

"*I* was asleep," said Shuthmili.

"Listen," said Oranna, chewing her lozenges. "You are very lucky, in a way that I hope you appreciate, not only that you have found someone whom you consider your equal in life, but that her interests align with yours."

"Well, to be honest, I'm lucky that she puts up with my interests—" said Shuthmili, already uncomfortable with this line of reasoning.

"What I am trying to explain is that one can't ask Belthandros for help, because helping is not what he does. And in my case, because he wouldn't approve of what I've done, or what I'm trying to do."

"Incarnation, you mean," said Shuthmili. She'd never considered confiding in Oranna, for obvious reasons, but for a moment the idea of being able to tell someone about Zinandour, someone who might understand what was happening to her, was almost tempting.

"Indeed," said Oranna. "The hypocrisy is quite astonishing, but then, it always is. Still, it hardly matters. I know how to do what he never could."

Shuthmili reflected that Oranna was right about one thing at least. Csorwe had been a lucky escape for her in more ways than one. She was certainly competitive enough to have ended up in some tangle like this, and it was so much more restful to know it would never happen now.

Among Oranna's books and papers on the ground was a sharp butcher's knife and a pool of black blood which splattered and trickled away into the sand. Oranna had laid down a sheet of canvas to catch the worst of it, a precaution so completely inadequate that Shuthmili could have laughed.

"What were you trying to do?" said Shuthmili.

"Something very difficult," said Oranna. "With success, I'm happy to say."

"If I've been talking to the Unspoken One all this while without noticing, I'll be ashamed of myself," said Shuthmili, in what was at least mostly a joke.

"No," said Oranna. "As I suspected, a radical transformation is required. The process is begun but not complete."

"Have you slept at all?" said Shuthmili.

"In my position, you wouldn't," said Oranna. She flicked her eyes up to meet Shuthmili's. They were a yellow so pale as to be almost white in this light, cool and appraising. Shuthmili blushed, and hoped it wasn't visible.

"Do you like him?" said Shuthmili.

"I'm far too old to talk about boys, dear," said Oranna. She pursed her lips. "To have an opinion about Belthandros would be to give in. Under other circumstances . . . perhaps. But the desire for companionship is not my ruling passion. And in any case, he is not mortal. Iriskavaal is a goddess of conquest and control. One cannot share with Belthandros unless one relishes the experience of extending one's hand in friendship to a rattrap."

She held up her hands: one freshly bandaged, one long healed. "And I have my own uses for these. I see you do not like the idea. But there is a kind of pleasure in taking control of one's own resources, exerting a will that goes beyond the survival instinct." Oranna smiled faintly, as though remembering a joke, and went on, more softly: "It is a condition of our existence that we must spend what we have, and hope to receive value in return. I lost more than a finger this evening. My path is set, and I will not turn away from it. I will live no longer than a year. I console myself that I have struck a hard bargain with the universe."

"What do you get in return?" said Shuthmili.

Oranna smiled. For the first time, the smile was in no way guarded or spiteful or mysterious. She looked exhilarated and not a little relieved.

"Eternity," she said.

They returned to the camp. Shuthmili settled into the curve of Csorwe's body and let her thoughts drift. Curled up here, warm, she felt there was a solid core to the world after all. Things might be all right.

But when she woke the next morning, Csorwe was gone, and Cherenthisse with her.

9

Pity and Mercy

Iᴛ ᴀɴʏᴏɴᴇ ʜᴀᴅ crossed the perimeter to take them, we would know," said Oranna. She looked bad this morning, worse than she had last night, with deep shadows under her eyes. She had staggered from the tent to the campfire and was lying beside it, clasping her hands before the embers as if trying to get warm.

"Could you have missed the alarm?" said Shuthmili. "Either of you? Could Atharaisse have crossed the perimeter?" Her nerves jittered, jangling out the awful possibilities. Csorwe dragged away in her sleep, the serpent's awful mouth . . .

"I very much doubt it," said Belthandros.

"Csorwe wouldn't just have gone without us," said Shuthmili. Csorwe was always practical, always vigilant; Csorwe had a sword and she knew how to handle it; Csorwe did this kind of thing for a living—and yet.

"She wouldn't just wander off," said Tal, "but she did keep going on about how she'd like to talk to Atharaisse."

"She's not that—"

"Don't kid yourself," said Tal. "She's exactly that stupid."

"Why on earth would she like to talk to Atharaisse?" said Belthandros.

"They knew each other," said Shuthmili.

"Atharaisse could have taken her as a hostage," said Belthandros.

"No," said Shuthmili, "it must have been Cherenthisse who took her—unless they're working together somehow, in which case . . ."

The panic which had been swirling round Shuthmili's skull began to tighten, like a diadem of hot metal. She took a deep breath, focusing as she had been taught in the School of Aptitude.

"It hardly matters who took her. Everyone is here for the same thing. Do you know where the Mantle is kept?" she said when she had recovered some composure.

Belthandros nodded. "In the main temple. It's on an island not far from here."

"Then I think we'd better beat them there and take Csorwe back," said Shuthmili. "Tal, how is your rib?"

"Fine," said Tal. He straightened up hastily, then winced, tensing in on himself. *"Fuck."*

"I could heal that for you," said Belthandros.

"I'm fine," said Tal, though Shuthmili saw the pain flicker like lightning across his face.

"You have *two* broken ribs," said Belthandros. "If you won't let me fix them, you should stay here with Oranna."

"Quite an assumption, that I'll be staying," said Oranna, though they all knew it was for the look of the thing. Her head rested on her folded arm, her dark hair spilling over her face in tangles, and her breaths came as little gasps of pain. Whatever magic she had done last night, it had taken all she had.

Shuthmili could see Tal was torn between two options he hated almost equally. "You should both stay," she said. "If Atharaisse comes back here, we'll need to be able to fall back to this perimeter. Belthandros and I will go."

"Where am I?" said Csorwe, when she woke. A reasonable question, given that Cherenthisse had bound her hands and dragged her into the temple while she was unconscious.

Cherenthisse did not answer. She did not understand why the Princess wanted to speak with this one in particular. Of all Shuthmili's party, she had found Csorwe the least communicative and most hostile.

They were in an upper chamber of the great temple, open to the sky overhead. It was immense even on an Echentyri scale, a vaulted bay which would have been large enough to house a thousand serpents when empty.

It was not empty. Occupying the whole space, like a beast in its lair, was a gigantic ship. Its silhouette was fuzzed with vines and drifts of dying leaves, but the sleek lines were unmistakable, silvered with wardlights like waves under the moon.

This was the ship which had brought triumph to the Thousand Eyes for a thousand years, whose shadow froze the hearts of kings. This was where Cherenthisse had been stationed almost all her career. This was the Imperial flagship, the strength of the God-Empress, the *Blessed Awakening*.

"Nice boat," said Csorwe.

Cherenthisse continued to ignore her. The Most High Atharaisse had not instructed her to say anything to the prisoner. She went on clearing vines from the side of the *Blessed Awakening*. She had found a knife in one of the storerooms, a stone-bladed sacrificial dagger whose edge was still wickedly sharp.

"So you're working with Atharaisse now?" said Csorwe.

Cherenthisse glanced over her shoulder. "How is it that you know the name of the Most High?"

"Long story," said Csorwe. "No need to tie me up, you know. I *want* to talk to her."

"Why should I trust prey?" said Cherenthisse.

"Take a look in the mirror," said Csorwe. "You're one of us now."

Cherenthisse hissed, but she was aware the sound was a paltry imitation of her real voice, thin and without resonance. "Never. Never. You have lied to me too many times. You brought me to despair. You made me doubt the justice of the God-Empress. Never again."

"The God-Empress destroyed your world," said Csorwe. "You don't think it's time to start doubting?"

Cherenthisse felt a sudden urge to violence, a vicious burst of energy, and wrenched a handful of moss from the hull of *Blessed Awakening* rather than hitting the prisoner. "No," she said. "Echentyr was hers to destroy, and I am one of the Thousand. Our loyalty is ever undimmed."

Csorwe's mouth turned up at the corner, twisted by some emotion Cherenthisse did not understand. "You know—" she said, in a rather different tone to any Cherenthisse had heard from her before. "You know you don't *have* to—"

Whatever she was about to say, Cherenthisse didn't want to hear it, and she was relieved when a rustling in the hall outside announced Atharaisse's return.

The Princess came gliding into the room, her ivory head held high. Cherenthisse was struck again by her beauty, the architectural precision of her bones, the clean smooth rightness of her scales, the brilliance of her eyes.

After so long looking on the misshapen faces of prey, it was like a drink of cool water.

"Csorwe, in truth?" said the Most High Atharaisse. She moved closer, her pink tongue tasting the air, scenting the prisoner. Cherenthisse ran her hands over her own ridiculous face, newly reminded of all the knowledge she was denied.

"Yes, ma'am," said Csorwe, and smiled, for no reason Cherenthisse could discern.

"Ah, little mouse, we did not think to see thee again," said the Princess, and she lowered her head to get a closer look at Csorwe.

Cherenthisse stared for a moment—*little mouse?*—then realised she was forgetting herself and returned to cutting vines off the flagship.

"I am glad to see you in good health, ma'am," said Csorwe. There was a smile in her voice. She only sounded like this when she was talking to Shuthmili and the two of them thought Cherenthisse couldn't hear.

"Despite the great efforts of thy master, the so-called Belthandros," said Atharaisse.

"I left his service," said Csorwe.

"He deceived thee also? A great pity, a great shame. We had forgotten ourselves, and the wrong that he had done us."

"Uh-huh," said Csorwe. "I know how that works."

"Unbind her, Cherenthisse. We would talk to her in a more civilised manner."

Cherenthisse complied, though she did not return Csorwe's sword. She was dying to ask how they knew each other. She had thought of the three thousand years since the fall of Echentyr as an abyss, a wound in time with no history but the mindless infighting of prey. She did not know what to make of the idea that the Most High Atharaisse might have played her own part in that intervening time.

"Csorwe did us a great service once," said Atharaisse, which really shed no light on the matter. "We desire her service once more in this matter. We know her of old as a destroyer of kings."

Csorwe stretched her arms and looked sheepish. "Hardly get any destroying done these days," she said.

"Belthandros means to claim the Mantle of Divinity," she said. "To despoil the goddess' rest and make of himself a greater tyrant still."

"He said it wasn't possible," said Csorwe. "He said it would take over anybody who put it on, or something—"

"Indeed. One who takes the Mantle trades self-will for undiluted divine power," said Atharaisse. "But to thy knowledge, which is greater in him, self-love or lust for dominion?"

"Huh," said Csorwe. "You know . . . that could actually go either way."

"A balance so fine it is not yet known even to him, perhaps. He would defile the tomb of our beloved Lady in order to discover the limits of his capacity. Sanctity is nothing to him, nor is there any cherished thing he will not burn to feed his ambition."

"Yeah," said Csorwe, "I know that, but . . ." She ran a hand back through her hair, uneasiness plain on her face. "If he takes it—what would change? He's got one bit of the snake goddess in him already. What's one more?"

"The difference between a candle flame and a forest fire," said Atharaisse. "Belthandros' incarnation has had three thousand years to dull its edges. He has settled in the mortal world, made himself comfortable, indulged a taste for mortal things. The true aspect of our goddess is a hunger which no mortal substance can sate."

Csorwe took a moment to think this over. Cherenthisse kept scraping at the wall of the flagship. Even knowing what the Most High had planned for her prisoner, it made her uneasy to bring prey into things. Why should Atharaisse need another servant, when Cherenthisse was right here? Cherenthisse would have done what she asked in a heartbeat.

"Should've known I'd get dragged back in somehow," said Csorwe. "You want me to help you stop him, I guess?"

"There is a great service you might do me, yes," said Atharaisse.

"There are others with me. Shuthmili and Tal," said Csorwe, and after a moment's thought, "and Oranna. I'll help you if you promise the others will be all right."

"Presumest thou to bargain with us, little crumb?" said Atharaisse. Her eyes gleamed approvingly.

Cherenthisse felt something hot and hard rise in her chest, as if she had tried to swallow a coal, but she said nothing, trying to focus on the weight of her stone knife.

"I mean it," said Csorwe. "I'm ready to deal with Sethennai, if I have to. But if you want me in on this, you have to keep the others safe."

"Time has done nothing to diminish thy audacity," said Atharaisse. "Very well. They will not be harmed, so far as their fates lie within our power. But now there is something we would show thee."

The temple island rose up from the mist, pale as the ghost of a palace. It was a stepped pyramid of white stone, overlaced with moss that coursed down the sides of the steps like spilling water.

Belthandros landed the cutter on one of the steps. Up close, the moss was a thick, soft blanket. It released a cloud of sweet-smelling spores when Shuthmili stepped down onto it.

Above them, set into the side of the pyramid with the first step as its sill, was a cavernous doorway, big enough to swallow a merchantman in full sail.

They climbed up to it without further discussion and came into a pillared antechamber. The weight of the air bore down on them, cooler and drier than the decaying warmth of the woods. Wardlights shone out from under a thick coating of moss.

Beyond was an immense atrium. It was laid out like an ornamental garden, a series of lowered terraces, clean and smooth as if they had been swept only that morning. Some of the terraces held shining pools filled with water lilies, miniature versions of those on the lake outside. In the gleaming of the wardlights they were beginning to open. The other terraces were lined with stone chests and pedestals of various sizes, and standing upon them were statues like the one Tal had found in Tvelujan's cutter.

Many of the statues were snakes, coiled or rippling at full length, but not all. Winged bipeds with heads shaped like flowers. Armoured exoskeletons. Mortal figures, locked into embraces that might have been amorous or violent.

"All the riches of the Empire of the Thousand Eyes," said Belthandros, with a melancholy smile.

There were huge amphorae, full sets of armour, and inlaid cabinets, like the portable shrines carried aboard Qarsazhi warships. Model seaships. Incense burners. Treasures upon treasures. Jade, lapis lazuli, cedarwood, marble, and gold.

Shuthmili did not have half a glance to spare for any of it. If she had still hoped to improve the gauntlets, she might have found some answers here, but they had slipped a long way down her list of priorities. Anyway, as far as she knew, they were still tucked inside Csorwe's coat—though that was a worrying thought in itself.

"The gauntlets," she said, breaking into a run to keep up with Belthandros. "Your gauntlets. Csorwe has them. If Atharaisse gets hold of them, is that going to be a problem?"

"Well, quite apart from the fact that Atharaisse doesn't have any *hands*," said Belthandros, "it's not first among my concerns. I made those gauntlets myself, back when I was still Pentravesse. They are intended to shield the wearer and to reinforce their connection with their patron divinity."

"Reinforce?" said Shuthmili.

Belthandros gave her a sharp look. "They were meant to prepare me for the incarnation. They allowed me to get closer to Iriskavaal, to talk to her without an intermediary."

"But I've been wearing them—" said Shuthmili, feeling sick. "I've been—you mean—all this time? That's why Zinandour's been in my head?"

A flutter of cherry blossom, of black feathers, of gold chains gleaming in darkness. The goddess was listening in on this, damn her.

"I did wonder how you were finding the experience," he said. "It's not for everyone."

It made such terrible sense. Such a cruel trap. And she'd thought she could use them to *fix* it.

"I should have realised—would have, if—"

"If you'd wanted to?" said Belthandros. "If you'd realised, would you have stopped? Given the chance to live forever? That's what the incarnation is, you know."

"I don't want to be immortal," she said, though billows of cherry blossom surged in her mind's eye. Immortality . . . the incarnation . . . so many nonsense words. None of it real, compared to what she might lose here. "I just want to make sure Csorwe doesn't get hurt. Why would Atharaisse take *her*—"

"I thought you'd worked it out," said Belthandros, striding ahead. "Atharaisse will not take the Mantle. She has guarded her sense of self through too many centuries to give it up now. But there is one way she might make use of the Mantle without ever having to touch it. She would gain a wellspring of power from which she could draw, a weapon against all enemies, a puppet God-Empress to control from the shadows—if she convinced someone else to take up the Mantle in her place."

"You mean Csorwe." Shuthmili's blood ran cold.

"I do. And whatever wrongs she feels I may have done her, I would not wish that on her."

They hurried on. Beyond the atrium was another chamber even larger. It was perfectly round, filled from edge to edge by a pool of dark water, as though the lake outside had found its reflection within. Like the lake, it was so deep you could not see the bottom, and it had a raised island at its centre. The island was a stepped pyramid, exactly like the temple but only the size of an ordinary house. At its apex was a square sarcophagus of white stone.

No sign of either Atharaisse or Csorwe. Had they made it in time? Had they guessed wrong? Could Shuthmili allow herself to hope?

Belthandros clicked his tongue and gestured over the surface of the water. There was a rumbling, and a row of white stone blocks rose up from the surface of the pool like teeth. They were wide enough to stand on, and close enough to hop from one to the next easily enough.

Shuthmili followed him out across these stepping-stones. They were horribly smooth and slippery, but she did not dare to fall behind.

Belthandros was already scaling the pyramid. He had shields up, three or four of them, thin as soap bubbles and invisible unless you knew how to look. The effortlessness of this would have been irritating under other circumstances—it would have taken Shuthmili whole minutes of concentration to raise a shield of her own, and that was time she did not have.

There was no sign of Csorwe anywhere. Shuthmili tried not to imagine how easy it would be for a body to slip away into the pool and disappear, and her chest tightened. No, she was being stupid—if Belthandros was right, then Atharaisse would not have drowned her puppet.

She skinned her knee on the edge of one step as she scrambled up after him, and scarcely felt it.

The sarcophagus was a great cube of unclouded marble, so white and still that it looked as though a hole had been cut into the universe to show a blank page beyond it. Someone must have made it, cut it from raw stone and polished its immaculate faces, but to Shuthmili it looked more as though it had taken form by itself, somewhere in the depths of the earth, like a diamond, secretly moulded and polished by the forces which shaped the worlds themselves.

Instinctively she reached out for it with her magic; it was like brushing away the dust from some buried fragment and realising that what you thought was a single glittering pebble was the tip of a mountain, older than the world. And then the mountain dissolved beneath you, giving way to perpetual abyss.

She must have gasped out loud, because Belthandros smiled.

"The Mantle," he said. "The last pure expression of Iriskavaal's power. Never broken. Never polluted. All that remains of her in death. And look, here."

Set into the side of the sarcophagus was a round indentation, so shallow that it was almost invisible. Shuthmili had seen enough Echentyri architecture to know this for what it was: a door.

Despite its apparent simplicity, the door to the sarcophagus was warded with hundreds of invisible sigils, ten times more intricate even than the mechanism of the hatchery door. The only thing Shuthmili had seen to match it for complexity was the interior of the gauntlets.

She couldn't read the sigils without looking closer, but she could feel the effects of them: cocooning the Mantle, sustaining it, shutting out the outside world.

Still no sign of Csorwe anywhere.

"You don't think they could be inside?" she said. "Could Atharaisse have opened the door?" The sarcophagus structure was the size of a small house. It was possible they were all inside. But if that was so, then they might already be too late—

"It's possible," said Belthandros. He sounded vaguely doubtful, but Shuthmili was already back at the door mechanism.

Come on, Adept Qanwa, think it through, she said to herself. *Imagine it's just an exam. You're good at those.*

She could do it. No use getting confused by all that filigree before she understood the basic structure. *Pay attention, don't rush . . .*

"Did you learn all this on your own?" said Belthandros, after she had worked for a minute or two. He sounded impressed, in the way you might be impressed by a child's drawing.

"You could help, you know," said Shuthmili, without looking round at him.

"You're really doing very well," he said. "But you've got it the wrong way round. Those linked pairs should be reversed." He positioned himself on the opposite corner of the door and set to work. With two of them, the work went quicker, and—she had to admit—it was easier with an example to follow. Belthandros knew this system as well as she knew the Qarsazhi style.

The worst thing was that if circumstances had been different, Shuthmili would have loved this. Getting to take apart an advanced Echentyri working was exactly the opportunity she had hoped for, but she'd imagined having the time to take notes, to cross-check some of her theories, to see if she could detect the style of the original Echentyri practitioner. Instead she found her mind wandering to what might lie inside.

How did the Mantle work? Did it hollow a person out and make a space for Iriskavaal to slither into them, or was it more like the gauntlets, opening up its victim to the voice of the goddess? What would happen if they were too late? According to Oranna, a divinity was a malleable thing. Shuthmili thought of the weeds in their garden, the way their roots split and spread, tendrils working their way into any available space, and shuddered.

At least they almost had the door open. All the outer wards disabled, leaving only a vulnerable inner defence which almost looked ready to come apart on its own.

"Ah, Belthandros," said Atharaisse from behind them.

The serpent was looped over the steps, like a casually discarded string of pearls. Shuthmili was struck again by how enormous she was, how silently she must have moved to creep up on them. Belthandros' outer shield fizzled like a film of water on a boiling pan, then reformed itself. Shuthmili got the sense of an unseen struggle.

"No need to panic," he muttered to her, sounding strained, as though his teeth were clenched around an iron bar. "I'll deal with her. You can finish it. Nearly there."

"Where is Csorwe?" said Shuthmili, ignoring him. Atharaisse's great head swayed like a pendant of ivory, and her eyes gleamed, reflected in the surface of the sarcophagus as twin points of red fire.

The School of Aptitude hadn't trained Shuthmili for war, which meant that everything she knew about violence she had invented for herself, and she doubted any of it would work on the serpent. To begin with, she knew nothing about Echentyri physiology. Atharaisse was like an ordinary snake only in the sense that a dragonfly is like a dragon. She wouldn't know where to start.

"Safe and unharmed," said Atharaisse. "Fear not, little hatchling. Our fight is not with thee."

"Where *is* she?" said Shuthmili.

"She rests close at hand," said Atharaisse.

"Do you believe her?" said Belthandros in the same choked voice.

Shuthmili had been told enough soothing lies in her time that she thought she could recognise them when she heard them. Atharaisse would give her nothing useful. Belthandros could handle this. She returned to the door. Only a few more loops to work through, and she would have it open.

"What didst thou say, Belthandros?" said the serpent. "We heard it not."

"Only that it's a shame for you to resent me so, Atharaisse, when we used to be such good friends—"

"Ah, Belthandros," said Atharaisse. "What wouldst thou think of me, if our positions were reversed? If thou hadst languished in the pit and we had reigned in thy beloved Tlaanthothe?"

"My dear, I had no idea about your captivity," said Belthandros. "I wouldn't have imagined General Psamag to be capable of overpowering you."

"It is the pity of the world that fools and dullards rise by chance," said Atharaisse, with a long hiss like the slow burn of a fuse.

"Oh, very good, I am wounded," said Belthandros. He smiled, cold and mirthless, splitting his handsome face like the stroke of an axe.

At the same time, space seemed to fracture around Atharaisse, faceting itself into crystal. The serpent screamed and recoiled, wounds torn in her flesh as though the air itself was barbed.

"Shuthmili, open it!" he said, breathing hard.

She broke open the final loop of the mechanism, and there was a quiet click like a mechanism sliding home. The door faceted itself into hundreds of triangles, which folded neatly in on themselves and away, as if they were paper rather than marble.

Shuthmili braced herself, pressing herself flat against the wall of the sarcophagus. Even Belthandros took a sharp breath.

Shuthmili had expected the whole interior to be hollow. Instead, there was a small niche, not much bigger than a person. Crammed into it, piled up haphazardly, were overlapping folds and layers of some pale translucent material, like a great cocoon of lace.

"The Mantle," he said, and frowned as though something was wrong. Perhaps he had expected to find it more neatly folded, thought Shuthmili, inanely.

No, something *was* wrong. Where was Csorwe? What *had* she expected to find, here?

What was it he'd said? *You've got it the wrong way round.*

If Belthandros was telling the truth, and the Mantle swallowed up any-one who touched it—if he was right that you could make use of its power by offering it a proxy to consume—if he really believed that was what Atharaisse meant to do—then wasn't it just as likely that he planned to do just that? With his very own ignorant sidekick, who had followed him all this way and done exactly as she was told . . .

Mother of Cities, how could she have been so stupid? First the gauntlets and now this. She was still just as naive as when she had first left the School of Aptitude. She drew back, stepping sharply away from the door.

"I know what you're doing," she said. "I'll fight you."

There was nothing she could meaningfully do to him, but perhaps if she could play for time—if Atharaisse wasn't lying and Csorwe was somewhere nearby—

She leapt back as Atharaisse struck again, her immense jaws snapping shut with a muscular thud in the space where Belthandros had been, mo-ments before. He didn't seem ruffled, and nor did he seem to have noticed that Shuthmili had said anything.

"Oh, Atharaisse," he said. "Why not give up? I would spare you."

"A famous jester," said Atharaisse. There was something wrong with her voice. It scraped across the surface of the brain in jagged leaps, making Shuthmili's head ache immediately. Dark blood poured from the wounds torn in her flanks, and every time she moved, her skin tore again, scales flak-ing like those of a skinned fish. "A renowned and adept jokesman. A clown, Belthandros. Is what thou art. Spare me? *Spare* me."

"I mean it," he said, with effort.

"Spare me as thou sparedst the Siren?" said Atharaisse. "Thou hast eaten all our hatchmates, and thou wouldst have me next." The snake made an awful hissing groan and blood poured from her mouth, steaming as it pooled on the white marble of the pyramid, and she made another lunge for Belthandros, her great teeth pink with blood.

"I would not offer mercy if I did not care for you," he said. Lying. Shuth-mili knew it. Knew the little falter in his voice was calculated. "I can stop the curse. You would live."

"Spare me as Iriskavaal spared Echentyr?" said Atharaisse. "We both re-made ourselves in the image of our goddess, Pentravesse, and we both of us are carnivores now. My fault was pity, and I am cured of it. And thy fault— thy fault, mine own heart—was ever *arrogance*."

It happened so fast that Shuthmili didn't see it. There was a flash of movement.

A sound like a needle piercing cloth. A gasp—a sigh. Belthandros slipped forward, his eyes wide with shock and pain. Surprise made him look young. And now she saw the point of the blade sticking out of his chest, silver and red and shining. His shields shimmered from nothing into nothing. He slid down to his knees and Csorwe stood over him.

10

Day of Ruination

Csorwe lifted Belthandros' body as if it were an empty husk, and before Shuthmili could understand what she was seeing, she pushed him into the hollow of the sarcophagus.

The sarcophagus, which was now empty. Where that mass of pale cloth had been was only a square stone cell. Csorwe must have been hiding there, among the folds of the Mantle.

Which meant—

Csorwe straightened up. The Mantle of Divinity rippled around her like a veil, gauzy white, wreathing her hair in a garland of twisted lace. She held her sword as if she'd never seen it before. She didn't react to Shuthmili's hand on her shoulder.

—which meant that Shuthmili had been too late after all.

"A shame, we know," said Atharaisse, triumphant despite the awful wounds in her side. "But she did well. An excellent child. She will make a fine vessel."

Shuthmili could not speak. She gripped Csorwe by the arm, brushing aside the folds of the Mantle, trying to see her face properly. If she could get Csorwe away from here—

"No, no," she muttered. Trying to wrench away the Mantle was like fighting the wind. One moment it billowed away from her, the next it stuck to her hands like wet silk, lapping around her as though it meant to swallow her as well—and all that time Csorwe stood still, not reacting to Shuthmili, nor to Belthandros' blood dripping over the edge of the hollow in the sarcophagus, nor to Atharaisse's blood steaming on the white marble.

"She was his creature once," said Atharaisse. "She now serves a far worthier master. Say thy farewells, if thou must."

"Csorwe, please—" said Shuthmili, hardly hearing the serpent at all. "Look at me, darling girl, it's me—"

Behind the veil Csorwe's eyes opened, a familiar flicker of gold, a distant, hazy recognition. Shuthmili looked up at her, her perfect face, all that guilt and fear and longing, and lurched violently from desperation to hope. She would kill everyone in this room if she could get out with Csorwe in one piece.

"Go," said Csorwe.

FLY FROM THIS PLACE! Zinandour's voice echoed like a distant bell. AN ENEMY IS HERE!

Shuthmili had wondered what it felt like, the moment when your courage failed, and it turned out this was it, this utter helplessness.

"Csorwe, please—please, look at me, come with me, you can fight this—"

"Go, love," said Csorwe.

"Forgive me," she said. "But I will never leave you."

She clutched at Csorwe's hand, but it slipped from her like water. Csorwe's expression slackened. Her eyes dulled, and the Mantle closed over her like a tidal wave engulfing a town.

Csorwe—whatever she was now—stepped away from the sarcophagus. The Mantle swirled after her in a ghostly, translucent wake. Her movements were slow but not jerky, as though she had woken from a long sleep and was well rested.

Atharaisse's eye flashed huge and red like a descending sun.

"Ah, thou wakest?" she said. "Pentravesse was neatly dealt with, as we reckoned—"

"The sarcophagus will hold him for a time only," said Csorwe. Her voice seemed to echo from some vast hollow space far away. Shuthmili found that she had slid to the ground, back against the sarcophagus, and that she was weeping.

Atharaisse laughed. "Little sister, hast thou no thanks for us? Thou wouldst sleep still if not for us, safe in the stone without body or breath."

"Then thy duty is fulfilled," said Csorwe.

"There is much still to be accomplished. With thy assistance—"

"Be at peace, Atharaisse," said Csorwe. "Thou hast accomplished all that we required of thee. Or . . . perhaps there is one further service you might do us."

Atharaisse screamed, a glassy chime of startled pain, like bells breaking. Whatever this not-Csorwe was doing to her, it hurt. She writhed, her great coils thundering like falling boulders as she thrashed.

All at once, her enormous head crashed to the ground and she went still.

Csorwe stepped toward her and rested a hand on her snout, almost affection-
ately. Atharaisse stared at her, red eyes glazed with pain, and began to fade.
Her scales, once ivory, turned as white as salt. The eyes were the last thing
to lose their colour, from blood red to dull pink and finally to the same pale
translucency. The serpent looked like a sculpture in snow. A pale, crumbling
husk.

Csorwe raised a hand to her mouth. Only now did Shuthmili see that her
arm was slick to the elbow with bright blood, as though she had plunged it
into the open wound in the serpent's flank, and in so doing drained all that
gave Atharaisse colour and substance. She chewed and swallowed something, then stepped back, looking blank.

Shuthmili knew that, in the same position, Csorwe's courage would
never fail, she would never run, she would never betray a friend—and she
knew what she would have to do, whatever it might cost her. She swallowed
her tears, and dragged herself forward in an ungainly half crawl.

"God-Empress," she said, and hoped she had chosen the correct title.

"Indeed. And what art thou?" said the Mantle, with Csorwe's mouth.
"No friend to either of these pretenders, we hope." She nudged the ashen
remnants of Atharaisse's body with her toe.

"No," said Shuthmili, her voice faltering, as though only just realising the
shocking danger of the course she had settled upon. "But a friend to you, I
hope."

"Oh?"

"I am a mage—quite a good one," said Shuthmili, and winced. This was
not the time for proper Qarsazhi modesty. "One of the best mages in my
country. I'm interested in power. I would make myself useful."

"Thou wouldst serve us?"

Shuthmili was still stumbling over her qualifications, wondering what it
would take to convince. But the God-Empress said this as though it was
the most natural thing in the world for anyone to fall at her feet, and in the
end, all Shuthmili had to reply was:

"I would."

Tal felt the rumbling from where he sat on the shore of the other island. Jagged little waves slapped at the shore. He'd once been in a minor earthquake,

on business for Sethennai in some distant world, and at first he thought it was the same again. The shaking hurt his chest.

Oranna burst out of her tent a moment later.

"Something's happened," she said, reaching for her staff.

"To the others?" he said, following. She was clearly moving as fast as she could. If she could run toward the explosion so could he.

"Such a bright spark," she said, hurrying on. "By the Unspoken—can't you feel it? The shadow?"

He couldn't feel anything but the persistent ache in his chest and the rumbling under his feet—and now a thundering sense of anxiety—but he didn't need magical powers to see what had now become visible behind the island.

Something had risen up from the water, raising with it a thick mist. Then the mist cleared, revealing a great tiered pyramid.

"The temple . . ." murmured Oranna. "You fool, what have you done?"

There was a kind of causeway they could cross to reach the temple, still ankle deep in water but rising fast, shedding clumps of weed. They struggled across it, and crawled round the tiers until they found a door. Under other circumstances, Tal might have objected to having to cling to Oranna, but needs must.

Inside, the temple was a changeful place. At times they found themselves hurrying along a narrow passage—now scuttling across a room so vast that Tal couldn't see the walls—now crossing a bridge above a chamber far below. The building flexed and altered all around them, compressing and distending like a squeezebox.

Then the light fractured, and he saw two or three temples at once, over-laid on one another as though on sheets of glass, with no way to tell which was real but to follow Oranna. She was panting, and the tapping of her staff on the tiles grew slower.

At last they emerged from another splintering corridor into a room where an island stood in a pool that shivered as though a rain was falling.

There on the island were Csorwe, wrapped in a strange filmy cloak, and Shuthmili, crumpled on her knees against a great block of white stone. Blood and ashes smeared everywhere. No sign of Sethennai.

Tal moved toward the stepping-stones which traced a path across the lake. Oranna grabbed his collar, yanking him back.

"Don't be an imbecile," she hissed. "That is *Tlaanthothei* blood."

It was true—the smears on the white stone were the vivid red which Tal thought of as the normal colour of blood.

Tal nodded, and drew his sword. God knew what was happening over there. He had fucked up before, when they had fought Atharaisse. He didn't plan to do the same again. No stupid stunts this time.

Oranna was barking some kind of instructions at him, and then stopped abruptly, as though her tongue had stopped working. All she said was "Oh. No."

Csorwe had stepped aside, revealing what lay bleeding in the hollow of the sarcophagus. The body of Belthandros Sethennai was unmistakeable.

"No, no," said Oranna, softly, a small noise of pain.

At that moment, Csorwe turned and seemed to notice them. Behind her, the white door closed on Belthandros' body, smearing blood on the marble. Tal's ears pricked up involuntarily, the hairs on the back of his neck prickling, as though his body knew something was wrong before he did. He felt the stone beneath his feet give way, and leapt back to the next. The ground collapsed beneath him and he had to fall back, again and again. He saw Csorwe approach in flashes, and at last, he saw her face behind the thin film of the cloak she wore.

Tal thought he knew all Csorwe's blank looks. The stiff glare of anger, the dull stare of loathing, the deadpan glance of a shared joke. He had, against his will, made a complete study of Csorwe's obscure nonexpressions. But here was something newly hollow, uncannily remote, alien and dead.

Whatever was here now, Csorwe was gone.

Later, in shame, he would realise that he'd never even considered whether Shuthmili or Sethennai might still be alive. He turned and ran, outrunning the pain in his chest, powered forward by sheer terror. He heard no sounds of pursuit. She must have let him go.

Some time later, Oranna caught up to him, gasping for breath in great retches.

"We should go back," he said, knowing that he wouldn't.

"Can't—help," said Oranna.

The pain had caught back up to him, but they seemed to have escaped their pursuer. The two of them limped slowly back out of the atrium, clinging together like two crabs with their limbs torn off. Tal could hardly see where he was going. Every time his vision blurred, he saw it happen again: the utter emptiness where Csorwe had once been.

"Move," said Oranna sharply. "If that creature decides to come after us, we are *dead*, Talasseres Charossa, and I do not plan to die with you."

"I don't fucking care," said Tal. It would have taken some effort to dislodge her from his shoulder or he would have shoved her off and crawled into a corner. Let it take him. It was over.

"Oh, kindly get a grip," she said. "I don't like it any better than you, but we are going to live. This isn't how it ends."

By the time they got out of the temple, Tal was bent double and felt as though he'd crawled over glass. Every breath felt like a knife in the lungs. But the cutter was there, still stowed under ferns. They hauled it out and climbed into it. Tal's hands felt slow and clumsy. He didn't think he could fly the damned thing if he tried.

"Get out of the way," said Oranna, climbing into the pilot's seat. "And get in the back if you want to survive this, but don't slow me down."

She took the cutter up, rising as fast as it could go toward the faint patch of sunlight above the temple. The darkness of the true deeps blurred into brighter green. Tal's stomach dropped. For a blessed moment he felt nothing but the pressure of the acceleration and a sharp pain in his ears, and then the whole of it struck him like an abattoir hammer.

His voice came out in a ragged whisper. "They're gone."

Oranna settled one hand on the wheel and buried her face in the other. For a moment he thought she was about to weep, and envied her, but instead she took a deep breath and looked back at him. "They were happy. They went together. That's more than most people get."

"Yeah," he said, though this was no comfort at all. "I guess. I'm sorry, about, uh . . ."

"Belthandros?" she said, and gave a shudder of laughter, indistinguishable from a sob. "Oh. Ha. Well. He—he served his purpose." Another strange choking laugh, bubbling up out of her like blood from a sucking wound. "I always meant to outlive him anyway."

The ancient flagship lay in its berth within the temple, a fragile shelter against the world outside.

Cherenthisse had trimmed away the worst of the vines and was now working at getting the main hatch open. She knew she would not make much of an honour guard, in her prey aspect, her clothes stained with sweat and sap, but the Most High Atharaisse had given her a job to do.

She had tried to make her case to the Most High—that she was a more worthy vessel for the Mantle than Csorwe, that without her true aspect this was the only meaningful service she could offer—and Atharaisse had only laughed at her and said that there was more ahead for Cherenthisse than she might think.

At last, with a groan, the main hatch of the flagship opened a crack. The smell of dead air seeped out like groundwater, and Cherenthisse stepped on board, the first person in more than three thousand years to enter the *Blessed Awakening*.

Cherenthisse knew the interior of the ship as well as she had known the grounds of her own estate. Once she was certain that the hull wasn't about to collapse on her, she made her way straight to the ship's chapel, as the Most High Atharaisse had instructed.

At the sight of what the Most High had promised her, Cherenthisse felt alien tears running down her cheeks. Her true aspect had never wept, but she could not restrain the reflexes of the prey body now, seeing what was here.

Here, in the chapel of the *Blessed Awakening*, was a stasis circle, exactly like the one which had sheltered her back in the hatchery, except that this one was much, much bigger. Its frail bounds had lasted, somehow, through all that had happened, and lying within the circle was an entire battalion of Thousand Eyes.

All of them in their prey aspect. All identical to Cherenthisse. That was no surprise. Atharaisse had told her not to hope for too much, that it was most likely they would be trapped in two-legged form as Cherenthisse was. Even so, it was not nothing. They lived. And while the Thousand Eyes survived, so did Echentyr.

She wiped her eyes and did her best to clean herself up before returning to the hatch. Just in time, in fact, because two small figures had entered the hangar chamber. There was Csorwe—or rather, the God-Empress, wrapped in the Mantle, just as she had been when Cherenthisse had stuffed her into the sarcophagus earlier. And beside her was—

"What are you doing here?" said Cherenthisse. "Where is the Most High Atharaisse?"

"You missed a lot," said Shuthmili. Her voice was hoarse. She moved like one who had sustained a mortal wound, yet she was clearly alive.

"Go back to your burrow and lick your wounds." said Cherenthisse. "There is nothing for you here."

"Oh, no," said Shuthmili. "We're on the same side now. Aren't you going to greet your Empress?"

Cherenthisse's cheeks flushed with shame, and she fell to her knees. This was not the introduction she had intended.

"Majesty, I am sorry—"

"Cherenthisse, first in loyalty," said the God-Empress, and gave her a smile that was as sad as it was kind, and as kind as it was terrible. "We sorrow with thee. Atharaisse was killed in the struggle with the Pretender Sethennai."

Cherenthisse reeled. The death of the Most High Atharaisse and the perishing of Echentyr each felt equally distant and equally vast. She no longer knew how to react in the face of so much loss.

"But I only just—" said Cherenthisse, and shut her mouth tightly. This was not proper behaviour before the Empress. The cold tears had dried on her face. She would have to endure this, as she had endured all else.

"She will not be forgotten," said the God-Empress.

Her grey skin was flushed. It was a pity that the vessel was so ill-used: scarred and weather-beaten all over. One of its tusks was missing, replaced with a gold prosthesis like a crude copy of an Echentyri war-fang. Cherenthisse still did not understand why Atharaisse had insisted on Csorwe, when Cherenthisse had offered herself—no matter. The vessel was what it was, and in any case hardly mattered. Here was the last of Iriskavaal, walking and breathing once more.

Shuthmili looked up at the God-Empress. Whatever expression flickered across her face, it was gone before Cherenthisse could understand it.

"When Echentyr lives again, it will be a fit monument to her name, and to all thou hast lost," said the God-Empress. "Take courage, Cherenthisse. When Echentyr is restored, we shall all of us take our true forms again."

All right, my lady. I know you're there.

GO! FLEE FROM HERE! IRISKAVAAL IS AN EATER OF WORLDS! DO NOT LINGER IN THE PRESENCE OF HER OFFSPRING!

Shuthmili sat on the floor of an empty cabin aboard the *Blessed Awak-*

ening. Csorwe's coat lay in her lap, discarded by a God-Empress who disdained mortal rags. She opened the inner pocket of the coat and pulled out the gauntlets. She tried not to think of Csorwe folding them neatly away. Another thing she might never see again.

I know what these do now. You made me an offer, didn't you? Beyond fear and limitation? I don't want that.

WHAT, THEN? NAME IT.

I want her back.

Shuthmili squeezed her eyes shut and pulled on the gauntlets. Zinandour seemed . . . relieved, as you might be to find some small thing, briefly lost.

Let's make a deal, my lady. Help me get Csorwe free of that thing, help me get her away, safe and alive, and I'm yours. This body is yours. You can do what you want with me. I will be the gate through which you return.

I AM WEAKENED BY CAPTIVITY. IRISKAVAAL WAS OLD WHEN I FIRST WALKED THE EARTH. I CANNOT BEAT THIS RELIC OF HERS BY FORCE.

Then you will never have me. I will fight you with everything I have, and I will destroy this body at the first opportunity I have. You will never escape the void.

HOW I HATE SENTIMENT. LISTEN TO ME. THERE ARE METHODS OTHER THAN FORCE, QANWA SHUTHMILI. I AM THE FLAME THAT DEVOURS. IF I DESIRE THE MANTLE OF IRISKAVAAL DESTROYED, IT WILL OCCUR. BUT YOU WILL HAVE TO BE PATIENT, AND YOU WILL HAVE TO ACCEPT MY INCARNATION IN FULL. CAN YOU?

When Csorwe lives again. Yes.

THEN IT WILL BE ACCOMPLISHED.

The rush of divine force came again, fast as a blush, vast as a tide. If she stood her ground, it would wash over her head, flood her lungs, tear her apart from within. Instead she let herself float, let the power swell around her, within her, and carry her forward.

11

The Last to Be Chosen

One Year Later

IN NORTHERN OSHAAR, in winter, the light thins. There is a pallid dawn, a fading dusk, and then darkness wraps itself again around the temple. Snow chokes the roads. The black cathedrals of the forest are lethal to a traveller. The Followers of the Unspoken Name expect no pilgrims until spring.

And all the same, one midwinter night, a pilgrim came to the House of Silence, like a dead thing returning.

Prioress Cweren was sitting up late in her study, with her eyeglasses pushed up her nose, gazing into her scrying-bowl. Her nightly indulgence of hot whisky and cloves sat beside her on her desk, its scent masking the bloody steam from the scrying-bowl.

The image in the bowl flickered in the lamplight, and she saw the pilgrim.

She was dragging her way through the snow, hauling her own body like a bag of rocks. She crawled at the foot of the road of white stones. She had dressed for a winter journey, but all the layers of heavy dark wool were now wet and ragged. Her black hair was not only threaded with grey but flecked with frost. Cweren could not see her face.

Cweren was foremost among the faithful of the Unspoken, and she knew the feeling of a true vision, the iron taste of it, like blood in her mouth.

She got up from her desk, thinking somewhat at random that she could consult *The Key of Waking Vision* or even *The Dream of Fly Agaric* for precedent.

The scrying-bowl flashed, startling her, and she fell heavily, cracking her elbow on the edge of the table. The glass of whisky was flung sideways and smashed. Cweren didn't hear it shatter, didn't feel the impact. She was only aware of the vision. It left all her senses ringing, pulsing, red and bright.

The crawling woman had fallen in the hollow her body had made in the snow, but she was alive. She was calling to Cweren by name.

Cweren, by the twelve thousand unspeakable names, help me.

It was a mortal voice, and one that Cweren recognised. And yet—behind it, somehow, or beneath it, she heard the voice of her god, rolling up like cold still air from an open grave.

Come to me, said the Unspoken One. *It is willed.*

In thirty-nine years of life, Cweren had heard the voice of the Unspoken in the mouth of three Chosen Brides—Ejarwa, Csorwe, and Tsurai—but it had never spoken to her directly. It knew her. It recognised her personally, and with that recognition came a searing clarity. There was something she had to do. A new and greater sacrifice, a purpose beyond any she had yet known.

Still, the House of Silence has ever taught practicality. Cweren wrapped herself in a heavy coat and strapped on her snowshoes before going out into the night. Swathed in wool and fur, with only a small gap between scarf and hood, she still felt the cold as a blow when she opened the door.

She crossed the courtyard garden. Her keys clanged like bells as she unlocked the boathouse. She dragged an oilskin down off the little cutter they used in summer to transport bales of lotus-straw. It might have been wiser to waken one of her seconds, to summon the librarian or one of the other high officers of the House, but she feared that explaining her vision to someone else would cloud that extraordinary clarity.

No, the Unspoken did not look kindly upon tongues that wagged. The vision in the scrying-bowl had been for her alone. Besides, if she was right about the identity of the pilgrim waiting on the hillside, she did not particularly want the librarian or the Keeper of Black Lotus to witness this exchange.

She hauled the cutter out and climbed in. As the engine warmed up, she glanced back up at the House. There were no lights in the windows. Cweren's home vanished behind her, its great bulk sinking into the greater darkness. She could see nothing but what lay within the circle of her own lantern, but she knew she was going the right way: toward the road of white stones, the beginning of the path to the shrine. That was where the pilgrim lay, half buried.

Cweren landed the cutter, set down her lantern, squatted in the snow beside her, and shook her by the shoulders, not gently.

The pilgrim choked awake, raising her head with what looked like an immense mechanical effort.

"Cweren," said the pilgrim. "I knew you'd come."

"Oranna," said Cweren. "I'm astonished you're not dead."

Oranna laughed, a wet rattle that sounded more as if she was choking.

"You're not the only one," she said, eventually. She certainly looked enough like a corpse. Her skin was mottled with broken veins, and her yellow eyes were grey with blood.

Under ordinary circumstances, Cweren would not have offered Oranna an arm. The former librarian of the House of Silence was an apostate and a schismatic, and she had betrayed Cweren in every possible manner over the years. At every step, Oranna had made it clear how easily Cweren could be put aside. And yet in all that time, Oranna had never once asked her for help. Cweren held out her hand.

Oranna did not get up. She was hunched over, clasping a kind of woven basket to her chest as if hiding a wound there. There came a sound Cweren had not heard for many years, a thin wail like a cat wanting to be fed. It was not very loud, but it pierced the heavy silence of the forest like a flash of red light, and it came from the basket.

"My word, a baby," said Cweren, and for a moment she might have been sixteen years old again, listening in scandalised horror to something her interesting friend had invented.

"Well *done*, Cweren, this must be the sharp logical mind which so impressed our schoolmistresses," said Oranna. Her mouth twitched into its habitual sardonic curve, then slackened again, weak with exhaustion.

When they were junior priestesses, Cweren and Oranna had officiated at the naming of hundreds of infants, and back then they had thought of them as props brought to the House for this purpose: to be pricked with pins, anointed with lotus, presented to the notice of the Unspoken One, and taken away again to be transformed into real people. How things changed.

"Let me help you up," said Cweren. Oranna shook her head. "Forgive me, but you can't walk, and if you don't already have frostbite, I'm sure it is imminent. And the baby—"

"That's a lot of assumptions this early in the morning," said Oranna. She held out the baby, who snuffled and started wailing again. "Go on. I can handle myself."

Cweren considered dispensing some sharp words regarding the fact that she was the Prioress of the House of Silence and Oranna was a murderous turncoat who had no authority over her, but that seemed rather childish under the circumstances.

The baby weighed almost nothing, the size and weight of a loaf of bread. Inside the basket, it was wrapped in a thick woollen shawl. Cweren twitched the shawl aside, trying to find where the baby's face was. It didn't even have its milk-tusks yet, and its mouth was stretched into a wide grimace of hunger.

"Is it yours?" said Cweren.

"What self-respecting necromancer would bear live offspring, I ask you?" said Oranna.

"I suppose you never could give a straight answer," said Cweren. She shrugged on the straps of the basket, bringing the infant close to her body. She could feel its little limbs twitching with hungry rage.

"So this is your triumphant return," said Cweren.

Many years ago, enraged by Cweren's accession as Prioress, Oranna had stolen as much as she could carry from the House of Silence and gone on the run with her own gang of followers. As far as Cweren had been able to discover, all the candlesticks had been sold, and all the runaway acolytes were dead.

"Not at all," said Oranna. She lurched to her feet and followed Cweren toward the cutter. Even the effort of rising seemed to strain her breath. "I have no intention to return. But the child—"

"Ah," said Cweren. "Yes, I see. We are to be left holding the baby, this time quite literally. This is new, even for you."

"This is willed by the Unspoken, I assure you," said Oranna. "And you can be sure the child is one of the faithful. I carried out the naming myself. Always was difficult to prick them with the pin. This one is a very enthusiastic kicker."

Cweren was being enthusiastically kicked herself. "You have always known so much about what the Unspoken wills," said Cweren.

"This is a matter of life and death, and not only yours and mine," said Oranna.

"Well," said Cweren. "The House of Silence is accustomed to receiving foundlings, I suppose." She took some comfort from the knowledge that Oranna apparently planned to go away again.

Oranna reached stiffly into the basket and touched the baby's cheek. It turned toward her, quieting for a moment.

"Come on, then," said Oranna to the child. "Back to the House of Silence, for our sins, to explain ourselves—oh, *damn*."

Cweren's own magic had always been weak, but it prickled at her then, a sharp jolt like cold metal.

A flash of movement had caught Oranna's eye far above.

Suspended in the sky above the sacred mountain, serene and deadly, was a warship. By a trick of the eye, it looked bigger than the mountain itself, speckled with lights as if the night sky had folded itself into the shape of a carrion bird about to drop.

Oranna cursed again. "And I thought we might have an hour or two."

The ship drifted out from the cover of the mountain and down toward them, all chill majesty. Then there was a flash of brighter light from somewhere in its underbelly. The baby was still crying, the sharp keening of a wild animal in distress.

"By the Unspoken, they're *firing* on us," hissed Oranna, more in aggravation than in terror. "Move!"

Cweren ran, shielding the baby as best she could. She skidded into the shadow of the cutter, and Oranna landed beside her, winded and gasping. The spot where they had been standing erupted in blue fire, with a vicious hiss like water on hot oil. The heat of the flames was so near, and their glistening blue light made everything else murky. The baby was still screaming, somehow louder than the fire.

There was another hiss and crackle behind them, and Cweren heard the snow sizzle from impact.

"Quickly!" said Oranna, and they climbed into the cutter. It was ungainly in a horrible way, trying to scramble in at speed without hurting the baby, like the recurring nightmare in which Cweren was being chased and had forgotten how to run.

Cweren automatically seated herself at the tiller, but Oranna gestured her into the back.

"You always flew like an old man," said Oranna. "Sit there and hold the baby."

The baby cried on and on, the sound like a red ribbon winding behind them. Oranna took them low, down through the trees, zigzagging between the trunks and branches and grinning to herself with a maniacal delight that would have been terrifying if Cweren hadn't already been at peak terror, coasting along on a kind of delirium.

"There, there," said Cweren, rocking the baby ineffectually.

Oranna's grin made her look like a young girl again, as though she had once again bullied Cweren into some scheme to steal whisky from the priestesses' stores. At the same time, her breath misted in the air like puffs of steam from a furnace that was running down. Cweren smelled flowers and metal in the air, blood and lilies, and knew that Oranna was dying. The mage-blight was not a gentle death. Among the Followers of the Unspoken, it was common to seal yourself into the crypt as an offering of starvation rather than face the blight in its full flowering. Of course, that would not be Oranna's way.

The cutter's old engine coughed and its timbers complained as they battered their way through the forest's understorey, and all the while Cweren was waiting for the fireball that would kill all three of them.

"Oh, here we go," said Oranna, her teeth clenched. "Really, Cweren, did you pick the clunkiest haycart you could—ah!"

But when the crisis came, it was pure accident, the same even-handed entropy Cweren had worshipped every day of her life. The engine of the old cutter choked, sending them careening sharply to one side. They struck a tree and spun out of control. Oranna cursed in a low furious hiss as she tried to regain steering, but it was no good.

"Have to land, if I can," she muttered. "Cweren, be ready to jump if you have to."

"With the baby?" said Cweren in disbelief.

"Of course with the baby, what kind of imbecile—"

Oranna swore again, and their cutter skimmed low over the snowy earth, the engine coughing up smoke. They leapt free just as it caught fire. Oranna screamed. The baby stopped crying abruptly, and Cweren thought for a horrible moment that it might have been crushed by the impact—but no, there it was, glaring out of the wrapper at Cweren with eyes of a dark inscrutable gold.

In her relief, it took Cweren a moment to realise that Oranna had fallen behind. She was sitting in the snow, back straight against a tree, face buried in one hand.

"What's wrong?" said Cweren, anxious to be moving, certain that at any second there would be another fireball.

"My leg," said Oranna. There was a matter-of-fact resignation in her voice. "It's broken, I think."

There was a hiss and a crash and the slithering of dislodged snow as something burst through the trees, a few hundred yards ahead. Not another fireball. Something much larger, a sharp black silhouette slicing down through the trees like a blade. Another ship, not much bigger than the cutter but obviously made for war.

"Cweren, take Tsereg and run," said Oranna.

"I can't—"

"You can. You'll have to," said Oranna. Her voice, which had always been the sweetest thing about her, sounded as though she had ground glass on her tongue. "Warn them at the House, for all the good it will do them, but there is nothing more important than keeping the child safe."

Oranna fumbled in her robes and produced a flat square object, thrusting it toward Cweren. It was wrapped in an oilskin, but Cweren knew a book when she held one. "This is for Tsereg. If anybody else opens it, they will die a most unpleasant death, so don't get too curious."

"You could lean on my shoulder," said Cweren.

"No, this is it, I think," said Oranna. "A pity not to make it back, but so it goes. *Nothing is to be preserved for all time.*"

"*What is saved can be saved only for a moment,*" answered Cweren automatically, and felt a wave of fury that Oranna thought she could leverage scripture against her. How dare she die before Cweren had a chance to set the record straight?

"I had longer than I deserved," said Oranna. "You would be the first to tell me that. And nobody understands better than I do the value of a willing sacrifice."

Oranna reached out and touched Cweren's forehead. At first her hand just felt cold, the wool glove scratching her brow. Then Cweren felt the power in that touch, cold and vast and hollow as a subterranean lake, and yet familiar, too, familiar as the crypts, familiar as the veins of her fingertips backlit by a lantern.

Oranna brushed her fingertips across the baby's forehead too, and drew them back. Her face was lit up by something brighter than the distant flames, though a trickle of blood ran from the corner of her mouth.

"*Thus shall we know thee,*" said Oranna. "Go."

Figures spilled out of the ship up ahead, and the light of the burning trees gleamed on metal visors.

The acrid smell of the burning cutter mingled with another sharp waft of blood and lilies. There was a strange high colour in Oranna's cheeks. She made the Sign of Sealed Lips to Cweren: three fingertips pressed to the lips, between the tusks, an ancient gesture of honour and reverence to the Unspoken.

"*Go*, Cweren," she said. "I'll hold them back."

It was hard to run in snowshoes, and harder still with the baby in the basket, but Cweren went as fast as she could. The burden grew heavier with every step, as if she were dragging a boulder behind her. After a while the pain and the fear were just more weights to drag along. She was a person who liked her comforts, liked her evening drink and her log fire and her lambskin slippers, but she was also the Prioress of the House of Silence, and this was her domain.

"Come on, Tsereg," she said, under her breath. The baby was no longer crying, at least.

If she could get through the forest, it wouldn't be far to the gate in the wall, and to the safety of the House of Silence and its ancient battlements.

Once she looked back, and saw Oranna in the clearing of pines. All around her, dark circles shimmered in the snow, black as blood but gleaming like wax.

The soldiers advanced upon the circle, as eyeless and single-minded as beetles, closing in with unhurried ease. The curved blades of their swords glittered like arcs of ice.

Cweren was too far away by now to really be seeing this. It was another vision. Oranna must have sent it to her. At the very last, perhaps even she did not want to die alone.

"Tell your mistress she will not find what she seeks," said Oranna.

"Witch of a false god," said one of them, laughing. "Take comfort. You will not live to see her triumph."

"No, you're right," said Oranna. "But neither will you."

Oranna raised a hand, her black robe flapping in the wind. You could have taken this for an idle gesture. Perhaps only Cweren saw what it really meant, the extent of the power she called upon. The depths of the mountain were in it, and the vastness of the night sky. All winter's cold, and the cold of the outer void, the implacability of stone and the implacability of time.

Oranna's lips were moving, this time silent in the silent forest, but Cweren heard what she said as if her old friend whispered it in her ear.

If Oranna was telling the truth, then there really was nothing more important than keeping this infant alive, whatever might follow.

Tsereg is the last to be Chosen.

Tsereg. It was a good old-fashioned House of Silence name: that which is without end. Even in peril of her life, Cweren knew her etymology.

"All worlds float upon the void," Oranna went on, her lips still moving silently. This was the first of the mysteries of the Unspoken, the words that each of them had spoken at their initiation, and which Cweren heard repeated every year by the latest class of acolytes. One could not fail to answer.

"And the hour of their fading is inevitable," Cweren replied, though the cold air burnt in her lungs and she could scarcely form words.

At once the first rank of soldiers faltered, as though some invisible barrier had risen up in front of them. That wasn't it, though. Oranna was not interested in postponing the inevitable, Cweren saw. She only wanted to do as much damage as she could. The soldiers seemed to crumple in on themselves, as though their uniforms had been sucked dry of flesh and bone, and then even leather and metal flaked away, leaving a ring of drifted black rust in the snow where they had been.

Cweren ran on through the snow as this nightmare unspooled across her mind's eye. There were more of the soldiers than she could have imagined. As fast as Oranna could fight them off, there were more of them, and the magic itself was taking a toll on her body.

"All form takes shape in emptiness," said Oranna, and the nearest soldier simply disintegrated, turning to a pillar of greyish smoke.

By unmaking is emptiness perfected, thought Cweren, though it was absurd to imagine Oranna could hear her.

Cweren stumbled on, and at last the walls of the House of Silence loomed up ahead, a dark bulk superimposed on the greater darkness. Cweren was too exhausted even to feel relief, but she was home, and both she and the baby unharmed. If the soldiers were still pursuing her, they were far behind. She stepped across the threshold, clinging to the basket. Behind her the gates swung shut.

Cweren and the baby were halfway back across the courtyard when Oranna was shot. Cweren almost felt the arrow herself, or at least the shock of it. A sharp thump in the middle of the chest, more like being punched than being punctured.

The vision blurred, and when it cleared, Oranna was looking down at the arrow, mildly, as though someone had tugged at her sleeve for attention.

Oranna smiled. She brushed a hand over the arrow and then let go, as if deciding against something. Her dark hair veiled her face.

The vision fuzzed and darkened and cleared over and over again, as if someone was rapidly blinking. Cweren badly wished it would end, that she would not be forced to see what happened next. One of the soldiers trampled through the circle toward Oranna's slumped body, and raised a shining sword.

"All voices sound in silence," said Oranna, and this was for Cweren alone. *And silence relieves them at last.*

At the moment of Oranna's death, the vision snapped apart. Cweren cupped the baby's head in her hand and stepped into the great hall.

High above, the bells of the House of Silence ended their long sleep and began to ring.

II

Common Enemies

Fourteen Years Later

Perhaps your teachers have encouraged you to think of the worlds of the Echo Maze as stones in a path: close, solid, and predictable. But like so many comforting notions, this is false. All the worlds that have ever existed are as dewdrops hanging on a spider's web: fragile, transient, and far distant from one another. The Maze that connects them is no more than a fine silk thread, and all around this brief glittering is the unsurpassable nothingness of the void.

from *Basic Precepts of Benthomancy* by Dr. Kaleni Tletharai

12

The Legendary Outlaw Talasseres Charossa

FAR OUT IN the desert there was a fortress, like a smoke-stained moon orbiting a dead and distant planet. This fortress was a prison, and it was called the Iron Hill.

It was a day of unmerciful heat. The sunlight hammered on the walls of the Iron Hill like a broadside, picking out every patch of rust, every creaking seam, every cloud of dirty steam that leaked from its vents.

A hatch in the wall of the Iron Hill slid open, and a child fell out. A bundle of grey cloth, bleached instantly white by the unforgiving sun, turning and spiralling in the wind. A brief pale flash against the blue unseeing sky.

No one saw them fall. If anyone had chanced to look up at that moment, the sun would have dazzled their eyes. The child fell out of reality, and entered it again several seconds later when they landed on the upper hull of the small Thousand Eye transport which was docked to the side of the prison. They lay there on the hot metal, among dust and smashed insects, clinging like a barnacle as the ship slipped its moorings. The canopies unfurled, the engines hummed to life, and the ship rose into the burning sky, oblivious to its strange new cargo.

A chain of hills ran through the desert, and on the largest of these hills there was a monstrous palace. In places, through walls of volcanic glass, behind its spines and towers, buried under the new fortifications that the God-Empress had made, you could see the shadow of Tlaanthothe, the city she had devoured.

The palace, which was called the Lignite Citadel, was encircled by an equally monstrous town, as ramshackle as the palace was impenetrable. The outskirts and remnants of lost Tlaanthothe had been glued together, like

the fragments of a broken vase, by a spreading penumbra of new facto-
ries, barracks, and slums. This was Ringtown, and down in the docks, the
convicts were scrubbing another poster off the wall of the Thousand Eye
barracks.

The poster depicted an athletic Tlaanthothei youth standing on a serpent's neck, looking young and muscular and waving a sword over his head.
Under the direction of a Thousand Eye officer who clearly thought she was
better than all this, the gang of convicts slopped at it with brooms.

Tal pulled his collar high and walked on by.

This shit was why Tal hated coming into town. It just made it more likely
someone would perform the complex imaginative manoeuvre—rare in Outer
Ringtown—which was necessary to picture Tal without his beard. Clean-
shaven, with his hairline free from grey speckles, he looked all too much like
the legendary outlaw Talasseres Charossa, the favourite topic of seditious art-
ists, greatly desired by the God-Empress as a traitor and ally of the pretender
Belthandros Sethennai.

It was all very funny, because Tal didn't know whether Sethennai was
alive or dead and would sooner ally with a scorpion.

And what kind of idiot would stick something like that on the walls of
the barracks themselves? Tal gave it two days before the culprit was caught
and drowned in the public fountain.

He put it out of his mind. The entire strategy which had kept him alive
for the past fifteen years of his life relied on not running toward trouble and
not being noticed. The secret of survival in Ringtown was to mind your own
business, and at this point in time, Tal's business was to consider a job offer.

He turned down a narrow alley and ducked inside the Lemon Tree. The
place was optimistically named, a bleak, windowless boozer that smelled of
stale wine and smoke. A while back, the old landlord had been executed for
distributing illegal pamphlets about the Snake Tyrant, and the place still
seemed to be in mourning.

Tal's brother was waiting for him at a basement table.

Niranthos had offered Tal work before, but it was the first time he'd come
down from his perch to do it. It had been years since the two of them had
met face-to-face, and the fact that Niranthos was here in person was un-
nerving. For one thing, Niranthos looked shockingly old. His hair was thin
and iron-grey, and his beard did not hide the deep lines around his mouth.

Do I look like that? Tal thought. Niranthos was giving him a forbidding look.

"Talasseres," he said, "you're late."

"Yeah, sorry," said Tal. "I guess everything up in the Citadel runs on time, but—"

"Not so loud!" said Niranthos.

"I'm not the one wearing my shiny fucking shoes under—what is that, a bedsheet?"

Niranthos' idea of a disguise was apparently to pull on a ragged cloak and wrapper over his immaculate palace livery. The sickening risk they were both taking made this less funny than it could have been.

Niranthos had some kind of dire administration job in the Citadel, and in his spare time he was the world's most boring Tlaanthothei loyalist, longing for the old order of things, in which he, Niranthos Charossa, had been the ultimate specimen of correctness. His rebellion was of a very Niranthos variety, trafficking information, funding propagandists, leaking the Thousand Eyes' secrets in measured drops. Tal didn't work for him when he could avoid it. Involving yourself with plots against the God-Empress was—as the former proprietor of this very pub had learned—a speedy way to get yourself executed. Sometimes, though, there were no other options.

Niranthos handed over a sheet of paper and waited while Tal read it. It was a Thousand Eye memorandum, detailing the route of a certain transport across the desert, from the Iron Hill to the Citadel.

"Commander Jatharisse was supposed to report at the Citadel yesterday. She left the Iron Hill as scheduled, but her transport never even arrived in Ringtown."

"You've lost a snake? Embarrassing for you," said Tal.

Niranthos lowered his voice to a hiss. Really, it was incredible that this man had survived as a double agent for so long. "Jatharisse is one of the Empress' high officers. She is deeply involved in what they're calling the *great work*. I need you to find out what's happened to her transport and get there before the official salvage team does."

"Right. Well, you know my usual fee."

Niranthos looked disappointed, as though somehow, after all this time, he expected Tal to volunteer out of the goodness of his heart.

"I need to eat," said Tal. It had been a bad winter. He had caught a fever and come close to death, shivering in a sleeping bag in one of his bolt-holes, and his resources were stripped to the bone. "We don't all have a nice town-house with proper plumbing, and if you think this job sounds like such a walk in the park, then maybe you should go yourself, or—"

"All right, Talasseres," said his brother, his shoulders slumping a little. "Yes. Fine. I can pay you."

Beyond the margins of Ringtown, the desert went on into a seeming eternity. Roads, like people, went out into the desert and disappeared. The God-Empress had taken territory in many worlds, but nowhere was her conquest so complete as here in Tal's homeland.

Tal's cutter skimmed low across the desert, cutting a winding path between outcrops of rusty stone and dried-up groves of acacia. He didn't want to be seen, not by the Thousand Eyes and not by any of the scavengers who made their living in the Speechless Sea by less official means.

Niranthos had given him the approximate location of Jatharisse's crashed ship. Tal tried not to think too much about how his brother even knew this stuff, but his sources must have been good, because there was the wreck. It lay in the shadow of a huge rock formation which cut the black sand like a shark's fin. Smoke rose in wisps from a hole in the hull, but in an unprecedented stroke of luck, it did not appear to be actively on fire.

Niranthos wasn't paying him to be curious, but Tal couldn't help wondering how this had happened. Why would Jatharisse have run her ship into a perfectly obvious rock like this?

Tal landed his cutter nearby and approached on foot. He recognised the ship's build—it was nearly as old as he was, and it had been a luxury Maze transport before they'd slapped a Thousand Eye insignia on its flank. Might never fly again now, given the damage.

Get on board, get whatever documents you can—don't bother trying to read them, you wouldn't understand them—and I'll pay for anything you can get, even if it turns out to be her shopping list. Those had been Niranthos' instructions. Unfortunately the way the ship had fallen meant there would be no access to the main hatch, but he could get in through the secondary cargo hatch which—yes—was still exactly where he expected to find it.

He climbed up to the hatch and began twisting the rings of the lock. With these old ships you could usually get the combination by feel if you had a few uninterrupted minutes to meddle with them. Tal remembered Sethennai teaching him that and felt an ancient and unbidden rush of blood to his cheeks.

The moment he solved the damn thing, the cargo hatch popped open and someone fell out with a shriek, right on top of him.

Tal did not jump. He did not yelp. It took many years' practice at self-restraint merely to curse in a clipped whisper.

It wasn't Jatharisse. It was a kid, not even five feet tall, squawking like an angry magpie.

"Shut up!" said Tal.

The kid didn't answer him. They'd already gone quiet, staring out over his shoulder. Tal turned, knowing what he'd see before he saw it.

Behind him was a Thousand Eye officer, her livery scorched, her smoked-glass visor cracked, and her sword already drawn. She must have heard the screeching. So *here* was Jatharisse.

Would she stab first and ask questions later?

Before Tal could find out, the child kicked him in the shins, pelted out of the cargo hatch, and was away the moment they hit the ground. Tal cursed again and followed suit. He heard Jatharisse snarl behind him.

Losing a pursuer would have been easier if he had been anywhere else but this. The desert was like an empty oven, and the snake was between him and his cutter. He zigzagged deeper into the shade of the rock, planning to double back round once he'd lost her.

He was all too aware that he was no longer as fast or as resilient as he had been. If he didn't get away from Jatharisse and back to his cutter before his first burst of energy ran out, he was a dead man.

God, but the snake was so fast! He glanced back over his shoulder, breathing hard, and saw that she was almost close enough to grab him.

"Hey!" came a shout from some distance away. "Hey, fucker! Leave him alone, it's me you want!"

It was the kid. Tal's lungs hurt too much for him to feel really bewildered by this. He had to assume they'd mistaken him for somebody else, because the life he was currently living wasn't one anyone else would risk themselves to save.

Jatharisse paused and dropped back, giving Tal time to dart deeper into the shadow of the rock. He didn't look back until he was beyond the out-crop and back in the blazing sun. He couldn't see the snake *or* the kid, and he had to catch himself before almost stepping back into a deep gully which trailed the outcrop as though the shark's fin had cut a wake in the earth.

"She's still coming, idiot!" said a voice from beneath him. It was the child again—what business did they have being that fast?—at the bottom of the gully, trying to climb up the far side. Without thinking, Tal dropped down after them.

"Go away! Don't give me away!" they hissed.

Tal stepped up on a rock and peered over the edge of the gully. Through a stand of dry grass he could see Jatharisse, silhouetted against a burning sky. Shit.

Option one, thought Tal. *Shove the kid back out in the desert as a nice distraction for the snake, and go back to Niranthos empty-handed.* It would be shitty even by Tal standards to use them as snake bait when they'd saved his life just now, but—well, it was a hard world, and if there was no other way—

"You were on the ship? Jatharisse's ship?" he said.

"I was stealing it," said the kid, ignoring him. They were trying to climb up the far side of the gully, but the sand slipped under their battered sandals.

"Yeah, that seems to have gone really well," said Tal.

Jatharisse was taking her time searching. Unhurried, relaxed, confident as only an apex predator can be.

"Get bent, old man, I'm not dying because of you!"

They scrabbled at the edge, slid down, and bounced immediately back up again, only to fall just as before. Tal knew the feeling.

Option two. Try to keep us both alive, and if we don't die, I can at least hand the kid over to Niranthos as proof that I tried.

"Leg up?" said Tal.

The kid was surprisingly sturdy, but Tal managed to hoist them to the top of the far side of the gully, and swung himself up after. Might buy them a little time, if they could at least get out of Jatharisse's eyeline.

"Who are you?" he said.

"Tsereg," said the kid. Oshaaru, probably, with dark grey skin and a mass of curly black hair that fell in loose ringlets over their face. Could have been a boy or a girl or neither. Tal didn't know enough about the Oshaaru to tell from the name or the hairstyle.

"No, I mean, what are you doing here?" he said.

"None of your beeswax," said Tsereg. "Get behind the rock before she sees us!"

They rounded the outcrop and kept going, close against its sunlit side. The heat was vicious. Tal felt like a blistered strip of paint flaking off the hot rock.

"*Why* exactly did you steal a Thousand Eye officer's ship?" said Tal, as they ran. No answer from the kid. "My cutter's nearby," he went on. "We can get away from here. Just need to know you're not going to knife me and take my ship too."

"Might do," said Tsereg. "Probably not. Had to catch a ride with Commander Snake-o to get out of the Hill, didn't I?"

"The Hill?" said Tal. "The Iron Hill? You were in prison?"

"Yeah, and I'm not going back," said Tsereg. They glanced back. Jatharisse was already past the gully and coming after them.

"Fuck! How can we lose her?" said Tsereg.

Short of splitting up and taking their chances, Tal had no idea. If Tal doubled back and charged Jatharisse directly, then he might be able to keep her occupied long enough for Tsereg to get away . . .

And god, for a moment, it was almost tempting. To die on Jatharisse's sword might just be the solution to all his problems. No uncertain future. No more memories. No more debt, no more fear, no more shame, no more regret, no more cold nights shivering in his tent alone, no more, no more—

But that had never been his style. He had bought his life dearly, and whatever he was these days, he wasn't the kind of person to throw it away for someone he'd just met.

His brain hovered around the thought for a while, like a fly inspecting a carcass, before alighting: he wasn't *Csorwe*, was he.

Then Tsereg tripped with a muffled scream, one threadbare sandal flapping off their foot, straps broken.

The smart thing to do would be to keep moving, away from danger and away from the small grey bundle that lay stunned on the ground like a dead pigeon. All he had to do was get round the other end of the outcrop and back to his cutter, and he would be safe, and Tsereg would most likely be dead. Just one of the many compromises one made to stay alive in the new order of things. If you had an ounce of self-preservation, you wouldn't slow down, you wouldn't turn back, you wouldn't draw your knife and yell—

Oh, for fuck's sake, thought Tal, as he did every one of these things.

By the time he closed with Jatharisse, Tsereg was back on their feet, and still shrieking, less with terror and more as if they had turned a spigot marked *yell* and the valve had broken off in their hand.

"Keep running!" Tal yelled, gesturing in what he hoped was the direction of the cutter. "I'll take her!"

Tal didn't carry a sword these days, not wanting attention from the Eyes—the irony was not lost on him—but at least his knife was the length of his forearm and could punch cartilage like a needle through canvas. Tal had as good a chance as he'd ever have. He sprinted toward her and tried to kick her backward. His boot connected with her ribs, but—god, *impossible*—she grabbed his calf and threw him back. He staggered and spun to keep his balance, but the Eye was upright now and facing him. Behind her cracked visor, she beamed, a crescent of gleaming white teeth. All the Thousand Eyes had the same face, but Jatharisse wore it crueller than most.

"Do try to fight, if you like," she said, as if she was being very generous in giving Tal the opportunity.

"Bite my ass, you crusty shit!" he said.

The Eye moved unlike anything Tal had ever fought, like a silk flag rippling in the wind. She twirled in circles round Tal. The sword drifted through the air in unhurried arcs, and yet Tal felt himself pinned in place, rapidly losing control of the fight.

He was horribly out of practice and he'd made an awful mistake and he was going to die. He feinted, retreating a little, trying to gain some space to breathe. If he could spin this out long enough, he might give Tsereg the chance to live a little longer, which was about as stupid a legacy as he deserved. He hoped they had run.

The Eye wasn't even trying seriously to kill him. She was having fun with him, tiring him out, in the knowledge that she could reel him in whenever she liked. Tal had *long* had enough of being treated like that. It made him angry enough that he actually had an idea.

He retreated further, moving back the way he had come, favouring his right foot as though injured.

The Eye pressed him as though her appetite had been sharpened by his yielding.

That's right, thought Tal. *That's me, I'm vulnerable as shit, come fucking murder me.*

The great thing about fighting to the death was that you had no time for doubt, no opportunity to worry about whether you'd miscalculated. Tal gave way and gave way until the Eye was almost on top of him, and then he dodged sideways so that she was between him and the hidden gully.

Tal spun and pushed the Eye back as hard as he could. She fell back in a perfect arc, head over heels into the gully. As she fell her head struck a rock, and by the time she hit the bottom, her body was limp and unmoving.

Tal straightened up, breathing hard.

"Fuck," he said, indistinctly.

Tsereg hadn't run. The little idiot had *followed him,* and now they were standing a little way off, an elbow-high pillar of silence.

"Is she dead?" they said, twitching aside a hank of hair to reveal their nose and a selection of teeth.

Tal gasped out a kind of laugh. He was still out of breath from the fight, which would have been shaming if he'd been able to experience such a sophisticated emotion in that state.

"Is she, though?"

The fall might well have killed an ordinary mortal, but you never knew with a snake. Tal hopped down into the gully. No, dead, neck snapped, no doubt about that. He set about searching the body.

Tucked into her outer sash was a wallet of papers. The first of these was a letter of marque in Tlaanthothei, confirming the snake's identity as *Jatharisse, Seven Hundred and Forty-Ninth of the Thousand Eyes,* and requiring all loyal citizens of the Empire to give her aid and succour.

Ha ha, succour, thought Tal, perhaps still shaky from the fight.

The rest of the letters were in Echentyri. Tal struggled to read Echentyri characters at the best of times, but these didn't make any sense at all—they weren't even grouped into sentences, just laid out in a dense grid. They must be encoded in some way.

Some of the papers had an unpleasant wriggling quality, the characters slipping from view like eels in a pond. Sethennai had sometimes received letters like this, and one of the few things Tal knew about magic was that this shimmery, elusive quality meant the papers were sealed under arcane cipher.

Well, bully for Niranthos, he thought. These must be the documents he'd been sent to find.

Tsereg had also shinned down into the gully again. They poked Jatharisse's shoulder with their toe, then looked from Tal to the corpse and back again, then grinned, a slow expression of pure glee which transformed their beetly, ingrown little face into something like a daisy opening.

Tal found that his face of its own accord relaxed into a grin. Maybe he had never enjoyed fleeing for his life over the rooftops; maybe the thing he enjoyed was surviving afterward.

"Wow, you really killed her," said Tsereg. "Nice."

"You are very damaged," said Tal. "But thanks. Now let's get out of here."

"So what were you in jail for?" said Tal, as Tsereg climbed up into the back of the cutter. Undoubtedly a breach of prison etiquette, but they could shiv him later.

"Killing old people," said Tsereg. "Asked me too many questions."

Tal laughed. "How old are you?" he tried instead.

They hunched up on the bench like a carrion bird guarding its kill, clearly enduring some kind of internal struggle over whether to divulge this secret information.

"Fourteen," they muttered.

"Right," said Tal. He tried to remember what he'd been like at that age, but recalled only a red fog of distilled embarrassment. Best not to dwell. "Well. Should I drop you somewhere? Where are you going?"

"On my way to Ringtown," they said, with great confidence for one who had broken their journey by crashing a hijacked transport into a rock. "I have a contact there, at the Lemon Tree. Let's go back there."

"We can't," he said. "Not for a few days, anyway. Place will be crawling with Eyes, all looking for you."

"I'll be fine. We have to go there."

"No, we don't," he said. "If you're meeting someone at the Lemon Tree, they're just going to have to wait. Who is it, anyway?"

Tsereg gave him a hard stare. For fuck's sake. This was going to be like dealing with Csorwe all over again, but worse, because at least he and Csorwe had been allowed to hit each other.

That made twice in an hour that he'd thought about her. It had been so very, very long. He didn't miss her, except in the way you missed the empty space when you stubbed your toe on something in the middle of the night.

The worst of it was that he couldn't think of her without remembering what she'd become. The Thousand Eyes scared him, but they were nothing compared to the Empress and her Hand. Csorwe and Shuthmili had died in the temple fifteen years ago. The fact that their bodies still walked the earth was just salt to the wound.

The cutter sped on across the desert, black sand glittering below.

"Someone told you this person could help you on the outside?" he said.

"I'm not telling you anything. Why should I trust you?" They bared a single tusk at him. There was a raw-looking gap of grey gum where the other one was waiting to grow in.

Tal raised his eyes to the heavens.

"No reason," he said. "Except that I could've avoided a lot of mistakes if I'd been a bit quicker to recognise what a common enemy looks like."

"Talasseres Charossa," they said, muttering it into the ragged shawl which served them as a cloak.

"What?" said Tal. He hadn't heard his full name for a very long time. The legendary outlaw Talasseres Charossa was a character from a wanted poster.

"He's the one I'm looking for."

Once upon a time, Tal had thought he'd survived every ambush this bitch of a world could try and startle him with. Some years later, he'd realised this was never going to be the case, and that all you could do was laugh.

Tsereg sat in the back quite calmly, as if they were used to people acting erratically.

"You got something wrong with you?" they said.

He just went on laughing. Maybe he did have something the matter with him.

"*You're* Talasseres Charossa?" they said, when he had recovered enough to explain himself.

"But you're . . ." They stopped, biting their lip. However Tal had disappointed them, they were—amazingly—too tactful to spell it out. They wrapped their skinny arms around their knees and stared at him. "Huh."

"Not like in the paintings, yeah," said Tal.

Once again Tal wondered why Oranna had thought it was a good idea to spread that particular story around. He'd never know, since she was dead, but it was a pain in the arse.

"I took a stupid risk in a fight that happened before you were born, and I got two ribs broken and my friends died. Great story. Love to be reminded of it."

"Hmm," said Tsereg. "Well, but you failed. I'm not going to fail."

"You're not going to what?" said Tal.

Tsereg narrowed their eyes. "I *am* going to assassinate the God-Empress."

They were so serious and so certain that Tal could almost have laughed again—it was like seeing a woodlouse with homicidal intent—but there was real venom in it. They'd do it, if they could. Or, far more likely, they'd make the attempt, and get themselves killed before they passed the walls of the Lignite Citadel.

"That's a hell of a death wish," he said, suddenly feeling very tired. Tsereg shrugged, like a pile of unclean laundry falling over.

"People are relying on me," they said.

Tal bet they were. Nothing like sending an untrained infant to die for you. He knew all about that. That was the shit that got into your bones, and there was nothing anyone else could do about it.

"That sounds like a problem for them," he said. "What are you going to do, anyway, just walk into Tlaan—into the Lignite Citadel and stab the Empress in the heart?"

"*No,*" said Tsereg, although their face wilted as if that had very much been the beginning and end of the plan.

Tal raised an eyebrow. As ever, when he thought of the Empress, he had to make a conscious effort to sweep away what he knew about the Empress, what she looked like, who stood at her right hand.

"I have a sacred duty," Tsereg added, which was the kind of thing that always made Tal's head ache. What people always meant by it was: I plan to commit an astonishing fuckup, and it will hurt my feelings if you try to stop me.

"The Abyss will consume the breaker of promises," Tsereg went on, coldly. "I won't turn my back on my people. And my god won't turn its back on me."

"Your *god?*" said Tal. Oh, great. "Trust me, I've dealt with gods, and they lie and betray just like anybody else—" Belthandros Sethennai was one of the most accomplished liars he'd ever met, for example.

"No," said Tsereg. "The Unspoken does not lie."

Tal jerked in surprise, sending the cutter sharply off course.

"Right," he said, when he'd recovered what little remained of his dignity and poise. "Makes sense. The Unspoken One loves an obstinate little shit." Tsereg gave him a scathing look, which did not help because Csorwe had given him exactly such a look on many occasions. He did not need this. He wanted Tsereg gone so he could get back to normal and not have to think about any of this past dead shit. "Look, I don't know who sent you to find me, but they picked the wrong guy—"

He paused. What *was* he going to do with them? Wandering round Ringtown with an escaped prisoner was obviously not an option, and he didn't think that even he could leave a kid in the desert to die, but where else? He still didn't have any money, and wouldn't until he could hand those documents over to Niranthos, and—

Maybe that was the answer. Niranthos had a nice setup in the Citadel proper, well out of Ringtown. Niranthos could take Tsereg off Tal's hands and give them an easy job as a servant or something, in his nice house away from prying Eyes. He might even pay Tal for the privilege, but if he decided to be a dick, Tal could make it a condition of the bargain. Take Tsereg, or you don't get the papers. Then Tal could get a little breathing space, pay off the people he owed, and start again somewhere else.

"If I can get you into the Citadel, will you do as you're told?" he said.

"I thought you were going to say no," they said. He should have known better than to expect any kind of relief or gratitude. They frowned at him. They had been frowning already, so their face now looked like a box that had been kicked.

"I changed my mind," he lied. They wouldn't be happy when they found out, but at that point it wouldn't be his problem anymore.

"Why?" they said. There was no suspicion in it. They were simply baffled.

He sensed that he would not get the desired reaction with anything along the lines of *because you may be mistaken for a spider and washed down the drain.*

"What can I say?" he said. "You remind me of a friend."

13

The Sovereign of All Space and Time

THE LIGNITE CITADEL engulfed the dead city of Tlaanthothe like a great bramble. Deep within that thicket was a prison, and within that prison was a close, dark chamber that smelled of hot metal and seared flesh, and within that chamber was First Commander Cherenthisse, listening—as usual—to somebody's complaints. The complainer was Bakranai, the God-Empress' chief interrogator, and the subject of his distress was the interrogation chamber's translator glyph.

"It's been misbehaving all week, First Commander," said Bakranai, a florid mortal man with thinning hair and pale, watery eyes.

The translator glyph was an intricate mesh of spellwork, wrought in a narrow band all around the walls of the chamber, its clean, bright quicksilver looking out of place among the filth. Cherenthisse couldn't see anything obviously wrong with it.

"What exactly is the matter with it?" said Cherenthisse.

"Couldn't say, First Commander," said Bakranai, "but we can't make head nor tail of the foreign prisoners. Not but what those Qarsazhi mages don't do nothing but spit anyway—"

"And the containment wards? Are they intact?"

Bakranai shrugged. "Wouldn't be surprised if there was a problem, First Commander. This is the third failure in a month. You know they're saying there's some kind of saboteur—"

Cherenthisse gave him a sharp look.

"An official of your station should not spread rumours," she said.

At the back of her mind, concern mingled with resignation. Concern, because the containment wards were the only thing that kept the Citadel's mage prisoners from bursting their bonds and wreaking havoc. Resignation, because there was only one person who could fix them.

"This does sound inconvenient, First Commander," said Qanwa Shuthmili.

The years had not done much to alter the person who was now known as the Hand of the Empress. She was small and thin, unarmed, austerely dressed, and she wore her hair in a severe braid coiled on top of her head. The only noteworthy thing about her was the pair of leather gauntlets she wore at all times, which made her look as though her hands and forearms were covered with smooth black scales. Nevertheless, as Shuthmili stalked into the interrogation room, Bakranai took a step back, as though an invisible wake radiated from her. The interrogator put the fear of god into most mortals and several of the Thousand Eyes, and even he would not look Shuthmili in the eye.

Shuthmili didn't appear to notice him. She spent a few minutes tapping and peering at the wall. Bakranai shuffled out, leaving Cherenthisse alone with Shuthmili.

"Apparently this is the third failure in a month," said Cherenthisse, relieved that she no longer had to be polite. "What's happened?"

"You ask as though I could possibly know," said Shuthmili, still inspecting the glyph.

"You wrote the translator glyph. And all the other containment measures," said Cherenthisse. "Either your work is failing, or somebody is deliberately meddling with it. You need to fix it."

"Is it any wonder so many people see you as my handler?" said Shuthmili. Her voice was as flat as ever. She still didn't deign to look up.

"This is your responsibility. And only attack dogs need handlers. The Hand of the Empress should be able to handle herself."

The Hand was the God-Empress' personal intelligencer. She reported directly to the Empress and had no part in the Citadel's factional politics, except when called upon from time to time to execute a traitor. Once you had seen Shuthmili exsanguinate some luckless aspiring regicide, it was hard to forget the sight. The worst of it was that her face never changed.

"The Hand of the Empress is an extremely busy woman, Cherenthisse. You called me away from ciphering a letter for Her Majesty. You might at least ask nicely."

Whatever it was Shuthmili did up in her turret all day, Cherenthisse suspected she had gone rotten up there, like a fruit left too long on the branch, turned in on herself until this kind of mind game was the only thing that entertained her.

"I am sorry to interrupt what I'm sure was important work," said Cherenthisse, bitterly. "But would you mind helping me?"

Shuthmili gave her a thin smile, clearly pleased at how well Cherenthisse had learned the trick. "Thank you, First Commander. Let us cut to the chase. How many prisoners are in the isolation wing just now? Who was interrogated most recently?"

"There are a few dozen, but Bakranai says he's been working over the two mages from the *Vehement Rejoinder,*" said Cherenthisse. This was a Qarsazhi warship, shot down months ago, with only these two survivors.

A sigh hissed between Shuthmili's teeth.

"One of them must have tampered with the glyph," she said. "It's subtly done, too. Only a mage could have done it. Goodness knows what else they're capable of. Rather inconvenient."

The God-Empress did not have her own client mages in this world. The death of the Siren had incapacitated Tlaanthothe's existing practitioners, and none of the children born in the Citadel since her accession had yet shown signs of aptitude. They would come in time, but in the meantime, the God-Empress only had Shuthmili, whose patron was some unpleasant-sounding Qarsazhi goddess, to help maintain the Citadel's arcane logistics and defences. An escaped mage could wreak all kinds of havoc before the Thousand Eyes could get them back under control.

"Can you fix the glyph?" said Cherenthisse. She had worked alongside Shuthmili for fifteen years now, and she didn't think this, at least, would take much cajoling. There weren't many reliable levers where the Hand of the Empress was concerned, but by god, the woman loved a puzzle.

"Yes," said Shuthmili. "But whoever has done this could be responsible for the other security breaches."

"That was my thought," said Cherenthisse. It hadn't been, but she refused to give Shuthmili credit for an idea anyone might have put together.

Rumour was everywhere, but it was a fact that there was a mole somewhere in the Citadel. Shipments went missing. A group of dissidents who operated an illegal printing press at the Lemon Tree public house had been warned, early enough that half of them had escaped before the Thousand Eyes raided the place. Someone was leaking information to the Empress' enemies.

"I think perhaps I'd better speak to these Qarsazhi," said Shuthmili.

They brought in the first of the Qarsazhi prisoners with her hands and ankles bound. According to the file, her name was Thurya Mishari, a fourth-year Adept of the School of Aptitude. When she saw Shuthmili, her face twisted and she spat on the ground.

If Shuthmili objected to this, she didn't show it. One of the things Cherenthisse most disliked about Shuthmili was that she had no sense of leadership, as if it didn't matter what anybody thought of you. Cherenthisse had made great efforts to understand the people working for her. It was on her initiative that the Thousand Eyes said *mortals* now rather than *prey*, for instance. It was important to set an example.

Still, Shuthmili's reputation could be useful under circumstances such as this.

Shuthmili raised an eyebrow, murmuring something in Qarsazhi. Without a working translator glyph, Cherenthisse couldn't understand what was being said, but Thurya responded with a stream of what were obviously curses.

Shuthmili went on in her usual indifferent drawl. Cherenthisse stood back out of spitting range. This went on for a few minutes to no avail.

"If she won't cooperate—" said Cherenthisse.

"Fuck you, snake," said Thurya, spitting out the foreign words as if they were jagged in her mouth. "Fuck you, Inquisitor Qanwa. Fuck you to hell, all snakes."

Shuthmili's face went very still, and then she leant in close, lifting Thurya's chin with one gauntleted hand. She held eye contact with the prisoner for a second. Thurya trembled in rage and terror, then Shuthmili released her, shaking her head.

"It wasn't her," said Shuthmili. "Not capable of it, unless they worked together."

"Inquisitor?" said Cherenthisse. "I thought that was a Qarsazhi title—"

Shuthmili twitched, clenching her jaw.

"It's what they all call me. A funny joke," said Shuthmili. "Thurya knows nothing. Let's talk to the other."

Cherenthisse chained Thurya Mishari to a bench by the wall and called for the second prisoner.

This one was old and shrivelled, with a completely bald head and a shrunken face. It wasn't immediately clear whether they were a man or a woman or a member of some other mortal class. Cherenthisse found it difficult to tell. In Old Echentyr, such distinctions had been exclusively a prey matter, unseemly and rather primitive, and in the new order of things, she generally had to rely on styles of hair and clothing to make a guess.

"What's their name?" said Shuthmili, flipping through the papers. "Oh, it says they won't admit it. My, Cherenthisse, your interrogators have not got far with this one."

"Qanwa Shuthmili," said the prisoner, now strapped into a chair in the middle of the interrogation room. Their voice rasped in their throat like a knife being sharpened.

Shuthmili's eyes widened—only a fraction, only for a second, but Cherenthisse caught it. She had been taken by surprise. The prisoner had recognised her, and there was no mistaking the look on *their* face. That was bitter, personal hatred.

The prisoner gave an empty wheeze of laughter and said Shuthmili's name again.

"Ah, of course," said Shuthmili, and then a word in Qarsazhi which Cherenthisse did not recognise: "Vigil."

There was a brief exchange in Qarsazhi, and Shuthmili rolled her eyes.

"You cannot expect me to believe you do not speak Tlaanthothei," she said.

Vigil said something biting, and then, in clipped but comprehensible Tlaanthothei: "This serpent is your master. Yes?"

"In a manner of speaking," said Shuthmili, giving Cherenthisse a derisive glance.

"Now I warn you, serpent," said Vigil, fixing their deep-set eyes on Cherenthisse. "This one, she is the traitor. She kills her aunt, she outrages her faith, she runs away from punishment. You trust her now, and she betrays you too."

If the prisoner thought Cherenthisse trusted Shuthmili an inch, they were dead wrong, but she said nothing.

Shuthmili's mouth twisted in a thin smile. "The prisoner is a Quincury Adept," she said. "Everything they see and hear will be received immediately in Qarsazh by the rest of Vigil Quincury. Yet another security breach. I hope your people have been discreet."

Not good. The war with Qarsazh had reached a kind of holding pattern, but in its worst years, the Imperial Quincuriate had been a real threat, perhaps the only real threat to the might of the God-Empress and her Thousand Eyes.

"You're certain?" said Cherenthisse.

"I know this one long ago," said Vigil. "She hurts many of me. She kills my bodies." Vigil looked up at Shuthmili again, their dry eyes blinking. "To be cut away, this is the worst pain. You know this, yes, I think?"

Shuthmili's lips curved up in something that looked quite like a smile. "No punishment worse than exile? I know *that* line. The kind of thing my aunt Zhiyouri used to say."

Only now did Cherenthisse realise something was wrong, and she didn't have time to warn Shuthmili before it happened. All the while they had been talking, the silver sigils on the wall had been shifting, so slowly and slightly that she hadn't seen it even out of the corner of her eye. Now they moved like water ruffled by the breeze. She could almost hear the breeze itself, though they were deep in the bowels of the palace, where the air never stirred.

"Look out, the wards—" said Cherenthisse, springing toward Shuthmili and Vigil. Before she could reach her, she was seized from behind as if by a gigantic hand, lifted and suspended, twisting in midair.

Thurya Mishari had been slumped on the bench, eyes fixed on the floor. Now the links of her cuffs fell away like sand, and the look of triumph on her face was unmistakable. Vigil had broken their bonds too, and they had Shuthmili pinned against the wall.

The sound of the wind rose. Behind Thurya, where once there had been a black wall of fossil-stone, there was a crude archway, and beyond it a dark passage, winding sharply away as though drilled into the earth itself. The wind whipped Cherenthisse's hair and clothing, but she still could not move. Every attempt just sent her spinning in midair.

Thurya's hands twitched. Cherenthisse knew the look of someone calculating whether they had time to kill her. Then she shook her head. "Vigil!" she yelled, then something else in Qarsazhi that was clearly *let's go!* She limped through the archway and disappeared.

As soon as Thurya was gone, Cherenthisse dropped to the floor.

Vigil's hands were braced around Shuthmili's throat. They still had some of their fingernails, long and black with dirt. If they heard Thurya, they showed no sign of it. So desperate to kill Shuthmili that nothing could have drawn them away. Cherenthisse supposed she knew the feeling.

"A little help, First Commander!" said Shuthmili, wriggling in Vigil's grasp.

Cherenthisse was a loyal servant and a dutiful soldier, but she would have needed the mercy and patience of the God-Empress herself not to enjoy the moment.

"Help?" she said, hooking her thumbs through her belt.

"If you have a chance to interrupt what I'm sure is *important work*—" said Shuthmili, kicking out at the Adept to no avail. "Would you *mind*?"

Cherenthisse grabbed Vigil by the middle and dragged them back. They were really very light, frail as an empty cocoon. All their focus and magic must have been concentrated on Shuthmili, because they came away from her like a bundle of dead ivy, and when Cherenthisse dropped them on the floor they crumpled.

Shuthmili stood over them, pinning one shoulder with her toe. She was wearing soft little slippers, but Vigil went as still as if they were manacled to the ground.

Vigil bared a row of small yellow teeth in a rictus of defiance, and the wind howled through the room like a wolf. "Very much you look like Zhi-youri today," they said. They opened their mouth as though to speak again, but a black tendril sprouted from behind their teeth.

There was a crisp squelching sound, like someone biting into a grape, and more tendrils burst through the holes in Vigil's ragged shirt. In a very short time, their rib cage was a nest of slithering things, looping in and out between the bones. Shuthmili's expression was dispassionate.

The wind died with the Quincury Adept, and the archway in the wall was gone.

"Was it necessary to kill them?" said Cherenthisse.

Shuthmili rose, brushing some invisible dust from her skirts. "You would never have learned anything from them. It was an absurd risk to hold them here. They will have reported everything they have seen and heard to the Inquisitorate."

"Of course you know best," said Cherenthisse bitterly.

It was typical of Shuthmili to make it sound as if she'd somehow done Cherenthisse a favour, when in fact it was a godawful mess. She would need to send someone to clean up the wreck of Vigil's body, she would need to explain to Bakranai why one of his prisoners was dead, she would need to explain to the God-Empress herself that Thurya Mishari had escaped . . .

"Thank you, First Commander," said Shuthmili. "Send some of your people after Thurya, if you like, but I doubt she will get far. She must have been relying on Vigil to sustain the passage. Opening that kind of door is more of a Quincuriate specialty."

Cherenthisse dimly recollected this was one of the reasons they had been holding Qarsazhi mages in the first place. As Iriskavaal's successor, the God-Empress was the sovereign of all space and time, and she resented any usurpation of that power by alien mages.

"Now, if you're finished with me, I really should get back to this cipher—" Shuthmili started to say.

"Another funny joke," said Cherenthisse. "We need to talk to the Empress."

The throne room of the God-Empress was vast and high-vaulted, and it altered itself constantly at the will of the goddess, expanding and relaxing like the ribs of a great animal. That day it was full of a mist, rising from the far end of the room and rolling over the dais. It smelled of ozone, like the air after a thunderstorm.

In it there were only two fixed and immutable things.

The first, set into the base of a pillar, was a tall cylinder of thick green glass. It was full of salt water, and suspended upside down in it was the body of the pretender Belthandros Sethennai. Its chest rose and fell as if it was asleep. Tubes and nozzles ran in and out of its mouth and nose, winding away into the fabric of the palace. They had retrieved Sethennai's body from the sarcophagus, back in Saar-in-Tachthyr, and it was now preserved here as a warning against defiance.

The second was the throne itself, a huge half-graceful fan of green chrysoprase. The God-Empress sat upon it, tapping her toe restlessly against her shin. The Mantle wafted around her, almost invisible, like a breeze made solid.

The God-Empress wore an enormous dress of layered translucent silk, every layer embroidered in gold so that she seemed to move within a gigantic mechanism, a cloud shot through with lightning. Beneath the Mantle, her dark hair fell to her waist, combed to the texture of silk and weighted with pendants of jade.

Her features were as lovely and as tranquil as ever, illuminating the crude vessel with divine power. As always, her lips were serenely curved, half in melancholy and half in sweetness. In these fifteen years, she had scarcely changed. Like stone, she did not age or yield. Like stone, the vessel had taken on a shimmering, translucent quality, hard and bright and impermeable. She had torn out the vessel's gold tusk and replaced it with another tooth cut from a single immense diamond. Even the scar that curved down her face looked more like a flaw in a jewel than the remains of a wound.

The whole throne room was full of her presence, a dark and stinging radiance, a weight and pressure like that of oceans. A mortal secretary stood at a safe distance at a lectern. His eyes were bloodshot, and his skin was thin, riddled with purplish veins. Spending too much time too close to the Empress could have this effect on mortal flesh, as though her very skin breathed out poison.

"Approach," said the Empress. Her voice crackled and sang with power. They knelt before her, Cherenthisse clutching her hand to her chest in a gesture of fealty.

"Well?" said the Empress. She raised a hand, bidding them rise. "Something troubles thee, First Commander?"

When Shuthmili used Cherenthisse's title, it was an insult. Hearing it on the Empress' lips more than made up for that. Cherenthisse had never hoped to rise so high. Every time the Empress spoke it aloud, Cherenthisse knew her true purpose again. Out of the dust of Echentyr new glory would rise.

Even so, it was uncomfortable to explain what had happened in the isolation wing, and Shuthmili—of course—remained silent throughout, letting Cherenthisse stumble through it.

When she had finished, the Empress considered them steadily.

"A catalogue of errors we do not expect from either of you," she said. "It is just as well that we had no further use for the Qarsazhi heretics."

"Majesty, there's something I had wondered," said Shuthmili, sounding not at all abashed. Cherenthisse darted a glance of disapproval at her, but the Empress inclined her head. "The presence of a Vigil Adept is a serious security breach. Could that have been the mole we've been dealing with? If Vigil was relaying information to Qarsazh, the Inquisitorate may have been passing it on to agitators in Ringtown."

Cherenthisse cursed her silently. Now Cherenthisse would get all the blame for the fiasco, and Shuthmili all the credit for the insight.

"It's not possible," said Cherenthisse. "Of course it's a security breach, but how would a prisoner in the isolation wing have known anything about our supply lines? What were we questioning them about? Qarsazhi magic?"

"The heretics have some limited capacity to manipulate space, as you two saw when you let them escape," said the Empress. "We had hoped it might be turned to the good of the great work. To no avail, however."

The great work was another phrase that sent shivers down Cherenthisse's spine. That was something Shuthmili could not steal from her. Cherenthisse had known and believed even before the Mantle of Divinity had been restored. Whatever Shuthmili might say about her loyalty and commitment, she was just a tagalong.

"Thank you, Majesty," said Cherenthisse. "I can't see any reason why the interrogators would tell a prisoner anything about Citadel logistics. The most they might have transmitted back to Qarsazh is the fact that we're interested in their magic. That can hardly have been a surprise to the Inquisitorate."

"We have been pursuing our own leads on the security breach," said the God-Empress. That was news to Cherenthisse. To her immense satisfaction, she saw it was news to Shuthmili too, and that she looked hurt by it. It was past time for Shuthmili to learn that the Empress did not have the luxury of trusting anybody. "We do not believe the Qarsazhi prisoners were involved. However, you have given us much to consider, and we appreciate your candour."

They both bowed and murmured their thanks, and the conversation moved on to the arrangements for the Midsummer Feast.

"My apologies, Majesty," said Shuthmili, as they were leaving. "I hope Cherenthisse and I have not offended—"

"Upset not thyself, Shuthmili," said the Empress. Her smile softened a little, and she reached out to brush a hand against Shuthmili's cheek. Cherenthisse's fists tightened with the usual resentment. "All is well. All is in hand. Until this security breach is remedied, we prefer to keep our silence on certain matters. But thou art ever dear to me."

Shuthmili made the appropriate expressions of gratitude, but Cherenthisse had not missed the moment of hesitation, the flicker of some other strange emotion that preceded it. This was exactly why Cherenthisse did not trust her. She just had the look of someone who was hiding something, and always had.

Cherenthisse shouldered her way down the corridor, with Shuthmili following in her wake. The Lignite Citadel wasn't usually so resistant, not to the First Commander of the Thousand Eyes, but when the Empress was in a difficult mood, the currents of space and time swirled wildly, and it took sustained effort even to walk in a straight line.

The inhabitants of the Citadel had come up with their own ways of dealing with it. At a crossroads they passed a group of mortal clerks in pairs, neat and serious in their green uniforms, all clinging to a rope that stretched ahead of them down a spiralling passageway.

At another intersection was a pillar of fossil-stone tagged with chalk sigils like tidemarks. Waiting for them at the bottom of the pillar was Shuthmili's secretary, full of some news. He saluted them both, but he clearly hadn't expected to run into Cherenthisse.

The secretary—Keleiros Lenarai—was a pretty Tlaanthothei whose anxious, delicate features were framed by a cascade of dark ringlets. Cherenthisse happened to know that anxiety masked a sharp eye and a very healthy self-interest. The boy had been reporting privately to her on Shuthmili's activities for a few months now.

Keleiros looked from Shuthmili to Cherenthisse and back again. Shuthmili raised her eyebrow.

"Did you have something to report, Keleiros?"

Whatever it was, she did not want Cherenthisse to hear it, but Cherenthisse had swallowed more than enough of Shuthmili's superiority for one day, and Keleiros knew which side his bread was buttered. She leant against the wall and waited.

"Ma'am—yes—I'm so sorry to interrupt you, but I assumed you'd want to be notified. One of your staff has been arrested, ma'am. They think he's been involved with the security breaches. Niranthos Charossa."

"Ah," said Shuthmili. Someone who knew her less well wouldn't have noticed the little twitch of startled disquiet. Shuthmili hated to be taken by surprise. "That's a pity. He was a good worker."

Cherenthisse was quietly pleased. If they really had apprehended the source of the leaks, that was one more problem off her desk. And she had to admit to a certain pleasure at learning it was one of Shuthmili's people who was to blame. After fifteen years, Cherenthisse had given up hope that Shuthmili might ever get easier to deal with, but she could do with bringing down to earth a bit. She thought her position as the Empress' Hand made her untouchable. It was about time she learned things could go wrong for her.

"If someone has been leaking information from my office, I need to know how much and to whom," said Shuthmili to Keleiros. Cherenthisse could have laughed at that. The Hand clearly had no idea that Keleiros himself was Cherenthisse's own man. "Tell Bakranai I would like to be present for the interrogation."

"That's highly irregular," Cherenthisse cut in. She was sure Shuthmili wanted to use the opportunity to try and smooth things over, to make herself look less culpable for Charossa's betrayal. "Bakranai won't allow it."

"Bakranai is an idiot," said Shuthmili. "Niranthos Charossa is quite diligent, but he does not have the initiative to do something like this on his own. Someone will have directed him. If we have an opportunity to find out who that is, we can't afford to pass it up."

14

Things Change

THE LIGHT OF Tal's lantern gleamed on the ancient pillars and tiles of the underground boulevard. By some minor miracle, the Thousand Eyes had never discovered Tal's old escape tunnel, and it was now the only way in or out of the Citadel without having to pass through their security.

He'd bought Tsereg a pastry from a roadside trader, hoping it would distract them from the enclosed space and the darkness. It seemed to be working. They ate it silently, eyes narrowed with puzzled concentration, and picked every crumb of almond paste out of the paper bag when they were finished.

"What was that for?" they said.

"What, was it not nice?" he said. "Thought you might like it."

"Yeah, but why?" they said.

He'd already begun to have the idea that the pastry had been a mistake, though he couldn't identify why. He'd expected some kind of gratifying reaction, maybe. Another smile, as when he'd killed Jatharisse. Now he thought about it, this made him queasy. He'd been careful to keep a certain distance from Tsereg. Partly because they would probably bite, mostly because—well, he wasn't used to thinking of himself as a man of power, but Tsereg was a teenage escaped convict, and these things were always relative. He didn't want to startle them, and he certainly didn't want them trying to ingratiate themselves with him.

He had been mad for ingratiating at that age. He had moved back to his mother's house after his expulsion from the Tlaanthothei Academy for Boys, and he remembered too well trying to make himself interesting and agreeable to her friends. The ability to make himself agreeable had served him well later in life, notably with actual men of power, but it had always required a calculated effort to suppress his real personality, and his real personality had never been happy with him afterward. At least Sethennai had known him for the nasty, spiteful creature that he was.

Still, Tsereg wasn't a performing animal, and presumably knew that people only did nice things if they wanted something from you, or if they were trying to pull the wool over your eyes. Which was exactly what Tal was doing, because he had not told them about his plan to dump them with Niranthos.

"Kept you quiet for a bit, didn't it?" he said. Maybe he should tell them. Maybe not everything, but enough that he didn't have to feel like he was *really* lying to them. "So when we get in, we're going to head to my brother's house—"

"Who's your brother?" Tsereg asked, later.

"He's some kind of city official," said Tal. Tsereg screwed up their face in preemptive wrath, and he shook his head. "No, he's really corrupt, it's all right."

"You mean, he's on our side?" said Tsereg.

Tal didn't know what to say to that. If he hadn't known for a fact that Niranthos was a turncoat, Tal would have said his brother was as disgustingly happy in the God-Empress' employment as he'd always been as a class prefect at the Tlaanthothei Academy for Boys.

"There's no *our side*," he said. "Niranthos is on his own side. He's a prick. But he's not on the Empress' side either, and I've got something to trade with him."

"Hmm. What'll you do afterward?" said Tsereg.

"What?" said Tal. He was still figuring that out. He'd only got as far as the idea that things would be easier for a while if he could get some money.

Tsereg's thoughts were clearly running on different lines. "When the Empress is dead. What'll you do?"

"I don't know, take myself on a bloody beach holiday," said Tal. "What will *you* do?"

Tsereg shrugged. "I'm going to die," they said. "So I don't need to worry about it."

"*What?*" said Tal. "What the fuck, Tsereg? You can't go in planning to die."

"I told you," they said. "It's my sacred duty."

"*What* sacred duty?" he said.

"As the Chosen Bride of the Unspoken," they said.

Tal had spent the best part of his early twenties wishing Csorwe had just fucking snuffed it in her cave, so he couldn't help knowing what this meant.

The Chosen Bride of the Unspoken went up the hill to the Shrine, where she probably got bored to death reciting verses or something. But all the same—

"How are you the Chosen Bride of the Unspoken? I thought it had to be a girl."

Tsereg rolled their eyes at him with deep scorn.

Tal bared his teeth to show off a general lack of tusks. "Don't know how you people do things, do I?" The only Oshaaru he'd ever known well was Csorwe, and he didn't think he could rely on her as an example.

Tsereg shrugged. "House of Silence was mostly girls, sure. Not like the Unspoken One is a man or a woman, though, is it? Gods aren't. So I'm *extra* Chosen, I feel like."

"Sure, fine, okay," said Tal, who always felt out of his depth with god stuff. "I thought you said you were in prison. Wouldn't have thought the Unspoken would want a baby shoplifter or whatever you are."

"We're all in prison. The Thousand Eyes burnt the House of Silence when I was three months old, and now we all hang out in the Iron Hill and have a great time sewing bags and stuff."

"And they still want you to die?"

"It's not *like* that! They don't want me to die, I'm just—I'm Chosen, so it's gonna happen one way or another, so I'm the one who's got to kill the Empress."

"And what, you don't have a choice?" said Tal.

"Yeah, that's sort of what being the Chosen one means," said Tsereg.

"The Unspoken One just . . . picks you out, and that's that? They just send you to die?"

"I'm not afraid of dying," said Tsereg. "I'm not a coward."

"You don't know what death *is*," he said. "You're literally a child! You don't know what you're throwing away."

"My mother died," said Tsereg, eyebrows drawn down so low that he only caught a flash of golden-brown iris, beaming hatred directly into his face. He felt guilty until he realised Tsereg clearly saw this as a winning gambit.

"When?" he said.

"When I was a baby," said Tsereg.

"Yeah, well then!" said Tal.

"What, does that not count or something?" they said, lip curled.

"God, you and the Unspoken One can both kiss my arse," said Tal. "It's like you *want* to throw your life away."

"Yeah, well. The world didn't used to be like this, did it?" said Tsereg, with a sudden solemnity that made Tal want to flick a piece of gum at them.

"I don't know what you've heard about the good old days, but I'm here to tell you it's always been a whole mess of bastards," he said.

"Yeah, but it wasn't like this," they said. "I heard about it. Tlaanthothe. Forests and seas and shit. No snakes. No Empress."

Sometimes he remembered Tlaanthothe with such painful clarity it was as if he was home again: the chatter of students flooding from the School of Transcendence after their exams, the blue aloes, the fountains, the exact smell of the bar where he had used to drink alone, aniseed liquor and candle wax and sawdust, spots of rain on dry stone. All carefully preserved behind one of those doors in his mind which he had done his best to keep closed.

"Yeah," he said. "You should've seen it. But it's gone."

"It doesn't have to be like this forever," said Tsereg. Their expression was one of utter and compelling faith in themselves.

Tal wondered if some people had a kind of switch inside them, some irreversible ratchet that saw things were bad and flipped over into *and I'm going to fix it*. He didn't have it. When things went wrong, the Talasseres way was to run.

A long time ago he'd thought he had something to prove, that he'd eventually be able to make people believe that he was brave and tenacious enough to be worth something. Or rather, let's be honest here, the person he was thinking of was Belthandros Sethennai—*who the fuck else*—and then that had fallen through, and then everything else had fallen through, and there wasn't much point being brave or tenacious anymore. He had seen what bravery and tenacity got you.

"And if you fix it," he said, "if you fix it and die fixing it. What's the point, then?"

"You are very damaged," they said. "Things change, Tal. And I'm the one who changes them."

"Sounds like you think this is going to be easy," he said.

"Been easy so far," they said. They were practically skipping down the passage in their eagerness to get going. "Maybe you're just lazy."

"Ha ha. Maybe you're just a kid."

"Maybe you're just a coward."

"Maybe you're just a *dumb baby*—" said Tal, and this was when something hit him hard in the back of the head.

It was a big stick. Holding the big stick was a skinny girl not much taller than Tsereg. Tal rolled over onto his back and tried to get to his feet, but something was holding him flat. His lantern bounced away across the ground and shattered, and before the light went out, he saw that the girl's teeth were bared as if she was about to rip out his throat.

Tsereg squawked and thrashed somewhere nearby, and Tal struggled against whatever was holding him, convinced the skinny girl must have an accomplice.

Then a bluish flickering light flared in the girl's hands—*magelight*, Tal thought, dazed—and he saw there was nobody there in the passage but the three of them. Tsereg was spinning in the air, held by whatever invisible force had Tal pinned to the ground.

"Let me go!" shrieked Tsereg, clawing at the air in rage.

The girl shook her head. Tal saw now that her clothes were ragged, her legs bare under a torn shift, and her feet bloody from walking on jagged stone. She was in her early twenties, but her cheeks were hollow and there were deep shadows under her eyes.

"Sorry," she said, in a thick Qarsazhi accent. "Sorry, sorry—"

Tal's Qarsazhi was rusty, but he still knew the essentials. "What the fuck is this?" he said.

She blinked at him. "I—I thought you were snakes," she said. She was shivering. "Look, I'm really sorry, but I still have to do this." She eyed the two of them up, and then spotted Tal's knife on the floor.

She fumbled for it, holding it as if she was about to cut into a steak. Her fingers didn't bend properly.

"Do you have any money?" she said.

"Tal, what is she saying?" Tsereg hissed. "Who is she?"

"She's robbing us at knifepoint, I think," said Tal. He struggled against the band of force holding him down. As soon as he got free, he could have the knife off her. He could incapacitate her without it, for that matter. She was no fighter, and she was shaking like a blade of grass.

"Yeah, I have some money," he said to the girl. "It's in my pockets. You'll have to let me go."

"All right. Maybe," she said to Tal. "When I do that, you need to take off your coat and put it on the floor."

"Why should I do that?" said Tal. "You know, this isn't the first time someone's tried to rob me, but I've never had to talk them through it before."

"Or I'll . . ." She looked down at the knife. "I'll cut the child. I will." She moved toward Tsereg, still holding the knife as if it might leap out of her hand.

Tsereg screamed at her. They really could use their voice as a blunt instrument.

"Shh," said the girl, wincing. "Please. The snakes might hear. They're looking for me. I'm serious, you don't know what I'm capable of. Tell your friend to shut up, or I'll use this. I mean it."

"Tsereg, shut the fuck up," said Tal obediently.

"Tell her I'll rip her eyes out!" hissed Tsereg.

Tal turned back to the girl. "Yeah, they're terrified," he said. "All right. I think you were mugging me?"

He didn't want to hurt her, which was a problem. He was surprised to realise that if she had a go at Tsereg, he *would* hurt her. She was certainly desperate enough to chase them if they tried to escape, and she was probably desperate enough to try and use that knife, and he knew from Shuthmili what a mage was capable of doing in a tight corner.

Not to mention that he hadn't forgotten what he'd told Tsereg about a common enemy. All in all, he didn't seem to have a choice. The girl let him go, he took off his coat, turned out the pockets, and held up his hands. The girl pounced on the coat hungrily and pulled it on at once.

"And your boots," she said, pointing the knife at him. It would be the easiest thing in the world to grab her wrist and snatch it off her. Instead he unlaced his boots, stepped out of them and kicked them toward her.

"Don't think I'm your size," he said.

She shook her head. "Doesn't matter. Thank you. I'm sorry to do this. I thought I was going to die."

"Hey, any time," said Tal. "Look at me, these days I'm a fucking charitable institution. Can I have my knife back?"

"N-no," said the girl. "I need it."

Tal stepped neatly over to her, plucked the knife out of her hands, and sheathed it again at his belt.

"Don't do yourself a mischief," he said. "Are we done?"

The girl flinched, flattening herself against the wall of the passage. She was a mage, which meant she could pull Tal's guts out of his nostrils, so this made no sense.

"We're done," he said, to clarify. "Get out of here."

She stared at him, uncomprehending. "I . . . I see. Thank you."

"Good job," said Tal. "Great robbery, let's do this again sometime."

"May the vigilance of the Mother of Cities protect you waking and sleeping," said the girl with a little bob of her head, and Tsereg squeaked as they hit the ground.

"Don't push it, you stole my bloody boots," he said. The girl grinned at him and limped off into the darkness.

As usual, Tal regretted this about five minutes later.

"What the hell," said Tsereg. "Why did you let her go?"

"She didn't know what she was doing," said Tal. Anyone less like a hardened criminal was hard to imagine. She'd had the same prissy cut-glass accent as Shuthmili. "Didn't you see? She'd been tortured."

"Yeah, I *know*," said Tsereg.

"I guess I just didn't really want to be a dick about it."

"Oh, yeah, I'm the one who's a dumb baby," said Tsereg. "Now you don't have shoes! And she was waving a knife at me!"

"Yeah, and I'm sure she would have done you a lot of damage if you'd run deliberately into it a few times," said Tal. "She could hardly hold the thing. Her fingers . . ."

It was just starting to sink in, now that the standoff was over and he could think. He knew what kind of things happened in the Citadel. Of course he knew. He'd seen the terror on people's faces as they were arrested.

It ought to have made him want to turn back. He ought to give up on this plan and scuttle out of town and find some other quiet hole to hide in. If he had any sense of self-preservation, he ought to tell Tsereg this little jaunt was over and that they were on their own.

"Do you really think you can do it?" he said. "Get rid of the God-Empress, I mean? You've got some kind of weird Unspoken scheme up your sleeve? You really think there's a way?"

"Yeah, I've told you," they said. "I know what I'm doing."

"Yeah?"

"There's a book. In the library, in the Citadel. Gotta get the book, and then I'll know."

"What book?"

"Just a book," said Tsereg, sounding cagey. "It's from the House of Silence library. The Thousand Eyes nicked it along with everything else, and now it's stashed away in some dungeon."

He didn't feel so good about the idea of leaving them with Niranthos anymore, and to be honest, he didn't think they would stay where they were left anyway. Maybe if they really did have a plan—as ridiculous as this book idea sounded—maybe if there was some way to bring down the Empress, maybe he should help them.

Except that they'd admitted the assassination would end in their death. Chosen Bride of the Unspoken, dying like Csorwe was supposed to have done. If they thought that was worth it, to fix the world, maybe it wasn't Tal's business to stop them—but then again, if they didn't have a plan, if they were running on pure faith in themselves and the Unspoken, then they'd probably be captured by Thousand Eyes first thing and drowned in the fountain like everyone else who had tried.

Tal did not enjoy complicated problems. He'd arranged his whole life to avoid them. If you saw a complicated problem, the only sane thing to do was to turn your back and walk away. All the same, he found himself dwelling on this all the way down the tunnel and up the hidden stairway.

Originally, the tunnel had emerged in a public park, among a stand of trees. This was now a huge dry stone garden, all gravel paths and bronze sculptures.

The bronzes had a half-finished, molten look, as though the sculptor had only vaguely imagined them and called them into being without thinking further.

Tal peered out from the stairway until he was sure the garden was empty, then called Tsereg up from below.

Looming at the far end of the garden, its apex brushing up against the panes of the dome, was the defunct Great Gate of Tlaanthothe, long since brought to earth from its original position hovering above the Gate-fortress. Before the accession of the God-Empress, the Gate had burnt as green as copper, but its light was long extinguished, leaving nothing more than a great circular stone frame, dull and sightless as the sculptures.

Beneath the dead Gate was a grand fountain, with steps leading up to a deep pool of salt water, and a large open space for spectators. Tal recognised it as the original on which the public fountain in Ringtown must have been modelled. It also reminded him, in a sickly way, of his mother's Midsummer's Eve party fifteen years ago—the ruined offerings, the withered body of the hippocamp lying in the dry fountain. These must be the Execution Gardens, where traitors were drowned.

The Gardens were very silent. The crunch of their footsteps on the gravel made Tal wince almost as much as the feeling of sharp stones on his bare feet. He hoped Niranthos would give him another pair of boots.

"Well," he said. "We're in."

It was not far from the Gardens to Niranthos' house, down narrow streets and covered alleyways. The shape of the streets was half familiar, like the mangled version of the old Charossa mansion that Tal sometimes saw in his dreams. The Citadel had grown on Tlaanthothe like a great crystalline fungus, a gigantic parasite that engulfed what had once been Tal's hometown. Here and there, a fragment of the old Tlaanthothei facade was visible behind the casing of fossil-stone. Niranthos' townhouse was a tall narrow sliver at the end of a long terrace.

Tal knocked at the door, and Niranthos himself answered. Tal should have known immediately that that meant something was wrong.

Niranthos gave him a forbidding look.

"Talasseres," he said. "It's six o'clock in the morning. What do you think you're doing here?"

"Long story," said Tal. "Uh, this is Tsereg."

He wasn't sure how to press on. He knew how Niranthos felt about anything he considered to be too risky, too outlandish, or simply beneath his dignity. *Take this foundling off my hands* was going to be a difficult proposition, whatever the child's provenance.

"Uh, they're from that shipwreck. You know, the one you sent me to investigate—"

Tsereg didn't say anything, apparently stricken by shyness.

"You always did know how to pick your moments, Talasseres," said Niranthos. A muscle was working in his jaw, and his long ears were flat against his skull.

"Can we come in?" said Tal.

Niranthos glanced back into the dark passage behind him. Tal really should have known then, really should have grabbed Tsereg's arm and turned and run, and later he would curse himself for not doing so.

"I suppose you'd better," said Niranthos. There was an odd intentful light in his eyes, as though he was trying to beam something directly into Tal's brain. They'd never been close enough for that kind of understanding. Tal didn't know what he meant. All he was thinking about was a cup of tea and a new pair of boots and maybe sitting in a comfortable chair for a while.

Niranthos led them to a small, dim sitting room. Where you might expect a window to be there was a huge tapestry depicting the God-Empress enthroned.

"Wait here a minute," said Niranthos. "I'll send for something to eat."

Tsereg watched him go and gave Tal the kind of look you might exchange with a friend when someone embarrassing left a party. It was all eyes with a little bit of face between them, goggling like two jar lids.

"I told you he was like this," said Tal.

After a few minutes Niranthos returned with a new look on his face, one that Tal *did* recognise. It was a very Niranthos expression. It meant *so be it, there's nothing I can do about it, it's not my fault if my fool brother gets himself into trouble.*

"What's going on?" said Tal, beginning for the first time to be alarmed.

At this Niranthos was overcome by a coughing fit. He held a green handkerchief delicately to his mouth, and when he pulled it away, it was stained dark. A handsome jade basin with a straw lid stood on a side table. It looked about half full of bloody handkerchiefs.

"Are you sick?" he said, casting at random for something to say. Niranthos seemed to be waiting for something.

Niranthos looked genuinely puzzled until he followed Tal's gaze to the basin of handkerchiefs. "I've been living in the Citadel for nearly twelve years," he said. "This happens to everyone eventually. I've . . . tried. Tal. I really tried. I thought I could do something. But I—"

Tsereg yelped at Tal's side, their pointed ears pricking up. "Tal, someone's coming," they said.

"What is going *on?*" said Tal.

"You shouldn't have come here," said Niranthos, and blew his nose bloodily into another handkerchief.

The door to the parlour opened, and three Thousand Eyes in full armour stepped into the room.

"Is this him?" said one of them. Her voice boomed behind her visor. Niranthos nodded.

Shock and inevitability collided, leaving Tal momentarily dazed. Then the world slid back into alignment and he realised . . . *Yeah, of course, this seems like Niranthos.*

"So you're with them now," he said.

One of the Thousand Eyes was barking some sort of command at him. He ignored her.

Tsereg was still and silent in a way he had never seen them before. Their hair fell down over their eyes as they hung their head, and Tal could only see their lopsided mouth, set in a dull line.

"They were going to hurt me," said Niranthos. "I'm sorry. I—I only *have* one life, Tal, I wasn't going to die down there, I had to—"

"So you flipped the first chance you got, and now you're selling me out?" said Tal.

"Anyone would have done the same thing!" he said. "You don't know what she's *like*, the Hand, you don't know what she was going to do to me—"

"That'll do, Charossa," said one of the Thousand Eyes, putting a hand on Niranthos' shoulder. He flinched and shut his mouth.

"Do we take the child?" said one Eye. Another one grabbed hold of Tal, and this combination of circumstances activated whichever one of Tal's base instincts made him fight like a wet cat. He kicked and elbowed and writhed and bit until one of them punched him in the face, which quietened him down a bit.

He blinked, his head swimming. Tsereg was still shrieking and kicking. Good for them.

When he was younger, Tal had been able to forget that every fight might mean death. It had been fun, sort of, a focus which sharpened everything to a single edge, cutting away all the idiot nonsense that bothered him the rest of the time. At some point—and it was probably about the same point that Csorwe had become the God-Empress—he'd lost that ability.

Tal did his best, but he was outnumbered, and tired, and he didn't have any shoes. One of them got his knife out of his hands almost immediately. They didn't even have the decency to kill him. They wanted to take him alive.

"What happened to your whole fucking *motto*?" he said. "What happened to *the city looks to us for leadership*, Niranthos? You fucker!"

The Thousand Eyes got him on his knees. One of them dealt him a backhand blow that made his head spin. His ears rang as if he'd been shaken in an iron drum, but he heard his brother's voice with clarity.

"I'm sorry, Talasseres," said Niranthos, "but things change."

Tal sat on a bench in a cell. His head ached in a way that made him wish someone would tap his skull on the top and scoop out the innards like a hard-boiled egg.

They had been locked in for a few hours, and he still hadn't got used to the smell. It rose from the sodden floorboards like marsh gas: blood and rot, warm and organic. At least he wasn't retching anymore. Tsereg was curled up on the opposite bench, grey jacket doubled around them like armour.

All the time the only thought Tal had been able to form was how stupid he was. Trusting Niranthos had always been a mistake. The Charossai ate their own. He ought to have seen this coming. He had wanted someone else to fix his problem badly enough that he'd got himself arrested by the fucking Thousand Eyes.

The Hand of the Empress wanted them. It was only a matter of time before they were handed into her custody. That much was clear from what the guards had said among themselves.

Tal's chest tightened.

He had never quite known what to make of Shuthmili. He'd taken her for another haughty wizard type, the kind to look down her long nose at Tal and curl her lip. He'd assumed she and Csorwe would be unbearable together. To his surprise, she'd been almost shy with him and somehow made Csorwe softer to deal with. They'd been so easy together, it had looked almost more like friendship than love to him, at least based on his limited experience of either concept. So when he'd first heard Shuthmili was still alive, he had assumed she must have some kind of clever scheme to fix everything. And even after he started to hear stories about the Hand of the Empress and the things she had done, there was still the hope. While he had been concentrating on staying alive, maybe Shuthmili had been playing a double game, trying to stay close until she could get Csorwe out of there.

But Csorwe was gone, and the years had passed, and nothing had changed, and whatever he might have hoped, Shuthmili was one of them now. The Empress was a monster, and the Hand was perhaps a greater monster still.

You don't know what she's like, the Hand, you don't know what she was going to do to me.

Even back then, he had seen the darkness in her. *Worlds die all the time,* she had told him, long ago in the deepwood, as if it was nothing to her. She could have killed him then.

He and Tsereg hadn't talked much. He hoped they were thinking about something nice, not wondering about whatever was coming, whether it would be a knife in the dark or the public fountain in broad daylight.

"Don't be sad," they said, catching his eye. "You tried. And at least we'll die fighting, when they come for us. Why are they leaving us so long, anyway?"

"I think they were probably hoping this place would crush your spirit," he said, weakly. He couldn't find anything to say to the rest.

"Ha ha," said Tsereg. "Good luck. We've got two whole benches *and* a bucket to piss in, nobody can break me."

They gave him a sunny little smile, appallingly brave, impossibly defiant. Tal felt sick.

Somehow, he remembered the first time he'd killed someone. A couple of dummies had ambushed Sethennai's retinue in the early days back in Tlaanthothe, and Tal had broken one of their necks without even really thinking about it. Csorwe had dealt with the other one and returned to her post without speaking to him. He'd been nineteen, and he hadn't slept for a week. He had lain awake staring at the ceiling, swallowing down justifications.

You were brave, Sethennai had told him eventually, and that had somehow made it all right.

It was no good to be brave, he thought. He had to stumble his way toward the thought in darkness. It was no good to break yourself and smile through it. He wouldn't tell Tsereg they were brave.

Not that it mattered, if they were both about to die. Or maybe it did.

"God, I'm sorry," he said. "I'm sorry. I wish I'd kept you out of it."

Tsereg's smile shattered like a dropped glass. "Shut up," they said, as if it had hurt them. "No. Don't be sorry."

"What?"

"This is my fault, not yours," they said. "I made you come here. Now they're going to kill you, and it's my fault."

They shut their mouth and stared at him, huge eyes like lanterns in the dark, and to Tal's utter horror and self-disgust, he saw those eyes were shining with tears.

Tal blinked. Why should Tsereg care so much for him? They hardly knew each other, and Tsereg mostly seemed to hate him. He'd only helped them get into the Citadel; that wasn't the stuff of life debts, surely—

But that was how they got you, Tal realised. It could happen more or less by accident. If you were entirely alone and someone paid you any kind of attention at all. All too easy to imagine Sethennai equally startled by the extent of Tal's adoration.

"Oh, well," they said, burying their head in their arms, so their voice was even more muffled than usual. "You were right. This was a stupid idea."

"Tsereg, no—" he said.

He was interrupted by a shriek of metal as the guard drew back the bolts to the cell door, and the Hand of the Empress stepped inside.

Shuthmili was older, although not as much older as she ought to be. The heavy-lidded eyes, the long nose, and thin mouth were all exactly the same. There were deep shadows under her eyes. She looked as tired as Tal felt, the weariness of the endless days and endless years bearing down, individual grains of sand that ground the rock to nothing. Her long hair and the skirts of her robe seemed all of a piece. She looked like a skeleton wrapped up in a single dark cobweb.

"Leave us," she said to the Eye.

The black lace robe drifted after her like a retreating wave as she came toward them. Her gauntleted hands were folded before her, shiny black spines, more like claws than fingers. The gauntlets were no longer recognisable as Sethennai's.

Whatever Tsereg had said about their plan to die fighting, they were frozen where they sat, their eyes empty with terror.

Shuthmili ignored them, looking straight at Tal. Her features were impassive, no hint of recognition. Tal was almost glad for that. It was better that she didn't know him. How much worse to be killed by a friend.

"So. You were working with your brother," she said. Her voice was as cold and inexpressive as her face.

No, thought Tal, *fuck this, I'm not dying sitting down, if she remembers me she'd better fucking remember me.* He was only going to get one chance to stick the knife in and he'd better make it good.

He looked up at her, folding his arms.

"You really think this is what she'd want?" he said.

He didn't know what he expected. He certainly didn't expect Shuthmili to laugh. It was a dry little laugh, only slightly sinister, as if she couldn't turn that off altogether.

"I expect I deserve that," she said. "Listen to me, Tal. You need to do exactly what I tell you if you want to get out of this alive."

15

The Hand of the Empress

B ᴜᴛ," ꜱᴀɪᴅ Tᴀʟ. "But Niranthos said—"

"Mother of Cities, Tal," said Shuthmili. "Your idiot brother managed to get himself arrested. Making a deal with him was the only way to get him out alive."

"What?" said Tal.

"They would have tortured him to death," said Shuthmili. "I told him we'd let him live if he'd give us everything he knew about you."

"Yeah. He sold me out. I got that much," said Tal. He looked deeply wary, flat against the wall, as far from her as possible. There was a child pressed into a corner beside him. Shuthmili hadn't expected *that* complication.

"He actually held out far longer than I had expected," she said. "Cursing me and the Empress. Some quite imaginative blasphemies. I would have been impressed, but I could really only spin the farce out for so long before Cherenthisse got bored."

Niranthos had never looked more like his brother than he had when spitting in defiance. He'd broken eventually, much to Shuthmili's relief.

"He promised to sell you out, and we let him go home," said Shuthmili. She hadn't known Tal was still alive. The knowledge had felt like a cold knife between the ribs, but she was well used to ignoring that kind of wound by now.

"Why?" said Tal.

"I do my best to protect my clerks," said Shuthmili. "After all, it's so hard to find the staff these days."

Tal look dazed. Eventually he managed: "But you—the things you've done—"

"Do you have any particular things in mind?" said Shuthmili.

Tal cast about for an example. "What about the Lemon Tree?" he said. "The old guy who used to run the Lemon Tree, the one with the pamphlets. You were there when they took him. People saw you there. They drowned him in the fountain."

"Well, yes," she said. "What is there to say? The God-Empress does not have a high tolerance for dissent. We were ordered to arrest the ringleaders and kill everyone else inside."

Tal flinched.

"And yet when we got there, the place was almost empty and the propagandist's family had somehow vanished," she said.

"I don't understand," said Tal.

"Try," she said. What had Oranna once said? Tal needs ideas broken down into digestible fragments.

"Niranthos was a saboteur," she went on. "He fed the dissidents in Ringtown with information about the Thousand Eyes, their supply lines, their movements, their operations. You knew that, yes? He warned the proprietor of the Lemon Tree, and gave his family time to escape. All true?"

Tal crossed his arms and glared at her, which made him look much more like himself.

"Come *on*, Tal. Your brother is a diligent man, but would you call him a natural agitator? Do you think he did all this on his own? Where do you think he got his information?"

"You mean . . . from *you*?" he said.

She nodded. The relief of talking to somebody who knew her was too good, after so many years, but it was poison. She couldn't tell him too much.

"People still died at the Lemon Tree," said Tal.

"Yes. As I recall, four people were killed at the wineshop, and a further three were executed later. Seven in total. I do what I can to keep the butcher's bill in the single digits."

"Oh, *good*, that's all right, then," said Tal.

"I can't do as much as I'd like," she said. "I am already walking a fine line. First Commander Cherenthisse thinks of herself as the Empress' watchdog. She dislikes me, and she is paying my wretched secretary to spy on me. I cannot slip even once."

"Right," said Tal. "Right." He let out a long sigh. "Bloody hell, Shuthmili."

"Tal," piped up the child. "Do you know *everybody*?"

"This is Tsereg," said Tal, after a moment, clearly feeling some explanation was needed. "They're, er—"

"Your child?" Shuthmili tried.

"What? No!" said Tal, and "Gross!" said the child. Shuthmili didn't think it was such an unreasonable suggestion. The child's Oshaaru heritage was obvious, but their ears tapered to leaflike points, and their hair was almost as tightly curled as Tal's.

"They're travelling with me," Tal managed eventually.

"You're travelling with *me*," said Tsereg. "I can't believe you know Inquisitor Qanwa."

Shuthmili did wonder who'd come up with that, originally. The worst of it was that she really did look like her aunt Zhiyouri. Seeing the old family bones in the mirror was still jarring.

"Shuthmili's a friend," said Tal.

Shuthmili ignored this. No use encouraging them to count on her. "Now, listen to me. Later this afternoon there will be a containment failure in one of the sealed wings of the palace."

"You really think you can make that happen?" said Tal. He looked exhausted. He'd never been one to take things on trust, even before.

"I know I can," said Shuthmili.

Shuthmili had become the world expert at manipulating the Citadel's wards. She had spent weeks shaving away at the containment wards in the isolation wing, weakening them to the point that Vigil and Thurya Mishari could break through them. It had taken the Qarsazhi prisoners an embarrassingly long time to figure it out. Shuthmili couldn't have risked speaking to them directly. She didn't want the Inquisitorate knowing anything that would give them power over her.

"The guards will leave this corridor to deal with the breach," said Shuthmili. "The locks on your cell will open. And you two will leave the Citadel by the way you got in, and go as far and as fast as you can from this place."

"No, we won't," said Tsereg.

Shuthmili gave them a sharp look. It did not have the desired effect.

"We won't!" said Tsereg. "We've only just got here!"

"Tsereg . . ." said Tal, warningly.

"What? Why?" said Tsereg. "If she's your friend, she should help us!"

"I am helping you," said Shuthmili. "I can't make you run. But I suggest you take the chance to save yourselves, because you won't get another one. Every time a ward fails, Cherenthisse has another chance to ask herself why my work is so unreliable, and I can only misdirect Keleiros for so long. If you get caught again, I am not going to help you."

Tsereg gave her a hard look. "Why not? Doesn't sound like you *like* the snakes much."

"Fifteen years of painstaking work—" said Shuthmili, and bit her tongue. Explaining herself to Tal was one thing. Justifying her actions to a strange child was another.

"Yeah? On what?" Tsereg folded their arms. "You're as bad as Tal! Oh, years of sitting around in the snake mansion and only doing a little bit of torture, so hard for you! None of you want to take responsibility!"

"For *what*?" said Shuthmili, not liking the sound of this at all.

"Dealing with the God-Empress. Getting rid of her once and for all," said Tsereg.

"No," said Shuthmili flatly.

Tal winced, and Tsereg opened their mouth again. Shuthmili raised a hand, and they fell silent at once.

"I think it's best for all of us that I assume that was a joke," said Shuthmili. "You understand that if I thought you were being serious, I would have to act on it."

"I knew it!" said Tsereg. "You're on her side really."

"I suppose so," said Shuthmili. "I'd prefer that the two of you don't throw your lives away, but I will die before letting anybody harm the God-Empress."

"Tsereg, you don't—I'll explain later," said Tal. There was some murky disappointment in his eyes. As if he'd really hoped Tsereg might win her over. "Do you really think—" he said, and cut himself off.

Tal Charossa exercising tact was one of life's true rarities, but Shuthmili was in no mood to enjoy it.

"That it's what Csorwe would want?" she said. "No. Of course not. Csorwe saved me once from a life in service to tyranny. But she is no longer with us, and I am selfish." She brushed a strand of hair back behind her ear, steadying herself. "And one thing I'm pretty certain she would not want is for you to be executed. When the door opens, you two need to do as I tell you and run."

"I was going to say, do you really think you can help her?" said Tal.

"Nothing has worked yet," she said. "But I haven't tried everything. If there's even a chance—do you really mean to tell me you'd ever stop trying?"

Back in her quarters, Shuthmili rinsed her face in freezing water and gave herself a reproachful look in the mirror. Her goddess looked back at her with her own eyes.

A FRUITLESS ENCOUNTER, said Zinandour.

Oh, there you are, said Shuthmili. *I was beginning to think you had left me in peace.*

RESPECTLESS INSECT, said Zinandour, not without fondness.

What was fruitless about it?

YOU SWIM IN FUTILITY AS A LEECH IN MUD. WORSE THAN FUTILE TO SAC-RIFICE OUR SECRETS TO A NONENTITY. IN YOUR SENTIMENT YOU HAND HIM A WEAPON TO DESTROY YOU. SUCH WISHFUL TRUST.

Tal won't sell me out, said Shuthmili, with more certainty than she felt.

Shuthmili felt Zinandour's presence as a physical weight, cold heavy coils nestled like a basket of eels in the base of her brain and at the back of her throat. When the goddess was thinking, she could feel them shifting.

YOU HAVE CHANGED. WHY SHOULD NOT HE?

I saved his life, said Shuthmili.

ANOTHER PIECE OF FUTILITY. MERCY COSTS.

Mercy pays, said Shuthmili.

IT DOES NOT. THEIR GRATITUDE IS THE VERY WORST OF YOUR SOFTHEART-EDNESS.

I don't know why you're upset. It's not as though I told Tal about you.

Zinandour hissed in grudging approval. There was nothing which Zinandour, goddess of hidden things and things decaying, enjoyed as much as a terrible secret, and what more terrible secret than the promises they had made to one another?

Shuthmili sent for Keleiros Lenarai and ate a hasty dinner, tearing apart an entire loaf of bread and shoving it into her mouth in handfuls. She was hungrier than ever these days. The Devouring Fire was no joke. By the time Keleiros arrived, there was nothing left but crumbs.

Shuthmili tolerated Keleiros for a variety of reasons. Partly because it was always good to be able to feed Cherenthisse false information in a way she wouldn't question. Partly because if she acknowledged he was a spy, she would have to kill him, and that would be a frustrating waste. Mostly because he was good at his job and not very scared of her. Her secretaries were always convinced that the Hand of the Empress was going to eat their hearts to slake her dark lusts. Sometimes they thought there might be something to gain by making themselves available for prompt slaking. Keleiros had figured out early on that her real dark lust was to be left alone.

"I need you to accompany me on a brief expedition out of the Citadel this evening," she said.

"Certainly, ma'am," said Keleiros. "Shall I request a pilot?"

"No," said Shuthmili. "This is a private matter for the Empress. I prefer to keep it to my own staff. I'll fly the cutter myself."

That was calculated to pique his interest, and she saw his eyes brighten. He would be glad of something good to tell Cherenthisse. Shuthmili hadn't given him anything substantial for a while.

She sent Keleiros to prepare for departure, and while he was gone, she opened the warded panel at the back of her wardrobe.

Inside were the fruits of the last fifteen years. All together, they looked pitifully meagre. She removed a small collection of private books and papers.

At the back of the niche was a jewellery box containing a thin bronze diadem. Shuthmili had salvaged it from a three-thousand-year-old shipwreck. Retrieving it without Cherenthisse's knowledge had been one of her earliest struggles. Its surface was now a patchwork of old Echentyri magic and sigils of Shuthmili's own invention.

Beside it was a lead-lined casket, which had itself taken Shuthmili and Zinandour years to prepare: it was heartwood from the true deeps, inlaid with gold and bone and pearls, sealed with wax and cord. Shuthmili would not risk opening that casket until the moment of need.

She took the casket and the jewellery box. Behind them, in a small leather pouch, was an even greater treasure. Shuthmili left that where it was.

STILL TRYING FOR YOUR FOOL'S ERRAND IN THE AERIAL VAULT, THEN?

Surely you don't expect me to become less of a fool at this point, said Shuthmili. Their plan to access the Empress' aerial vault had been over a decade in the making, and she knew Zinandour's mockery was a facade.

IT DOES SEEM TOO LATE TO HOPE.

Vigil told me what I wanted to know. Folding space is a Quincuriate specialism.

IT IS A PERVERSION OF MY GIFTS.

It's what we need to get into the vault. You know how this works, Zinandour. You cooperate with me, and eventually we both get what we want.

AID AND OBEDIENCE ARE NOT IN MY NATURE. DIVINITIES DO NOT "COOPERATE."

So I've learned, my Corruptor. The God-Empress has forbidden us to enter the vault. I would have thought that alone would have you scratching at the door to get in.

TRUE. SHE CONCEALS BY NATURE. SHE IS REPLETE WITH SECRETS, said

Zinandour, with the air of one resisting the temptation of a small sweet-meat.

When Csorwe lives again, you will have full control of this vessel, said Shuth-mili. *You will have your true incarnation, and all the secrets of this accursed palace will be yours for the taking.*

I WILL REND THIS CITADEL TO DUST. I WILL FLAY THE CITIZENS TO RAGS. WHEN ALL THIS WORLD IS A WASTELAND, I WILL CAST DOWN FAITHLESS QAR-SAZH AND EAT THE MARROW FROM ITS BONES. I WILL MAKE ALL THE WORLDS MY DOMINION, AND ALL SHALL FEAR ME ALONE.

Of course. That was our deal, my lady.

Tal sat in the cell feeling as though the universe had slapped him in the face.

"I know what you're going to say," said Tsereg at last. Their eyes glowed like hot coals in the darkness of the cell. "You're going to say, *Tsereg, we really should do what she says—*"

"No," said Tal. He rose to his feet. The shock had passed, and now some unexpected fury bubbled up in him. "*Csorwe wouldn't want you to be executed*—screw you, of course she would, she'd love it, how do you know?"

Tsereg raised one beetly eyebrow at him.

He loped the six feet to the other side of the cell and back again. Restlessness crackled in all his limbs. "Think you can tell me what to do. Can't fucking tell me Csorwe would run away. Fuck you," he muttered.

He went on pacing, waiting for the rage to die down so he could come to his senses and do the smart thing. The smart thing would be to run for his life, whether Tsereg agreed to go with him or not. The smart thing would be to let go of this stage of his life like a lizard dropping its tail to get out of a trap, to find work in some dreary desert town and go on the way he always had, bored and alone and alive. He might live a long time like that. He might get to be properly old, and the Thousand Eyes might forget about him, and one day he'd die quietly of pneumonia and that would be the end of that, and the world would go on just the same, with the God-Empress piloting Csorwe's shell around and Shuthmili crawling after her like the universe's saddest spider.

"Shit," he said, coming to a stop.

"What?" said Tsereg.

"Let's do it," he said. "Let's assassinate the bloody God-Empress."

Tsereg gave a sigh of mock relief. He didn't miss the flicker of real relief, though, or the way they bobbed up and down in their seat like a small grey balloon trying to free itself.

Just as Shuthmili had promised, a few hours later, there came the sound of a distant alarm, and the bolts of the cell slid back of their own accord. The door swung open, revealing a dark and silent corridor. Tsereg and Tal exchanged a silent glance.

"Really hope you weren't making it up about this stupid book. Or about having a plan," he said.

They flashed him a row of pointy little teeth. "I always have a plan," they said. "Just, sometimes I make it up as I go along."

16

Form Shapes Function

THE AERIAL VAULT was a needle-shaped obelisk that hung in the middle atmosphere above the Citadel. Like all the Empress' buildings, it was made from petrified wood and vitrified sand, black fossil and black glass, layered together in coils. Up close, its masonry looked less like worked stone and more like the shell of some unimaginable creature. The rough grain of petrified wood, laid alongside the gleaming smoothness of volcanic glass. The two together seemed to make figures: serpents, lichen, waves, maps.

Shuthmili landed the cutter on the ledge at the base of the vault, and she and Keleiros disembarked. The ledge ran all the way round the base of the vault, but each face of the vault was a blank expanse of fossil-stone. As Shuthmili had anticipated, there was nothing resembling a door.

This was nothing new. In the Lignite Citadel were many rooms without doors: cisterns of dark water large enough for the drowning of thousands, still and silent hothouses, colossal statues in darkness. This was why she had taken the risk of speaking with Vigil, back in the interrogation chamber. She needed their knowledge. She would have to fold space to get inside.

She pressed her hands against the wall. She sent a brief, weak pulse of energy into the stone, listening for its echo, searching for the next door. There were hollow vaults above and many stairwells syringing up into them.

The stone was thickly warded. There were weapons inside the walls, half alive and sleeping. Luckily, the careful breaking of mechanisms was a specialty for Zinandour. Shuthmili rested a hand on the smooth surface of the door and began to feel her way through them.

Once the weapons were disarmed, it was time to open the door. She had not had much liberty to practice the discipline of folding, so it took a few attempts, but at last it did work.

There was—not a sound, but a feeling, as if a key had turned in the lock of the world. The tower opened. There was no slithering of stone on stone, no creaking of ancient hinges. It was like the opening of a flower, the beating of a bird's wing, either too slow or too fast to witness with mortal eyes. There was a way in where none had been before.

If Keleiros was surprised by any of this, he didn't show it. He had lived most of his life in the Citadel, after all, and knew its ways. At twenty-three, he might remember the years before the God-Empress' accession, but Shuthmili wouldn't have bet he thought about them often. He was a creature of the times. He didn't question what she was doing here, either, in what was clearly a forbidden area: probably storing it up to report back to Cherenthisse.

A passage opened into a high-vaulted hall, lined with dozens of doors. The black stone was ribboned with moon-coloured wardlights, which gave the room a faint warmth and an uneasy, quivering illumination. Keleiros followed her inside, his bright eyes darting here and there. He was smart enough to know that Cherenthisse would pay well for this information, and not smart enough to wonder why Shuthmili was letting him see it all.

Certainly not smart enough to keep Shuthmili within view. She pretended to move from door to door, drifting out of his sphere of vision. The spell she had prepared required only the faintest touch at the base of his skull. He dropped as though his strings had been cut.

She checked his vitals—healthy, but sound asleep; good, that spell could take people the wrong way—and carefully moved him to a corner.

NEXT TIME I WILL KILL FOR YOU, said Zinandour. YOUR HESITANCE TIRES ME.

I don't want him dead, my lady.

YOU KNOW AS I DO THE PUNISHMENT OF A TURNCOAT.

I still have use for him, said Shuthmili, although she wouldn't need him, if she needed him—she wasn't going to think about that just yet—until later.

The door she wanted was on the far side of the room. It had no keyhole or handle. It would open in the presence of one only. Shuthmili set the lead-lined casket on the ground before the door and, with the care of one removing a crucible of molten metal from the furnace, severed the wards and seals holding it closed.

The wood of the casket smouldered and began to char, and fell away to ash. Within, in a scorched shell of lead, was a pale little crescent of green stone, as small and sharp as a clipped fingernail. It was an inert shard of the throne of Iriskavaal, perhaps one of the last remaining. For thousands of years, it had slept in a ruined watchtower in some forgotten world, over-looked even by Belthandros and Atharaisse.

The door slid open, revealing a narrow stairway rising into darkness.

Shuthmili secured the fragment in a circle of black ash from the casket and went on up the stairs, leaving Keleiros safe in his corner.

Beyond the door were an exhausting number of floors, stairs, and corridors. The aerial vault held every artefact of power that the Thousand Eyes had looted in the past fifteen years. A younger Shuthmili would have been wild to catalogue everything here. Today she had only one thing in mind.

She had spent a whole year gaining access to the Empress' secret libraries, and months afterward scrutinising the maps and blueprints she had stolen. She had run through this expedition in her head a hundred times: up four floors, then turn left, then take the third right, then on up, and up, until you reached the final door.

As it came into view—a plain iron door, unornamented, one among many others—Shuthmili had to stop. Her breath seized in her throat, and she leant back against the wall.

After working so long and sacrificing so much, she hadn't let herself believe it would really happen. She had failed so many times. Fifteen years of schemes, most of which had died in their cradles, and this was her last resort. If there had been any other hope, she would not have come to this.

There was still so far to go. So much to do. No guarantee of success. She had done things that had made her glad Csorwe was not there to see what she was becoming.

She saw Csorwe's face almost every day, and she thought it was still the same: the sharp cheekbones, the angular nose, the eyebrows like two dark brushstrokes, the soft mouth slightly roughened by the elements. In daylight the eyes were the colour of clear topaz. The scar that curved from brow to lip had been smoothed out by the years, but Shuthmili ought to know its line. She had traced it often enough with her fingertip. And yet, if something was different, would she really know it? Time took so much from her, always. All she could do was stand and endure as the only person she had truly loved was made alien to her.

ALWAYS DWELLING UPON PAST REGRETS, said Zinandour. If it were possible for an ancient goddess of fire and dissolution to sound like a mother hen, she would have done. *I WAS TORN DOWN AND CAST INTO THE VOID BY*

THE HERETICS OF QARSAZH. I DO NOT DWELL IN REGRET BUT NOURISH MY VENGEANCE. YOU MUST DO THE SAME. TAKE YOUR MOMENT OF VICTORY. THEY ARE FEW ENOUGH.

Apologies, my grim Corruptor, you know it is a terrible struggle for me having to operate this primate, said Shuthmili, grateful for the chance to squabble with the goddess as a distraction.

Zinandour laughed, a rattlesnake noise.

Very well, said Shuthmili, and returned to the iron door. If she was right, this door would open on the vault itself.

The last fifteen years had been, if nothing else, a lesson in her own fallibility. She was wrong. She stepped through the final gate and fell straight into the void.

The void beyond all worlds is a place of neither form nor substance. No light survives there, nothing lives, and it knows no limit in time or space. Its only properties are vastness, darkness, and terror.

Vastness, darkness, and terror surged around Shuthmili as she fell. Worse than the dark was Zinandour's panic, breaking and crashing within her.

Zinandour screamed, and all Shuthmili understood of the screaming was DEATH BEFORE THE VOID! I WILL END THIS WORLD IN FIRE BEFORE I RE-TURN! IT WILL NOT TAKE ME AGAIN!

Shuthmili could keep herself breathing by magic for a while, but eventually she would suffocate faster than she could fix herself. She was one of the most powerful mages who had ever lived, she was the living vessel of a goddess, but she needed air or she was going to die.

Shuthmili had never been very good at despair. Despair was another kind of acceptance, and she had burnt through her whole stock of acceptance early in life. She could not die. Nobody else knew or cared what had become of Csorwe. She was the only one who could help her.

She gathered herself as best she could. This couldn't just be a trap, it had to be another security measure. Zinandour had been imprisoned in the void for good reason: it made an excellent prison. But a prison needed a door.

Yes, there was a light—some kind of structure—not far. Another door, with faint light shining through it.

She kicked out at the dark and managed to flail her way to the doorway, and collapsed on the threshold, gasping for fresh air.

Buried in her brain stem, Zinandour howled like an animal in a trap. For the past fifteen years, Shuthmili's dreams had been haunted by an emptiness, a dark and cold without surcease. Shuthmili felt the pressure of the memory, swelling like a blood clot. Shuthmili knew isolation—she had fed on it and nursed it all these years alone in the Citadel—and she knew how it ate away your sanity like waves lapping at a sandcastle. Those thousands of years of loneliness were torture to a divinity, annihilation to a mortal mind.

IT WILL NEVER LEAVE ME. IT IS HERE ALWAYS. AT YOUR FINGERTIPS. WITHIN YOU FOREVER.

I know, said Shuthmili. *I was there with you, was I not? You were my goddess in imprisonment. We called to one another. You are still here with me now. We are both alone, but one of these days we will both be free.*

At least calming Zinandour down left her no room to panic on her own terms. She did her best to be stern.

Next time let us not forget that you need my body alive. Recall that I need to breathe.

Her limbs were numb and aching. Her clothes felt as if they were woven from lead. Inside the gauntlets her fingers were stiff, the shooting pains in the joints ever more difficult to ignore.

Maybe we're just getting old, she said to herself. She was forty years old. She had never imagined she would live this long.

INFANT, said Zinandour, sounding more like herself at last. LARVA. HATCHLING. YOU LIVE THIS LONG AT MY SUFFERANCE AND FOR NO OTHER REASON.

Shuthmili smiled with weak relief and hauled herself to her feet.

She had emerged onto a flat-topped turret, open to the elements. Above them, a cupola was supported by eight narrow pillars, and apart from these there was nothing to stop anyone falling over the sheer edge.

An expanse of night-blue sky spread from horizon to horizon. It was piercingly cold, and the air was thin here. There was no land below, only clouds that billowed like clean washing.

She reached for the comfort of Zinandour's presence and found her very distant. The gods loved the earth, the great, cold mineral mass of the seas, the yolk of hidden fire. In the high air their powers began to fail.

When you considered who was imprisoned in the vault, it made sense that the God-Empress had put him up here.

Under the highest point of the cupola was a table of white stone, shaped like a sarcophagus, but Shuthmili knew without checking that there would be no body inside it.

Surrounding the table were nine concentric grooves in the stone, warded with brine, myrrh, and bone, and puddled on its surface was a dark shape. As she approached, it coalesced upward into an arch, its hooked tail wavering over its head like that of a scorpion.

It was a dead cat. Unkindly dead, and mummified as if in hot sand, without care. Its dry skin was hairless, clinging stickily to its ribs, drawn back from its mouth to reveal a jagged row of little black teeth.

It stretched each limb languorously before bothering to notice her.

Ah, it said. *Company. How wonderful. Why don't you come closer so I can talk to you?* said the cat. Its ears had withered into perfunctory little flaps, flat against the back of its skull. The notches in its spine moved like gear teeth.

Well, well. You, again?

"Hello, Belthandros," said Shuthmili.

The desiccated cat gave an eyeless impression of staring.

I suppose you're here to ask me for something, he said.

It had been hard to believe that the creature was really Belthandros Sethennai until it spoke. The voice was exactly as Shuthmili remembered it. His tail swished like a dry reed.

So these days you're—remind me?—that's right. The Hand of the Empress.

"Correct," said Shuthmili. "What do they call you these days? The Pretender?"

So I hear. Although really, if anything, the God-Empress is the Pretender to the Throne.

"And now you're a cat," said Shuthmili.

I'm sure the God-Empress thought it was a funny joke to imprison me in this vessel. How long has it been? Ten years?

"Fifteen," said Shuthmili.

The cat stopped pacing and perched on the edge of the sarcophagus, and Shuthmili realised she didn't quite know what to say. She didn't trust any iteration of the snake goddess; she'd hated Belthandros on first sight, and he'd never done anything to improve her opinion.

You're not Shuthmili at all, are you? he said. *Or if you are, there is something very strange about you. What are you?*

Shuthmili shrugged. "You told me the gauntlets were created to prepare you for incarnation. It turns out they still work."

Ah, the Devouring Fire, said Belthandros, with the kind of knowing drawl that meant this was in fact a surprise to him. *Yes, I see it now, your incarnation is true, if strange. Welcome to the club. Oranna will be unhappy you got there first.*

"Oranna is dead," said Shuthmili.

A pause, akin to an intake of breath. *My mistake. Of course.*

Did he sound thrown? Shuthmili didn't read into it. Csorwe had wasted an extraordinary amount of time and energy trying to invent a softer side to Belthandros Sethennai. Even years after leaving him behind, she would occasionally turn to Shuthmili with a frown and say something like *but what if he really did like her?* Privately, Shuthmili had wished she would stop torturing herself with it. Tal was even worse. When they got together they had been like two dogs chewing over the same old bone.

It is a pity what happened to Csorwe, he said, so now it was Shuthmili's turn to steady herself, although the absolute calculation of the manoeuvre blunted its effect a little. *Curious that you're still prepared to serve the so-called God-Empress. Given that she stole your lover's body, I am startled to find you so loyal.*

"Do you find me loyal?" said Shuthmili.

As a matter of fact, I do not, he said. *I don't think you'd be here if you were, since the God-Empress has taken pains to shut you out. What is it that you want?*

"Why don't you take three guesses," said Shuthmili.

If you were Zinandour alone, I would say you wanted to rule in place of the God-Empress. That has ever been her motive, since the days of High Qarsazh. She is a byword for usurpation, so reliably unreliable as a second-in-command that I become almost nostalgic for Olthaaros Charossa. He paused midturn, tail held high like a feather. *But I know better than most that a true incarnation is not as simple as that. Form shapes function. You are not solely the Dragon of Qarsazh but also a renegade Qarsazhi Adept, an archaeologist, and a murderer of aunts.*

"I have murdered so many more since then. And I think I've changed my mind: you can have one guess."

I am, as they say, just kidding, he said. *You're much more transparent than you think. It's perfectly obvious that you're here because you think I can help Csorwe.*

It was almost a relief to hear it. The years had made their slow progress and dragged Shuthmili after them, and with every ditch and furrow, she worried that she'd lost her purpose, as if it hung on a chain that could break. Maybe, she thought, it was just the excuse she clung to, justifying her continued existence. Maybe it was what she had to tell herself, to endure bowing to the God-Empress. A daydream of rebellion.

"Yes," she said. "Of course."

Touching fidelity, he said. *But I don't know that it can be done. For all intents and purposes, Csorwe is dead, and the God-Empress haunts her corpse.*

"Perhaps you're right," said Shuthmili. "That said . . . consider that, between you and me, one of us is the greatest magician of the age."

The cat paused and looked up at her. She felt the click of satisfaction at having guessed right: however old and however brilliant, some people responded to challenge like sunflowers turning toward the light.

Bold claim, he said.

She smiled. "If it can be done, we can do it. If it can't be done, I will die killing the Empress and leave a clear path for you to reclaim your throne."

You think you can kill her? Interesting.

"You know so much. Do you know about the Empress' great work?"

The cat put its head on one side.

"She means to undo the withering of Echentyr. To bring back the world that was."

Hah! said Belthandros. *Necromancy on a grand scale?*

"No," said Shuthmili. "Not necromancy. Real new life. Regenerating the Echentyri homeworld, making it habitable again, bringing back its people. She has promised the Thousand Eyes a return to their true aspects."

The dead cat's tail flicked thoughtfully back and forth. If Belthandros was startled, he didn't show it. *Ambitious,* he murmured. *But it might be done—it might perhaps be done—I wonder . . .*

"I've been assisting her with some of her experiments," said Shuthmili. She did not go into detail: months in the Citadel's laboratories, up to her elbows in formaldehyde as the God-Empress attempted to restore life to her specimens. The results had been more or less grotesque, but the Empress' mastery of her craft was undeniable. "I think it could be done, if you had the right source of power."

Perhaps, said Belthandros, doubtfully.

"She's a long way from pulling it off," said Shuthmili. "But the nearest source of power she has is the population of Tlaanthothe, as was."

The dead cat fixed its eyeless sockets on her. *Do you think so?*

"She'll do it if she can. She will drain this whole world if she thinks she can get back what was lost."

Belthandros averted his eyes discreetly.

"Yes, thank you, I know, I'm in no position to judge her," said Shuthmili. "But I need your help, and I think our interests are aligned. You want her out of your city, and I want Csorwe back."

Well, then. I suppose we have a deal.

Shuthmili responded by neatly breaking the three wards around the sarcophagus. The cat Belthandros hopped down from the sarcophagus and, without hesitation, crossed the broken circles. He moved almost as quietly as a real cat, but his claws clicked on the stone like dice.

Pleasant to stretch my legs, he said. *You know about the void-trap?*

Shuthmili nodded, unwilling to admit it had taken her by surprise the first time. She told the door firmly to send them back to the stairs of the isolation vault, and it obeyed.

Belthandros followed her down the stairs, almost invisible in the half dark.

You found him, then, said Zinandour, deeply suspicious, when she resurfaced and caught sight of him. *A foolhardy plan, as I have told you. One head of the snake is no better than the other.*

No going back now, my lady, said Shuthmili. If there had been any other way—if any of her other ideas had worked at all—she would have left Belthandros to rot. But it was done now, and she would just have to make sure she saw the inevitable double-cross coming.

They were almost at the bottom of the stairs, descending into the eerie gleam of the central hall, when he spoke again.

You must have thought about how you're getting me out of here, he said. *I cannot leave in this vessel, and with respect, I don't much like the idea of playing house with you and Zinandour.*

The ward keeping Belthandros' cat-vessel inside the prison was beyond Shuthmili's ability to unpick without being detected. So she needed to give him a new vessel. She had seen this coming. After all, Belthandros' original body was still in its jar in the throne room, even as his essence was trapped inside the cat.

She held out the jewellery box containing the diadem. It was green with verdigris, pitted and mottled by the years, gleaming with the gold tracery of magic.

Impressive work, he said.

Shuthmili squashed the fleeting sense of gratification at having her work admired. Belthandros was altogether too good at that.

"It's based on the Mantle," said Shuthmili. "And the gauntlets, actually. Can you use it?"

I imagine so, said Belthandros. *Do you have a vessel in mind? Oh. I see. Yes, that will do.*

Keleiros lay where she had left him, his delicate features picked out in the light from the door.

"Can you do it without killing him?" said Shuthmili.

If he doesn't fight me, said Belthandros.

There was always a moment, in Shuthmili's experience, where you stood on the brink of a sudden drop and some internal voice said, *Is this really going to happen? Is this what I'm capable of doing?*

With real effort, she reached for the old memories, trying to remember exactly how Csorwe had looked on the day they'd run from Qarsazh—tired and resolute and young, just impossibly young, the hair blowing into her eyes as they stood on the deck of the ship that carried them away.

Every time she returned to this memory, she tarnished it a little more. Every time she used it to steel herself against what she was going to do, it became a little more hollow. She'd become a carrion bird, picking over her old life for whatever might nourish her another day.

As the years passed, the teetering moment of doubt got shorter and shorter, and the answer was always *yes.*

Shuthmili lifted Keleiros Lenarai in her arms with an awful tenderness and placed the diadem on his head.

Again the lurch of recollection—Csorwe's face, Csorwe's eyes bright with Iriskavaal's malice. Again the mocking voice which started up in the back of her head: *After all this time, aren't you over it? Trying so hard to convince yourself that you still feel what you've forgotten? You are a broken thing, and she would despise what you've become.*

HUSH, said Zinandour, and Shuthmili had a feeling as if someone was stroking her hair, although nobody had touched her for a very long time.

She laid Keleiros down again and rose, pacing, trying to calm herself, counting out the seconds. The claws of the cat clicked on the tiles.

When she could bring herself to look again, Keleiros Lenarai was sitting up, idly scratching behind the ear of the undead cat, which nuzzled against him as if it appreciated the thought. The diadem suited him. He looked like a prince.

"Well," said Belthandros, looking up at her through Keleiros' eyes. "It'll be good to get out of here."

Shuthmili had to fight the palace all the way to get back to the Turret of the Hand. The Empress must be fretful tonight.

Belthandros took Keleiros' body back to his usual quarters for the night. This was for the best—it wouldn't do for anyone to notice that the Hand's secretary was acting differently—but it still left Shuthmili with the unease of one who has seen a large spider disappear under a bookcase.

On her desk was a half-finished report and an abandoned cup of coffee. Shuthmili didn't have the energy to heat it, even by magic, so she drank the whole lot cold. It hardly affected her, since Zinandour purged poisons from her system with obsessive vigour, but sometimes it was nice to pretend.

It had been strange to discover that the worst could happen, and the world as you knew it could end, and you would still take your coffee the same way. You still had to eat. You still got dressed. You still brushed and braided your hair. And if you were very lucky or very unlucky—Shuthmili was certainly one of those two things—you still had a job.

She also had a tin of biscuits in her desk for emergencies. She sat mechanically eating one after another until her hunger was beaten into submission. She could send to the kitchens for a proper dinner, but the idea of thinking of something she'd like to eat and describing it to someone else was just too much.

The problem with committing to something when you were young was that you had no idea how long time was capable of taking. When she was twenty-five, the years had felt like an infinite resource, and she'd had so little idea what would be involved in selling herself in service for all of eternity that it had felt essentially meaningless. The fifteen years that had passed felt like stones on which she had blunted herself.

AGREED. I AM AGELESS AND IMMUTABLE, AND YET THESE YEARS HAVE BEEN THE LONGEST OF MY EXISTENCE.

You're unhappy? said Shuthmili.

JOY AND GRIEF DIMINISH BEFORE ME. I AM GLORY AND CARNAGE. YOU ARE UNHAPPY.

Shuthmili ignored her and got on with the report, until her wrist ached and her eyes blurred with tiredness. She yawned, and tried to spike her own adrenal glands, and felt Zinandour's opposition as a fog of stubbornness.

YOU HAVE NOT SLEPT FOR THREE DAYS.

Well, if I don't sleep for another three, that'll be a new record for me.

IN ANCIENT QARSAZH I DRANK HONEY FROM THE SKULLS OF QUEENS. DO YOU THINK IT AMUSES ME TO PLAY HANDMAIDEN TO YOUR BLIGHTED CAR-CASS?

I didn't ask you to, said Shuthmili.

BELTHANDROS IS A DANGEROUS ALLY. WILL YOU MEET HIM HALF SHARP? HE WILL NOT PITY YOUR INCAPACITY.

Shuthmili had to admit this was true. She took herself to bed, an absurdly huge four-poster draped in brocade.

Csorwe's coat was still hidden folded under one of the pillows. She brushed aside Zinandour's pitying disdain and reached for it, at first just to touch the sleeve. It was lamb's leather, warm grey like a pigeon's wing, patched at the elbows, with deep pockets inside and out. Csorwe had owned the coat longer than she'd known Shuthmili, and it was one of only two things Shuthmili had managed to retrieve from her body.

Shut up. It's cold.

AGAIN YOU ATTEMPT TO JUSTIFY YOURSELF TO ME. NEEDLESS, FRUITLESS.

The lining of the coat had once had some kind of print, and was now faded to a dull, soft dust colour. The collar no longer smelled like her hair. Shuthmili lay in bed with her knees drawn up to her chest and the coat pressed to her cheek and felt the old impulse to scream, lodged in her throat like a fishbone.

Instead, she returned to the safe at the back of her wardrobe and reached for the last of her treasures.

It was a small drawstring bag of kid leather, bound with a cord braided from Shuthmili's own hair and laced with the worst curses she knew.

She loosed the cord and tipped the bag out into her palm. It contained a single object, slightly hooked, smaller than her little finger, white and gold.

One of the God-Empress' first acts upon getting control of Csorwe's stolen body had been to wrench the gold tusk from her own jaw. Shuthmili, ever a scavenger, even then, scrabbling indiscriminately for scraps, had gathered it up and cleaned off the blood and hidden it away.

The tusk was both oddly heavy and oddly light, for what it was. Shuth-mili raised it to her lips and kissed it.

"I am going to win this," she said. "I promise you."

III

Two-Headed Snake

O, serpent! said Najalwe. How grand you are! How bright your eyes! How sharp your teeth!

The Empress was flattered. Perhaps we will not eat thee, she said.

The servant girl smiled and curtsied and said that she would be honoured to be eaten, or not, as the Empress pleased. That was politeness in those days.

from the Oshaarun folktale "The Empress' Tooth"

17

The Glass Archive

THERE WERE NO windows anywhere in the belly of the Citadel, just endless dark rooms and halls and staircases, spiralling down like screwthreads driven into the ground. Tal and Tsereg crept from one dark cellar to another, all the time without meeting another living soul. Tal had the seasick feeling he always got from divine spaces. Sometimes you would emerge from a passage and find yourself walking across the ceiling of a chamber you had already crossed. Tsereg was dead certain that this time they knew how to find the library where the books stolen from the House of Silence would be kept. Tal had slept badly on a damp stone floor and was still feeling nauseous, so he agreed just for the sake of something different to do.

Tsereg led him to a corridor where the fossil-stone masonry of the palace gave way abruptly to a wall of smooth greenish glass. In the eerie illumination of overhead wardlights, tiny flecks and bubbles were visible in the solid glass, as if a whole volume of seawater had been vitrified. Tsereg paced up and down the glass wall, occasionally tapping it.

"There's supposed to be a way in," they said. "The House of Silence archive is in there. My mother said so."

"I thought your mother was dead," said Tal.

Tsereg shrugged. "I'm a prophet of the Unspoken. The dead speak to me."

Tal laughed. "What, so belonging to your spooky skeleton club means you can talk to ghosts?"

"Not like that," said Tsereg. "I take the lotus, I enter a trance—"

Tal had tried the black lotus once or twice when he was young and only remembered waking up with a blinding headache.

"That stuff stunts your growth, you know," he said, doing his best to mask his discomfort. The smell of lotus always reminded him of dark places underground, of blood and ice and sacrifice—in other words, of all his previous encounters with Tsereg's spooky skeleton club. "No wonder you're so short. Anyway, where would your mother be getting all of this? If she died when you were little, how the hell would she know where they're keeping some book?"

"*That which is dead, that which is dust, that which lives in the present moment, and that which is yet to come,*" said Tsereg, their scrawny face becoming very solemn. "The Unspoken has dominion over all knowledge."

"Well, when we get out of this, you'll do really well as a professional gambler," said Tal, and regretted saying it because it only reminded him that Tsereg didn't plan to get out alive.

"Mm," said Tsereg, staring into the glass so intently that their nose bumped the surface. "All right, I see how to do this." They took a step back and rolled their shoulders as though limbering up to lift something heavy. "Tal, get behind me and cover your eyes."

Tal by now knew better than to argue, not because their ideas were good but because they wouldn't pay any attention if he objected. He ducked out of the way and covered his face with his arms.

There was a single quiet *plink,* exactly like someone tapping a fingernail against a glass window. Then, a flash of searing light and a noise like a window breaking, if the moment of shattering could be prolonged into a screech of whole seconds. It made Tal feel as if his skin was shrinking in on itself.

The light died slowly, but when Tsereg said, "You can look now," it was still bright enough to make Tal's eyes ache. The entire glass wall was a brilliant orange, as though a segment had been sliced from the setting sun, and he could feel dry heat pouring off it.

Sunk into the middle of the wall was a passage, rimmed in a brighter white glow. Tal could never resist sticking his finger into a puddle of molten candle wax, and this was exactly what it looked like.

"You're a *mage?*" he said.

"Sure," said Tsereg. "Why do you think they put me in jail?"

"I thought it was probably because you're a pain in the arse," said Tal. He looked back at the glowing wall, which looked like a really fun new way to die.

"It'll cool off in a minute," said Tsereg, although they were eyeing the wall in a way that suggested it wasn't cooling quite as fast as they'd hoped.

"I can't believe you're a mage," he said. He knew how long Shuthmili had trained to keep her powers under control, and that had barely worked. Tsereg's training had probably been delivered by a bunch of old ladies in jail or, given recent revelations, by a drug-fuelled hallucination of their mother's ghost. Not exactly encouraging.

Tsereg wheeled round to glare at him. "Oh, sorry, forgot you weren't a fan, let me just turn it off for you," they said.

Tal rolled his eyes. "Do you mean you could have got us out of that cell the whole time?"

"No, they had some kind of weird dampener in there. Takes a *long* time to wear those down." They trailed off again, then reached out to tap the lip of the passage in the glass. The orange glow had faded by now, restoring the glass to its original colour, a green so deep it was near black. Tsereg stepped up onto the lip of the passage and their shoes didn't catch fire, at least.

"Come on, Tal," they said, taking a few steps down into the passageway. "It's fine. It's not even hot anymore."

The passage descended rapidly, and it was hard going to keep your balance on the glass, especially given that Tal had to stoop to fit.

"I've been thinking," said Tsereg. Tal recognised this from long experience as a phrase that didn't mean anything good. "About your friend."

"What, Shuthmili? She was pretty clear that she's *not*—"

"No, the other one. Csorwe."

They pronounced it crisply the first time, which was more than Tal could do without making an effort. There was something eerie about that.

"What about her?" said Tal, loping down the dark passage after them.

"Are you going to be all right?" said Tsereg. "I mean, we're going to have to kill her body."

Tal had told himself that the thought didn't bother him at all. Whatever the God-Empress was, she wasn't Csorwe anymore. Shuthmili was delusional if she thought there was anything left of her. It would be a kindness to put Csorwe's body to rest. Anyway, when the time came, he'd take care of it, and if he felt weird about stabbing her in the back, he would just have to suck it up. Better that than letting the kid do it.

"It'll be fine," was all he said.

The dark passage opened up and spat them out. A library was not Tal's natural home, but you didn't grow up in Tlaanthothe without coming to recognise what a huge room full of books sounded like: a particularly dry, muffled kind of silence, which always made Tal feel he was about to be told off. Overhead was a heavy dome of the same greenish glass as the passage, and the glass walls were lined from the floor to the base of the dome with immense bookcases, most of them far too high for a person to reach. Walkways and galleries stretched overhead, all crammed with more shelves.

The place was lit by high wardlights laced through the glass dome above. The misty light and the thickly crowded shelves gave the place the feeling of a moonlit forest, except that the cold air was utterly still and the sweet dry smell of old paper had no freshness in it.

"Oh, wow," said Tsereg. *"Wow."*

Tsereg moved toward the shelves as though enchanted, not watching where they were going. Their toe brushed a triple ring of inlaid gold set into the floor.

"Look out!" said Tal.

The tiled floor was engraved all over with lines and curves of gold, marking zones like a map of the Maze. Tal knew a security bound when he saw one.

"You need to go round them," he said. "Bit of a joke if we come all this way and set off the alarm now."

They nodded, still bouncing a little with anticipation. Their eyes were wide with the kind of greedy excitement which most people reserved for free food. Normally Tal's feeling on other people's enthusiasm was that it was embarrassing to be excited about anything and they ought to be ashamed of themselves. Getting invested was a quick way to open yourself up to disappointment, as he well knew.

Still . . . it was nice to see Tsereg pleased for once, without that little notch of worry between their eyebrows. Hard to feel sour about it, even if he truly did not understand what was meant to be so appealing about a huge collection of books you would never have the time to read even if you liked reading. A quick scan of the spines of the nearest books revealed that most of them were in languages he couldn't even recognise.

"Where'd you learn to read, anyway?" he said.

They gave him a withering look, though there was no real anger in it. "Prioress Cweren taught me."

"What, in prison?"

"Literally where else, Talasseres?" they said. "Do you know what the House of Silence archive looks like?"

"Literally how would I?" he said, in what he thought was not a bad impression of Tsereg's gruff squeak.

"Ooh, litewally," they said. "In that case shut up and let me concentrate. Go and rest your old bones."

He ignored this, following them on down the library's close avenues, although now they mentioned it, he wouldn't mind sitting down. The life he had led had not been easy on his joints.

It had startled him, before, when Shuthmili had thought Tsereg might be his child. They didn't look anything like him, but more to the point, he hadn't thought of himself as being that old. He didn't have any of the things people had at his age—job, house, family, any of that. He'd never considered the prospect of having children, and thinking about it now was like peering in at a stranger's window. He'd never liked any of his little cousins, but they were all Charossai, and therefore whiny little connivers from beginning to end.

Tsereg hummed as they darted from shelf to shelf, a soft tuneless drone like a bee going from flower to flower. Tal smiled to himself.

Some time later there was a cry of triumph from up ahead. They'd found what they were looking for. The House of Silence archives turned out to oc- cupy one whole gallery, half filled with books and half with sealed wooden crates. Tal couldn't see anything special about the books—they were, if any- thing, duller and shabbier than the rest of the holdings. Presumably the Thou- sand Eyes had dumped the whole lot in crates when they looted the House of Silence, and nobody had bothered with them since.

Tsereg looked at them as though they were holy relics.

"This book you're after," said Tal, wondering if he could help.

"I'll know it when I see it."

"Great," said Tal. "What did your mother say, exactly?"

"Ugh," said Tsereg. "It's not like that. It's hard to explain. It's like . . . I go into the trance, and I'm in a dark place, and I can ask questions. And then I hear her voice, or sometimes I see things, or just *know* things. You can ask where's something you've lost, or where are the guards at the moment, or what are we going to get to eat—anything. She always knows. And she's always right, but sometimes . . . it's fuzzy. I saw this place and a book. It's *her* book. She left it for me. I just have to find it." They chewed a fingernail thoughtfully and seemed to come to some conclusion. "It has to be here. She's always right."

"You said."

"No, I mean it, she's always right, but sometimes she doesn't think about things like living people do. Like, uh, I asked her once what she looked like, and I saw . . . something weird."

They moved off, scanning along the shelves. Tal followed, looking vaguely along the spines of the books. All this was so far outside his expertise, but he at least knew better than to press them after a statement like that.

"What's this thing?" he said, pointing to a large metal bowl that stood on a nearby shelf. It was dull cast iron, standing on three taloned feet.

"It's a scrying-bowl—don't *touch* it, it'll drain your blood."

"Looks like you could roast a leg of lamb in it," said Tal, but he kept his hands to himself.

"Don't be rude, it's really holy." They peered closer. "I wonder if it still works? Maybe I could have a go . . . It's not *that* much blood."

"If you pass out, I'm not going to carry you," said Tal.

"I was just thinking I could send Cweren a vision, let her know I'm doing all right . . ." They read Tal's expression and shook their head. "No, fine. Let's get the book first. And don't touch anything, all right? A lot of this stuff is cursed. Just wait for me."

He didn't have to wait for long. Tsereg yelped and pulled something out from one of the shelves. Tal had expected some huge fuck-off tome covered in gold squiggles, with a skull or two and some gems set into the cover. This was a battered little book, brown and spotted with damp.

When Tsereg opened the book, a letter fluttered out. They unfolded it and made a quiet, sad little noise, like the sound of a snail being stepped on.

If not for this, Tal might not have peered over their shoulder, and might not have read what the letter said. He half expected Tsereg to snatch it away and hide it—pretty soon he would wish they had—but Tsereg didn't seem aware of anything around them.

> *My dear Tsereg,*
>
> *Do not grieve for me more than is convenient. I have lived my life in the mouth of death, and I have enjoyed myself immensely. I go now to my final rendezvous with curiosity but no fear.*
>
> *There are things which must remain concealed from you, and for this I apologise. This is not the world I had hoped to leave to you. My intention was that you should live and learn as I have not, without constraint. This book contains most of my discoveries of the past thirty-eight years, which have been won at some pains and may be of use to you. I hope you have not grown up unduly squeamish about bones.*
>
> *We are small, and the forces which bear down upon us are great,*

*but your existence is a proof that the odds are not insuperable. May
the tyrant learn what we have ever known: that no dominion lasts
forever.*

May you strike your own bargain with the universe.

Until we meet again,
Oranna

Tal scanned through it again. The handwriting was difficult. Maybe he
had made a mistake.

"*Oranna?*" he said. "Your mother was Oranna?"

"What?" said Tsereg, distractedly. They folded the letter very small and
slipped it into a pocket of their horrible jacket. "Did you know her?"

He wasn't sure what to say to this. They frowned at him, then shrugged
and returned to their book, huddled over it like a seabird protecting its eggs.
The pages were covered in the same close, spidery handwriting, diagrams
and charts showing god knows what.

He wasn't going to get any sense out of them for a while. Tal leant back
against the bookcase and tried to make sense of this strange new set of facts.

So. Oranna had a kid. Probably not that shocking. Tsereg was really good
at bossing him around and telling him he was stupid, so maybe that ran in
the family.

He bumped his head deliberately against the hardwood of the bookcase.
Idiot. Of course it was Oranna who had given Tsereg his name. Yep, that
made sense, just assume Tal Charossa has nothing better to do, that he's just
available to dance on a string for you whenever you ask, that even after everyone else is dead, he doesn't mind running around mopping up after them.

Oranna had never mentioned to any of them that she had a child, but
then, she wouldn't, so—

No, that didn't make sense. Tsereg was fourteen. The last time Tal had
seen Oranna had been . . . about fifteen years ago, escaping from the temple
after everything went to shit. He wasn't all that clear on the dates, but as far
as he knew, Tsereg had been born after the ascension of the God-Empress,
which meant—

Did Tsereg know exactly when they had been born? Exactly when
Oranna had died? Possibly not. Tal couldn't bring himself to look at them.

Even if he could pinpoint all the dates, it wouldn't answer his actual question, which floated around him like a miasma, refusing to actually coalesce

into words. Not exactly a question, in fact, because once you saw it, it was impossible not to see: in their gestures, their smile, the completely appraising quality of their gaze, as if everything in the world was something that could be assessed and measured.

He wondered if Tsereg knew who their father had to be.

Looking back, he saw now that Tsereg was *much* smarter than he had realised. They'd broken out of the Iron Hill on their own. They'd survived this long by sheer force of personality. They could talk to the dead at will, and they had bored a passage through solid glass.

And they looked like him. They looked exactly like him, much closer to him than Oranna, so much so that Tal couldn't believe he hadn't seen it sooner. Belthandros Sethennai's broad, handsome features floated un-formed on Tsereg's face, as though waiting to take on their final shape.

And only a few minutes ago Tal had been feeling all . . . familial. What a fucking joke.

He should have known just from how excited Tsereg had been about the stupid library. Both their parents had been tiresome scholars who had loved to bore everyone shitless. He had to wonder what the hell Tsereg needed him for.

"No chance of going back now, I guess," he muttered.

Tsereg glanced back at him. "What?" they said, absently.

"You've got what you want," he said, pressing on. He'd been even stu-pider than usual not to figure this out. "You're here. You're a mage, you don't need my help."

"I—yeah, obviously," said Tsereg, folding their arms. "Why would you think I need your help?"

"I just don't want to die," he said. "And that's definitely going to happen if we get caught. And—and I don't like being tricked. Especially being tricked into doing shit I don't understand."

"I didn't!" said Tsereg. "You said—you said you were staying. You said you wanted to assassinate the God-Empress, I thought."

"What did Oranna tell you about me?" he said.

The frown deepened. "*How* did you know my mother?"

"What did she tell you? That I'm a big dumb idiot who does whatever anyone tells him to do?"

"No," said Tsereg. "She said I could trust you."

"Well, she was wrong," said Tal. Somehow this was just unbearable. It just proved Oranna had thought he was predictable enough to take advantage of, even postmortem. "She didn't know me then and she doesn't know me now and maybe you shouldn't be taking so much advice from someone who's fucking dead!"

Tsereg gave him a caustic stare. "You said all that stuff about how you'd help me. So what, you're some kind of coward now?"

"Yeah, probably!" said Tal. "I didn't know then—"

"About my mother? You're such a dick! I never met her! And I didn't trick you into anything."

Tsereg drew back. Their mouth was drawn tight as if they'd eaten something bitter. Contempt radiated from them like heat off a hot stone.

"Look at you," they said, "acting like you've done me this huge favour by getting us both arrested. You're not that helpful. If you want to go, then fucking go. You're right. I don't need you."

"Fine," said Tal. "Fine, I will."

Tal's body had run through this whole scenario so many times that it had turned him on his heels and started walking him away down the aisle before he could think his next thought.

His next thought was this: behind the scorn and anger in Tsereg's voice there had been something else, a misery that wasn't even surprised about this. They'd half expected him to go.

He kept walking. He couldn't turn back now. He was really good at this. Conjuring up some stupid fight out of nowhere, any time things got complicated, any time he might have to face something difficult. That was the whole way he got through life.

Never break first, that was Tal's motto.

Everything was fine before they turned up, he tried to say to himself. *I didn't have to think about so much shit—nobody had their claws in me—I was safe and now I'm in danger—I was nice to them, wasn't I, I didn't ask for this—*

Except that he knew how that felt, huh. For someone to treat you nicely for a bit and then change his mind.

Nice going, Talasseres, you giant fuckup. Tsereg was a child, and they'd obviously never met either of their parents. Belthandros and Oranna had abandoned them like they'd abandoned everyone else.

"Oh, fuck *this*," he said, and turned round.

Tsereg was striding off in the opposite direction, pretending with fierce determination to read Oranna's book.

Before Tal could call out to them, they had stepped straight through three security bounds.

Instinct snapped its jaws around Tal's heart, and before he consciously understood why, he lunged forward and grabbed Tsereg around the middle, hauling them back. They squeaked and flailed, elbowing him in the face.

"Shut up!" he hissed, narrowly dodging a claw. "Look where you're bloody going!"

Tsereg goggled at him, clearly about to spit venom, before focusing on the bound in the floor.

"Shit. Did I step over it?" Before Tal could answer, their eyes widened. "D'you hear that?"

A regular metallic sound, as though someone was running their hand again and again through a bag of coins. The sound came up from among the bookshelves—*clink, clink, clink*—soft but getting louder.

"That's *footsteps*," said Tsereg under their breath.

Tal moved back the way they had come, towing Tsereg after him, and as he did so, he caught his first glimpse of what was making the noise: a tall, angular shadow, moving out from behind a bookcase.

Long gilded limbs, slender jointed fingers which ended in knifelike talons. It was all gilded metal, darkly glittering. Some kind of automaton. To judge from the length of its arms, it was at least twelve feet tall.

"*Be quiet,*" he mouthed at Tsereg, and the two of them shrank back against the wall.

It didn't move like any automaton Tal had ever seen, but with a terrible slow fluidity, its clawed fingers waving and uncurling as if plucking at the air. Could it somehow smell them? Tal immediately regretted wondering.

It moved out from behind the bookcase. It seemed impossible that something so huge should move so quietly, with only that soft clinking sound to warn you it was near.

It was man-shaped and skeletal, with two pairs of jointed arms. It had no head, but set into the centre of its rib cage, in place of a breastbone, was a large oval vessel of clear glass. Something dark floated inside it.

It stopped, dead still but for its fingers, endlessly writhing. Then it turned toward them.

At Tal's side, Tsereg was shaking like a frightened animal. As Tal noticed this, he found that he was not frightened at all, but furiously calm, the blessed incandescent calm which only ever came to him in moments such as this.

"I've got this," he murmured to Tsereg. After all, if there was one thing he knew, it was fighting some big fucker that got in his way.

He slipped sideways into shadow, springing up toward the nearest bookcase and landing on the edge of a shelf. As he crossed the boundary line, there was a louder metallic noise. The creature must have realised he was there. Good. Get its attention away from Tsereg. He climbed quickly up the bookcase, propelling himself from shelf to shelf. Not as easy as it would have been when he was twenty-three but not very difficult either.

He reached the top of the bookcase and allowed himself to look down. The creature loped toward the place where he'd crossed the golden boundary. It moved much faster than he had imagined, its quiet footsteps like a peal of little bells. He broke into a run, sprinting along the top of the bookcase to keep up with it.

Tsereg had frozen where he left them, hands clenched at their sides. Weird that this should be their breaking point after everything they had been through, but Tal knew better than most that sometimes there was just one thing too many.

Tal paused at the edge of the bookcase, tensed to spring, and as the creature passed just beneath him, he leapt. There was no time to panic. He'd calculated this perfectly. He landed on the automaton where its head ought to be, in the dip where its first pair of clavicles met.

The thing was lighter than he'd expected. Its limbs were not solid metal, but gilded bone. For a second Tal had to cling on for dear life, thrown from side to side as the creature swayed under his weight. Its arms flailed in surprise, then began reaching for him, whipping blindly at its own upper body to try and catch hold of him. The point of one talon sliced across Tal's cheek, but he didn't feel it.

There was a gap at the top of its torso, just wide enough for him to wriggle through. He squeezed down into the opening and dropped into the rib cage. There was no solid base for him to stand on, but he wedged his feet onto a lower rib and clung on with both hands.

The creature thrashed with panic and discomfort, lurching back and forth as it clawed at its own rib cage, trying to rid itself of the intruder.

Ha ha, thought Tal, as it closed one clawed hand on its own rib and yanked. The rib came away with a horrible crunch and clattered on the floor behind it. Tal scrambled out of the way of the hand as it reached in after him.

Some part of his brain knew this plan was not a good one, that he was caged in a small space with twenty wriggly knives all going for him at once. He did not care. He laughed aloud and dodged another swipe from the creature. If it wanted to get at him, it was going to have to pull itself apart.

It seized another rib and pulled it out with a scream of metal on metal. It reeled sideways, nearly dislodging Tal from his perch, then staggered sharply in the opposite direction, hopelessly off balance. Tal was flung loose. He slammed into the edge of the glass vessel with a bruising impact, but he managed to grab hold of another rib and climb back up again before the thing could shake him free.

He was laughing hysterically, as if every time the creature lurched in another direction, it dislodged new bubbles of delirium.

Then it careened into a bookcase and Tal felt something shatter. The automaton wavered unsteadily and collapsed. Tal fell six feet to the ground and landed heavily, all breath knocked from his lungs. Bones and books thunked into the floor around him, and he curled up, shielding his head.

The glass vessel hit the ground nearby with a splintering crash that vibrated through Tal's body, jarring the wild laughter out of him all over again. If that had landed on him, he would've been dead for sure. This was somehow very funny.

Some kind of liquid was pooling across the floor, cold and sticky. *Blood?* thought Tal, still rather delirious. No, it was clear, more like spit, and it smelled like turpentine. *Ugh, I should get up or it'll get on my face,* he thought, and laughed again.

"Tal!" he heard someone calling. He managed to raise his head.

The glass egg that had been at the heart of the creature had cracked open as it hit the ground. The cold liquid seeped out of the egg, and that wasn't the only thing.

A bald, ragged figure crawled out of the jagged opening. It was about the same size and shape as Tsereg, and it had probably been a living person once. Its skin was wet and shrivelled, shrunk onto its bones. It had huge cloudy eyes and sharp little teeth.

Tal blinked, all laughter startled out of him. It didn't seem real. Just a nightmare. Then the thing bounded across the floor toward him, on its toes and knuckles, and it landed on Tal's chest, pinning him.

He squirmed back, growling, and tried to throw the thing off, but twisting like that sent a white-hot jolt of pain through his body. So he'd got hurt after all. Nice going, Talasseres.

Its flesh was withered and purplish, like grapes that had gone bad. Its breath smelled of turpentine. It ran one long, ragged nail over Tal's eyelid as though contemplating putting his eye out.

Then all the colour drained from its skin. It turned grey as rain, then white as ice, and then it disintegrated. The bones of its skull appeared like rocks in mist, and then they too went to dust, just a settling cloud of shreds.

Behind it was Tsereg. Their mouth was pinched with concentration. They were holding the little book open in one hand, and they looked as though they were trying to solve a difficult maths problem. They reached for Tal with the other hand. It moved in the air like a waterweed uncurling.

The automaton was dead. There was just Tal on the floor and Tsereg standing over him, and he thought for a second he knew how a spider felt before someone stamped on it.

Then Tsereg laughed, their whole face crinkled up with wicked glee.

"What the fuck!" said Tsereg, bobbing from one foot to the other as though it was a real effort not to float away. "That was incredible!"

Tal lay back on the floor and laughed with them, because, well, why not? It seemed as good a response as any.

A flash of movement caught his eye. Behind Tsereg's shoulder, he thought he saw something on one of the upper levels of the library. A small dark figure, peering down at them. He blinked again, and it was gone.

"That was so sick!" said Tsereg. "You just got *inside* it, what's wrong with you—"

"Uh," said Tal. "I think I might have cracked a rib, actually. You didn't mention you could disintegrate things."

"I didn't know!" said Tsereg. "It's from the book! Did it look cool?"

"Sure," said Tal, deciding he'd deal with the implications of this later. "What the hell was that crawly thing?"

"Probably one of their nasty snake experiments," said Tsereg.

"Looked kind of like you," he said, grinning.

"Should've let it poke your eye out," they said. "Are you hurt?"

Tal sat up carefully and prodded at his chest, wincing. His ribs hadn't quite healed right after his injuries at Saar-in-Tachthyr, and it would be just his luck to break them again in the same spot, but on further prodding, he thought it was just bruised.

"I guess your mother didn't warn you about that," he said. "Tal Charossa, you can trust him to constantly trip over and fall on his stupid face."

Tsereg gave an involuntary snort of laughter. They brushed their curls back out of their eyes. "Look—" they said.

He had a sudden horrible premonition that Tsereg was about to try and apologise to him. As if *they* were the one at fault here. Disgust at himself twisted in his chest, far worse than the bruises.

"Fuck," he said. "I'm sorry. I'm an idiot. You didn't do anything wrong."

"Yeah, I *know*," said Tsereg, with obvious relief. They crossed their arms and scowled, for the look of the thing.

"Your mother was a heinous bitch, and I hated her"—*wow, great apology so far, Talasseres*—"but you're obviously not her. I don't get on that well with my family either."

He wasn't even going to address the other thing. He wasn't going to think about that. No point. Nothing to do about it. Best to pretend he didn't know.

"Yeah, I sort of got that from how your shitty brother sold us out to the snakes," said Tsereg. "So what, you're staying now? Make your mind up."

"Yeah," he said. "Yeah, I'm staying. I said I would. And Oranna's right, you know. No dominion lasts forever."

Tsereg grimaced, clearly embarrassed by this, but he went on. "I don't know how to kill a god, and I bet neither do you. Just have to hope there's something really fucking good in that book."

18

The Fallacy of Sunk Costs

SHUTHMILI WAS WOKEN by the creak of a floorboard next door, in her study. Nobody else should have been in her chambers—she had managed to terrify the latest maidservant away—but she was pretty certain who it was.

She pulled on Csorwe's coat over her nightdress and went to see. As expected, the body that no longer belonged entirely to Keleiros Lenarai was standing at the desk in her study.

"What brings you here?"

"The palace opens to me," he said. "I've been exploring." He had arranged Keleiros' ringlets into a fetching cascade, which just happened to conceal the diadem, and outlined the boy's eyes with his usual fine line of kohl. The eyes were as bright and open and friendly as ever. It was only the power of the imagination that added a knowing glint. For that matter, Shuthmili's own eyes were the same undistinguished dark brown that they had always been.

"Well, I hope you're doing a convincing job as Keleiros," said Shuthmili. His features might be unchanged, but his posture was visibly different, relaxed and authoritative. She might not have noticed unless she'd been looking for it, but someone who knew Keleiros well might spot it.

"People aren't very observant, really," he said, shrugging. "But *you've* really made a name for yourself. I've only been here three days, and I've heard all about you. People fear you as much as the Empress."

"I do my best," she said. "Do sit down."

Shuthmili's study was built of the same intricate black fossil-stone as the rest of the Lignite Citadel, but the walls were hardly visible between the bookshelves that rose from floor to ceiling on every wall. There was a high narrow fireplace whose iron chimneypiece was in the shape of a cobra's hood, and two deep leather armchairs.

She snapped her fingers and lit a fire in the grate. A languid blue flame sprang up halfheartedly, casting only a shadow of warmth. It was always cold in the Lignite Palace, regardless of the desert sun outside. The fossil-stone seemed to drink up light and heat and swallow them down.

Shuthmili boiled water and made tea and porridge. There was something unpleasantly vulnerable about cooking in front of him, but it would be worse to have to deal with him on an empty stomach.

"Ah, the tyranny of breakfast," he said, as she set down the tray on the table between them. "You and Csorwe were well matched. Although that coat is too big for you."

He was only probing her defences. She ignored him and ate her porridge. It was, as usual, grainy and slightly burnt.

"So," he said, when they had eaten. "You want her back. The question is, what is left of her?"

Shuthmili nodded. Belthandros was not to be trusted. He was not her friend, not her colleague, not her ally. She had to keep that in mind. And yet, all these years with nobody else to share her plans . . .

"She is still there," said Shuthmili.

"The mortal apparatus is not designed to sustain two minds," Belthandros went on. "When a god possesses a mortal for any span of time, the weaker mind tends to waste away. Remove the parasite, and you are left with a shell. You *know* this, Shuthmili."

"What about you?" said Shuthmili. "What about me? We're both living proof that it doesn't have to be true, not always."

"Neither of us is possessed. True incarnation is an exchange between equals, brought about by consent and sacrifice. I cut out my beating heart and placed it in the Reliquary. No doubt you have given Zinandour something of equal value."

Do you think so, my lady?

Zinandour preened distantly, emanating distaste. *HIS HEART IS FIT ONLY TO BE EATEN, AND ONLY IF ONE WERE IN GREAT NEED. EVEN YOUR FEEBLE HUSK IS A MORE PROPER OFFERING.*

Belthandros picked up his teacup, swirling loose the black tea leaves that had settled at the bottom.

"I don't see how this is relevant to Csorwe," said Shuthmili. "If you think there's no hope, then just say so, but I don't believe she's gone. Even after she put on the Mantle, she was still there—I spoke to her, she tried to fight it. Do you think I should just *give up?*"

The alternative was more than Shuthmili could bear. Every moment she spent in the God-Empress' presence, it was impossible not to look for signs. She had searched every word and every expression for some sign that Csorwe was still there. She didn't know what was worse: that Csorwe might have lived through the past fifteen years with some conscious knowledge of what was being done with her body or that she might be gone altogether.

"I do not know," he said, rather dreamily, as if ignorance was a pleasant novelty. "Csorwe survived the first fourteen years of her life in direct contact with the Unspoken One, and she is terribly stubborn when she chooses to be. Perhaps her mind is intact. Perhaps the God-Empress chose to preserve her. Or perhaps not. A mortal soul is like salt. In contact with the divine—in time—it dissolves."

Shuthmili flinched, and realised too late that a small sound had escaped her throat, an inarticulate mew of distress.

There was a curious expression on Keleiros Lenarai's face, like a machine that had discovered the concept of pity. "Shuthmili—are you sure that what you're doing here is the best use of your time?" said Belthandros. "Fifteen years in service to the Empress? The fallacy of sunk costs is a terrible thing."

She swallowed, twisting her hands together in her lap.

"Csorwe was dear to me, too, you know." he said. She could tell he was trying to be gentle, but this still made her want to scream all over again. "She was my companion in exile. I would not willingly have let her go, but it is sometimes easier, in the long run, to recognise when something has slipped through your fingers."

"It's not the same thing at all," said Shuthmili. "She was happy with me."

"And you think you can get that back?" he said.

"No," said Shuthmili. She knew she couldn't. She'd never had any hope of that at all; those weren't the terms of her deal with Zinandour. When Csorwe was saved, Shuthmili's body would belong to the goddess altogether, and it would be her turn to dissolve.

"Thinking like this about mortals will break your heart, you know," he said. "But you'll come to see it. After three thousand years, no mortal seems all that extraordinary. There are only so many types. Beauty and courage and intelligence recur again and again, and they fade almost immediately. It's a mistake to become too attached."

Shuthmili laughed abruptly, surprising herself. "Listen to yourself. That is monstrous."

"Well," said Belthandros. He leant back in his chair. "We *are* monsters. You have a lot of laudable mortal feelings, and if you're wise, you'll squash them as quickly as you can. They're maladaptive for your current situation."

"You mean to say you think I should give up on Csorwe because pretty girls are a renewable resource?" said Shuthmili. "Fine—I don't think you're a monster, I think you're an idiot."

"I think you're denying reality. Even if we do manage to bring her back— for however long—do you really think there is such a thing as a love eternal? I suppose there's no point trying to warn you, though. It's a hard lesson. If you try to hold on to mortal things, you will lose and lose and lose. Enjoy them, and let them go."

"I suppose what I'm meant to take from this is that you've suffered nobly and learnt your lesson, but I don't think you'd know a lesson if it slapped you in the face," she said. "This explains so much about you. Is this why you treated Tal so badly?"

"I tried to give Talasseres what he wanted," he said levelly. More level than Shuthmili was managing, which was embarrassing.

"And Oranna? Do you know how she died?"

He paused. "No."

"The Thousand Eyes executed her," said Shuthmili. She had a report on it somewhere. She had looked hard for both Tal and Oranna. She hadn't found Tal until now, and it had been a kind of relief, to think that perhaps he'd been able to find his way out. But by the time she'd got word of Oranna, it was too late. "Beheaded," she added, with a hot flash of cruelty, quite badly wanting to hurt him.

Immediately she felt grubby for using Oranna's memory to wound. At the time of her death, Oranna had been no older than Shuthmili was now, though she had looked older. Much later, Shuthmili had seen what was left of her, laid out in two pieces in the morgue of the *Blessed Awakening*. Some part of her hadn't believed it could actually be true until she'd seen her, even though Oranna herself had predicted she'd be dead within the year. Whatever had happened, the year hadn't been kind to her. The familiar features and the new lines of suffering were all blurred by death into a uniform, slack blandness.

"That wasn't how it should have been," was all he said, and then looked up at Shuthmili, a gleam of vindictive malice in Keleiros' bright eyes. "I suppose I should start wearing her clothes, then? I might live another three thousand years, should I spend all of them weeping?"

Shuthmili shook her head, a bitter smile twisting her features. "They both deserved much more than they got. And we both got much more than we deserved."

Somehow this had been the right thing to say. Belthandros leant back, and the malignancy faded from his expression.

"I mean to redress the balance," said Shuthmili. She didn't intend to tell him anything about the fine detail of her deal with Zinandour. The less he knew the better. "Do you think you can help me, or not?"

Belthandros leant back in his chair, crossing Keleiros' elegant ankles.

"As a matter of fact, I do. If we can persuade the God-Empress to re-move the Mantle of her own volition—if you are right that there is some fragment of Csorwe's personality remaining—that would give her the best possible chance to reassert herself."

"Of her own volition?" said Shuthmili. "That can mean a lot of things. And if she notices we're acting against her—"

"No need to get ahead of yourself," said Belthandros. "I told you, I can help you."

"Then where do we begin?"

"Well," he said. "For one thing, I will need my body back."

Shuthmili tucked her elbows in. It was a good thing that she had never been claustrophobic. Around her was a shimmering bubble of air and light that would hold for only as long as her concentration. Beyond that was solid glass and stone, glowing as the heat of the bubble melted it. Belthandros' bubble was yards away, ahead and slightly below, twinkling dimly through the glass. It was a slow business, burrowing down through the fabric of the palace, never moving fast enough to risk detection by the God-Empress. The bubbles were a spell of Belthandros' devising, and Shuthmili was de-termined not to show how difficult she had found it.

Zinandour disliked the confinement so much that for most of the de-scent she had managed nothing but a silent scream of hatred.

This does not help me focus, Shuthmili thought, for the third or fourth time. *Drowning in molten glass would be an unpleasant way to die.*

I WILL REVIVE YOUR BODY TO KILL YOU AGAIN IF YOU DO NOT RELEASE ME. YOU HAVE NEVER KNOWN SUFFERING UNTIL THIS DAY. LET ME GO OR I WILL RENDER YOU TO OIL AND ASH. I WILL NURTURE TEETH IN YOUR GUT. I WILL OPEN MOUTHS IN YOU TO DEVOUR YOUR ORGANS FROM WITHIN.

My Corruptor, this is hardly the time to flirt with me. We will be there in less than five minutes.

I WILL NEVER RETURN TO THE VOID! I WILL DIE FIRST! I WILL INVENT DEATH FOR MY KIND AND I WILL TEACH IT TO YOU!

Shuthmili rolled her eyes and focused on piloting the bubble, down through the glassy veins and flesh of the palace.

Belthandros had spent the past few days holed up in Shuthmili's private training room, having given out some story about the Hand of the Empress needing Keleiros for a secret project. He had left it full of detritus: experimental doves, both living and dead; burnt-out candles; stacks of books; huge closely written sheets of paper. But there was a limit to what they could achieve through theory alone, and so it was time to pay a visit to the heart chamber.

The bubble breached the outer shell of the chamber and Shuthmili halted its descent, cooling it as rapidly as she dared. She was in effect standing on the lip of a pockmark set into a great domed ceiling.

Their magelights cut through ink-black darkness to reveal that the heart chamber was one huge round bubble, without doors or windows, sealed within a stratum of volcanic glass deep beneath the palace. Glass tubes and pipes grew everywhere from floor to ceiling, as though the place was haunted by the ghost of a pipe organ. Some of the tubes ran with clear or yellowish fluids, others with what was unmistakeably red Tlaanthothei blood. The thunder of a distant pulse could be heard, huge devices turning over in the depths of the palace.

Shuthmili had spent a lot of time setting up the heart chamber before the Empress sealed it. She knew that some of the glass pipes ran up through several levels of the palace to emerge in the throne room, and some connected to the jar containing Belthandros' body.

Belthandros emerged from his own bubble a few yards away. He had made a pet of one of his experimental doves, a round and self-satisfied creature which liked to perch on his shoulder and eat seedcake from a silver dish. She fluttered after him out of the bubble and landed on his shoulder again as he descended.

"Oh good, I'm so glad you brought the bird," said Shuthmili. She found the dove infuriating. It was such an obvious piece of ostentation to bring the wretched creature safely down here.

"I'm training her as my assistant," said Belthandros. He clicked his tongue, peering at the pipes and valves.

"I don't know why you want your body back so badly," said Shuthmili. "I would have thought you'd be glad to trade in for a younger model."

He laughed. "Keleiros Lenarai has a doting mother. I can't get away from her. Not to mention the fiancée."

"Don't even think about it," said Shuthmili. She hadn't known about either the doting mother or the fiancée, but she didn't have time to give in to pangs of guilt. She had work to do.

High above them, up in the throne room, Belthandros' body was joined to the machinery of the Citadel by a number of fine tubes which grew from the jar like the bundle of veins and arteries which grow from the upper portion of the heart. These tubes emerged here in the heart chamber, a thick bundle of pipes which branched and divided, growing back into the floor like roots.

"Here we are," said Shuthmili. She tapped one of the tubes, and it gave a bright, glassy *tink!* "Salt water, alchemical solutions, preservative."

"All this, just to sustain my body?"

"The God-Empress likes her trophies," said Shuthmili.

"So I see," said Belthandros, looking around.

There were larger glass bubbles in among the tubes, like fruit swelling on some unearthly tree. Some of them were bigger than Shuthmili. Most of them contained the discarded results of the Empress' experiments: slippery, half-living things, which followed Belthandros with their great eyes as he moved down the walkway.

A WRETCHED BLASPHEMY, said Zinandour.

"So this is the *great work* . . ." said Belthandros. "If this is as far as she got, I think Echentyr is still some way off," he added, leaning in to look at one bubble. The inhabitant, a foetal amphibian thing, reached for him with pale webbed fingers. It seemed a miserable existence, sealed alone here in the heart chamber, kept alive only by magic, but the Empress never threw away anything that might be of use.

"This was as far as she had got ten years ago," said Shuthmili. "This one was from the marshes of Tsortanapan," she added. "Conquered by the Thousand Eyes and destroyed by the curse a few centuries later. The God-Empress told me they had beautiful singing voices."

Like songbirds, she remembered, unwillingly.

"Bringing back the old order of things will solve nothing," said Belthandros. "Even if the God-Empress succeeds in resurrecting Echentyr, she will not find what she looks for." He gave her a double-edged smile, which she ignored.

It took quite some time before Shuthmili found what she was looking for, a huge glass amphora shaped something like a hanging flower bud, filled with red liquid.

"Here we are. This is your blood."

"Goodness, is it?" said Belthandros, looking up at it with mild interest. "I'm sure it could be anybody's blood."

"Your body was exsanguinated fifteen years ago, and the Empress keeps the stuff here," said Shuthmili, ignoring him.

She set about reconnecting the amphora to the jar systems. Belthandros watched thoughtfully.

"So tell me," she said. "When are we going to do this? The God-Empress never leaves her throne room, and it's unbelievably hard to distract her."

"What about the Feast of Midsummer?"

"Don't mock me, Belthandros. A glass tank of blood is so breakable."

The Midsummer Feast was still celebrated every year in the Citadel, although rather than honouring the Siren, it now commemorated the destruction of Echentyr. Every year it struck Shuthmili as a worse and more gruesome charade.

All the usual tedious parades and sacrifices, with Cherenthisse at the head in her full regalia. All the most important families of Tlaanthothe-That-Was were also invited to celebrate the Feast at the God-Empress' table. Shuthmili suspected that the families selected their representatives by short straw. The God-Empress' presence was at its most malignant during the Feast. Watching five hundred mortal dignitaries struggling to maintain composure as they wept blood into their goblets was never an edifying spectacle. This year Shuthmili meant to arrange for extra handkerchiefs.

"I've always thought that if you're going to steal something, it's a bad idea to do it specifically on the night when a few hundred delegates are going to be in the throne room looking directly at it," said Shuthmili.

She gave a vicious twist to the nearest dial and stepped back as the tube began to fill with blood, siphoning out of the glass tank.

"No. They will be looking directly at the God-Empress. And she will be occupied by whatever tiresome ceremonial rigmarole she has devised for the occasion. If she never leaves, our only option is to act while she's distracted."

"And afterward? I want Csorwe safe and out of the palace. That's my only condition."

"Once I have my body back," he said. "That's *my* only condition. Can you arrange for me to attend the party?"

"The Lenaraii have already selected their representative," said Shuthmili. She'd seen their elderly patriarch at previous feasts. "It would look odd for Keleiros to suddenly receive an invitation."

"Can't you bring a guest?" said Belthandros. "It wouldn't look *that* odd for you to favour your pretty secretary."

Shuthmili made an involuntary noise of disgust. "I doubt it'll win me any favours with the doting mother or the fiancée," she said.

She did not, personally, give a damn whether Belthandros got his body back, but at least if he did, then Keleiros would be off the hook. She really did not want to do the stupid boy any more injury than she had already.

She adjusted another dial. The blood was flowing freely now. If she had done her job properly, it would be pumped back into the veins of the body in the jar, but she wouldn't be able to see for certain whether it had worked until the next time she was in the throne room.

"I'll get you an invitation," she said, "but if we get caught . . ."

"Oh, no need to worry on that front," said Belthandros. "I never get caught."

19

Learning Lessons

TAL RETURNED TO the Glass Archive with an armful of pilfered rations, wondering how he could get Tsereg to leave the book alone long enough to eat something. When he reached their hiding place among the House of Silence papers, however, there was no sign of Tsereg, and a stranger was standing quietly among the shelves. Tal reached automatically for his knife.

The stranger was a young Tlaanthothei man, dressed in a palace uniform. He didn't seem at all startled by Tal's appearance, or by the knife. A white bird perched on his shoulder, peering at Tal with pink beady eyes.

"Talasseres Charossa?" he said. He sounded surprised and delighted, as if they knew each other. Which wasn't likely, because he was half Tal's age and—actually just impossibly beautiful, what the fuck. He had soft chin-length ringlets which framed his face like a jewel in its setting, and long eyelashes, and a surprisingly strong chin to set off the rest, and . . . none of this had ever been Tal's thing, at all. Tal's tragedy was that he liked bad men who could break him in half. Presumably the weird ache he was currently experiencing was to do with the fact that he'd been twenty once himself.

"Uh, sure," said Tal, intelligently. "Not how I look in the murals, I know."

The young man smiled. He had a dimple, of course. The bird on his shoulder fanned its wings and settled like a powder puff. "Close enough," he said. "I saw the two of you kill the security construct. Impressive."

That explained the distant figure Tal had seen just after the fight. He had completely forgotten about it.

"Thanks," said Tal. He still wasn't sure what was going on here. The young man didn't seem to be about to call for the guards. Another thought lurched into his brain several seconds late. "What have you done with Tsereg?"

"Your friend?" said the stranger. "Over there. I didn't want to interrupt, since I prefer not to be disintegrated." His ears gave a little flutter of amusement.

He waved over the balustrade. Tsereg was sitting cross-legged on the floor, with Oranna's book open before them, surrounded by a hand-drawn circle of wards. They had found a handful of bone amulets in the House of Silence archive and these were arranged at various points around the circle. Whatever they were trying to do wasn't going as planned, so the ritual was punctuated by cursing.

"My name's Keleiros, by the way," said the stranger. "Keleiros Lenarai."

Tal had been at school with some Lenaraii, but he didn't remember anything about them. Another Tlaanthothei noble family, similar rank to the Charossai, probably just as unbearable.

"I know who you are, obviously," said Keleiros. "You wounded the God-Empress."

"Not sure about *wounded*," said Tal. The mural painters had a lot to answer for. He rubbed a bit of sleep out of his eyes. He might have been out for longer than he'd thought. "I thought it was a brilliant idea to jump on a big snake to try and impress someone, and I nearly got drowned, so. Learned my lesson."

"Personally I think learning lessons is overrated," said Keleiros. "Who were you trying to impress?"

"Er—" said Tal. "It was a long time ago."

"Anyway, I don't believe you," said Keleiros, drifting closer. "If you'd learned your lesson, you wouldn't be here."

"Er," said Tal, again. Tal realised dimly that he was being flirted with. It had been such a long time. What was he supposed to do? Who *was* this?

"Oh, don't worry," said Keleiros. "Do you think you're the only one who wants the God-Empress dead?"

"How did you—" said Tal, not sure where Tsereg would stand on admitting this.

"I didn't. But perhaps this was meant to be," said Keleiros. "There are forces at work that are larger than either of us, you know. Sometimes an opportunity comes along"—he shrugged, a movement of impossible grace that made Tal's stomach do an acrobatic flip—"and what can you do but take it?"

Before Tal had to think of anything to say to this, Tsereg came rushing over, their arms full of books and bones. Keleiros' bird fluttered up from his shoulder, startled, then landed again and began a catlike preening.

"*Tal*," they said, "guess what I—oh!"

Keleiros smiled and gave them a little wave, looking mildly embarrassed. "You must be Tsereg," he said.

"Hmm," said Tsereg. "I might be. Who are you?"

"Well. Among other things I'm the person who's going to help you assassinate the God-Empress."

Shuthmili returned to her study to find Belthandros waiting for her there. He was sprawled in one of the deep armchairs with an enormous book spread across his knees and a glass bowl balanced unsteadily on his chest. The dove perched on his shoulder, asleep.

He had lit the fire, and it crackled away merrily, a much brighter and warmer yellow than she'd ever managed with it. This wasn't her fault—the Citadel fought her every moment—but there was still something galling about it.

At first Shuthmili thought the bowl might be part of his workings, but on closer inspection, it contained rose sherbet flecked with almonds.

"Where did you get that?" she asked.

"Ordered from the palace kitchens," he said. "There are *some* rewards to being trapped in this place. Oh, don't look like that, you've virtually told everyone I'm your concubine, ordering up sweetmeats is one of the accepted perks."

"I'm just glad to see you're taking the work so seriously," said Shuthmili.

He ate another spoonful of sherbet, picked a fragment of almond off the rim of the bowl, and raised an eyebrow. The dove fluffed its wings, opened a ruby-red eye, and nuzzled his cheek with its smooth white head. "You are *very* opposed to ever enjoying yourself, aren't you?"

"Famously," said Shuthmili. This made him laugh, which felt briefly like an achievement, though she was wary of this feeling. It didn't pay to be eager to please around Belthandros. "I've sorted your invitation to the Feast, by the way."

"Ah, excellent," he said. "I'm glad you're back. Time for the next step."

He unfolded himself from the window seat and sat himself cross-legged before the hearth, where another crystal bowl was set out, this one full of water, as if for scrying. The white dove flew down and perched in his lap, nuzzling his hands for attention.

"I still don't really understand why you want the thing back so badly," she said.

"My original body is perfected for my inhabitation. Keleiros is not. I could squeeze a few years' good use out of this vessel, no more than that. And if you want your secretary back in one piece, I'd better not keep him much longer."

There was a soft crunch. Shuthmili glanced over her shoulder, wondering if they had been interrupted, and only realised what had happened when Zinandour flashed her an image of a loose vertebra crushed underfoot.

Belthandros had killed the dove, snapped its neck midsentence. Keleiros' fingers were stronger than they looked. She really ought to have predicted this, given the way the foolish creature had cooed and preened over him, given what she knew of how he treated those who trusted him.

And after all we've seen, this is what shocks me? she thought to herself.

It wasn't pity that moved her so much as fear. Belthandros could have killed the bird by magic, instantly, just as Shuthmili had once laid waste to the whales of the deepwood, and he had chosen to do it like this, to show her how easy it was to destroy some harmless thing.

"This is the next step?" she said, repulsed.

He beckoned her closer. She watched him spread the dead dove out on a cloth, and did not look away as he drove a small knife into its breast, cutting down and opening up the ribs to expose the red interior, with the businesslike efficiency of one peeling back the pith of a pomegranate. With a single, certain stroke of the blade, he snipped out the dove's heart and swallowed it, whole and raw. The tip of Keleiros' tongue flicked out to dab the smear of blood from his lower lip.

This was not a magic she recognised, although she suspected it had something in common with Oranna's preferred technique; it occurred to her that she had never seen what Oranna did with her severed fingers and that it was perfectly possible that she had eaten them, and somehow this—the knowledge of all the little bones and tendons, the scrabbling openmouthed desperation it would take to go through with it—was what finally made her retch, undisguisably.

He held the dead bird open over a bowl and let the blood drain down into the water, pink and then deepening red. He must have done something to the water to keep the blood from darkening: as they sat there minute by minute, it retained its colour as vividly as ever.

"I don't see why I had to witness this," she said.

"If I gave you a bottle of blood, you'd only get suspicious," he said. "Easier if you know from the start." He put aside the drained corpse of the dove, picked up a small dropper, and began decanting the contents of the bowl carefully into a glass vial. "If we were to smash open the jar and haul my body away like a side of beef, we would gain nothing for our trouble but a wet corpse. I must bind myself to it first, and the simplest method is by a ritual offering. Fortunately, my body is woven directly into the palace, so by the principle of exchange—"

"Mother of Cities, Belthandros, I do not care," said Shuthmili, feeling her last thread of patience snap. Once upon a time she could have stomached playing the grateful audience if it meant learning some of Belthandros' arcane secrets, but no longer. "Just tell me what you need me to do."

"A libation of blood is ancient magic," he said, unruffled, "as I'm sure Csorwe could have told you. To complete the ritual, we will need to find a way for you to spill this in the throne room of the so-called God-Empress. Directly before the throne, if possible, but anywhere on bare stone will do. Once that takes hold, I will begin to regain some power over my body."

"I can't just walk in and smash it on the ground. She'll realise I'm up to something."

"Almost certainly," said Belthandros.

"There would be a way," she muttered, wheels already starting to turn. "There would be a way to do it, but it can't be me . . . When do you need this to happen?"

"Before Midsummer," said Belthandros. "I will need at least a full day and night to regain total command of my limbs in time for the Feast."

"Even if you're right and the God-Empress is distracted during the Feast . . . people will notice if the body goes missing. People will notice if you're suddenly walking about wearing it."

Belthandros shrugged, as if this were a very minor consideration. "Please, Shuthmili, give me some credit. You do your part, and I will do mine. The God-Empress defeated and imprisoned me. I will not risk exposing our presence before we know how to handle her."

NOT TO BE TRUSTED, murmured Zinandour.

I don't trust him either, my lady, but I do trust that he knows his own interests.

HE IS AN INVETERATE DECEIVER.

I know, said Shuthmili. *I know, but what other resources do we have?*

The guests began to arrive, by mazeship or caravan, from their own dominions, and as Hand of the Empress, Shuthmili was required to receive some of them.

Halfway through the morning, the Charossa carriage rolled in. The Charossai were represented by their matriarch, as ever. Niranthe Charossa stepped down from a carriage, leaning on the arm of a footman. Shuthmili almost liked Tal's mother, because she was one of the few people who looked Shuthmili in the face and did not flinch. Her hair was by now more white than grey, but still arranged with great pains into an elegant garland of braids.

"Ah, Madam Qanwa," she said, as if Shuthmili were just another palace functionary. It was so unusual for any mortal to address her as such that Shuthmili almost smiled despite herself. "We can look forward to the usual guest rooms, I assume?"

At Feast time, the palace repopulated itself with guest chambers, rows and rows of them, swelling around the turrets like oak galls. Most were well formed, but there were always a few that took shape without ceilings, or with the doors sunk halfway through the floors. Some contained beds, but a majority were furnished with stone blocks or empty sarcophagi. Occasionally there was something stranger still: a tank of deep-sea fish, a gigantic quartz crystal containing a fist-sized bubble of blood, a bed-shaped machine which Shuthmili took to be an instrument of torture.

"Indeed," said Shuthmili, recalling that she'd quietly managed to reserve one of the decent ones for Niranthe.

"Do you know, I've attended the Midsummer Feast every year since I was your age?" Niranthe added.

There was a look of cloaked resentment in her eyes, painfully reminiscent of her youngest son. There were so many Charossai in the Citadel that Shuthmili really should have got used to running into Tal's relatives, and yet every time she felt as if she'd pushed with her full strength on an open door and fallen through it. The Charossai were a lichen that grew in every crevice, and they had adapted to the accession of the God-Empress as they had to every tyrant in Tlaanthothe's long history.

The city had bounced rapidly from one Chancellor to another over the past seven decades. Usurpation had been commonplace, and duelling a previous incumbent had been a perfectly legal way to claim control of the city—but Shuthmili got the sense that before the advent of the God-Empress, this had been something like a game. A way for the ruling class to entertain themselves, while the scholars and students and citizens got on with their lives in comparative peace.

"Tlaanthothe has known so many rulers," said Niranthe, echoing Shuthmili's thoughts. It was a remarkable piece of daring to speak the old name in front of the Empress' Hand. Shuthmili wondered what she thought she was doing. "I remember the reign of Chancellor Lathraai," she went on. "Before Sethennai. Then my brother Olthaaros. Then Sethennai again. And now—her Gracious and Immortal Majesty."

"Now and forever," said Shuthmili.

"So we devoutly hope," said Niranthe, without expression. "Thank you for your hospitality."

The encounter with Niranthe left Shuthmili feeling strangely compromised, though she had said little and Niranthe had come very close to actionable treason.

On the subject of actionable treason, I hope Belthandros knows what he is doing.

BELTHANDROS LIES. WHAT HE INTENDS IS NO OFFERING BUT A PROFA-NATION.

Surely that rather depends on one's perspective, said Shuthmili, knowing she was kidding nobody, least of all herself.

Like every other room in the palace, the Empress' wine cellar didn't seem to have been designed for mortal use: too grand, too dark, all the surfaces cold and slippery. Each cask was the size of a wagon, and they were stacked in deep columns, but in this immense room they still felt mortally insignificant.

Keleiros had arranged to meet them here, in what was clearly a private bolt-hole for him, to judge by the stacks of books and cushions piled on crates. Tal didn't know what to make of the four or five white doves who lived in the rafters, fluttering in the dark like huge moths, but Keleiros had put out a bowl of birdseed for them.

"Do you reckon he stole these?" said Tsereg, throwing themselves down on a pile of cushions.

"They're silk, so probably," said Tal, distracted. "He definitely stole *that*."

The scrying-bowl they had found in the House of Silence archive was sitting on one of the crates. The spiral patterns hammered into its dull surface gleamed even in the low light.

Tsereg shrugged. "Well, if it hasn't drained his blood by now, he's probably okay. Maybe I could try it—"

"You think he's making us wait on purpose?" said Tal hastily, keen to get them off the topic. "Something off about him."

"He's not a snake," said Tsereg.

"That doesn't mean he's a friend," said Tal.

Tsereg shrugged as if it was good enough for them.

"We have no idea who he is or what he really wants," said Tal. "Things don't just fall into your lap like this. People don't just turn up and offer to help, and if they do, they've got an agenda."

Tsereg scowled. "You helped me."

"Yeah, but as we've already established, I'm an idiot," said Tal.

"My mother says in the book that playing off your different enemies against each other is usually a good way to win, so it doesn't matter who he is."

"Of course she does," said Tal. "I thought your book was supposed to help. Isn't there anything useful in there?"

"Yeah, loads, it's really good," said Tsereg defensively. "Just . . . a lot of it's about skeletons. I think she thought I'd have masses of them lying around. Nothing about the God-Empress yet. This is why we need Keleiros. We need *information*."

They reached out as if to run a finger round the rim of the scrying-bowl, then stopped abruptly, their ears twitching at something Tal couldn't hear.

It was Keleiros, carrying a basket. Two of the doves flew down to greet him, and landed one on each shoulder.

Tal unfolded himself from the crate where he was sitting. "Listen," he said. "We want to help. But we need to know more about what you're planning."

A curious smile flickered at the corners of Keleiros' mouth. "Of course," he said eventually. "I wouldn't expect anything else—" He went still, and Tal followed his gaze to the scrying-bowl, which Tsereg was still peering at. "Have you two been going through *all* my things?"

"Nasty habit," said Tal, raising an eyebrow at Tsereg, who glowered back at him.

Keleiros didn't seem upset, exactly. He wrapped his hand in his sleeve to pick up the scrying-bowl, and put it out of reach on top of a stack of barrels. "Someone ought to have a stern talk with the pair of you about touching strange artefacts. You don't know where they've been."

There was a note of warning in his voice, and his ears had flicked straight up in displeasure. Strange to see this in such a young man, a face completely unmarked by stress or fear. Then any sense of danger was gone, and Keleiros returned to his basket.

"Palace livery for you both," he said. "You can't go on lurking about the underpalace. Plain sight is much safer."

Tal's uniform fit him surprisingly well, considering that Keleiros must have guessed at sizes. And, thank god, there was a pair of shoes for him too.

"Suits you," said Keleiros, offhand, and perhaps held Tal's gaze for a half second longer than necessary. Tal ignored it. Surely he was imagining it.

"I look like I've run away from the fucking circus," said Tsereg, looking disconsolately down at their outfit. The green palace tabard reached almost to their shins, and their hair escaped from the cap in billows.

Keleiros tried not to smile. Tsereg objected to the non-smile in strong terms. It wasn't lost on Tal that all this horseplay had allowed Keleiros to neatly sidestep explaining anything.

"What's the point of all this?" he said.

"So that you and Tsereg can attend the Midsummer Festival as palace servants," said Keleiros.

"I thought you said—"

"That I wanted to kill the God-Empress? Yes," said Keleiros. "What did you think that was going to entail, breaking into the throne room and sneaking up behind her with a big sword?"

Tal and Tsereg schooled their features.

"She is capable of healing almost any wound, almost instantaneously," said Keleiros. "We have to pick our moment, and I believe the Feast of Midsummer is our best shot. I will be attending alongside the Hand of the Empress."

"What, *really*?" said Tal. "Is Shuthmili in on this? I used to know her, maybe—"

"She is the Empress' creature now."

"About the Empress," said Tsereg. "You said she could heal wounds, but I was thinking what if we cut off her head?"

Keleiros' expression made Tal glad he hadn't had time to volunteer the same suggestion.

"So she can't even die?" said Tsereg, as if this were a personal failing of the Empress. "What do we do?" Tsereg was keeping Oranna's book very close, tucked under their jacket.

"Oh, no, I am quite certain she can die," said Keleiros, tossing the wine bottle from hand to hand. "But we will need an unconventional weapon. Talasseres, can you still handle a knife?"

Tal blinked. His full name sounded strange coming from Keleiros.

"I don't have one on me," he said.

"That won't be a problem," said Keleiros.

"And it's been a while, to be honest—"

"I have confidence in you," said Keleiros, and from within his jacket he produced a small dagger sheathed in a filigreed scabbard. It looked like a child's toy, much showier than Tal would ever have bothered with.

"Unsheathe it," said Keleiros.

Tal did so, thinking it was just as well to check the thing was actually sharp. A strange mixture of smells wafted from the scabbard: one part the electric blood-scent of magic and another part like perfume, austerely floral, both inviting and forbidding.

"As I said, not a conventional weapon," said Keleiros. "Try not to prick yourself with it."

"Got it," said Tal. He had used a poisoned blade before and felt it was more trouble than it was worth, but whatever.

"What about me?" said Tsereg.

For one blessed moment, Tal thought Keleiros might be about to tell Tsereg that their job was to stay hidden and not get killed, but instead he said:

"You're a mage, I think? Nothing like magic for causing a distraction. You and I will make something loud and diverting happen, and Tal will be on hand with the weapon."

All right, thought Tal, *so this is really happening.*

Up until now, the entire plan had seemed like a kind of game, something to keep Tsereg occupied while Tal tried to figure out what he was really going to do. Keleiros was quite serious, though, and Tal was in favour of any plan that didn't put a weapon in Tsereg's hands. He would be able to keep an eye on them, at least. And all he had to do was carry this special knife and stab Csorwe with it? Sure. Fine. No problem.

Keleiros was still talking, though. "We'll discuss this further, but you may not see a great deal of me between now and Midsummer, so I should mention . . . there is one other minor complication."

The casual way he said it made Tal's hackles rise. Nobody said *one other complication* like that unless they meant a gigantic fucking spanner in the works.

"The Empress is planning something for the festival of Midsummer. I don't know the details. She hasn't spoken of them even to her closest advisors. But on Midsummer's night, the world is going to change, and I quite like this world as it is. So we have this one chance and no other."

20

Kindly Bane

CHERENTHISSE STRODE INTO the infirmary wing of the palace and was met by a mortal medic and one of her junior officers.

"How is she?" she said, as they showed her into one of the private rooms. "Can she speak?"

"A little," said the medic.

A newly recovered Thousand Eye lay on the bed, her eyes open but bleary.

"Remind me where she was found?" said Cherenthisse.

"Aboard the wreck of the *Kindly Bane,* First Commander," said the officer. "No way to know who she was, I'm afraid. Her stasis circle had been buried in sand some distance from the ship, which accounts for why it took us so long to find her."

The majority of Cherenthisse's troops were those of the Thousand Eyes who had been in stasis aboard the *Blessed Awakening,* but over the past fifteen years they had recovered a few dozen more. As a matter of principle Cherenthisse met with each of the newly awakened, however busy she was, even now when the preparations for Midsummer occupied almost every waking hour. The Thousand Eyes had served loyally, through many lifetimes. This was the least they deserved from their First Commander.

She sat down beside the bed, a respectful distance from the Thousand Eye on the bed, and dismissed the others. She remembered the pain and confusion of her own awakening, and preferred to do this alone.

"Do you remember your name?" she said softly.

The Thousand Eye made a strangled noise, trying to speak.

"Take your time," said Cherenthisse. The impulse to take her hand was very strong, and Cherenthisse had to remind herself that it would be no comfort to the soldier on the bed, not yet.

The Thousand Eye coughed, doubling up with a painful tremor. "Thalarisse," she managed. "Eight-Five-Two."

Cherenthisse nodded, and marked it down on her tablet. Thalarisse,

Eight Hundred and Fifty-Second of the Thousand Eyes, woke again for the first time in three thousand years. Cherenthisse would see what could be found out about her, if any of her history had been preserved in the *Blessed Awakening*'s fragmentary records.

As Thalarisse struggled to marshal the fleshy tongue of her prey aspect and to make sense of her new helplessness, Cherenthisse introduced herself and began to explain what had happened, to her and to them all. The curse of Iriskavaal, the destruction of Echentyr, the loss of their true aspects. She paused. It usually took a few minutes for the full import of this to sink in, but none of the others would have to suffer as Cherenthisse had, with the knowledge of what was lost and without hope. She told Thalarisse of the sacrifice of the Most High Atharaisse, the dominion of the God-Empress, the new place of the Thousand Eyes in upholding her law.

"My ship—" Thalarisse managed. "Lost too?"

"Yes," said Cherenthisse. It was no good softening the blow. The warship *Kindly Bane* had been shot down by rebels one month before the cataclysm, lost in the Maze with all hands. They had recovered much from the wreck, but there had been only a few Thousand Eye officers in stasis on board. The rest of the crew were dead, and would stay so.

Thalarisse was silent a while longer.

"We have been given a second chance," said Cherenthisse. "We have a new God-Empress, a new chance to prove ourselves. We have been given a gift."

A fleeting expression of misery and terror contorted Thalarisse's face before she could suppress it. "I know my duty," she said.

"I know," said Cherenthisse. "You served bravely. You fought for many centuries. You have done what was asked of you."

"Injured before," said Thalarisse haltingly. "Many times. Hurts." The *Kindly Bane* had burnt, Cherenthisse recalled. The wreck was little more than a smear of black ash splashed across the abyssal plain.

"I know," said Cherenthisse. At Tsortanapan, on her first assignment, Cherenthisse had almost drowned in mud. She remembered the feeling of it clogging her mouth and nostrils, the panic and then the utter darkness.

"The gift we have been given is a choice," she said. "Fight for Echentyr again, and the strength of the goddess will be with you. But if you cannot—if you have given all you can—then we do not ask more than that. I can give you a peaceful end, and your memory will strengthen us."

There was a long pause. Thalarisse squeezed her eyes shut.

"I would fight," she said. "I would serve. But—not like this. Not in this form."

"I understand," said Cherenthisse.

This was part of the cost of what they were doing here. Some could not accept what the worlds had become. If they could not bear it—too revolted to be severed from their true aspect, too heartbroken by the destruction of Echentyr, or simply consumed by a soul-deep exhaustion after lifetimes spent fighting in vain—Cherenthisse could not blame them.

"It won't hurt?" said Thalarisse. The spark of hope in her eyes cut Cherenthisse like a knife.

"No, it won't," said Cherenthisse. She took her sheathed dagger from her belt and laid it on the table beside the bed. "The mercy of Iriskavaal. The kindly bane indeed." She smiled weakly at her own joke.

The God-Empress had granted Cherenthisse a private stock of the ancient venom for this purpose. It killed instantly and without pain.

"You don't have to decide at once," said Cherenthisse. "Take your time."

"No—First Commander—please. I know."

Cherenthisse touched Thalarisse's cheek. It was cold, damp with sweat.

"Everyone dead. All gone. I can't," said Thalarisse. "Please."

"You're certain?" she said, and got a look of such agonised assent that she felt a pang of guilt for asking.

"*Your will is just, beloved Lady,*" said Cherenthisse, and drew her dagger.

The blade was very sharp, with a faint iridescent sheen. A small nick was all it took, made delicately in Thalarisse's wrist. Death followed at once, like a veil drawn closed.

Cherenthisse brushed Thalarisse's hair back from her brow and closed her eyes.

Not everyone had the courage to struggle on through this diminished world. Thalarisse had needed rest, and deserved it. Once upon a time Cherenthisse had longed for rest herself, but she had found the strength to endure, and now—well, now she was First Commander of the Thousand Eyes, and all would be well, and rest would come when the great work was done. She could last that long.

The God-Empress was merciful. When Echentyr was born anew, those who endured in patience and loyalty would be reborn, restored to perfection, and Cherenthisse would be whole again. In the meantime Cherenthisse kept Thalarisse's vigil, as she kept it for all the dead.

She sighed, running her hands back through her hair. It was never easy, but at least there was a purity in it. Dealing with Thalarisse had not made her feel tainted and dishonourable, as this next meeting certainly would.

She got back to her office to find Keleiros Lenarai already waiting there.

"You're walking a fine line, Lenarai," she said.

"Am I? Usually, I suppose," he said.

"I asked you to keep me informed of the Hand of the Empress' activities. Not to *seduce* her."

"She's a very lonely woman," he said, with a hint of a smile.

Prey coupling had always been a rather unclean topic, and all these years in the shape of prey had brought Cherenthisse no closer to understanding the appeal of an activity that sounded messy and undignified. Some among the Thousand Eyes had begun to experiment, but Cherenthisse felt that was their own business. They all had to cope with this new world as best they could, and if they found some aberrant solace in their prey aspects, then who was Cherenthisse to judge?

Still. She did not like Keleiros Lenarai's faintly mocking expression, and she did not like the idea that there might be some region of Shuthmili's motivations that she hadn't fully charted.

"She may be more likely to confide in you," said Cherenthisse.

"You'll be the first to know if she does, First Commander," he said. "But I wanted to tell you, there is *something* that's been bothering me."

Cherenthisse stalked into the Turret of the Hand without knocking and found Shuthmili sitting by the fire, staring into a cup of coffee. She looked translucent with exhaustion, pale as a shed husk of skin. Cherenthisse's lip curled. Hollow, that was right.

"So, here's what I'm wondering, Shuthmili," said Cherenthisse.

Shuthmili looked up vaguely. "Oh, First Commander," she said. Her eyes were unfocused. Cherenthisse wondered if this, like so much else, was a pose. "What brings you here?"

"So," said Cherenthisse, standing over her. Shuthmili did not rise, which aggravated Cherenthisse still further. "Suppose I know who the saboteur is."

It had all made sense. She could have kicked herself for failing to see it sooner. The translator glyphs, the prison wards, and possibly worse. At this point she would believe Shuthmili capable of anything. Behind Keleiros' self-satisfaction she had seen real fear of his supposed mistress.

"I am supposing," said Shuthmili. She didn't sound worried, only bored and tired as always, as though Cherenthisse were a hatchling that she tolerated only because it was easier than putting her out of the way. Cherenthisse crackled with fresh anger. "Go on."

"Suppose I don't yet have hard proof," said Cherenthisse. "Do you think I should wait and see if they slip up, or should I just kill them before they can make a mistake?"

Cherenthisse had brought her sword. She meant it.

"Are those your only choices?" said Shuthmili. "I mean, *nothing, or else murder* is a very Thousand Eyes approach—"

"Do you have other suggestions?" said Cherenthisse.

"Well. I certainly don't recommend confronting the object of your obsession, particularly if the two of you are alone in a confined space and the other significantly outmatches you," said Shuthmili, languidly. "Interrogate your feelings, Cherenthisse. As I'm sure one learns in snake school, emotion is weakness. Has it occurred to you that what you are experiencing is not suspicion but jealousy?"

Cherenthisse shrugged. She could tell Shuthmili was trying to rile her, but her anger had crystallised into something pure and unbreakable. Knowing what she knew now, Shuthmili had nothing to hold over her.

"I suggest," Shuthmili went on, "That you focus on being the very best little soldier you can be, and don't compare yourself to others. Concentrate on your own achievements. What makes you *you*? What do you have that nobody else has?" She gave Cherenthisse a smile whose sweetness rang utterly false. "I'm sure there's something."

Cherenthisse still said nothing. Her mistake in the past had been to react to this kind of needling, to let it throw her off course. Her silence seemed to unsettle Shuthmili, who tried a different tack.

"I know you do not trust me, Commander," said Shuthmili. "But I assure you, and the Empress knows it, that all I have ever wanted is to share a place at that table, to be trusted as you are trusted. Let's put this aside. Surely you've had enough of fighting like children?"

"Fighting?" said Cherenthisse. "Who's fighting? I came to ask your advice."

Shuthmili rolled her eyes. "What's brought this on, Cherenthisse?

You've been accusing me of treason about once a year for the past decade, and you've never had the guts to do more than threaten to tell the Empress. What makes you think you're right this time?"

Cherenthisse took her time over this next bit, savouring the moment of her triumph.

"Keleiros," she said.

Shuthmili rose, and there was no vagueness in her eyes now. They were hard and black as beads of onyx.

"What have you done to Keleiros?" she said. She tried to keep up that languid tone, but Cherenthisse could hear the cracks in it now. She sounded genuinely angry. Perhaps she really did care for the secretary.

"He came to me," said Cherenthisse. "He told me what you've been up to. Profaning the wards."

"And does he have any proof?"

"Would I tell you if I did? Do you really think I'm that stupid?" said Cherenthisse. She had all the proof she needed in her pocket. The God-Empress would see that.

Shuthmili seemed to make an effort to restrain herself, and then— something Cherenthisse could not recall ever seeing before—that restraint failed. "Yes," she said, quite simply.

Cherenthisse felt a flush rise to her cheeks, but she held steady. Shuthmili stared at her, open loathing contorting her features. This was new. If Cherenthisse hadn't felt so certain of that bright diamond of rage that burnt in her heart, she might even have been alarmed.

"You know what I wonder about *you*," said Shuthmili, almost spitting the words. Her eyes were wide as though startled by the venom spilling out of her, but once a person lost control, it was hard to stop. "When you're off duty, do you ever read? Do you enjoy long walks on the beach? What is it that makes life worth living for you?"

"None of your business," said Cherenthisse. "Still trying to make me lose my temper? As if it'll help you?" It was almost working. The sheer calculated rudeness of it. Shuthmili ought to be afraid and ashamed. She was in Cherenthisse's power now, even if she didn't realise how much, and she ought to show some respect.

"Do you lie on your bunk in the dark and think about drowning people?" said Shuthmili. "I suppose there's no accounting for taste, but I think I'd get bored."

"No. I serve the Empress. I don't need *distractions*," said Cherenthisse. She thought of Keleiros, and her lip curled. Shuthmili had always tried to seem so aloof, so detached from mortal things, but she was prey, tangled in base instincts like all the rest. How had Cherenthisse let this prey creature manipulate her for so long? She couldn't believe how long she had been taken in.

"This is what fascinates me," said Shuthmili. "What is it that makes you think our beloved Empress cares for you personally? Why are some people so keen to strap themselves to the wheel of whatever megalomaniac can treat them worst? I suppose what I'm trying to say is . . . who hurt you, First Commander?"

Cherenthisse moved without knowing it, and hardly felt the impact. The next thing she knew, Shuthmili was thrown back across her chair, limbs awkwardly askew. Blood dripped from her nose to her chin, splattered across the arm of the chair.

Cherenthisse grabbed Shuthmili's head by the braid and pulled her upright, leaning in close to hiss.

"Talk about her like that again, and I'll break more than your nose."

The potential of the moment sang in Cherenthisse's blood. They'd never come to open violence before. It might really be this easy. Shuthmili wasn't even fighting back. Cherenthisse didn't know what she might do next.

"This is extremely forward of you, First Commander," said Shuthmili coldly. She managed to sound almost calm. Blood dripped down her chin and onto the neckline of her gown. "Get your hands off me, or I will start to take it the wrong way."

Cherenthisse let go. The moment soured. Solid certainty began to crack under her feet. Her heart pounded in her head, no longer energising but sickening.

Shuthmili stepped back out of reach, dabbing at her bloody nose with one hand.

"Fine. Let's take this to the Empress, if you're so certain," said Shuthmili. "Otherwise, get out of my quarters."

Shuthmili's nose was still bleeding by the time they reached the throne room. Cherenthisse was certain she was doing it on purpose.

That afternoon the throne room had opened to display a map of the imperial territories. It was set into the floor, inlaid in slivers of agate and chalcedony, bounded in gold. The Empress stood over it, wreathed as always in the Mantle, layers of translucent matter that made her look like a statue, as though she had risen up herself from the glossy surface of the map.

Her eyes were fixed dreamily on the expanse of jasper which represented the Speechless Sea. She was always so beautiful, a changeless and perfect beauty that was all of a piece with an unending weariness. Cherenthisse felt a tightness in her chest, a yearning that felt very much like her yearning for Echentyr.

The God-Empress looked up at Shuthmili and Cherenthisse as they entered, and her lips curved up in distant amusement, which did not so much cut through her weariness as cast new light upon it.

"Majesty, the saboteur—" Cherenthisse began.

"I would like to lodge a complaint against First Commander Cherenthisse, Majesty," said Shuthmili coolly, speaking over Cherenthisse as though she had not heard her.

"Perhaps one of you had better begin at the beginning," said the God-Empress, still smiling. She seemed almost mortal, though in Cherenthisse's vague recollection, the mortal Csorwe had never looked so lovely.

"Oh, by all means, explain yourself," said Shuthmili sourly.

Cherenthisse explained what Keleiros had told her, concluding, "And finally, my informant tells me that this morning he followed the Hand to one of the outer security bounds and observed her produce a bottle of some reagent, which she poured upon the wards and rubbed away certain among them with a cloth."

"Yes, and I suppose he heard me say to myself, *Ha ha, what a lovely morning for crime?*" said Shuthmili. "This is ludicrous. Ma'am, this morning, as you know, I was receiving delegates for the Feast. Niranthe Charossa can confirm it, if you're really thinking of giving this any credence."

"My informant—"

"First Commander Cherenthisse does not explain that her informant is my companion Keleiros Lenarai," said Shuthmili. "Keleiros has been upset with me recently, for reasons I don't entirely comprehend. I have no doubt this is his attempt to cause trouble for me."

For a moment all Cherenthisse could do was stare at her. She sounded entirely composed, despite the blood speckling the front of her dress. There was no trace of the anger Cherenthisse had noticed earlier. There was something Cherenthisse had missed. Something was going wrong, and she had hardly even had a chance to put her case across.

The Empress no longer looked particularly amused. "We have better things to occupy our time than mortal squabbling. Cherenthisse, did thy informant give thee anything in the way of proof?"

"Yes!" said Cherenthisse, feeling her way back to solid ground once more. She had the bottle Keleiros had given her, a small, insistent weight in her coat pocket. She was right. Shuthmili was lying. She produced the vial. "This is the reagent she used."

"Let me see that," said Shuthmili irritably, reaching for it. Cherenthisse held it away from her.

"My informant was able to retrieve it from her desk when she returned to her office," Cherenthisse went on.

"Is that so," said Shuthmili. "For heaven's sake, First Commander, how can you expect me to defend myself if you won't let me see the evidence? That is certainly one of my reagent vials, but I have no idea—" She swiped for the bottle again, and Cherenthisse jerked it back. "You are behaving like a *child*," she said, and tried once more to snatch it. Cherenthisse felt the sharp, insistent jab of magic trying to unbalance her. She tightened her grip on the bottle, but it was too late.

The vial slipped from her hands and shattered on the stone map, splashing the jasper desert with blood.

For a moment, Cherenthisse just stared at it. "This is a blatant attempt to destroy the evidence, Majesty," she managed. Blood trickled into the crevices of the map, making red rivers.

"I'm not the one who dropped it!" said Shuthmili. "Majesty, you see what this is—Cherenthisse knows she does not have a leg to stand on. This is entirely manufactured. I don't believe you even spoke to Keleiros," she added, darting Cherenthisse a poisonous glance. "You must have stolen the vial from my office yourself."

"I—" said Cherenthisse.

"Perhaps we should bring Keleiros up and see what he says about it," said Shuthmili.

The God-Empress sighed. "No, that will not be necessary. Cherenthisse is not a liar. We are inclined to blame the mortal boy for this. Let him be put to death in whatever way seems best and let us hear no more of this."

Cherenthisse hardly heard Shuthmili's objections. She wasn't a liar. She had clung to her faith, even in this place of liars and false images. The God-Empress understood that her heart was still true. Shuthmili was irrelevant. She was a mortal, and no doubt a traitor, but the God-Empress saw all things as they truly were.

"Majesty, you have always permitted me to discipline my staff as I see fit," Shuthmili was saying. "Keleiros meant nothing by this, I am sure."

"He meant to deceive us," said the Empress. "We know he is dear to thee, but a traitor cannot be pardoned."

"Dear to me—" said Shuthmili.

Cherenthisse heard the ripple in her composure and smiled to herself. She did not doubt that Shuthmili had manufactured this situation some-how. Perhaps she and Keleiros had stitched it up between them. She had always longed to see something blow up in Shuthmili's face.

"There are so few things that are dear to me," said Shuthmili, controlling herself. "In your mercy and your wisdom, I would request that you leave me one."

The Empress reached for Shuthmili and carefully dabbed at her face with the corner of her sleeve, cleaning away the blood that had dried there. Shuthmili went very still, not even blinking.

"Why should such a small thing matter so greatly to thee?" said the Empress softly. "Have we not given thee all that ever thou desired? Power, and knowledge, and liberty, and the esteem of all as our Hand. Is that not sufficient?"

"It is certainly far more than I deserve," said Shuthmili. Her voice caught again.

The Empress' smile faded. She looked bewildered, as if she had been presented with a wailing infant and was not sure what to do with it.

"He meant to turn us against thee, little one," said the Empress. "Out of jealousy, no doubt. It is not seemly for thee to beg for such a life."

"Seemly or not," said Shuthmili. She swallowed, seeming to gather herself. "You know what it is to forgive treason, ma'am. Echentyr turned against you, and even so, the great work—"

"Yes," said the God-Empress. "Very well. Deal with Keleiros as thou wilt. But leave us now. We would have words with Cherenthisse."

Shuthmili murmured her thanks and left. For once, Cherenthisse almost wished she hadn't. She didn't know whether she was pleased or angry or disappointed, and being left alone with the God-Empress was like looking directly into the sun.

Somewhat to her relief, the God-Empress did not immediately say anything, but wandered away from the throne. The splash of blood had drained away into the floor, and the shards of glass were gone as if they had never been. The Empress shed her outer robe, inspecting the sleeve which was now stained with Shuthmili's blood.

"There is little liking between Shuthmili and thee," the Empress reflected.

"No, ma'am," said Cherenthisse. The Empress understood she was not a liar. "I have done my best, but—"

"But?"

"She isn't one of us, ma'am," said Cherenthisse, because to complain about Shuthmili's personality did seem immature. "She talks well, about the great work and the return of the empire, but she can have no personal stake in the matter. She is faithless to her own country."

"Thou wouldst rather an honest Qarsazhi patriot than a turncoat on our side."

"Well, I—yes," said Cherenthisse. She thought she could have respected Shuthmili as an enemy. Having to work with her sullied them both.

"She is crafty and tenacious," said the Empress. "Thou art a true lodestone. We need metals of both tempers."

"Thank you, Majesty," said Cherenthisse, feeling herself blush. "All the same, there is something about her that shifts. I do not understand her."

"Thou hast the right of it in one respect," said the Empress. She paused, running a fingertip over the diamond tusk. By now even the tusks suited her, Cherenthisse reflected, close enough to fangs that they seemed perfectly fitting. "Her loyalty is all to us, to *me*, for love of the vessel, and thou needst not doubt it. She will die before she sees us harmed."

"As any among the Thousand Eyes would," said Cherenthisse, feeling she ought to stand up for her own people. Willingness to die for the God-Empress was not a unique quality, after all. "Our loyalty is ever undimmed."

"Of course," said the Empress. "But—as thou hast observed—she has no true commitment to the restoration of Echentyr. Come, Cherenthisse, we would show something to thee."

She took Cherenthisse's hand in hers, cool and surprisingly strong, and the palace shifted around them. An archway opened, swallowed them up, closed behind them, and Cherenthisse found herself in a vast greenhouse.

High overhead, a dome of paned glass glittered like a wasp's wing. The air was thick with the cool metallic smell of wet soil, the heavy perfume of blossoms on the brink of overripeness, the sharp astringence of sap. Vivid mosses blanketed the walls, looking soft enough to sink into. Trees swelled with fruit, pink and gold like small suns glowing among the leaves.

Cherenthisse felt tears start in her eyes. She couldn't at once tell why, and then:

"It's home," she said. "It's Echentyr." She had hunted among forests of such trees on her own estate. Here were the meadow grasses, with their nodding violet flowers—there were the blue-green creepers which had grown on the walls of the hatchery. All this life which had died with their world.

"Yes," said the Empress. The light that came in through the glass roof rippled over her face like sunlight on deep water.

"*How?*" said Cherenthisse, wiping her eyes fiercely with her knuckles.

"A cache of seeds aboard the *Blessed Awakening*. Shuthmili has been of assistance. Though she has never visited this place," the Empress added, and Cherenthisse's heart swelled.

The Empress plucked a fruit from one of the trees and handed it to Cherenthisse as if this impossible treasure were nothing at all.

Cherenthisse had eaten these fruits back at the hatchery: one of the few pleasures she remembered from that time, all the more clearly because the demands of her training had otherwise been so bleak. She peeled it herself, watching her strange little hands carry out the task with the ease of years of practice.

"Back in the hatchery a servant would have done this," she said. She hadn't intended to speak it out loud, but the Empress did not seem to mind.

She ate a segment of the fruit and had to stop. The sharp sweetness was almost too much for her, the flood of memories even sharper.

The Empress picked another fruit for herself and began peeling it. She wore claws of polished jade on her fingertips, and they cut through the peel like knives.

"There were a hundred of us in my year," said Cherenthisse. "A dozen of us left by graduation."

"Our world could be a merciless place, could it not?"

"We were tempered in fire, ma'am," said Cherenthisse.

"A very correct formulation," said the Empress. She pulled away a coil of white pith and twirled it around her index finger. "Echentyr asked so much of thee. So very much."

Unwillingly Cherenthisse recalled the death of Thalarisse, and of all the others who had been unable to face the future.

"Your will is just, beloved lady," she repeated, without thinking.

"Nevertheless . . ." said the Empress. "Doubt never troubles thee?"

It sounded almost as if she were asking for reassurance. Cherenthisse's every instinct was to offer it, but the Empress deserved her honesty.

"I have doubts," said Cherenthisse. "I doubt sometimes whether the price is too high. Whether our people can keep paying it, when they have already paid so dearly. Whether we will have the strength to carry through to the end. Whether it can be done at all. But a noble cause *does* demand much. I was proud to serve Echentyr and to serve you, and I am still proud."

The Empress let another loop of peel fall from her hand. "I am glad," she said, and caught Cherenthisse's eye with a gleam of delight. Her unhappiness was gone, almost as if it had been a mask. She held up the peeled fruit in one hand, a translucent globe like a small shining world, and bit into it with evident relish.

Cherenthisse realised, with mingled relief and disappointment, that it had been a test, and that she had passed.

"We will show thee what we truly brought thee here to see," said the Empress, when she had finished eating, and led her further into the garden.

Here they were almost in darkness, under the shade of great broad-leaved trees. It was eerie to stand in a forest without wind, without the sound of birds. Cherenthisse felt as though she had walked into a tapestry. In the place of deepest shade was a great stone basin, freckled with moss and brimming with dark water. The surface of the water was almost entirely covered with giant water lilies, each one large enough for Cherenthisse to curl up inside it.

"The water lilies of Saar-in-Tachthyr were sacred to us," said the Empress. "From their nectar the priests distilled a swift poison, a killing agent of tremendous purity and gentleness. It destroyed without pain. It was said that its victims experienced great joy in the moment of death. It was reserved for the most perfect sacrifices. The highest form of the kindly bane."

The water lilies floated like pale moons. Knowing that each one was freighted with poison did not diminish their beauty.

"Thou knowest not *whether it can be done at all*," said the Empress. "It is true that to regenerate a blighted world is a very great magic, but most certainly it can be done. And it will require a truly great sacrifice."

All at once they were back in the familiar throne room. Cherenthisse felt dizzy, and not only from the sudden shift.

"What are you asking of me, ma'am?" she said, and yet she saw now that it had been inevitable, that all this talk of doubt and pride had led to this moment. That it was her death which was called for.

To Cherenthisse's great shame, there was a part of her which did not welcome the honour. A large part. In fact, she did not want to die at all. It would be a noble cause to restore Echentyr, yes, but she had always imagined she would be returned to her true aspect, she would see the orchards and the rivers for herself again, she would play a part in putting it all back as it had been.

And yet, if her goddess asked it of her, she could not decline. Would she fail her people and her world, even if it meant she would never see them again? Of course not. *I am a true lodestone.*

The Empress' eyes widened, gold as the pollen at the heart of a lily. "Oh, Cherenthisse. Oh, my dear. Best of all the daughters of our dominion. No. Thou wilt taste the fruit of victory. We would not ask this sacrifice of thee. Besides, thy life alone would not suffice, though we doubt not thou wouldst give it gladly. The resurrection of Echentyr demands the blood of this vassal world."

21

Midsummer's Night

IN THE HOURS before the Midsummer Feast, the walls receded and the throne room of the God-Empress opened like a bud. Great chandeliers, like fireworks stilled in motion, hung in rows, turning the vaulted ceiling as dark and impenetrable as the night sky.

Tal's palace uniform made him almost invisible, just as he remembered from his days as Sethennai's bodyguard. The guests' eyes flicked past him, and from time to time someone gave him a tray of drinks to carry round.

Between the chandeliers, tapestry banners wafted. To look at them directly, the banners were blank, shifting, colourless, gauzy, like breeze given form—but when you saw them from the corner of your eye, each one showed a scene woven in rich colour and deep shade. All of them were scenes of cruelty, though it was sometimes hard to tell victim from torturer, weapon from limb, blood from ornament. These probably had something significant to say about the long and gory history of the God-Empress. Tal just kept his head down and tried not to look at them.

Despite the scale of it all, there was still something dark and narrow about the place. Tal couldn't place it. There weren't enough guests to fill the cavernous space, not enough light to extinguish the stains of shadow that crept down from the vaults. He had never felt claustrophobic in such an open space before.

Long tables stood around the edges of the room, already laid for the banquet: heaps of cakes and sweetmeats, silver bowls overflowing with candied fruit and nuts, crystal-glass decanters of wine, an enamel punch bowl of shaved ice jewelled with pomegranate seeds, gleaming piles of grapes and apricots and tangerines. It was more food than Tal had seen in one place for years. None of the guests were eating or drinking yet, waiting for the entrance of the God-Empress.

The tables surrounded an open floor where the guests milled around talking. There were hundreds of them, mostly Tlaanthothei but plenty of

Oshaaru and others too, all dressed up in their finery. They reminded Tal of dolls wrapped in rolls of silk and propped upright on spindles, spinning in empty spirals from one conversation to another. The room was filled with a low and uneasy buzz of chatter. Perhaps the crowds were waiting to see what kind of mood the Empress was in when she appeared.

"Resin wine, ma'am?" said Tal, holding out a tray to an elderly Tlaan-thothei woman who stood among several hangers-on in a great ceremonial monster of a gown.

"Thanks," she said absently, and took a glass. Tal only caught sight of her face as he was walking away. It was his mother. He had known she might be here, but he hadn't been prepared for how old she was, how gaunt and grey. She was too frail and thin for the gown she was wearing.

He should have felt something. Some kind of protective instinct. Some kind of yearning to go and talk to her, even though he was already walking away as fast as he could. Instead, nothing. Almost a bit of a relief. If he had wanted confirmation that the Charossai had no more hold on him, here it was. He glanced back, but the crowds had moved, and a long row of shuffling snake cultists had severed her from view. Their masks nodded mockingly, huge painted eyes staring at nothing.

He stalked on through the crowds, resisting the urge to elbow someone, and then a path opened and he was standing in front of a cylinder of green glass, wider than his arm span and twice as tall as he was.

The cylinder was surrounded by urns of flowers and fruit as if it were a sculpture to be admired. Inside it was the pickled corpse of Belthandros Sethennai.

Sethennai's hair floated out around his head in a dark halo. The green glass turned his skin a burnt and sickly shade. His face hadn't changed, exactly, hadn't bloated in death, but his expression was slack and his eyes were wide and staring. He looked as he had never looked in life, vacant and uncomprehending.

Tal looked up at the body with much the same expression.

If Tal had ever wondered how he'd feel to see Sethennai again, he would have said he'd be angry. Furious with the way Sethennai had treated him, and the way he'd fucked off and died before Tal could ever tell him what he really thought of him.

He didn't expect this wave of grief. He had never been so happy as he'd been with Sethennai when it was good, when he had really thought that this extraordinary person had noticed him, had laughed at his stupid jokes, had held him and looked at him as if he was worth something.

Oh, god. I loved him, he thought. *I really did.*

He'd fooled himself into thinking it had been anything else. He'd idolised him. It had been a twenty-year-old's obsession, never reciprocated. Something pretty pathetic and sad, all things considered. Sethennai had done it all on purpose. Sethennai had done it all by accident—

—and all that was probably still true, and yet. That twinge of misery, deep in his chest, as if the wound had closed around the knife, but now, *now,* after all these years, someone had taken the handle and given it a twist.

He turned away, no longer hesitating to shove his way through the crowd, and dropped the tray on the nearest table. If anyone noticed he was behaving oddly for a servant, they didn't say anything. He reached for a jug of water and poured himself a glass, hoping it might pull him together.

Get a grip, Talasseres! Don't blow this!

Eventually the cold water seemed to do its job. He picked up the tray and turned back toward the floor, except that everyone seemed to have turned toward the immense double doors at the far end of the throne room. They opened slowly, with a sound like the stone slab sliding off a sarcophagus, and two people walked in.

One of them was Shuthmili. Her dress was a plain dark blue, austere by comparison with the other guests. It left you no doubt that she was an unobtrusively sheathed weapon. She wore a pair of spiked gauntlets, and she carried herself as if she was thinking all the time about where she could hide your body.

It was easier if you pretended she was someone else, no more herself anymore than Csorwe was Csorwe. Keleiros was right, and Shuthmili had been clear enough about it herself. She had made her choice. She was the Hand of the Empress, just another monster who'd taken away one of his friends. Just another body floating in a jar, laughing at him.

At her side, dressed in matching blue-purple and looking like a freshly picked violet, was Keleiros Lenarai. He was holding on firmly to Shuthmili's arm, huge dark eyes gazing out across the throne room. Tal was pretty certain the expression of starstruck amazement was feigned. The young man they'd met in the library hadn't seemed capable of being startled by much. Well, no time to think about that now. He had a job to do.

Keleiros' appearance meant that the clock was ticking on the diversion.

There was no sign of Tsereg so far, but they could have been hiding out of sight, or masked like the snake cultists. Only a few minutes now until the God-Empress showed up.

The unconventional knife was still tucked into his jacket. It was heavy for such a small blade, hard up against his ribs.

He wasn't sure how he was going to kill Csorwe with it. It had been surprisingly difficult to think about. A cut throat was quick, or through the eye into the brain, but it might be easier if he didn't actually have to look at her stupid face.

He brushed his hand over the handle of the knife and felt an odd rustling. There was a scrap of paper in the pocket. He unfolded it and read in growing alarm:

> do not panic!!! bit of a change of plan
> i know what im doing. sorry i didnt tell you but you would of been weird about it
> everythings fine just do the plan like we said but dont trust kelearos!!!
> tsereg x

A familiar dread came over him, as if it had been with him all along and only just put a name to the tightness in his chest, the cold weight in his belly.

No sign of Tsereg anywhere. What were they *doing*?

I didn't trust him from the start, you idiot! he thought. *You were the one who trusted him!*

Although, if Tal was honest with himself, it *had* been a relief to have someone else making the decisions for a change, to be given clear instructions to follow. He'd forgotten the other side of that, which was having no choice and being kept in the dark.

Not for the first time in his life, Tal had the sense that something was about to go horribly wrong.

Shuthmili was not in good spirits for a party, for one thing because she disliked parties, and for another because she had been in the throne room in the small hours, covertly weakening the bounds around the jar according to Belthandros' instructions.

How pleasant it would be, to float mindlessly in a jar of slightly warm water, nourished intravenously. When this was over and Zinandour claimed her body, she thought she would go to that oblivion gladly. At least then she wouldn't have to attend state functions.

Belthandros appeared just in time to accompany her into the throne room. He looked dazed. His smile was flimsier than usual, like a pane of distorting glass. When he was close enough to touch, she sensed distress like a contaminant in his bloodstream. His pulse fluttered, fast and irregular.

PERHAPS HIS PRESENCE STRESSES THE VESSEL, said Zinandour. ALL TOO LIKELY THE POSSESSION IS FAILING. That would make sense. Shuthmili doubted he had been taking good care of Keleiros. All the more reason to get this over with.

They made a slow circuit of the room, and Shuthmili greeted the assembled aristocrats with as much chilly menace as she could summon, struggling to remember their names.

Belthandros hung on her arm, uncharacteristically silent. He seemed to have lent Keleiros a persona of silent, staring astonishment, which was inoffensive but gave Shuthmili the sense of steering deadweight. He was wearing some kind of floral cologne, not intrusive but compelling and rather unlike him.

They glided past the jar where Belthandros' body was preserved, and she was careful not to look round at it, not to show any interest at all. This was easier than she'd expected: as they passed the jar, she felt Keleiros' vitals spike, a shock so vivid she might have thought he was going into seizure. Belthandros had said it was sentiment that attached him to his old body: perhaps he'd underestimated the shock of seeing himself dead.

"Ah, Keleiros!" came a voice from one side, before she could dwell on it further. She spun round, turning her iciest gaze upon the speaker. It was the Lenarai patriarch, greeting what he presumably thought was some kind of grandson. The old man faltered. "Are you quite all right, my boy?"

Blood was trickling from Keleiros' nose and down his upper lip, leaving a dark and sluggish trail. Shuthmili remembered Belthandros eating the dove's heart and felt newly nauseous.

"Uh?" he said, blinking huge eyes as if struggling to focus on the old man.

Shuthmili made an impatient noise, withdrew a handkerchief from her pocket, and dabbed away the blood. This was, she hoped, in keeping with their roles.

"If the palace has so weakened my nephew's constitution," said the old man, extremely daring, "perhaps a rest cure at the Lenarai estate? You would be welcome also, of course, my lady—"

She had misjudged Lenarai, not reckoning he was the kind of person who would risk himself like this, and somehow the misjudgment made her feel sicker than ever. Even if this was all a cruel sham of Belthandros' devising, they had hurt Keleiros worse than the palace ever could, perhaps broken him forever.

"The invitation is noted," she said. Lenarai flinched. "And appreciated," she added, cursing herself for a softhearted imbecile. She hurried away from him as soon as she could, leading Belthandros to a quieter corner.

"What are you doing?" she muttered. "What is this?"

He stared at her, eyes wide and dull with pain, and clearly tried to speak. The words seemed to melt as he spoke them, fusing into a jagged unintelligible mass.

"Is this meant to happen?" she said. "*Talk* to me, Belthandros."

She managed to get him into a chair and pressed her fingers ungently to his throat. His heart raced. Sweat glittered on his forehead. He was shaking now, more than just a tremor. She had to hold him still to get a better look at his eyes. It was hard to tell what she was seeing, like trying to count the legs of a panicked insect, but it was clear enough that the pupils were hideously dilated, seeming to overspill the narrow ring of iris that bound them in.

"What *is* this?" she hissed. He just stared at her, opening his mouth in a way that suggested he was trying to speak, but could produce only a choked yelp.

Zinandour must be right, and the possession was failing. Either that, or someone had poisoned him with something slow-acting and nasty.

She pressed a hand to his sternum and did what she could for Keleiros' body, at least, steadying and soothing, repairing the damage as far as she could, trying to relieve the pressure on his heart and brain. The rest she could fix later. Gradually his body went quiet. The pattern of the damage was strange, ebbing and returning. It had to be poison.

Keleiros' breath smelled of lilies. She had taken it for perfume, but it was coming from his own body. Perhaps if Belthandros had found some secret cache of Echentyri venom while he was exploring the palace—but he wouldn't be stupid enough to touch it. Somebody must have poisoned him deliberately. Who could have done it? She could think of plenty of people who might want Belthandros incapacitated, but nobody knew who he was, and who on earth would poison Keleiros?

"Did someone give you something to eat?" she said.

He looked up at her and said, in a painful whisper, "Where am I, ma'am?"

Keleiros Lenarai's dry mouth. Keleiros Lenarai's bewildered eyes. Keleiros Lenarai's mortal terror.

Shuthmili brushed his hair back from his forehead and found the diadem broken in two pieces.

"Oh, that *bastard*," she said.

Whatever Belthandros was up to, he wasn't here. He had poisoned his own vessel and left. Was he already in the bloody jar?

"Listen to me, Keleiros," she said, glancing back over her shoulder. Nobody had noticed Keleiros' illness, or else they were exercising the valuable survival skill of studiously pretending that nothing awful was happening. "Everything's going to be fine. Your grandfather's going to take you home, all right? I just need you to hold it together for two minutes, and—"

At this point, the grand double doors which had formed like fresh buds at the far end of the throne room opened with a sonorous clang and the Empress' retinue entered. Cherenthisse led them, her armour gleaming like polished jet. Behind her, two of the Thousand Eyes carried their banner. It was emblazoned with the Empress' crest, and the motto LOYALTY UNDIMMED, truly one of the phrases Shuthmili had come to hate most in the world.

After her retinue came the God-Empress. She was dressed in a gown constructed from translucent scales of jade, as if a suit of armour had become malleable and flowed like silk. Her face shone with some unfathomable triumph, and in that moment she did not look like Csorwe even a little.

Cherenthisse held a silver wine jug and a chalice, and the Thousand Eyes who followed her carried identical apparatus. Dozens of them. Odd, for the Empress' honour guard to double as waiting staff, thought Shuthmili distractedly.

The guests began to move to the sides, forming into two columns, facing each other. Shuthmili and Keleiros were pulled along with the rest, and bowed along with them as the Thousand Eyes processed down the centre of the throne room, handing out cups and pouring wine. The room reshaped itself, forming a kind of aisle, with the jar containing Sethennai's body standing at the far end and a table beneath it like a sacrificial altar.

The Thousand Eyes fell into formation, and the God-Empress followed them down toward it. The train of her gown rattled on the tiles like wind on rough sand.

Cherenthisse and her people moved down the lines, passing out the chalices. Cherenthisse herself handed cups to Shuthmili and Keleiros, solemnly, as though this were part of some obscure sacrament. Another Thousand Eye poured a thin stream of black wine into Shuthmili's cup.

"What is this?" Shuthmili mouthed at Cherenthisse. Cherenthisse was impassive. There was to be a toast, presumably. But Shuthmili had been briefed on every detail of the ceremony that was to follow, and she had been told nothing about this.

Keleiros' hand shook as they poured wine into his cup, slopping some of the liquid down the front of his clothes.

Shuthmili mopped at him with her sleeve, desperately trying to keep a semblance of order. Something was going wrong. Belthandros had lied to her, one way or another. None of this had been part of the plan they'd discussed.

Her sleeve came away smelling strongly of that same white-lily scent, somehow overpowering the sharp smell of the wine. She raised her own cup to her lips and sniffed it.

THE KINDLY BANE, said Zinandour, with a sudden flash of alarm so vivid that Shuthmili nearly dropped her own cup. WE ARE DECEIVED!

"Keleiros," she hissed. "Keleiros, don't drink that. It's poisoned—they all must be poisoned—"

There was no sign of Tsereg anywhere at the party. Maybe they'd run off to some other part of the palace, with some other stupid secret plan. Or maybe they'd already been caught, and the Thousand Eyes were already interrogating them, or maybe they were already dead. For all that he'd warned them, he'd almost forgotten it was a possibility. Tsereg acted as if faith and courage really could save you, and he'd somehow started to believe it.

He scanned the crowd, no longer making any kind of effort to look like a servant. He hardly heard the double doors opening, but he found himself drawn into the lines of people as they began to form up for the arrival of the God-Empress.

Tal had never seen the God-Empress in person, not since the last few moments in the temple at Saar-in-Tachthyr. He could feel the pressure of her arrival as a pain in his inner ears, a headache insinuating its roots into the joints of his skull. He kept his eyes down. If he looked up and saw Csorwe like this, clean and polished and stately, it would be like watching her die. He'd been an idiot for imagining he could keep Tsereg safe.

The God-Empress took her place, and the Thousand Eyes formed up around her, smoothly correct, looking like the pieces of a machine which had at last been put together correctly as intended.

Someone presented Tal with a cup and poured wine into it, and he took it mechanically.

"We welcome our loyal subjects," said the Empress. "Representatives from all our territories, from every part of this new empire. We come together to remember the world that was. Still, to remember is not enough. Here, in Tlaanthothe-That-Was, Echentyr will be born anew."

There was a cheer with every appearance of enthusiasm. The diversion was meant to happen any minute now. Keleiros wasn't a mage, as far as Tal knew. He couldn't do it without Tsereg.

"All of you have a part to play in bringing it to life," said the God-Empress, and then broke off as a loud, choking cry sounded from the opposite side of the aisle from Tal, where the other column of guests stood with heads bowed. Keleiros Lenarai had fallen to his knees. Blood was pouring from his nose and mouth. You could have taken it for an overeager display of devotion, except that he was also screaming, a high note of agony, like a single splash of ink on an expanse of white paper.

Shuthmili knelt beside him, taking his shoulders in her hands, clearly trying to steady him. Tal tried to push toward them, but there were lines of people in front of him and it still might be part of the plan, Keleiros still might be doing this deliberately—

"Shuthmili," said the Empress, in a voice that made Tal feel that something held his heart in its claw and was starting to squeeze. "Control your concubine or remove him."

"Apologies, Majesty," she said, without looking up, her voice strained. She glanced up, perhaps looking for the Empress, and noticed Tal across the aisle. Her eyes widened in naked shock.

"As I said, all of you have a part to play in bringing it to life," said the God-Empress. "We raise our cups to a new dawn. To Echentyr restored."

"To Echentyr restored," the crowd of guests began to say, and Tal raised his cup to his lips, thinking he might as well have a drink since everything else was spinning out of control.

He smelled the poison before it could touch his lips. The same flower-metal scent that lingered on the blade of Keleiros' special knife.

"No! Don't drink!" said Shuthmili, stepping out of line. She threw her own cup into the aisle, with a clang and a dark spray of wine.

Before anyone could react to this, there was a single sharp noise, impossibly loud, metal resonating with metal, like a hammer striking an anvil the size of the palace itself. The fabric of the throne room shook. Tal's first impression was that he was aboard a mazeship and that it had run into the rocks. Then the echoes died away and people were screaming.

Tal reached automatically for the knife inside his jacket. The Thousand Eyes had drawn their weapons, but the guests were already scattering, spreading toward the edges of the throne room, trying to remember where the exits had been. Even if they knew, they were out of luck. The throne room no longer had any doors.

An eerie light emanated from behind the God-Empress, and a mist that smelled of blood and salt. The light was the same unearthly green as a maze-gate. Tal stood where he was, looking into the light, dazed, as fleeing guests pushed past him. Those who hadn't tried to escape had fallen to their knees. He didn't see what had become of Shuthmili and Keleiros.

The jar which had contained Belthandros' body was cracked in half, and the green light seeped from the cracks, making rays in the mist. The God-Empress stood frozen before it. She looked translucent, precious but unreal, as if carved from glass.

Tal elbowed his way to the front of the senseless crowd, and now he saw Shuthmili, half carrying Keleiros and half dragging him. Tal saw her open her mouth to call something, but nothing could be heard over the noise. It was hard to get any closer to the broken jar. It felt as though time itself was pushing back against him. At least this close at hand the screaming of the guests was deadened.

With a noise that was almost soft, almost like a sigh, an inevitable giving way, the jar shattered. The crystals flew outward, briefly formed a glittering sphere in midair, and then fell away to no more than sand.

Standing on the base of the jar was Sethennai. His hair and clothes were damp with brine, and Tal remembered how he had looked when he'd stepped out of the lake, all those years ago. Despite it all—despite literally everything that had intervened—before Tal's shock and outrage kicked in, he felt a little rush of pride and fondness to see him standing there, eyes gleaming, beaming in triumph, just extraordinarily pleased with himself and glad to be alive.

"*Pentravesse*," said the God-Empress. Tal tasted iron and realised his nose was bleeding. Her voice was alien, a cold, buzzing roughness drowning out anything familiar about it.

"Quite right!" said Sethennai. "What a nice party. I suppose my invitation got lost in the post."

"What are you doing here?" she said. Her voice rasped with malice, like a saw cutting stone.

"What do you think?" he said. "I challenge you. Before the people of your city and according to its ancient law."

He grinned, spreading his arms as if to show to the assembled crowd that he had no weapon.

"By the way, friends, I would not recommend that you drink any of that wine," he said. "I hear the lily of Saar-in-Tachthyr is a very pleasant death, but as pleasures go, it's quite *final*."

The tide of people had reversed: the Empress' guests were pressing closer to see what was going on, and Tal didn't need to listen very hard to hear what they were saying. Sethennai was back! Just as they'd always hoped! Long ago, Tal had felt the same way. It was so nice and easy and comforting to imagine that once Sethennai showed up, everything would be all right.

"I'll give you this," he said, quite softly, to the God-Empress. Tal only heard because he had moved unobtrusively closer, still hoping blindly that Tsereg might show up. "Your technique is irreproachable. You would have killed them all. There were *gallons* of the stuff in your wine cellar. Enough to kill a whole world. Enough to regenerate Echentyr. Such a blood offering . . . it would have worked."

"Of course," she said, coldly.

"But I don't see the point," he said. "Echentyr was just a place. One mortal world among thousands."

"Echentyr was the cradle of our people," said the God-Empress.

"And eventually one grows up and leaves the cradle," said Belthandros. "You should look closer at what you have here and now. These are a people as good as any other."

"Still a prey creature, after all these years, Pentravesse? Is this where your loyalties lie, with warm blood and soft skin?"

"All that really matters is power. And yours is ending."

"You really believe you might win," said the God-Empress.

"In a fair fight I think either of us might win," he said, and then he spoke up, loud enough to be heard throughout the hall. "Don't you think we ought to settle this? Before them all?"

"I can't say that I do," said the God-Empress. She tapped her fingernails on the glassy surface of her stone gown.

"You haven't figured it out, have you?" said Sethennai. "What makes their tiny lives bearable? They fight for what they have, knowing that it can be taken from them. They stand up for themselves. They struggle, and the struggle creates meaning." He beamed at the crowd, turning the full force of his admiration and approval on them like a searchlight. The crowds murmured and jostled, and Tal wanted to shrink to nothing, recognising all this as the purest bullshit.

The God-Empress looked out across the crowds of people, perhaps noting the way they were looking at Sethennai; just the way Tal had looked at him once, he assumed.

"What I'm saying is this," said Sethennai. "Fight me and prove yourself. Strike down the Pretender once and for all. Or have your Thousand Eyes cut me down, I suppose, and let your subjects know you a false queen, a coward who fears defeat. I know which I would choose."

The tension in the room hummed like a plucked string. Tal himself, and Shuthmili, and Cherenthisse, and hundreds of guests and guards and servants, all fixed upon the scene as if strapped to a rack.

"Very well," said the God-Empress. "Name your terms."

22

A Speck of Dust

THE CROWDS BACKED away to the edges of the throne room, pressing themselves against the walls of fossil-stone. The room rippled and flexed as Belthandros and the God-Empress faced one another, fighting for control of the space. The air itself iridesced, flickering bright-dark-bright like oil on water as one divine aura refracted through another.

Shuthmili crouched on the floor of the throne room, holding Keleiros together through determination alone as the world around her went all to chaos.

LEAVE HIM! Zinandour insisted. THIS EFFORT IS WORTHLESS. BELTHANDROS KNOWS YOUR PITIABLE SOFTHEARTEDNESS. YOU ARE TO BE DISTRACTED WHILE HE ACCOMPLISHES HIS ENDS.

The God-Empress will kill him, said Shuthmili. Give me a moment, my lady, please—

She kept her grip on Keleiros' heart and did not relinquish it, though it was like clutching a living eel, feeling it thrashing in her grip, slippery and desperate to destroy itself. He had to live, or else she might as well have killed him, like all the rest.

IF THE EMPRESS DEFEATS BELTHANDROS, YOU CANNOT IMAGINE SHE WILL BE MERCIFUL IN VICTORY, said Zinandour. SHE WILL DISCOVER OUR PART IN THIS, AND SHE WILL DESTROY US. SHE WILL KILL YOU AND SEND ME BACK TO THE VOID, AND YOUR BELOVED WILL BE HERS FOREVER.

At last Keleiros sighed and stilled, his heart beating by itself. He was no longer twitching and staring, so perhaps she had managed to purge the worst of the poison.

AND IF BELTHANDROS WINS, said Zinandour, without mercy, DO YOU THINK HE WILL SPARE HER VESSEL?

Shuthmili's breath caught. Of course he would not. Whatever the bargain they had made, if killing Csorwe was what it took to get what he wanted, he wouldn't even hesitate.

She laid Keleiros to one side and looked about her.

Two throne rooms now overlaid each other, architecture ghosting in and out of existence. Neither Belthandros nor the God-Empress could force the other out. Walls flexed, columns bent, clouds seethed, and here and there fragments of the night sky shone through.

The floor of the throne room had become a labyrinth of pits and spikes, with the two combatants facing each other at its centre and the guests clustered in terrified rows around the far edges.

We can make it through, said Shuthmili. *I can shield us.*

YES. Zinandour sounded almost proud.

Shuthmili disintegrated her ball gown and grew herself an exoskeleton. It was a complicated magic but not really so much harder than growing out her hair or nails. Petals of hard keratin scaled themselves over her whole soft body, leaving only her face and her gauntlets exposed.

Zinandour admired the exoskeleton as Shuthmili flexed her fingers. The armour plates had the texture of tortoiseshell, hard and dark but somehow luminous, flecked and veined with brightness. Finally Shuthmili raised a shield, as bright and vicious as she could make it, imagining herself as a hot needle, and walked into the labyrinth.

"Tsereg!" called Tal, scanning the crowds of guests for any sign of them, without success. The bright colours of their party clothes were incongruous against the blackened and broken stone of the ruined throne room. Tal grabbed the nearest guest, an old Tlaanthothei man.

"Have you seen a kid? Oshaaru, pretty short—"

The old man ignored him, and Tal noticed that behind him a group of people was cradling someone in a blue suit stained with wine and blood.

"Oh, shit," said Tal. "It's Keleiros. What *happened?*"

Dazed and wounded, Keleiros looked very young, closer to Tsereg's age than Tal's, but at least he seemed to be alive.

"Where is Tsereg?" he said, elbowing past the old man, ignoring the objections of the rest of the crowd. "What did you do?"

"Who are you?" said Keleiros, in a whisper roughened by pain, so soft that Tal had to lean closer to hear him. His eyes had the dull blankness of someone who had been hit in the face too many times.

"What are you talking about, I'm Tal, we—"

"Talasseres?" said a voice above him.

It was his mother. Niranthe had cast off the outer layer of her gown—he saw now that Keleiros had been laid down upon it—and she looked almost how Tal remembered her, in the last years of Olthaaros' reign: anxiety sharpened and tempered to a hard shell.

"Mother," he said. "You recognised me," he added, uselessly.

"I think Keleiros has a concussion," said his mother. "You won't get any sense out of him."

The hard shell was opaque. If she was surprised or moved to see Tal, she didn't show it. Tal couldn't say what kind of reaction he would have looked for, anyway. *How you've grown, are you hurt, where have you been* would all have been frighteningly out of character.

"He doesn't remember anything. For the best, I think, since he has been in the clutches of that awful creature for only the Exalted Sages know how long. You're working with Chancellor Sethennai, I assume?"

"What?" said Tal. "No, I . . ."

He trailed off. He wanted to be flattered by the assumption. It was nice that anyone could imagine he'd been by Sethennai's side all this time, that he knew what was going on or had done any of this on purpose.

"Keleiros was carrying a package for you," said his mother, which seemed so incongruous it took Tal a moment to understand the sense of the words. She held it out to him, a slim paper packet, flat and squashy. Scrawled on the paper was *Talasseres. Bring this with you. Keleiros.* The handwriting was familiar but unplaceable, in a way that made Tal feel queasy.

Well, Keleiros was down, and the plan was well and truly fucked. Tal tore the package open. Inside was a folded length of slithery jade-green silk, patterned in gold thread, beaded with tiny fragments of ivory. Among the embroideries was a gold cup borne up by two fish-tailed horses. Tal recognised the crest of Tlaanthothe before he realised what it was he was holding, though he had seen it many, many times.

"That's the Chancellor's sash," said his mother. "If you're not here with Sethennai, why do you have that?"

He looked from his mother to the sash to Keleiros' body, crumpled like a discarded wrapper, and he knew how he recognised that handwriting.

"No idea," he lied. He knew it all, every miserable fact of it, the kind of hard, sharp knowledge that made you long for the soft fog of ignorance.

There had been no *reason* for Sethennai to trick him. If he'd asked, Tal would have helped him anyway, because he was one of the world's biggest idiots.

He thought of the things he had said to Keleiros and wanted to die. Sethennai had enjoyed it, obviously. Having that kind of power over him. Giving Tal his cryptic instructions, holding back as much as he could, presumably just for the pleasure of knowing that Tal would do whatever he asked without question, because it was hardly as though Tal was an important part of the plan. He was unarmed, and even with his sword there was nothing he could do against a goddess, so Sethennai must have done this just for fun, unless—

He froze, crushing the sash in his hands, looking at nothing.

I know what I'm doing. Don't trust Keleiros.

"Oh, fuck," he said. "No, it was never about me."

Tsereg was a mage. Knowing their parents, they were probably a disgustingly powerful mage. And Sethennai had always liked getting other people to fight his battles for him. Sethennai had recognised Tsereg—perhaps not as his child, but certainly as something he could use. And even if Tsereg had seen Keleiros for what he was, Tal knew from bitter experience that the knowledge was no defence. Tsereg would have followed him out there, into the labyrinth.

"Talasseres?" said his mother, but Tal shoved the sash into his pocket and was gone.

Zinandour's power gave Shuthmili access to all kinds of hidden things. She knew in intimate detail the function of every speck of meat that made a living person; she could kill or mend with a thought, all language and mathematics opened to her, and so did every kind of lock and seal and cipher—but Iriskavaal swayed space and time. This was not a fight she could win. All the same, as Shuthmili approached the centre of the labyrinth, she reached for the glass sword, and felt it shimmer into reality at her side.

THAT WAS MINE. IT HAS BEEN SO LONG. WHERE DID YOU FIND IT? said Zinandour, with barely masked pleasure.

When I killed my aunt, said Shuthmili. She remembered it very clearly, half a lifetime ago. The weight of it, the wicked edge glittering, as though it had been waiting for her just out of sight. *Clearly you and I were always written in the stars.*

THE STARS ARE INSENSIBLE FIRES, said Zinandour. *I CHOSE YOU.*

"Shuthmili!" came a familiar voice, hoarse with pain, and Tal stumbled round a corner. "Tsereg's out there—we have to get to them before he does—"

Tal's eyes were milky, his eyelashes mostly gone, his lips cracked and bleeding, but Shuthmili couldn't fail to recognise him now. He had made it this far into the labyrinth with what had to be the last of his strength. His face was streaked with mud and blood, his clothes were ragged, and given what the spatial distortion had done to his organs, he should not still be conscious.

Not for the first time, Shuthmili wondered who had made mortals so fragile and so persistent, and who had made Talasseres the flimsiest and most bloody-minded of them all.

THE MOTH THAT BEATS ENDLESSLY AGAINST THE LANTERN, said Zinandour.

Shuthmili ignored her. "Tal, why didn't you run?"

"Ha ha," said Tal, in barely more than a whisper. "Listen, we have to get Tsereg, Belthandros is planning something, I think he's planning to *drain* them or something—"

They pressed themselves against the grey wall of the labyrinth, peering through the opening. The stone of the duelling ground was scarred and cracked all over, rippled with damage.

Belthandros and the God-Empress fought in a blooming cloud of dust. The cloud reformed itself and burst again as though tugged back and forth in time. The Empress' long hair hung loose over her shoulders, her robes were shredded, the Mantle hung about her like a loose wing case, but she showed no sign of relenting.

Belthandros dodged to one side, making too ambitious a feint—his foot slipped, his ankle turned, and he went down. His head hit a chunk of loose rock, and he did not get up again. The God-Empress reared above him, a spark of rage in her yellow eyes.

Tal pushed forward, as though—even now, after all this—he couldn't watch Belthandros die. The God-Empress bared her teeth, tusks curving up like scythes, meaning to tear out Sethennai's throat. Csorwe's face twisted with rage, and Shuthmili winced.

"Stop," said a voice. Not very loud, but somehow still perfectly audible.

Beyond the combatants the dust cleared, revealing a small figure with one fist raised.

"*Tsereg—*" said Tal.

In one grubby hand Tsereg clasped a small, battered book. The other hand was wreathed in a distorting haze. Even at this distance Shuthmili recognised raw magic when she saw it.

The God-Empress hesitated.

Shuthmili resisted the urge to run to intervene, and she had to wrestle Tal back to stop him bursting on the scene himself. It was horribly easy. Tal could hardly hold himself upright, and every breath felt like a shudder of pain through his whole body.

"God-Empress," said Tsereg. They folded their arms and stood their ground, looking like nothing so much as a small cairn of stones. "Inheritor of Iriskavaal."

"What manner of thing art thou, little one?" said the God-Empress.

"I am the last Chosen Bride of the Unspoken," said Tsereg, "and my name is forsaken."

The God-Empress smiled. "Nameless slave of a nameless god. Is that all thou art? We would make thee great. Thy allies are all defeated. We are a kinder master than the Unspoken."

"Ha ha! Fuck you!" they said. "No. I don't think so. My name is Tsereg. You work for me now."

The God-Empress only laughed at this coldly, with tolerance but no real amusement.

"This is some scheme of Belthandros' invention," she said.

"Nope. He doesn't know about this. Listen to me," said Tsereg. "You made a promise. I demand three days' service."

The God-Empress froze. Her eyes widened. To Shuthmili this was a shock as sharp as an unexpected fall.

"Three days'—*ah!*" She twitched, and clutched at her left hand as if it burnt her. "No!" The word was drawn out into a shriek of pain, and she clenched her bare hand to her chest.

It had been a long time since Shuthmili had remembered the scar on the back of Csorwe's hand. It was still there, intricate as a nest of earthworms, except that now it was glowing with a flickering phosphorescence, beads of light moving over the whole sigil, pulsing and wriggling. The God-Empress screamed.

Shuthmili dropped Tal, abandoned any pretence at stealth, and ran toward her.

"How?" The Empress gasped for breath. "We have never made thee any promise." She doubled up, falling forward on her knees in the black mud. She stared down at her hand, now glowing brighter than the dim light above, squirming and twitching.

"Your vessel owes a debt," said Tsereg. "A pledge in blood is binding beyond life and death. You know what that means?"

The God-Empress pressed her forehead against the cold earth and groaned.

"What have you *done*?" said Shuthmili, trying to lift her.

The child ignored her, poking the Empress with one sandalled toe. "It means that my mother made a deal with your vessel. It means we both got what they left us. It means you owe me three days' service."

"No," said the God-Empress, without conviction. Shuthmili had never heard her sound defeated before. It tore at her heart to hear Csorwe in pain, although—if Tsereg was right—if this could really work . . .

"Not that hard to understand," said Tsereg. "I don't even want the whole three days. There's only one thing I want. Take off the Mantle."

The God-Empress raised a hand and lowered it jerkily, with obvious effort, her fingers clenching and unclenching. "I—will—not," she said, her voice ragged with pain. "I will kill you all first."

"Take off the Mantle," said Tsereg again. Their jaw was clenched. The scars and grazes on their face and arms glowed faintly, as though a light burnt within them.

Slowly, and then with convulsive speed, the God-Empress tore off the Mantle of Divinity.

Even on her knees and in pain, the God-Empress had been defiantly alive. Falling, she was a candle snuffed out, just a limp mortal body, lying on its side in the mud.

As she fell, her pale hand flew up, almost accidentally, and brushed against the child's arm.

Tsereg gave a strange little yelp, a very mortal cry of shock and pain, and then their resistance failed, and they fell to the ground, utterly limp. Far away, Shuthmili heard Tal cry out.

The Mantle of Iriskavaal floated to earth and landed in a shallow puddle of water, a drift of translucent snakeskin. Shuthmili reached for it. Before she could touch it, another hand plucked it out of the water: an elegant, long-fingered hand, bearing a gold signet.

"Ah, Shuthmili," said Belthandros. "I told you all would come right in the end."

He smiled to himself, a private and triumphant smile, and lifted the Mantle to his mouth and *ate* it. The Mantle crumpled and shrank like rice paper in water, but it still took a horribly long time, chewing up mouthfuls of lacy snakeskin and swallowing them down.

When it was done, Belthandros looked just as he always had, but brighter, happier, no longer tired or ruffled in any way.

"It's done," he said. "You were right, you know. Between you and me, one of us is the greatest magician of the age."

He smiled. It was clearly meant to be a smile of warmth, brilliance, welcoming magnificence. Shuthmili saw the teeth behind it. Belthandros had absorbed the Mantle. All the God-Empress' presence was in him now. It made for a kind of luminous vitality, all that power charged in him like a taut bowstring.

The throne room was already contracting. The labyrinth was gone. They were in a wintry garden, surrounded by colonnades. The God-Empress' body—Csorwe's body—lay now in a kind of sunken bed. She looked like a carving on a tombstone: grey marble, swirled dull with black bloodstains.

"Will she wake?" said Shuthmili, not quite daring to voice it. She had been so deep in defeat. She couldn't believe that it might have come good at last.

"Yes. As we arranged," he said. "Just as she was, if you are very lucky."

Shuthmili knelt beside the grave, brushing aside the wards. Csorwe looked as though she was sleeping. Just as she was. After so very long dealing with the God-Empress, Shuthmili couldn't quite bring herself to touch her.

"You should come and work for me," said Belthandros. "There is much to do."

"Just as she was," said Shuthmili, hardly hearing him. Cautiously she reached out, leafed back her exoskeleton, and brushed her fingertips against the back of Csorwe's hand, feeling strangely furtive, and not only because Belthandros was watching.

"You understand how things are managed here," he was saying. "I need a second-in-command. At least consider it."

He didn't know about her bargain with Zinandour. She wasn't going to be the one to tell him. If he thought he'd get a helpful little sidekick out of this, let him think it.

She retrieved the gold tusk from beneath the armour plate that covered her collarbone. It was warm from resting next to her skin. She pressed it to her lips and held it up to show him.

"I want to put this back first," she said.

"How gruesome," he said. "Very well."

He took the tusk from her. She resisted the irrational urge to snatch it back from him. It was worse when he pulled out the diamond tusk, with no more effort than it took to uncork a bottle. Pinched between two fingers and plucked neatly from her jaw, with a crack like an icicle snapping. Shuthmili had to drive her claws into her palms to keep from doing something she would regret.

She replaced the gold tusk herself, telling herself that this was a medical procedure, that there was nothing strange about touching Csorwe's mouth for the first time in so many years, and nothing terrible about the fact that she was still lying there, near dead, and nothing awful about the fact that Belthandros would speak to Csorwe again, when Shuthmili never would. If she focused on sterilising the site, bonding the living root to the bone, she could almost believe it.

When it was done, Csorwe really did look just the way she had. Shuthmili lay down on the ground—*let* Belthandros stare, she hoped he would die from staring—and curled up against Csorwe's body, on that cold bed of broken stone.

So, WE COME TO AN END, said Zinandour. Softly, and oddly without triumph.

Funny, really, that after all Shuthmili's striving, the endless days and years of frantic activity, she had accomplished almost nothing, and all her efforts had been outdone by a child.

Still, when Csorwe lived again, Zinandour would have her full incarnation, never mind the circumstances. That was the bargain they had made, and Shuthmili could not even claim it was a bad one.

She hadn't been sure how it would feel, to surrender control altogether. She'd thought it might be like falling, tumbling away into darkness, as in a nightmare. In fact it was more like lying on the shore of a warm sea, as the waves crept up bit by bit, dissolving her away. It wasn't so bad.

Will you remember me? I hope you might, if only as a speck of dust in your eye.

The goddess showed her a picture or a memory—bright sunshine through blossoms, pink and white, familiar-unfamiliar all over again. Petals falling in the courtyard of the Qanwa townhouse.

I CHOSE WELL. HAD YOU BEEN LESS THAN WHAT YOU ARE, I WOULD BE IMPRISONED STILL. I WILL NOT FORGET.

Will you do something for me, my lady? I'm out of leverage. I can only ask.

ASK.

Don't let her get hurt.

With the last of her control, she propped herself up on one elbow, looking at Csorwe's face, serenely still and perfect, and thought, *Well, here we are, it's been a long time, my love, I have missed waking next to you.*

Csorwe opened her eyes.

As the waves of oblivion closed over Shuthmili's head, she thought, *No! Wait! Let me back! I made a mistake*—and then no more.

TOO LATE, MY SPECK OF DUST. TOO LATE.

23

A Better World

"TALASSERES?" SAID A VOICE.

It wasn't the first time Tal had dreamed about Sethennai. It wasn't even the first time he'd woken from such a dream immediately ready to kill someone.

It was the first time Sethennai had actually been there when he'd opened his eyes, though. His dark eyes were soft with concern, and he was brushing Tal's cheek with the back of his fingers, and for a moment all Tal's more pressing questions such as *why am I still alive?* were annihilated by an overwhelming fury.

"You," said Tal. He jerked away from Sethennai's hand, drawing his knees to his chest. "You were Keleiros all the time, you motherfucker, you—"

"Well, obviously, yes," said Sethennai. "I'm sorry, of course, I suppose I should have told you—"

Tal found he did not give a shit about any of this. He saw Sethennai watching him with a kind of indulgent caution, as if Tal were someone else's dog, and behind that, endlessly, he remembered Tsereg falling to the ground, their eyes as flat and dead as stones.

He struggled to his feet, up out of the shallow grave he'd been lying in.

"You're in remarkably good shape, given how close you were," said Sethennai, rising to face him. "And in general, you look well—"

"Shut the fuck up," said Tal. "You might as well have killed them yourself."

"Who?" said Sethennai, with genuine confusion.

Tal punched him. It wasn't his best punch of all time. He hadn't planned to do it, so the angle wasn't great, and his arm was half dead from lying in the grave. It still connected with Sethennai's shoulder, a flat and heavy impact like punching a slab of solid oak, and Sethennai still stumbled back, startled.

Under other circumstances, this might have made Tal feel better, in a *notice me now, you prick* kind of way. Now all it did was add to the weight of grief a twist of panicked guilt and horror. He backed away, not knowing what to do with his hands, which felt awkward and alien to him.

Sethennai rolled his eyes. "You're lucky I wasn't shielded," he said. "You mean Tsereg, I take it."

"I should have known it was you," said Tal. "Right away. Getting a teenager to fight your battles for you. You can't resist."

"It was Tsereg's battle too," said Sethennai, mildly. "They wanted the Empress dead, and so did you. They wanted to help make a better world. They knew that it might mean their death. You brought them to the Citadel yourself, and you're lying to yourself if you think you didn't know what you were getting them into. Nevertheless, I don't think it's worth fighting about who has a stronger handle on Tsereg's best interests, since in point of fact, they are not dead."

Tal clenched his fists at his sides, silent because he didn't trust himself not to lash out again. At last, with enormous effort: "Then *where are they?*"

Tsereg was curled up against a rib of stone, like a castaway sleeping in the wreckage of their ship. They were dusted all over with ash, buried in it to the knees, hair and skin and clothes all ghostly white. When Tal shook them, he only detached a cloud of dust. They didn't open their eyes. Their eyelids and lashes were thick with powder. Tal stopped shaking them, suddenly afraid that they might be nothing but ashes settled into the parody of a mortal form.

"But I saw them die," said Tal. He lifted them in his arms, loosing another cascade of ashes that prickled his nose and mouth. They were certainly light enough. "I saw them fall—"

He regretted speaking it out loud. It made it too real, undeniably something he had really seen, not a nightmare.

"I don't doubt it," said Sethennai. "They are an exceedingly powerful mage. Amazing they've lived so long without training."

Tal adjusted Tsereg's weight in his arms. Could he feel a heartbeat through the ash, or was it his own pulse? Tsereg didn't stir or sigh as a sleeping child normally would. It was like carrying a bundle of wet paper.

"Hey," he muttered into their ear. "You're not dead. You'd better not be. You're fine."

The space shifted around them, reconstituting itself into an actual room, with walls and a ceiling.

"I do wonder where Oranna found them," Sethennai murmured. "But the Unspoken does pick a winner from time to time."

He doesn't know, thought Tal. *Oranna never told him.* For perhaps the first time in their association, he knew something Sethennai did not. He felt like he'd swallowed a marble. This cold, undeniable secret was in him, and he didn't know what to do about it.

He said nothing, still cradling Tsereg, letting Sethennai focus on reassembling the throne room. Tal saw the outlines of doors and even windows, such as the God-Empress' throne room had never had, with sunlight pouring in.

Sethennai didn't know. How would he react if Tal told him? Would he be happy about it? Indifferent? Would he be stricken with guilt to know he had put Tsereg at risk? That was almost good to imagine: that if it was his own child, he might learn what it felt like to regret, and that if Tal told him, then he might get to see that realisation.

Tsereg lay limp and motionless. Without their usual scowl it was too easy to imagine the skull under the ash. Then they moved in his arms, and took a breath that stirred a wisp of dust from their upper lip, and their brow creased, forming its usual deep notch of displeasure.

Abruptly he realised that he didn't care how Sethennai would react. Tal wasn't going to tell him. It didn't change who Tsereg was. If Sethennai hadn't already recognised that they were worth something, then he didn't deserve to know.

The throne room was almost back to normal now, flooded with the light of dawn. The guests were standing around in loose crowds, their party clothes ragged, their expressions somewhere on the spectrum from bewilderment to defiance, giving way to a thin and halfhearted hope as they saw who was standing on the dais before the throne.

Chancellor Sethennai! was the whisper. The people of Tlaanthothe remembered. Tal saw his mother among them, in a gaggle of other Charossai. They were looking at Tal too, standing at Sethennai's side in victory, just as he had always imagined it might happen. He had to resist the urge to hide his face in Tsereg's shoulder. After so long on the run, a crowd of people looking at him made his hackles rise. The old vision of triumph felt so far away it might have been someone else's fantasy.

"Thank you, everyone," said Sethennai, with a nicely judged humility. "I knew you hadn't forgotten me. It's all over now. Your patience and tenacity are rewarded. You're all safe."

For a moment it seemed this might really be true, and then there was the sound of running feet and a group of soldiers in ceremonial armour parted the crowd and pushed through to face the dais. They were Thousand Eyes, doing their very best to exude confidence and menace, but unable to disguise the uncertainty hanging around them like mist. It was true what they said about cutting off the head of a snake, then.

"Pretender—" said Cherenthisse, at the head of the group.

Sethennai parted his hands and smiled. A whole sequence of snake names came hissing off his tongue like sparks from a whetstone. "I am no impostor. I am your God-Emperor. I am Iriskavaal's last incarnation. Will you turn away from me?"

The Thousand Eyes stood looking at him. They had formed up into perfect rank and file, but there was still a sense of milling about.

"I offer you free choice," said Sethennai. "You have your freedom, granted in recognition of your faith and your service. Your lives are yours to use as you will. Leave if you wish. I hope you will stay, but I will bear no grudge against any who leaves, and all who stay will keep their rank, their privileges, their position of honour and confidence among my Thousand Eyes. To each of you I say, take your time, consider your choice, be assured that my love and gratitude are yours always."

The Thousand Eyes glanced at each other. Perhaps they had expected to be the ones who would offer a choice—surrender or die, surrender and die anyway, that was about what you usually got from the Thousand Eyes—and this had taken the wind from their sails.

Sethennai clearly had a whole lot more speech to make. Tal had worked security for plenty of Chancellor's addresses in the past, and he knew Sethennai was capable of going on almost forever, regardless of whether he'd had time to prepare remarks. Tal's arms were beginning to ache. He wondered if there was a chair where he could put Tsereg down, but in the presence of so many snakes, he was reluctant to let go of them.

So he stood there waiting while Sethennai went on and on about loyalty and honour and citizenship, and everyone seemed to drink it in, and Tal felt an unaccustomed stab of the emotion known as pity. They all wanted to believe it. He could see his mother, overcome with an almost impossible relief, leaning on the shoulder of a younger relation. They thought it was over, the long tyranny, the cruelty and despair. They thought Sethennai was here to save them.

He was tired, he realised, the sick, numb tiredness that sometimes followed after a fight, when all the spark drained away and you were left feeling no better for having won and survived.

There was no sign at all of Shuthmili, or of Csorwe's body.

He heard his own name and looked up. Sethennai was smiling at him, a genuine and encouraging smile.

"The sash, Tal," he said, very quietly, so that nobody else would hear, a kindly reminder of something Tal should have remembered.

The ceremonial sash of Tlaanthothe was still, somehow, crumpled in Tal's pocket. Everyone was watching. A Thousand Eye stepped up on the dais and reached out helpfully to take Tsereg off Tal's hands. Tal made a strangled noise and drew back, clutching Tsereg to his chest, though his shoulders were now aching so badly that he would have quite liked to put them down.

He felt the assembled eyes on him, every gaze like a physical touch. This was clearly something Sethennai had stage-managed from the beginning. The only part Tal had actually been intended to play was enacting this little coronation, and Tsereg's presence was making it awkward.

If he'd had the presence of mind, he would have said something or run away. Later he would wonder why he hadn't. He laid Tsereg carefully down on the ground at his feet, and retrieved the sash, and—oh, god, Sethennai wasn't just going to take it from him, Tal had to put it on him. He looped the green silk band over his head and smoothed it down over his shoulders. It was impossible not to look at his face. If Sethennai had smiled at him, it would have been easier to hate him. Instead he gave Tal a searching look, curious, almost worried.

"Not long now," Sethennai mouthed.

Tal nodded, and turned back to face the crowd, and managed a kind of smile.

24

A Place for You

SOME TIME LATER, Tal woke up in barely controlled panic, in an unfamiliar tangle of quilts and bedsheets. From the dark he imagined it was the middle of the night, but then a servant drew back the canopy and he saw that a warm and rosy light was streaming in through the windows. Either it was late afternoon or something was on fire.

The servant wanted to make sure that everything was all right. Tal had been shouting, apparently. That sounded about right. He lay back on the bed.

Right, of course. He had slept in a real bedroom, in a real bed, in the guest wing of the Lignite Citadel, and he wasn't dead. They had put Tsereg in the next room, with a real medic to keep an eye on them, and they weren't dead either. There was a Thousand Eye guarding the corridor, and this was supposed to make them feel safe.

He was in a clean nightshirt, which was concerning because he didn't remember undressing, and he couldn't see where they'd put his clothes. He peered round the connecting door into Tsereg's room. They had a canopy bed of their own, on which they lay utterly still, deep pink in the light of the sinking sun. Someone had managed to dab away most of the ash. Their hands were folded neatly on the white sheet.

"How are they?" he said. The medic gave him a weary look, as though it wasn't the first time he had asked. He couldn't remember. She was the same doctor who had examined Tal himself, on Sethennai's instructions.

"No change, sir," she said. "I said I'd tell you if anything happens."

The servant was still hovering in the room behind him, and seemed very keen to get Tal washed and dressed. They had drawn up a nice hot bath for him, if he would wish it?

The bathroom itself was a cold windowless cavern of vaulted fossil-stone, but the bath was scented with orange-blossom and someone had put out a plate of apricots for him to eat while he was in it, taking the trouble to halve and stone them. Tal ate them all without thinking. As he was towelling off, another servant appeared with a pile of clean clothes and tried to shave him. Tal, who had what he thought of as a normal distrust of blades near his face, insisted on shaving and dressing himself. His face looked strange in the mirror without the fuzz of stubble and ill-trimmed beard, but he hadn't aged as badly as he'd feared. The lines of his jaw and cheek were sharper than he remembered. The rest of him looked as narrow and lean as ever, weather-beaten into a kind of compactness, like a fork of driftwood with its grain polished to the surface by the waves.

There was a shirt and leggings, both clean and soft in the way he had forgotten clothes could be. They ran through Tal's hands like water. After them was a smart buttoned tunic and sash. Tal had never been all that bothered about clothes but could not help noting that the tunic was a dark moss green, enough like the Citadel livery that he would not stand out, but not enough to feel like anyone was staking a claim.

"Do you know where the other Charossai are being kept?" he asked the servant.

"The Charossa apartments are on another floor of the guest wing," said the servant. "Your lady mother Niranthe is very eager to see you, sir, whenever you are well enough, but the Chancellor has ordered that you are not to be bothered until you seek company yourself."

Tal turned this over in his head. On the one hand, this was how they got you. You were tricked into being grateful and then they turned around and said, *Well, I fed you, I clothed you, I hid you from your enemies, don't I own you now?* On the other hand, he *was* glad not to have to deal with his family before he was ready. He pulled on his shoes and stared at himself in the mirror, a clean-shaven and neatly dressed citizen.

Maybe that was how things were going to be for him, now. Just an ordinary person in this new world. Had he imagined what he might do, if the reign of the Empress was ended? No, because he'd never really believed it would happen, or if it did that he would live to see it, he alone of all the rest.

"What do I do now?" he said to the servant. The servant gave him a frightened look and eventually said that sir could return to his room if he wished.

Back in his room, they'd put out tea and pastries, which Tal ate in small bites, wondering when the blow was going to land. Tsereg never stirred. The original doctor was replaced by another. Tal loped back and forth between Tsereg's room and his own.

He had to climb up on the table to get to the windows, and when he did, he couldn't see anything out of them, only the turrets of the palace and that warm pink sunset radiance. It had been a long time since he'd had the leisure to be bored, and he'd forgotten how he hated it, especially when it was underscored by the constant thrum of anxiety.

Eventually there was a knock at the door, and Tal answered it, expecting it to be another servant, wondering whether he could ask for something to do—and it was Sethennai.

"Can I come in?" he said.

Tal stepped back into the room to make way for him, his heart blundering up into his throat like a wasp trapped in a bottle.

Sethennai closed the door behind him and stood for a moment, not quite making eye contact, as though—however briefly—tongue-tied.

"It's come to me that I owe you an apology," said Sethennai. "If you'll hear it."

Tal felt as if the room was shrinking around them, as if he might elbow through the wall if he moved too quickly. "Do you want to sit down?" he said.

They sat at the table, and Sethennai poured Tal a cup of tea, although Tal had been certain the teapot was empty.

"It was a mistake to conceal my identity from you," said Sethennai. "I wasn't sure of your motives. If I'd known I could still trust you, I would have chosen differently. I'm sorry for that."

"Did you trust me?" said Tal. He'd always thought of himself as a bit of a liability. Csorwe was the one who had been trusted. Tal was unreliable.

"Tal!" he said, genuinely taken aback. "Truly. Of course."

There was another silence. Tal looked down at his hands.

"Listen—" said Sethennai, and Tal heard the whole machine of rhetoric start up and then, abruptly, run down again. "How have you been?" he said.

Later on, Tal would be embarrassed that his resistance lasted only for a moment. It was just so long since he had been able to talk like this, to someone who knew him. He explained about his escape with Oranna and his years wandering the desert. A few near misses with Thousand Eyes, his illness a few years ago, his encounter with Tsereg and the events that had brought them to the Citadel. Put like that, the years felt like nothing, like a small handful of sand trickling away through his fingers.

"I'm sorry to hear you were alone all that time," said Sethennai.

Tal looked up at him, startled. He hadn't thought of it like that in a while. It was possible to get so tired you no longer felt sleepy or so parched you no longer wanted water, and so too with isolation.

"I'm used to being by myself," said Tal, wanting Sethennai to understand that he hadn't completely lost control of his life. "I don't mind it—" He realised abruptly that the look on Sethennai's face was one of terrible sorrow. "Don't pity me," he said, irritably, without thinking about it.

"I'm not," said Sethennai. He smiled with undiminished sadness. "I understand you, I think. Easier to have nothing when you know how quickly the loss becomes unbearable."

"How is this not pitying me?" said Tal.

Sethennai grinned, the old rueful grin, the real one. Tal hadn't expected it to hit him with such force, but it really did, inescapably, the same way he thought every year that he wouldn't be surprised by the spring and still liked it when the leaves came back. Tal blinked.

"If anything I was feeling sorry for myself," said Sethennai. "I'm functionally immortal. The only way to survive that is not to hold out much hope. Things slip away. It happens. So you know, I try not to get attached— but, god, I'm glad you lived."

Tal was trying so hard to stay cynical and aggrieved. Cynical and aggrieved were at the core of his being, so this should have been easier than it was.

"But I'm not the same," said Tal, recalling how he'd looked that morning, not bad but certainly no longer twenty-two.

"Oh, Tal," he said. "None of us are the same." He looked down, his smile fading. "I never wanted to treat you badly," he said. "I want to make it up to you. Is there any way I could?"

Tal swallowed. It was an awful power to hold in his hands, and he couldn't think what to do with it. He tried to remember all the things he'd once wished Sethennai might say to him. They had seemed very important at the time, but most of the time they didn't count if you asked.

"Do you want me to stay?" said Tal. He'd assumed he was being kept here until someone could figure out what to do with him.

"Do you want to stay?" said Sethennai. Tal couldn't explain that it wasn't the same thing at all.

"I don't know," said Tal, trying to be honest. "Until Tsereg's better, at least."

This broke the moment, somehow. Tal was almost grateful. The weight and pressure of it had become too much. Sethennai rose from the chair and went into the sickroom. Tal followed. Tsereg hadn't moved since the last time he checked on them.

The extraordinary sunset made both Sethennai and Tsereg into crystal statues, luminous from within. The stillness made even Tsereg's snub, mundane profile look like something architectural. It made the family resemblance harder to miss. Tal had to lean hard against the doorway.

"I understand if you can't forgive me for this," said Sethennai at length. "There might have been another way. I could have looked harder to find it."

"Can't you do anything for them?" said Tal.

"I've done as much as I can," said Sethennai. "Even in death, the God-Empress is vindictive. It will take time."

"I tried so hard to keep them safe," said Tal.

"They wanted to keep you out of it, too, you know," said Sethennai. "They were worried you'd get yourself hurt."

Tal dug his nails into the doorframe. This misery of this just went on and on. It was too much. Looking at Sethennai hurt too. He didn't trust himself to react to anything.

"You want to make it up to me?" he said, when he could make himself say anything coherent. "Just leave me the fuck alone."

He did. Tal was left to his own devices. The light outside the windows never changed, orange-pink, like the roses which had bloomed in the palace gardens in the old days, poised on the moment just before the sun sank beneath the horizon. Presumably, elsewhere in the Citadel there were all kinds of consequences of the Empress' defeat. Tal didn't leave his quarters. He took a lot of baths and changed into different but identical sets of clean clothes. He sat by Tsereg's bedside and tried to think of what he wanted to say to them. He walked up and down the corridor and tried to think of what he wanted to say to Sethennai.

Sethennai had cared for him once and cared for him still. If that was true, then the whole story could be different. Some of the things he'd lost might be found again. It might mean he'd survived for a reason.

Tal insisted he wasn't fooling himself. He knew what kind of person Sethennai was. He'd always known, really. It wasn't as though Sethennai was the first bad man he'd ever met. But—and he'd always known this too—

Tal wasn't a good enough person to care about that if Sethennai thought he was worth liking and wanted to be forgiven.

After a few days of this, Tal received a note.

Would you join me for dinner?
S

The servant who handed it over waited in the doorway for a response, which was a mercy because it meant Tal couldn't agonise about it. He nodded once and shut the door.

An invitation to dinner turned out to mean a visit to Sethennai's private quarters, a new suite of rooms opened up on a mezzanine above the bookshelves in the Glass Archive, and Tal was the only guest. The pink light filtering through the dome of blue-green glass turned everything a dusky violet, and reflected candle flames floated on the lacquered table and the gleaming tiles like the moon on water.

Dinner was lamb casserole with figs. Even from the smell Tal could tell it would be the best thing he had eaten for a long, long time. Sethennai poured him a glass of wine.

"I hope you haven't been too bored," said Sethennai, when Tal sat opposite him. "As you can imagine, things have been busy."

"Always are," said Tal, with an ease he hadn't expected. It felt so much like old times.

"Help yourself to rice and things," said Sethennai. "There's a lot to do. It's not just a matter of putting everything back how it was. Sometimes that's impossible, for one thing."

"Yeah, I bet," said Tal, thinking of Ringtown, and of the wounded girl they'd met in the tunnel. "People have got used to it."

"This is an opportunity," said Sethennai. "To change things for the better. To make a better world. I had an empire once, Tal. A real one, not this mad dolls' house. People were happy in Echentyr. Thousands of years of scholarship, peace, stability."

"You don't have to give me the hard sell," said Tal. He took a gulp of wine and peered over the rim of the glass at him.

"Ha. Call it force of habit. I'd forgotten that I don't have to, with you."

Tal didn't know how to answer. His great weakness with Sethennai was that he never had a smart reply. Even when he tried to think of them in advance, he never had the chance to use them. The conversation moved on to other things. There weren't many harmless topics available, but they talked about the food and the wine and the palace, until eventually—without warning—Sethennai said:

"You said the other day that you wanted to be left alone. Is that still true?"

Tal had come to dinner with every intention of telling Sethennai that he was leaving as soon as Tsereg was better, and yet. Perhaps it was the wine and perhaps it was the way Sethennai sat in his chair, relaxed at last, crisp shirt collar unbuttoned, or perhaps it was just the knowledge that running away would leave him more alone than ever.

"If it wasn't," said Tal. "What would you have in mind?"

Sethennai sipped his drink and set down the glass, seeming to consider his words before he spoke. "There is a place for you here, if you want it."

"To work for you?" said Tal.

"Is that what you would want?" said Sethennai. He reached for the salt, leaving the question hanging, a small burning sun suspended in midair above the table.

Tal didn't later recall how he came to end up in Sethennai's lap, his hands pressed flat against Sethennai's shoulders, pushing him back into the dining chair as he kissed him. All he remembered was Sethennai's murmur of surprise, and his own sense of triumph, followed by a flash of horrified embarrassment that perhaps this was not welcome.

"Should I not—" Tal said. He pulled back, suddenly very aware of what he was doing, every point of contact between them, the weight and pressure of all his limbs.

Sethennai grinned and his hands found the small of Tal's back, running his nails up and down the curvature of his spine, idly and apparently without thought. Tal was so sensitive there that he felt each fingertip even through two layers of clothing, and it knocked every half-formed thought sharply out of his head.

When Tal recovered any presence of mind at all, he thought, *Oh, he remembers what I like.* He was so torn between whether this was good or whether it hurt or both that he kissed him again, tangling one hand in Sethennai's hair to hold him in place.

The silence of the Glass Archive wrapped around them, the dark expanse of the bookshelves absorbing every echo, like the night sky itself.

"Do you have a bedroom in this place or what?" said Tal.

"Are you sure?" said Sethennai. He drew back, biting his lip. This was obviously meant to indicate concern, but it made Tal ache.

"I'm too old to do it in a chair," said Tal, in the flattest possible drawl. Let this mean nothing. Or, better, let him forget about whether things meant things for five fucking minutes.

"No, I mean, are you sure this is really what you want?" said Sethennai.

"What are you talking about," said Tal. He leant down and kissed him again, hard, digging his nails into his shoulders. It was true. He was fine. If he wanted badly enough for this to be fine, then it could be fine, and he wouldn't have to leave.

Sethennai brushed the back of his hand against Tal's cheek and ran his thumb over the curve of Tal's ear. Tal shivered, trying to focus on how this was nice and not on how it made him feel like he'd been laid open.

"It's been so long," said Sethennai. It wasn't exactly an objection. He sounded persuadable.

"I *know*," said Tal without thinking, too far gone even to be embarrassed. "Please."

He felt Sethennai smile against his mouth. "I forgot how you say that," he said. "Say it again."

Tal awoke in the crook of Sethennai's arm. His whole body ached in a dim, fuzzy kind of way, and he didn't want to move, except that he was cold. He curled up against Sethennai, trying to absorb some of his body heat without waking him. It was oddly gratifying when Sethennai wrapped a warm arm round his shoulders and pulled him closer.

"You're awake," he said, his face pressed to Sethennai's rib cage.

Sethennai yawned, stretching underneath him. It was like being part of a tectonic disaster. "Sleep well?"

"Mm," said Tal. Better than he had in years. He couldn't tell what time it was now. The blue-violet light was soft but disorienting. He closed his eyes, pressing closer, hoping it might make him feel steadier, or more certain of what he had done. He didn't know how to find his footing. There was still that terrible familiar vacancy, an emptiness without definition. This was supposed to have fixed things. He was supposed to feel better.

It was what he had wanted, wasn't it? What more could he possibly ask for? Maybe the gnawing sense that something was wrong was just always present, even in the best-case scenario.

"Everything all right?" said Sethennai, absently scratching the back of Tal's neck. He sounded as if he was about to fall asleep again.

Tal mumbled assent. It was fine. He was fine. He just had to stop thinking so much. He'd managed not to fret about Tsereg for a few hours, but the tightness in his chest was back with a vengeance now, and he kept seeing Keleiros Lenarai, too, on hands and knees, with blood pouring from his mouth and an expression of dull, paralysed terror on his face.

Tal could ask what had happened to him. Sethennai might say *who?* or he might say *he's recovering with his family and I've sent the best doctors to attend him* or he might say *I'm sorry to say he didn't make it.* Tal didn't think he could handle any of those options, so he didn't ask. He knew exactly what he was getting into here. He had his eyes open.

That being the case, he didn't know why he felt sick. It was dread, or guilt, or something, but he was sure it would go away. He remembered that marble stuck in his throat. If he was going to stay here, Tsereg would stay too—safe, with everything they wanted, and that was worth bearing in mind too, probably—and it would all come out in the end. Maybe he had to say something.

Sethennai had trusted him. He didn't want to lie, not even by omission, and if he put it off, he might never say anything. Maybe he had to say something *now*.

"Tsereg is your child," he said, just like that. He didn't move. If he sat up, he would have to see Sethennai's expression. "Yours and Oranna's."

Sethennai went very still. If Tal had expected some kind of relief, it didn't come. The hairs rose on the back of his neck. He was still held securely in the loop of Sethennai's arm, bare skin to bare skin, and nothing changed, and still it was as though Sethennai had turned to stone around him.

"What makes you think that?" said Sethennai.

"It's obvious," said Tal.

Sethennai sat up, leaning over Tal. The mattress tipped Tal flat, and he had no choice but to look up into Sethennai's face. The expression he saw there was so unfamiliar that it was like looking into the eyes of an alien creature.

Sethennai hadn't expected this. He was startled.

Then shock passed, and he gazed down at Tal: curiosity without the thinnest veil of tenderness. Tal was already naked and sprawled on his back, and he hadn't thought it was possible to feel more exposed than that, but it turned out he'd been wrong.

"I'm not making it up," said Tal.

"No, why would you?" said Sethennai, drawing back. He reached for a shirt, and his expression clouded beyond Tal's ability to decipher. He got out of bed, pulled on the shirt and a loose robe, and moved from his desk to the dresser and back, somewhat at random. Tal lay back on the bed and looked up at the ceiling. The smooth glass of the dome made him feel like a beetle trapped under a bowl.

"Are you *sure?*" said Sethennai. "It's extremely rare for mages to conceive, let alone bear a living child."

Tal told him as much as he knew, and Sethennai listened, his expression grave, his fingers drumming on his thigh.

"How old are they? Twelve or thirteen? Oh, I see—well . . . technically it's possible, I suppose," said Sethennai. "Although Oranna, the last time we—huh." He sat up straight, looking at nothing. Tal had never seen him like this before. "That night, in the temple, her hand was injured. I wondered then why she hid it from me."

Tal didn't understand. He wished he could see where his clothes had gone. By now he was very cold, not just because the room was huge and draughty and the sheets were thin. The last time he had seen Sethennai like this had been back in the day, when they'd got a lead on the location of the Reliquary.

Sethennai sat down at his desk, pinching the bridge of his nose between his eyes. "Of course it isn't over," he said, softly. "There is no rest."

"Sir?" said Tal, and realised what he'd said with an instant flip backward into a black pool of self-hatred. Sethennai at least didn't seem to notice. He was staring down at something on his desk, shaking his head slightly. Tal followed his gaze and saw the iron scrying-bowl from the House of Silence archive, looking rather dull and crude among Sethennai's other possessions.

"Does Tsereg know?" said Sethennai abruptly.

"That you're their father?" said Tal. "I'm not sure."

"No, do they know what they are?"

"What, a mage?" said Tal. "Er, I think so."

That wasn't the right guess either. One corner of Sethennai's mouth jerked up in a parody of a smile, and he returned to his thoughts, resting his chin on his folded hands. He looked like the silhouette of a mountain when the sun was behind it.

The silence crackled. Tal found he couldn't bear to look at Sethennai, so he searched around the edges of the bed for his clothes, eventually finding at least the shirt and leggings. He put them on, and when he glanced back Sethennai still hadn't moved.

"I knew something wasn't right," Sethennai muttered.

None of this fell anywhere in the region of the reaction Tal had expected. He could imagine Sethennai being unhappy not to have known about Tsereg—regretful that he'd exposed his child to danger—melancholy that Oranna was dead or angry that she'd apparently deceived him—but Tal realised he'd assumed Sethennai would eventually settle down to pleased pride. The man was always so satisfied with his achievements.

But even indifference or displeasure would have been better than this, whatever it was. This cold focus. The same chilly analysis Sethennai applied, in general, to threats.

Do they know what they are? Tal rubbed his forehead with his thumbs, trying to banish the wine headache that was creeping in, and the dread that crept in after it. He couldn't quite pin down why, and then he remembered— the lake in the dark wood, and the serpent, and what the serpent had shown them.

He's been killing the other fragments, and he's been eating them.

That had been the purpose of all this. With the death of the God-Empress, Sethennai had thought he was the last. And now he'd found out he was wrong.

In the quiet room in the guest wing, Tsereg slept on, defenceless. Tal wondered whether Sethennai was struggling with the thought of killing his own child, or whether he was just thinking about how to do it.

Tal made himself stretch and yawn. "I'm going to go and take a bath," he said. Long practice kept the tremble out of his voice. "If you don't mind. Seems like you've got stuff to be getting on with."

Sethennai nodded without looking round at him, then turned abruptly, just as Tal reached the door, making him jump. "Tal," he said. "I meant what I said last night. There would be a place here for you."

Tal smiled. "Yeah. Thank you. I'll think about it."

Tsereg didn't stir as Tal lifted them out of bed, wrapped them carefully in a blanket, and carried them out of the guest wing. They didn't make a sound the whole way, not that it mattered, given that Tal had already strangled the Thousand Eye who'd been guarding their corridor and taken her sword.

He reached the hangar and looked along the row of cutters. There was a large handsome-looking one called *Red Kite* which he thought he could fly. He bundled Tsereg aboard, opened the hangar doors, and climbed into the pilot's seat. The *Kite* slipped its bonds, gliding out into the night.

Tal wasn't going to fool himself. He'd done enough of that for one night. They didn't have long. The Thousand Eyes would be after them as soon as Sethennai realised what he'd done. His only thought was to get them away, as far and as fast as he could. That meant a Gate, and the closest was now to the north in Grey Hook, and from there to anywhere that wasn't here.

Outside the Citadel it was dark, and worse than dark. Tal had known the sugar-pink sunset light had to be a lie, but he as he brought the cutter out from among the turrets and into clear air, he pulled up sharp from pure shock.

Ringtown was gone. Where Tal had expected to see the messy scatter of lights, the dilapidated houses—it was all just *gone*. Where the town had been, a crown of new towers stretched into the desert, glossy spires tendrilling up into the air or reaching hungrily across the sand. Each one gleamed as if polished, obscenely shiny, and as the light shifted they seemed almost to move, wriggling like a colossal blue-black anemone. Each tower was as tall as the old city walls, or taller. Tal couldn't understand the scale of it. Thousands of people had lived in Ringtown—tens of thousands of people, almost the entire displaced population of Tlaanthothe—but there was no sign of anybody inside the towers, no windows and no lights.

Tal remembered Belthandros Sethennai standing on the dais inside the Citadel, telling the crowd *you're all safe*, and his hands tightened on the wheel of the cutter. How long had he been inside the palace, eating fruit in the bath, while this had been just outside?

He wove the cutter between the forest of spires as fast as he could go without risking a crash. They were even bigger than he had imagined, towering but sleek as eels. Passing close to one, he saw person-sized shapes inside them: skeletal, faintly glowing even through the black glass walls. He swallowed, keeping his eyes fixed on the way ahead. He could feel bad about this later.

It wasn't over. On the horizon, the earth cracked and another tower sprouted like some hideous fungus. The city was spreading. Was this Sethennai's doing? Did he even know he was doing it?

Tal clung to the controls as if they were the only certain thing left, and kept flying.

At last, Tsereg's forehead creased, and they turned over in their blanket cocoon.

"You there, Tal?" they said. Tal had propped them in the copilot's seat. Their eyes were still half closed.

"Yeah," he said. "I'm here."

"Is it over? Did we win?"

"We won," he said. "You can go back to sleep."

IV

Mortal Coil

At the last, all worlds fade
All strength fails, and nothing is to be saved.
Only I am without end, for desolation is my watchword.
Yet nothing is to be forgotten that belongs to me.
All things that are lost come into my keeping.

                    from the litany of the Unspoken One

Before the oceans and the Maze, even the gods are small.

                              sailors' proverb

25

The Philosopher-King

ALL AROUND THE Citadel of the God-Emperor, the dead city grew like a ring of mould on the surface of a rotten fruit. Since the duel on Midsummer's Night, it had spread constantly, the shadow of Belthandros Sethennai's influence reaching further across the black-sand desert until it was all eaten up. There were no more dunes and no more aloes, only a great glassy tangle of empty buildings without doors and twisted streets without destinations. Not even the little foxes and scorpions which had dwelt in the desert could find any shelter here.

The Citadel curled up at the centre of the dead city, a flower turned in on itself, walled in among its own brambles. There was no leaving. In that thorned labyrinth you would die of thirst before you made it out of sight of the Citadel, and it was said that worse things than thirst lurked in the shadows of the spiked towers.

Cherenthisse tried not to think about any of this. There was too much work to do. Everyone who had been within the walls of the Citadel on Midsummer's Night was now a permanent inhabitant, and all these people—mortals and Thousand Eyes alike—needed to be fed and housed and clothed. So there were patrols to schedule, and scavenging parties to provision, food and medicine to distribute, morale to sustain. Doing the work kept her sane, and it felt right to have her people to look after.

Still, sometimes her mind wandered, and she caught herself looking out at the monstrous city, as though that bright hot desolation had some power to draw the eye. They had meant to make Echentyr live again, and all they had achieved was to make this world share in Echentyr's ruin.

At least the Glass Archive had no windows. Now that Belthandros Sethennai ruled in the Citadel, the Archive was its heart, and he kept his private quarters here. Cherenthisse approached the grand table, trying not to show her distaste at its contents: game boards, musical instruments, bowls of fruit, boxes of sweets and cigars, carafes of wine, and dozens of books in haphazard piles.

The Pretender himself was sitting at the table playing a board game against Niranthe Charossa, who held a cup of tea very tightly between her thin fingers. Cherenthisse didn't recognise the game. Something with many counters of different colours, all in dyed ivory.

The Pretender liked games. In Echentyr, cards and dice had been diversions for servants, something to keep them distracted from their short lives. Some of the Thousand Eyes had taken to them in this new existence, and Cherenthisse did not begrudge them, but Sethennai seemed to love all mortal pursuits. There was something grotesque about it, a god stooping to this kind of frivolity.

"I hope you aren't letting me win, Niranthe," he said, with a brittle smile.

"I'm offended you would think it, Chancellor," said Niranthe, with an equally transparent attempt at good humour. Niranthe Charossa had emerged as Cherenthisse's opposite number among the palace's mortal inhabitants, a woman of good sense and perspective. She could not disguise a flicker of relief on catching sight of Cherenthisse.

"Ah, yes. The First Commander wanted to see me. We'll have to finish this another time," said Sethennai, with the usual thin lacquer of languid amusement over some deep abyss of boredom and frustration. At least the God-Empress had worn her weariness openly. Cherenthisse didn't know who Sethennai thought he was deceiving.

Niranthe cleared out with a brief backward glance at Cherenthisse, a faint warning look. Cherenthisse took her seat at the table, eyeing the counters to avoid making eye contact.

"Well, Cherenthisse?" said Sethennai, pouring himself a glass of wine.

Where to begin. "Sir, the Thousand Eyes have been wondering—that is to say, I'm here for myself but also representing their views—and they—we—have been wondering—"

"Yes?"

"We have been wondering what the plan is now," she said. "We have been wondering about Echentyr."

Sethennai leant back in his chair. "Of course. My predecessor promised you a triumphant return to the old country, and no triumphant return has materialised. I can see that's very disappointing for you."

Cherenthisse held her chin high, doing her best to compress and ignore her feelings. Whatever she thought of Sethennai, she had sworn fealty to him.

He had defeated Cherenthisse's empress, whom she had served through all these years, who had trusted and relied upon her.

Nevertheless, Cherenthisse's duty was clear: she had been hatched and educated to serve the goddess Iriskavaal, and if any trace of the goddess remained in any world, it was in this man, Belthandros Sethennai, the one and only remaining incarnation of her goddess. It should have been easy for her: no division, no doubt, the blessed certainty of orders to follow.

The trouble was that Cherenthisse hated him. She hated his pose of sleepy amusement, his endless tolerant irony, as if everything was rather funny and nothing meant anything, as if her own concerns were fundamentally small and laughable. She hated his voice, his face, his self-indulgence. Everything about him was wrong. She missed her own God-Empress with a sleepless, dismal yearning.

"Tell me, Cherenthisse," he said. "What do you imagine it would have felt like to return to Echentyr? There is an emptiness in you, no doubt, some formless need which you think would be satisfied if you had your own place again, if you had your original form."

This was so far from what she had expected that she had nothing to say. The Pretender rose from his seat, picked up a cigar, and beckoned her after him, leaving his glass of wine forgotten and unsipped. She followed him up a flight of stairs and down a hallway to a balcony that looked out over the dead sprawl below.

Cherenthisse's choice was to look at the blasted city or to look at Sethennai. She focused on the horizon and tried to remember what the skyline of Echentyr had looked like. Was it true, what he said?

"All mortal creatures think this way," he said, behind her. "I understand that, because I felt it myself. Before I knew myself for what I am, I thought—"

He paused, and stepped in front of Cherenthisse, giving her no choice but to make eye contact.

"I was born a mortal, you know," he said, another change of subject so sharp that Cherenthisse was taken by surprise. "As Pentravesse I was a prince of my world. Even that was a pretty dreary existence. I felt all the time that there must be something more, that if I had this one short life, there must be some greater thing to do.

"And then I came to Echentyr, to the court of the Empress. I'm sure you can imagine the impression it made on me. I felt that if I could make a place for myself there, among all that beauty and luxury and power—then I would be content at last.

"My disillusionment came slowly. The Echentyri squabbled, reproduced, and died like anybody else. I studied, I gained power, I became a favourite of the Empress. There was always more to gain, and whatever I gained fell to ashes as soon as I had it. The only real thing, the only true power, was the power of Iriskavaal, and sooner or later, that was mine too."

He put his head on one side, watching Cherenthisse thoughtfully. She refused to give him the satisfaction of reacting in any way to the name of her goddess or the slander of her people.

"I would never die. I had everything I wanted. And it was so unbearable that I forgot as soon as I could. I imagined myself to be a mortal man again. I returned to the striving, the endless rivalry, the pursuit of futile gain, earthly power, fruitless territories. To live a mortal life is to yearn for completeness, and there is nothing in mortal life which satisfies that particular hunger."

He glanced at the unlit cigar in his hand, no longer smiling. "Even now I seem to want to believe that there is some relief to be found in temporal things. So I do understand why you and your colleagues wish to return to your own homeland. But Echentyr is just a place, just something else to strive for to no real end."

"You're wrong," said Cherenthisse, before she could think about it. She shut her mouth abruptly, feeling horror close around her like a strangling cord. What had she said? What had possessed her to say it? To all that remained of Iriskavaal? What was the matter with her?

"Am I?" said Sethennai. He smiled, but his eyes were cold and still. "Well . . . you're very young. But tell me, how am I wrong? What do you disagree with?"

"I don't know," said Cherenthisse. She didn't think she could explain her feeling of wrongness, even to herself.

"Do you think Echentyr was so very great? You lived in fine style as one of the Thousand Eyes, I do not doubt, but to be a slave, or a vassal, or even a lower-caste serpent, was no great delight."

"Please forget it, sir, I didn't mean anything by it—"

"I think you did," he said. "Do you miss being a serpent so very badly?"

Cherenthisse shook her head. Sometimes, still, yes, but only in the way he had described, a vague sense that something was missing or unsatisfactory.

"Well?"

"There are things worth doing," she said haltingly. The God-Empress had known that, surely.

Sethennai managed to look both relieved and disappointed, as if he had both hoped and feared she might have a better answer for him. "Perhaps," he said. "But there is no way to make them endure. Funny—that always was Oranna's creed. Nothing lasts. Nobody lives. Not even her, in the end."

He leant on the balustrade and gestured out at the necropolis below: the blasted sand, the barbed and lifeless spires, the towers of glass. "All this is my earthly mansion, Cherenthisse. All that remains of Tlaanthothe. All this and more than you can see. I am no longer interested in playing the philosopher-king. This is how a divinity should rule."

26

The Prioress

PRIORESS CWEREN LAY in a crevice beneath the Iron Hill and knew that she was dying. The prison-fortress where she had spent the last fourteen years of her life was on fire.

All over the plain, new towers sprouted like mushrooms, and one of them had pierced the jagged bulk of the prison all the way through, and stuck there. Both prison and tower, wedged firmly together, were burning steadily despite the heavy rain. Cweren herself had crawled into a sheltered place to die.

Well, Cweren thought, *I always intended to get out. I just meant to make it a little bit further.*

She was in considerable pain, but she had long experience of simply putting the pain somewhere else. All form took shape in emptiness, and that included her own form, and any pain and indignity it might suffer.

At least she was out of the rain, and warm. Warmer than she'd been in years, even this far from the fire. The Iron Hill shed sparks like clouds of midges from a core of flame. Yes, if she had to die so far from home, it was pleasant at least to see the prison burn.

Then a shape emerged from the smoke, a single seedpod picked out by the lightning.

It was a small two-canopy cutter. Two people in it. *That's dangerous,* thought Cweren distantly. *They're flying towards the fire.*

It grew closer and closer and landed somewhere Cweren could not see. It was hard for her to turn her head. Two people got out. She could hear them talking to each other, but not what they said.

One of them knelt beside her, taking Cweren's hands in their own.

"Prioress Cweren," said a small voice.

"Tsereg," said Cweren. She reached out to touch the top of the child's head with a trembling hand. She had not thought to see Oranna's child again. And yet there was a rightness, that Tsereg should be here to witness her death as Cweren had witnessed Oranna's.

"What happened, Prioress?" said Tsereg. "Where is everyone? What happened to Tsurai and Narwe and—"

"We tried to escape when the prison broke," said Cweren. It was hard to speak. Her throat was parched and she had to shunt her words carefully into place. "It was no good. The Thousand Eyes caught up to us. They took the others to the Citadel, and left me as I am. Child, what has happened? We knew nothing until the disaster came."

Tsereg explained what they could. Cweren found herself wishing she could offer the child some kind of comfort or consolation, which was strange, since this had not been her business in life. A darkness clouded her vision. There was something she should tell them. Something to do with Oranna.

"Then she is dead? The false God-Empress?" said Cweren.

"Yes," said Tsereg. "I was there. I helped."

Cweren shut her eyes for a moment as a tremor of pain ran through her. What should she feel? Pride, relief, triumph? No, overwhelmingly what she felt was guilt. That this child had done what she herself could not, and that Cweren had nothing to offer them in return but loss.

"Then we are avenged," said Cweren, "and the will of the Unspoken is done."

Was this really the best she could manage? What was it she had been meaning to say? Tsereg had kept them all alive inside the Iron Hill, by their very existence. Feeding Tsereg, teaching them, raising them as one of the faithful, all that had been the thing sustaining everyone's hope. Cweren did not know how to explain it.

"Your mother," Cweren went on, "I knew your mother—we were friends—" No, that wasn't it.

"I know, Prioress," said Tsereg gently.

"No, no," said Cweren, impatient with herself. Darkness swirled around her. Despite the heat of the fire, she was starting to be cold. "She told me— she told me—you need to know—"

"Let's get you out of here, ma'am," said Tsereg.

The chill deepened, as though the forest of northern Oshaar had lived in her all this time. That was a good thought. Death might mean going home after all. "Listen, Tsereg—that which is without end—"

"Can we lift you—Tal, could we lift her?"

"No. Listen to me," said Cweren, mustering as much force as she could, and she felt for a moment as if she were really Prioress of the House of

Silence once more. "You need to know what you are. Go home. Go to the Shrine."

"But it's all gone," said Tsereg. Cweren herself had seen the House burn, shackled among the rest of the faithful as the Thousand Eyes had marched them aboard their ship.

"Of course," Cweren managed. "By unmaking is emptiness perfected. Go home. You'll see."

"We need to get you to a doctor," said Tsereg.

Tsereg did not look much like their mother, and never had, but the luminous determination in their small face was all Oranna. Ever hopeful, ever confident that all would come good.

Maybe they were right.

No wonder Oranna had left the House of Silence. It had been nothing to do with Cweren at all. The creed of the Unspoken was the endless fading, the world that slipped away like water, like dust, and could never be held. But perhaps—perhaps—

Cweren said no more. Tsereg sat there with her, holding her hand.

Tal stood a little way off, and could not help wincing every time the burning ruin creaked. It was all going to collapse eventually, and Tal did not want to be there when it did. Still, Tsereg deserved at least to say their goodbyes.

"All things that are lost come into my keeping," said Tsereg softly, and made a gesture Tal had seen Csorwe perform sometimes, the tips of three fingers pressed to the lips. They touched the Prioress' forehead and got back to their feet.

The two of them sailed away in silence. It would have been better if Tsereg had cried properly. They just stared at Tal, the usual flinty glare dull with grief, as though something in them had finally burnt out.

"I could have got her out," said Tsereg, when it was no longer visible. "At least her. They were all meant to get away. This is—"

"If you're going to say *this is my fault*," said Tal, "just give me a moment to scream into a bag first. Sethennai did this, and the snakes."

"If I hadn't believed Keleiros—" they said.

Tal shook his head. "Trust me. He was going to do what he was going to do. You couldn't have stopped this."

"You don't understand," said Tsereg.

"Pretty normal to feel like it's your fault," he said. "But sometimes things don't work out. People die, and it's the fucking worst, but it's not—"

"I was Chosen," said Tsereg, hitting the capital *C* hard enough to crack its skull. "It was my job to make sure this didn't happen. It's the only thing I was ever supposed to do."

"*Tsereg*—"

"I was meant to die back there in the Citadel, and the others were meant to live," they said. "I knew it was going to happen. I was fine with it."

This was every bit as fucked up as the first time Tal had heard it.

"So, what, you actually think if you'd died fighting the Empress that this wouldn't have happened?" he said.

They faced him, glaring. "How do you think I'm alive? The only reason I survived the Iron Hill is because everyone covered for me. I always got food and medicine even when the others didn't."

"It's not like you asked for it," said Tal. "You were a little kid—"

They stared at him. "Why would that matter? They kept me alive to save them, and I failed. So don't tell me this isn't my fault."

Tal clenched his fists on the wheel of the cutter and swallowed his outrage.

"People do this all the time, you know," he said. "Make you believe you owe them something just by existing. It's not *fair*, Tsereg! Why should you get Chosen? Not like you get to fucking choose."

"My mother—"

"Yeah, actually, whatever they've told you about her, I think they lied to you," he said. "I knew Oranna. I didn't like her. But she didn't act like she was doing you this huge favour by kicking you in the nuts. She was honest about what you were getting into. More or less. Most of the time, anyway."

"Why would they lie to me?" said Tsereg, equally angry. "They wouldn't. They didn't need to. And now they're all dead, all my friends, so fuck you."

"She said they were taken to the Citadel—"

"Yeah, and what just happened to the Citadel?" said Tsereg.

"Some of them might have got away," said Tal, though he didn't have much hope.

Tsereg slammed a fist against the inner hull of the cutter and swore. "It's not *fair*! It wasn't going to be like this! We won! I did everything I was meant to do!"

They buried their head in their hands and screamed silently into them. Tal reached out cautiously to pat their shoulder, but they threw him off, curled into a tight knot of anguish.

When they spoke again, it was in a disturbingly flat, even tone, with an iron self-control which seemed alien to them.

"Do you know Belthandros Sethennai very well, Tal?" they said.

He blinked, taken aback. "I—uh—I used to work for him."

"But do you know much about what he's like?" they said.

"What's brought this on?" said Tal, unease prickling at him.

"He's my father," said Tsereg, just like that.

"You *knew?*" said Tal. He had been agonising about when to tell them. It was obvious that they needed to know, at least so they'd understand why the Thousand Eyes were chasing them, but there did not seem to be a good moment.

"It's in the book," said Tsereg, as if that were obvious. "Didn't mean much to me to begin with, just a bunch of stuff about *if you meet him, don't even think about trusting him,* but I figured he was dead so it didn't matter. But now—knowing he was Keleiros, and knowing he's got a fragment of Iriska-vaal inside him—I mean, if there's some mystery about me, about *what I am,* it doesn't take a genius, does it."

"No," said Tal. "Even I figured it out. He thinks you're . . . part of what he is. That you're another fragment, somehow. Like you've inherited it from him."

"So I've been on the snake side all along. Yeah," said Tsereg. They weren't looking at him. Their face was half hidden behind their hair. "Cweren knew all along. I wonder if they all knew. And they never said anything."

Of course they hadn't, Tal thought bitterly, because it would have thrown off their whole story about how Tsereg was the Chosen whatever and destined to die young.

"Listen," he said. "We don't have to do what she told you."

"I'm not a coward," said Tsereg.

"Nothing wrong with wanting to live," said Tal. "Fuck 'em. This time we both have a choice. If you just want to get out of here, we can, even if you are part snake, who cares? They don't own you. Nobody does."

He had his doubts about how long they could run from the Thousand Eyes, but he wasn't going to throw Tsereg under the wheels of anyone else's plan. Maybe there was a world out there that the God-Empress hadn't touched. He could try and send Tsereg to school, find some wizard who was prepared to teach them, find some kind of job to pay for all that.

Sethennai had taken so much from them both. They deserved a chance to make their own way. He braced himself for his usual attempt at not thinking too much about Sethennai. Usually this took a lot of effort and felt like poking himself repeatedly in the eye.

But now . . . Well, it still hurt, and he wished he hadn't been taken in by Keleiros, but there was no clamour of inner opinion burbling about how this was Tal's fault for asking too much or being too stupid, fretting about what Sethennai thought of him now, weighing and measuring how much he was worth and whether he had done well. It didn't matter. It was over. He was done.

He expected another snap from Tsereg, another flat denial. Instead they rested their head on their folded hands and looked at him curiously.

"It wasn't an accident, you know, whatever it is I am," they said. "My mother meant it all to happen. Me getting born and everything." They rolled their eyes, embarrassed. "I want to know for certain. Then we can run, maybe. But I want to know first. We have to go to the Shrine."

"Yeah, I know," said Tal. "I just hope you know the way."

27

Well Done, Talasseres

THE WHITE STAIRS that led up to the Shrine of the Unspoken were buried under feet of snow, the shed skin of an entire winter. That route would not be passable for months, so Tal and Tsereg landed their cutter higher up on the mountainside and trudged down toward the plateau.

Below them, the hungry forest lapped around the House of Silence, cloaking it in pine boughs and settling snow as if to hide what had been done to the only temple of the Unspoken One.

It was a ruin. What was visible from above resembled the body of a beached whale: a huge grey bulk, rotten and collapsing, with rows of pillars standing out like ribs. The roof of the Great Hall had fallen in, leaving it open to the sky.

The Shrine itself was nothing but a dark hole in the mountainside. Tal thought it was a bit of a letdown. It was just the entrance to a cave, cold and dark, ominous and probably dangerous, but there was no crackle of power, no magnetic draw, no sense of an immortal presence reaching out to grasp you. Tal had experienced quite enough immortal presence to know what it felt like.

"So do we just—" he said.

Tsereg had been very quiet on the walk down, eerily so. Tal couldn't see much of their face behind the scarf, but what was visible was a fretful combination of reverence and anticipation and frank ambition, all simmered together.

"Yep," they said, and strode into the cave.

Tal had to hurry to keep up, faster than he would have liked, given that the passage was icy and sank rapidly into total darkness. They had stopped on their way to scavenge clothes from an abandoned village, so now Tsereg was wrapped in a padded coat of bright yellow wool that made them look spherical. The bobble on their woolly hat bounced with every step. They should have looked out of place here; Tal should have found the whole thing funny, or at least sad, but in fact there was nothing incongruous about it at all. Tsereg was meant to be here.

As they emerged into a larger chamber, the last of the light from the entrance faded altogether and Tal reached into his pack to light a torch.

"No," said Tsereg. "No light. Listen. Watch."

Tal did as he was told. There was silence. The distant plink of water. The pressure of the dark all around him.

"Think we need to go down deeper," said Tsereg. He felt them take his hand and squeeze his fingers through two layers of mitten. "Don't worry," they added.

This ought to be frightening. It was all absurdly ominous, and Tal didn't like enclosed spaces at the best of times, and he ought to make some crack about *yeah, let's stumble around in the dark until I trip over and break my neck*—but he didn't. He wasn't scared at all. He felt certain, in a way he had not felt certain for a long time, that everything was under control.

"Follow me," said Tsereg. "I know the way."

Fear had filled him up for so long, a great bubble occupying most of his skull. Walking into darkness and doubt, he had expected the bubble to swell to bursting, but instead it felt more like finding your way through your own house at night, certain of the path, and returning securely to your warm bed.

"I'm going to let go of you for a second," said Tsereg. "Stay still, or you'll fall."

Their footsteps moved softly away. The two of them were in a larger chamber again, to judge from the echo and the way the air moved. Still Tal wasn't scared. The future was as open and as unreadable as the black void ahead of him. When he had been very young and the whole world had hummed with possibility, this had been a good feeling.

A soft light gleamed up ahead, illuminating the cavern. It was vast, and longer than it was wide. Tal was standing at one end, and all around him—in heaps, like drifts of fallen leaves, like so much ossuary debris—were hundreds of shrivelled corpses. Most of them were little more than bone, held together by shreds of shrunken skin and wisps of hair and the tattered remains of white dresses.

—and *still* Tal wasn't scared. The bodies were whole, not scattered. From the way they lay, they seemed to have curled up together to sleep, except that they were all of them holding hands. They made a great chain that ribboned through the chamber toward the far end, where Tsereg stood, holding a single flame in their hands, before a tall, rectangular hollow cut into the back wall.

Tsereg climbed up onto the lip of the hollow and sat on the edge, as if waiting for something to happen.

"You sure you should be doing that?" he said, with a prickle of true alarm, as though he had woken and seen for the first time where he was standing.

They didn't reply. And then, abruptly, they began to sing. There was no warning of this; it sounded as though they had perhaps been singing for their entire life and someone had just removed a bag from over their head.

The spectacle of someone else bursting solemnly into song was one of those things which should have made Tal's insides shrivel up biliously with secondhand embarrassment. It should have been all the worse because it was Tsereg, who never had any idea that what they were doing was appalling. Tal shouldn't have known where to look.

In fact, he couldn't look away, not from Tsereg's solemn little face nor from the great yawning space above them, the empty hollow, which he now recognised for what it was: an immense granite throne. A throne, with Tsereg sitting upon it, in their yellow coat, feet neatly tucked in.

He didn't recognise the song. It had the thudding repetition he associated with something *religious*. Tsereg's singing voice was, if nothing else, strident. Then, just as abruptly, they stopped.

The song did not. Elsewhere, out of the darkness, in the other hollow places of the Shrine, it continued, in voices rough and scratching, small and high and piping, in whispers and in echoes.

"Tal," said Tsereg, with the slightly wheedling briskness he had come to recognise and dread. "Something's happening. Try not to panic."

To the song, there was added a sound as soft as rain falling, and all throughout the chamber the dead unlaced their shrivelled limbs and began to rise.

"Try not to *panic*?" said Tal. He didn't move. Couldn't, in fact. He'd heard of being frozen in terror, but he'd always assumed it was just an expression, because when he was terrified he only wanted to move, preferably *away*— but he couldn't think straight enough to make his legs move.

The skeletal fingers uncurled from one another and reached up like new shoots, pale and pointed. Gradually, and then all at once, as though they had been playing a game and now it was over, all the dead children rose to their feet.

"Try not to panic, *Tsereg?*" said Tal. The false sarcasm cracked like old paint.

"Yeah, for once in your life!" called Tsereg.

Hundreds and hundreds of Tsereg-sized ghouls, and as they rose, they all let go of each other's hands and turned to face the throne. They were singing too. The voice of each was no louder than the sifting hiss of sand, but hundreds of them together were dreadfully audible.

Another light flared, just behind him, and he jumped. Two revenants, much bonier than the others, without even a shred of lingering cartilage, came past him and on down toward the throne. One of them had a single candle on a stone dish. The other was carrying a long and fraying length of embroidered yellow silk, folded many times and tattered at the edges.

The other revenants formed up into rows on either side of the chamber, and the chanting song grew louder, somehow more purposeful. Tal had the sense that he was about to witness something of awful spiritual import and prepared to be bored as well as terrified.

Then he noticed that the cloth was the same colour as Tsereg's coat, and he was back to being terrified. He had been so sure that Tsereg knew what they were doing, that they knew all about the Unspoken and would be able to avoid its pitfalls. He'd forgotten how the cult habitually treated its children.

"Leave them alone!" he said, but the revenants continued to pay him no attention. "Don't you dare—"

It wasn't just fear that held him to the spot. He tried to move now, really tried, but it was as if Tsereg's injunction to stay still had fixed him in place. He would have drawn his sword if he wouldn't have ended up waving it around like a statue with its feet stuck to a plinth.

The two revenants reached the centre of the chamber, still facing Tsereg on their throne. Ceremoniously they set down the cloth and the candle, so that the flame cast up flickery shadows, shining up through their rib cages.

And then with a suddenness that made Tal throw up his hands to protect his face, they exploded.

There was no detonation. There was no sound at all. The bones floated in the air in two small clouds, illuminated from below by the light of the single candle. The small bones glittered: metacarpals, phalanges, teeth. The two skulls and four femurs tilted slowly among them like larger fish within a shoal.

Then there came a faint, sandy grinding noise as the bones began to reconnect. They danced in bony constellations, turning and wheeling in place or in great arcs. The vertebrae locked into solid curves and the loose limbs began to articulate themselves. There was a soft rattling, like wind in dry reeds.

A single skeleton stepped out of the cloud, adjusting its skull on the fragile stem of its neck. It pressed its second tusk back into place with an indescribably unpleasant pop.

Tal had watched all of this in the assumption that he had finally gone mad, that all this bone stuff had been the last straw for one T. Charossa, and that that was it, thanks for nothing and goodnight. The reconstituted skeleton did nothing to dispel this impression by turning and walking toward him. Its bony feet crunched on the stone floor, sounding like someone walking on dry bread crumbs.

Tal leant back as the thing approached. He did not want it to touch him. He was sure it had more bones than it ought to. It was slightly taller than either of the original two, for one thing. It held out its hands to him and gave him what was unmistakably an expectant look.

"What?" he said.

It just kept holding out its hands. The smallest finger on each was no more than a stump.

Its empty eye sockets seemed to reproach him. It made sense that this might be the last thing he saw—stared into passive-aggressive oblivion by a corpse—but he didn't have to like it.

"*What?*" he said. "You missed a spot, it's not my fault."

He looked at his own hands, still not understanding. Tsereg had picked out these mittens for him. They were lumpy and orange and matted with melted snow.

The yellow robe on the ground floated up around the revenant's shoulders, and fastened itself into place. The revenant pulled up the hood of the robe and drew it down to veil the gleaming cranium. The fabric was translucent, embroidered with some swirling design, and it framed the fleshless grin with a fringe of tiny pearls.

All the while it looked at Tal, apparently watching for his reaction. Then it lifted his chin with two bony fingers, and a familiar voice said:

"Well, you look much better than you have any right to."

The freezing hold on him collapsed and his legs seemed to turn into bags of water. Only the fact that it would have been incredibly fucking embarrassing to fall on his face at this point kept him upright.

Tsereg stood up on the edge of the throne to see over the crowd of revenants, quicker on the uptake, as ever, than Tal had ever managed to be.

"Mum?" they said. Just in case Tal's heart had needed breaking again, there was an undisguisable hitch in their voice. They hastily pulled off the woolly hat and stuffed it into their coat pocket.

"Oh, well *done*, Talasseres," said Oranna, and—proving there was a first time for everything—she sounded completely sincere.

Tal toyed with a series of smart responses from *what the shit* to *what the fuck* and eventually, with great poise and deliberation, sat down on the floor.

28

Salt Water

Csorwe woke, with the floating disoriented sense that you got from napping too long in the afternoon. She had been asleep for a *long* time. She had no idea where she was.

She had the vague sense that she was being carried by a gigantic bird. Something huge and dark which had swooped down and picked her up. That made about as much sense as anything.

It didn't usually take so long to remember where she was. She might have been hit on the head. It was hard to feel very worried about that when she was held so securely. She had the feeling of travelling by night as a passenger in an open boat: the cold wind nipping at her face, the rest of her wrapped in a warm blanket, the sense of the dark landscape passing away below in a sleepy, distant blur.

Her limbs felt mainly numb, but her cheek was buried in something soft and feathery.

"What time is it?" she murmured, nuzzling against it.

"Late," said a rather distant voice, after a long pause.

Well then, thought Csorwe. She closed her eyes and went back to sleep.

The next time she woke, she was lying on the shore of a still green sea. The beach was coarse white sand, like flakes of salt, and the light was clear but distorted, as if it had filtered down through crystal. She was very cold. The cold had woken her. She felt something brush against her neck, like a loose and prickly scarf. She pulled at it and winced. She didn't remember growing her hair so long.

Uneasiness crept in with the cold. She was alone. Something bad had happened. The sand shifted under the press of her hand, and she felt the particles of grit under her fingernails, much too real for this to be a hallucination. The last thing she remembered—but no, trying to remember anything came with a soft, fuzzy sense of warning.

"Better for you to remain asleep," said the same distant voice.

She sat up and looked around. Further down the beach, looking out at the sea, was a small dark figure. The figure was oddly familiar. Something about the slim build, the focused composure, the sense of force controlled by tremendous self-discipline. Something kept her from calling out at once. Not just the fact that this woman was wearing armour in a style Csorwe had never seen before—dark overlapping lamellae with a sheen that looked more like carapace than metal—but something else too, a warning beacon which flickered hot across all the disconnected fragments of her memory.

"Who are you?" said Csorwe, when she realised she had to say something, or the stranger might look out to sea forever.

The woman turned, her armoured feet crunching on the sand, but before Csorwe saw her face, she raised a hand and Csorwe slumped backward, dropping instantly into sleep.

She woke for a third time, hungry and terribly thirsty, seated upright in a hard white chair, in a grand shadowy room whose exact bounds were hard to gauge. The same cold, crystalline light came in through a row of high windows that reminded her of a chapel. It felt desolate, wind-scoured, as though moss ought to have grown between the flagstones—except that there were no flagstones, and whenever she looked at any one surface, her eyes seemed to slide away.

There was a monumental table before her, banded white in the light from the windows and stretching away into the indeterminate darkness beyond. On the table was a goblet of thick clear glass, bulbous and misshapen, as if viewed through flowing water. Beside it was a black stone bowl of what looked like broken eggs, though to judge from the salt-water smell, they were actually shellfish, cracked raw into the bowl.

"It has been many hours," said the cold voice from before. "You must eat and drink."

Csorwe's hunger wasn't up to the shellfish, but she picked up the goblet, finding it too large and heavy for comfort, and sipped. It was brine, bitter and sharp.

"I can't," she said, spitting it back into the goblet.

The dark figure swam into view and stood over the table, some distance from Csorwe. "I am bound to keep you from harm," it said. "But your dignity is of no concern. Drink or I will find other methods."

"It's seawater," said Csorwe, her dry lips stinging from the salt.

The stranger passed her hand across the goblet, palm up, and tipped a meagre handful of salt flakes onto the table. "Drink."

Csorwe sipped from the goblet and found it more or less fresh, though now the temperature of blood. She was too thirsty to object. She drank, and found that however much she drank, there was enough in the glass to quench her thirst.

"You must eat, also," said the stranger. The light did not fall on her face.

Csorwe looked down at the bowl of raw mussels. Now she had drunk, she felt the gnawing of a long-term hunger. She had certainly eaten worse, but there was no cutlery.

"What do you want me to do, sip it?" she muttered. She scooped up a handful of shellfish and slapped them into her mouth before they could escape between her fingers. They were cold and powerfully salty, like drinking directly from a rock pool, but they weren't too bad as long as you didn't dwell on the texture.

The stranger waited, silently. Her expression was not visible, but it was clear there was nothing to talk about until Csorwe had finished the bowl. There were some strands of green and brown seaweed mixed in, which made for a difference in chewiness if not in taste.

"These are from outside," said Csorwe. She had the sense that it hadn't been so long since the beach. "You pick them just for me?"

"Return to sleep," said the stranger. She raised her hand into the sunbeam, and dropped Csorwe back into sleep with the attitude of one heaving a corpse into a river.

The next time, Csorwe was ready. As soon as she was awake, she kicked the chair back and rose to her feet, grabbing the heavy goblet; never a bad idea to have a blunt instrument ready.

"What the fuck is happening?" she said, but the stranger rose with her, and her face came into the light, and it was Shuthmili.

She looked thin and ill in a way that made Csorwe think hopelessly of blankets and soup. There were dark shadows under her dark eyes, new lines of age and tiredness. These would have worried her in themselves, but the expression was worse: wearily bland, bleak, corpselike. Even in the worst times, she had never looked like this, never looked at Csorwe with such a complete lack of interest or tenderness.

"Shuthmili?" she said.

"No," said the stranger. "No longer."

It was like a dream, seeing the face of someone you loved and knowing it to be a mask—but Csorwe looked down at her hand, her own familiar tendons and knuckles, resting on the table beside the bowl of glutinous yellow shellfish, and knew this was no dream.

Her memory cleared, as though she had been looking without knowing it through smeared glass. She knew who she was. She remembered the House of Silence, and Sethennai, and Tal, and the temple in the deepwood. She remembered the Mantle, the powerless terror, the obliterating darkness. *Forgive me, but I will never leave you.*

"Where is she?" said Csorwe. Cold terror pierced through her confusion like a needle going in.

"Gone," said the stranger. She sounded almost exactly like Shuthmili—like Shuthmili when Csorwe had first met her and mistaken her reserve for haughtiness.

"What happened?" said Csorwe. The stranger moved to put her back to sleep, but Csorwe had already lunged forward to grab her arm. "No! Tell me what happened!" The plates of her armour weren't metal or leather but part of her body—something like horn or bone, rough and warm to the touch.

The stranger made a disgusted noise and twitched Csorwe instantly into unconsciousness.

Csorwe came awake feebly, with a pounding headache and a thick, stupid feeling. She realised distantly that she was severely dehydrated.

"What happened?" she said again. "Let me go! What happened to Shuthmili?"

"I have no obligation to keep you in comfort," said the stranger, who was sitting on the edge of the table. To Csorwe's distaste, she was holding a bowl of seaweed in one hand and the goblet in the other. "Compliance is rewarded."

Csorwe was too thirsty to tell her to fuck off, as this clearly merited. She drank from the goblet held to her lips, lukewarm water slopping down her chin, and she ate bundles of seaweed from the stranger's clawed fingertips.

"I complied," she said, when the stranger stepped back. "What happened? Who are you, if you're not her?"

She didn't want the stranger to answer. Every word made it clearer that it had really happened, that Shuthmili was really gone.

The stranger shrugged. Her face didn't change—Shuthmili's eyes were dead behind lowered lashes—but there was a visible impatience in her posture.

"I am Zinandour. It is by my grace that you live, and the next time you touch me, I will put out your eyes. I must go away for a time. Chambers are prepared for you. You will feed yourself. You will not leave those chambers. You will not harm yourself."

"Sure," said Csorwe, privately deciding that she would throw herself out of the first window she saw.

"Do not lie to me," said Zinandour. She pressed the tip of one claw under Csorwe's chin and looked into her face.

"Don't *touch* me," Csorwe snarled, jerking her head back. The look of routine displeasure was very like Shuthmili's expression when confronting a poorly indexed reference work, and she couldn't bear it.

Zinandour clicked her tongue and then frowned, as if it hadn't come naturally to her. "It was sentiment to spare you," she said. "If you attempt to escape or to harm yourself—"

"What?" said Csorwe. "What can you possibly do to me?"

The goddess hissed, reaching for her throat again, and Csorwe sprang out of the chair. Or rather, she tried to spring, but weeks of Zinandour's ministrations had left her with the muscle tone of boiled carrots, and she tripped to one side, scraping her calf against the leg of the bony chair with a stinging pain.

"Fuck *off*," said Csorwe. She was aware that she'd become pathetic, but at this point she was out of other options.

"Stand," said Zinandour, looming over her.

Csorwe struggled to her feet, light-headed, but before she could get her balance again, Zinandour had pinned her to the wall, one hand holding her shoulder, one barbed forearm pressed loosely across her throat.

"Wiser not to contemplate what I can possibly do to you," said Zinandour.

"Wow," said Csorwe, the words burbling out of their own sweet accord, with no regard for the thorns of chitin poised close to her jugular. "I hate contemplating, you'd better tell me."

Zinandour made a sound of profound disgust and dropped her. Csorwe sat down heavily and stayed there, a dull blush crawling up her cheeks. She'd forgotten for a second where she was and what had happened. It was a miserable insult that it was possible to forget. It was extremely unfair that Zinandour had never looked more like Shuthmili than when she'd had Csorwe pushed up against a hard surface. It was a whole new territory of bleakness and guilt that she was going to have to trudge across.

"Coming on a bit strong," she muttered eventually.

Zinandour was swishing around somewhere in the middle distance. "Silence," she said. "Fifteen years was superfluous for me to learn of your relations with the vessel. I have no desire to—"

"Fifteen *years*?" said Csorwe, startled out of misery. Zinandour started saying something, but Csorwe could not let this go. Certain things clicked into place, such as why Shuthmili looked so very tired. "*Fifteen* years?"

"As I said," said Zinandour, returning to look down at her. "I am leaving. You will—"

"I won't do shit," said Csorwe. "You want me to behave, I want information."

"No," said Zinandour. "It is tedious, and I have other tasks to accomplish."

"Yeah, I bet, and one of them's going to be fishing my mangled corpse out of the sea unless you tell me what the hell is going on."

Zinandour sat down at the table, weariness creeping across her features like a drift of cobweb. "Even the threat of self-annihilation loses its potency," she said, propping her cheek on her gauntleted hand.

"I'm working with what I've got. If you give me a sword, I can do other threats."

Zinandour rubbed her forehead between her eyes and exhaled; the gesture was so mortally familiar that Csorwe almost wanted to apologise. "Very well," she said. "Obey my edicts when I am gone, and when I return, I will tell you the truth."

The earthly mansion of Zinandour, the Flame That Devours, hung suspended in the Maze like a jewel in the throat of a giant, high above the sea below. It was called the Pearl of Oblivion, and there was no way out.

The walls of Csorwe's chambers were curved, made of some hard, smooth pearl-stuff. The windows on one side of the bedroom looked out on an unpeopled and alien palace, all apparently wrought from the same shell-like matter, whose keeps and towers and domes all had a soft organic curvature, like wax or petals. Every time she looked out at it, her brain threw up some other idiot comparison, such as *meringue*. On the other side of the bedroom was a balcony which looked out over the ocean, a deep and uncanny green, so still and so clear that Csorwe could have seen a long way down into it if there had been anything to see.

Her quarters had a bathroom, an apparently well-stocked pantry, a rudimentary kitchen, and nothing resembling a door. She couldn't remember quite how Zinandour had brought her in here; she seemed to remember that the goddess had drawn aside the wall like a curtain and pushed her inside. There was of course the balcony. She wondered if Zinandour had left it there on purpose.

A shifting light reflected up from the waters below and glowed through the shell stuff from within. The next-door bath was a cup of shell grown up from the floor, and so was the bed, except that it had been filled to the brim with soft pelts. The rest of the furnishings suggested that Zinandour's idea of mortal tastes had been shaped by a very singular source. The bedroom was lined almost wall to wall with books. There were three different jars of pickled vegetables on the desk, and a tin of watercolour paints, and the wardrobe contained a wide selection of drifty robes, half of them embroidered with pearls. Csorwe's heart ached.

The labels on the pickle jars were faded and peeling. Everything else was washed out and battered as if it had been recovered from a shipwreck.

While Zinandour was gone, Csorwe returned to her old training regimen gradually, with the suspicion that she'd been absent from her body for a long time and that she'd better treat it gently.

She'd always been good at dealing with boredom. She could thank the House of Silence for that much. She could operate pretty much all day not thinking about anything. Not thinking, for instance, about how goddamn unfair it was, about how little time they'd really had, about her creeping doubt that there was really any point in doing anything now.

One evening as she was about to go to bed, something plummeted from the sky in a steep arc and crashed into the balcony.

At first she took it for a gigantic seabird, which would have been a smarter guess if she'd seen anything flapping about with a six-foot wingspan. It battered against the doors and fell still. The impression of wings subsided, and instead what she clearly saw was Zinandour, curled over on her face in a pool of blue-black feathers.

Csorwe opened the door, and the goddess fell inside. As she struggled to her feet, shadows poured off her like water, and her dark hair fell over her scaled exoskeleton like a veil.

"Csorwe," she said, reaching vaguely for her as though blind, and stumbled to sit on the edge of the bed.

"What happened?" said Csorwe.

"Always the same question," said Zinandour. Her voice was strained, which made it curiously softer, weathered to gentleness.

"Are you injured?" said Csorwe. Zinandour's robe was shredded, and underneath it she was shedding tarry ichor from between the plates of her armour. Could a goddess be injured?

"Belthandros is—so depressingly eager," said Zinandour, pressing a hand to her rib cage. "To enlist me."

"You mean—" said Csorwe, hardly knowing how to react to this. "He's here?"

Zinandour shook her head. "He is uncounted worlds away. I killed a dozen of his Thousand Eyes at the far boundary."

Csorwe stared at her.

"I told you I would explain," said Zinandour. She lay back on Csorwe's bed, heedless of the trails of ichor still trickling from her abdomen, and she explained.

The story was in some ways very complicated and in others very simple. As far as Csorwe was concerned, the significant thing was that Shuthmili had meant at least some of this to happen, somehow, that it had all been part of a plan which had kept her going for more than ten years. And the rest of it was all Belthandros Sethennai.

"You knew him," said Zinandour.

"Uh," said Csorwe. "Yes."

"Then you know his dreadful persistence. I must rest," said Zinandour. She closed her eyes, and her clawed hands went slack on the wolfskin comforter.

Csorwe realised she was not going to get her bed back any time soon. Well, no matter. She had too much to think about. If Shuthmili had done this on purpose, perhaps there was a loophole. It might be something that could be taken back.

Zinandour fell silent, and after a while, she appeared to fall asleep. Csorwe didn't know whether she was really unconscious, whether she *could* sleep, but she wasn't going to interfere. Instead she went to the wardrobe to find something warm, so she could go out on the balcony.

At the back of the wardrobe was a single dark and ragged object which looked more battered than the rest. Csorwe shook it out and recognised it, almost beyond belief, as her own old leather coat, the same one she had owned since she was a teenager. It had been patched and mended, let out and taken in, and the mark of the Grey Hook tailor stamped inside the collar was now as unrecognisable as the pattern on the lining. There was no other coat like it. It was unmistakably the same.

She pulled on the coat over the loose nightshirt she was wearing and stretched her shoulders. It still fit. She almost relaxed into it, before feeling something in one of the inner pockets. There was a crumpled piece of paper shoved inside it. She unfolded it and saw a familiar scrawl:

Darling girl,
Don't hate me for this

There was nothing else written there. She stood for a long time, looking down at Shuthmili's handwriting.

"Wish I could," she muttered.

The next morning Csorwe found a new door leading out of her quarters, and took this for permission to explore.

Most of Zinandour's palace was empty, but before long she found a row of storerooms, filled with heaps of shipwreck goods. Mostly junk, but among the broken timbers and rotten barrels, Csorwe found cases of lost apricot wine from the orchards of Qarsazh, a Gate-compass which still worked despite its cracked and misted face, and a box of loose assorted teeth. When she found a way outside, she discovered a series of walled and terraced gardens. She recognised at least some of the plants, and the promise of fresh food occupied her for long hours, picking fruit and wondering whether she might find a trowel in one of the storerooms.

When she caught herself having hopes such as these, she felt like the world's greatest traitor. Surely after losing what she had lost she shouldn't be able to think about anything else, she should lie down and refuse to eat and waste away—but then, she could hardly think about the loss directly, either, and she'd never been dramatic like that.

She never saw Zinandour in all this time. This was for the best. Seeing Zinandour vulnerable had not made anything better. Until now she had almost managed not to dwell on the fact that her jailor was not only occupying Shuthmili's body but had taken it, deliberately, intentionally. A spark of sympathy for the goddess burnt like a drop of acid.

Still: no dark silhouette drifting up a distant walkway, no spectre brooding on the loggia. The goddess was absent, or avoiding her, or the palace was just so vast that they kept missing each other. Csorwe had looked for Zinandour's living quarters without really admitting to herself that she was looking, and found nothing, until one afternoon the goddess fell from the sky again, with a hiss like a blade in the wind, and landed on the next terrace over.

Csorwe's reaction startled her, in that she dropped her basket into the rosemary bush, vaulted over the low terrace wall, and sprinted toward the small crater the goddess had made in the onion bed.

Zinandour's armour was partially retracted, drawn up to expose one bare brown arm and most of a shoulder, which would certainly have made Csorwe's heart seize even if it hadn't been splashed red to the elbow with blood. Csorwe picked her up with only a little difficulty, and thanked the Unspoken wildly that she'd coaxed her muscles back into form.

"What," said Zinandour, "are you doing."

"You're hurt," said Csorwe.

"It is the blood of the foe, you unpitiable wretch. Put me down."

Reflecting that it was probably a win that Zinandour had not simply dissolved her kneecaps, Csorwe did so. The goddess immediately crumpled to the ground again, puddled in the black rags of her cloak. She tried to close up her armour again. There was a soft rattling, like a pinwheel in the breeze, but her arm remained bare and bloody. A bitten-off snarl of frustration escaped between her teeth.

"Sure you're not hurt?" said Csorwe.

"Not in any way you can fix," said Zinandour, wrestling her bare hand with her gauntleted one, making an awful smearing of blood. The pungent smell of crushed onion leaves wafted around her, not something Csorwe had ever expected to associate with a malfunctioning divinity. "A failure of—*ugh!*—conjunction. Will you remember me? Easier to forget a leech, you sawtoothed little parasite—"

She went on like this for some time, thrashing around among the broken stems, and Csorwe stood there, startled to attention by *little parasite* and the first spark of true hope she had experienced in this lifetime. Hope was like trying to keep a hot coal alive between her palms. Not to put too fine a point on it, it hurt like fuck, but she didn't want it gone.

At last Zinandour struggled to a sort of half crouch, re-formed her cloak around her, drawing up shadows from the garden as if soaking up water with a sponge, and stumbled toward the nearest wall of the palace. She raised her gauntleted hand with the weary finality of one falling into bed, and a roughly door-shaped opening dilated into the shell stuff. Zinandour stumbled through the door, her cloak floating out behind her, and disappeared down the staircase beyond.

Csorwe followed.

If these were Zinandour's living quarters, they weren't what she'd expected. It was a small room with high windows. A tiled pit was sunk into the ground at the centre, filled with fine black dust. Candles burnt in sconces, lending the room a multitude of shadows. Zinandour had fully retracted her exoskeleton and had burrowed to the shoulders into the dust. Her hair spread out in a dark flame behind her. The sight of her naked collarbones did renewed murder to Csorwe's heart.

Csorwe sat down on the edge of the pit, keeping her eyes firmly on her lap. She had not forgotten the whole pinned-to-the-wall episode. There were clearly parts of her which hadn't got to grips with the new state of affairs, and looking at Shuthmili's bare shoulders made her whole brain remember how they had felt in her hands, and other things too, all of which was like pressing on a bruise. All the more so after what Zinandour had said on the terrace. Little parasite. If Shuthmili wasn't all gone after all—

"Another incursion of Thousand Eyes," Zinandour said, interrupting this train of thought, thank god. The goddess seemed to have taken in Csorwe's presence with equanimity. She was scrubbing her nails in the dust to get rid of the blood. "This time they reached the second boundary. Belthandros is determined, and they are warded against me."

"If he wants to recruit you, he's going about it a weird way," said Csorwe. "Would have thought he'd have other options."

"Oh, they come bearing gifts and promises," said Zinandour. "Belthandros seeks his offspring, and it seems the Thousand Eyes do not live up to their name. He needs my help."

"His offspring?" said Csorwe. Now, there was an idea that was hard to reconcile. Zinandour leant back to rinse her hair in the dust, and Csorwe was so arrested by the idea of Belthandros' *offspring* that she could almost avoid noticing the shallow curve of hip this brought closer to the surface of the dust-bath.

"Yes," said Zinandour. "Either that, or he believes I am concealing the child here. In any case, the implicit choice is fealty or death. What he cannot assimilate he destroys. There is no margin of safety, though I had hoped for more time than this. When the time comes that they reach the third bound, we must leave this place." She sank lower in the dust, as if the idea wearied her, and her waxen face twisted briefly in what was unmistakably frustration with herself. Not an especially divine expression, but one which her features were used to. Shuthmili had never liked to make a mistake.

"Can I help?" said Csorwe.

"Help?"

"Let me fight. Maybe we can keep them off for a bit."

"You are a mortal swordswoman. Do you truly believe you can fight alongside a divinity?" said Zinandour. She didn't sound scornful, but Csorwe suspected she was being humoured.

"I'm not bad for a mortal," said Csorwe. "Didn't the vessel ever reflect on that? Would have thought she'd give me some credit."

Zinandour appeared to search her memory, and a curious avarice flickered on her face in the candlelight: unmistakably Shuthmili's expression on learning of a new type of cake.

"No," said Zinandour. "You are not to be harmed."

"If you won't let me fight, let me be useful," said Csorwe. "Come to dinner with me. I know you need to eat." She had witnessed the goddess gnawing through a packet of ship biscuit as though it was a hated chore.

"The weakness of the vessel is not your concern," said Zinandour. "But very well. If it will quiet you."

Csorwe gathered what she needed from the gardens and around the palace storerooms. She still yearned for eggs and cheese and butter, and a proper oven to make bread, but there was plenty you could do with just a fire and a mysterious bottle of Salqanyese seed oil. She bound potato dumplings with flour and fried them into chewy little clouds. She didn't recognise most of the herbs in the garden, but she had tested them by trial and error in the mortar, and now had a pleasantly sharp green sauce to accompany the dumplings.

She set the table in her room, and began to wait. Quite soon she found that she couldn't bear to sit and wait, or stand and wait, or read a book and wait; her usual reserve of calm had run dry. She had to go and stand on the balcony with her back to the door to still the jitters that simmered in every nerve.

When Zinandour actually turned up, Csorwe managed to tell herself that she had known this would happen and hadn't been worried about it, and that there was absolutely nothing strange or upsetting about spending all day cooking an elaborate meal for Shuthmili's animated corpse. As she served up dinner, the dishes did not at all tremble in her hands.

Zinandour sat very upright, unspeaking, and held her cutlery like surgical instruments.

"Eat," said Csorwe. "It's better than biscuits." She poured a glass of wine for herself and one for Zinandour, interested to see the effect of alcohol on a divinity.

"What is the purpose of this charade?" said Zinandour. She picked up a single, unseasoned dumpling and regarded it with great weariness.

"You don't like food?" said Csorwe.

"The demands of the flesh are dismal and unending," said Zinandour. "The Lady of the Thousand Eyes finds something entertaining about aping mortal fashions. I do not."

"Shuthmili liked this," said Csorwe, and felt at once like a sulky child.

"I do not recall Shuthmili liking anything very much," said Zinandour.

"Why did you bother to be alive, then?" said Csorwe, with a flash of anger that startled her. "Why did you have to—if you didn't *want* to—couldn't you have left her alone?"

"It was the only way out," she said. "For both of us. I assure you. I did not want to go insane. I bore four millennia of imprisonment, I could not bear another, and Shuthmili—"

"What?" said Csorwe.

"She wanted to save you very badly."

Csorwe had not thought her soul could put forth any more hateful emotions at this whole scenario, and yet there it was, a deep and miserable flush of shame.

She stalked back to the kitchen, ostensibly to fetch a jug of water, in fact to calm down. This had been the worst plan of all time. As though she was so special and so desperate that she could call Shuthmili back from wherever she was gone. Now she'd have to finish this parody of a dinner while looking at Shuthmili's face and then go to bed with no plan at all.

Don't hate me for this. She couldn't even be annoyed with her for it. How could she blame Shuthmili for doing anything when the idea of getting through the day without some scheme was unbearable?

She returned to the table to find that Zinandour had almost finished her plate.

At the sight of this chitinous undead monster sitting at the dining table and meekly sipping a spoonful of broth, Csorwe's anger slipped away, replaced with a bubble of weird, hopeless laughter, that got stuck in her throat and refused to escape. "Pleasant in its way," said Zinandour.

Csorwe hadn't realised until this point that Zinandour was trying very hard with her even though it did not come naturally. Now she really started laughing, great miserable sobs of laughter that doubled her up, so that she had to lean on the back of her chair, water spilling from the jug she was holding.

The goddess did not hiss at this. She simply said, quite mildly, "I do not understand. This was your plan? To feed me and talk to me?" Csorwe nodded, still choking, and then Zinandour too started to laugh.

The laugh was a hoarse rattle, completely at odds with her lovely face, completely unlike Shuthmili's laugh as Csorwe remembered it. She sounded as though she was choking to death in a bed of dry reeds.

"Oh," she said. "Oh, Csorwe. My—" She paused, blinked, frowned hard, her claws scraping pale traces in the tabletop. "So valiant and so futile. This would never have worked."

"No!" said Csorwe, her heart pounding against her ribs. She felt as if her chest was no more substantial than a paper bag. "Please, it did work! Come back—bring her back!"

Zinandour dug her claws deeper into the surface of the table. "I thought you meant to poison me." Now she hissed, a cry of pain that boiled off like water on a hot stove, and Csorwe was torn between running to comfort her and running for the door.

"No, I—" she said. "With Belthandros—he was still himself, right? There was a fragment of Iriskavaal in him, but they kind of merged. I thought . . . with you and Shuthmili, maybe it could happen like that again."

"You cannot *imagine* how it hurts," said the goddess. "To find your infantile schemes so—to sit and eat with you as if—"

"I didn't know," said Csorwe.

"I should eat you alive. This place is not for mortal habitation—your presence is a defilement—" said the goddess, doubled over in her chair, her face buried in her hands. "I should flay you. I should *dissolve* you. Why won't you be quiet?"

"I'm sorry," said Csorwe, although Zinandour no longer seemed to be talking to her. At last she looked up at Csorwe through her claws, eyes wide with alien pain.

"The flesh is an unbearable burden," she said. "All I wanted was to be free, but this is an imprisonment worse than the void." She drew her claws thoughtlessly down her own cheek, leaving a trail of four thin cuts, weeping ichor.

"Stop that," said Csorwe, and grabbed her arm. Zinandour blinked in what could have been fury or spasm, rose up from her chair and kissed Csorwe hard on the mouth.

Csorwe recoiled from pure shock—it had been a bruising thing, all teeth—and the goddess stood staring at her with bleak horror.

"*Vile*," said Zinandour. She opened a new door in the nearest wall, and left. This time it closed sharply after her.

Csorwe stood there for some time, hand pressed lightly to her mouth, gazing unfocused at the empty patch of wall where the door had been.

Then, because practicalities outlive all else, she cleared the table and washed the dishes, and tried not to think too hard about the feeling or implications of being kissed. Salt, burnt and bitter like an olive with a stone in it. And yet if Shuthmili was still there, even just a trace, still fighting for control, there was no end to the bitterness she could swallow.

29

Eternity

ORANNA WAS—AND THIS was really a testament to what Tal's life had become—not an ordinary skeleton. He tried not to pay close attention to whatever was going on under her robe. From unavoidable glimpses he got the sense that there were certainly a *lot* of bones under it. They often took on the form of five-fingered hands, but the exact number of hands was variable, and the presence of a solid spine and rib cage seemed to be optional.

In case he needed proof that it was really Oranna, though, she ignored him almost completely. She and Tsereg were sitting on the floor in a side chamber, talking in their own language, too fast for Tal to really follow. He stalked around the heart of the Shrine with one of the candles, pacing and waiting, and trying to get to grips with what he should have known from the start, which was that Tsereg had their own family and he wasn't a permanent part of it.

He had known it at the start, in fact, before he'd lost all self-respect. He'd started out meaning to palm Tsereg off on someone else and get back to his real life. He should have tried harder to keep that in mind. It would have been a lot easier now if he could look back and think, *Well, I knew they weren't sticking around, I knew it all along.*

People did not stay in his life. And that was how it was, and it was fine. He'd kept Tsereg alive for as long as he could, like he'd said he would, and now they weren't his responsibility.

The walls of the Shrine were painted, though the pigment had faded until it was close to stone-grey, only visible if you held the candle close. The frescos depicted Oshaaru gods and saints whom Tal did not recognise, often dying in unpleasant ways, pierced with swords or spontaneously bleeding from the eyes. Many of them had their lips sewn shut.

He found the entrance to the side chamber where Oranna and Tsereg were talking, and leant against the door.

"Just like old times," he muttered. He'd spent such endless days waiting, guarding Sethennai's door through some important meeting, and usually Csorwe had been glaring at him from three feet away then too. Then she'd met Shuthmili, and Tal, obviously, had not been on the inside of that. Now Shuthmili was gone, and Tsereg was going to stay with their mother, and Csorwe was, presumably, dead.

The minutes slipped by, and Tal's mood bounced from restless misery to restless boredom. He could feel his ears starting to twitch. At last, Oranna spoke up from inside.

"You can come in, you know."

Tal wished he hadn't got so self-pitying. He sidled in and sat on the floor opposite the others. Tsereg beamed with excitement and satisfaction, although in this mood Tal didn't feel lightened by it, and couldn't help noticing how much it made them look like Sethennai.

"So you're alive," said Tal. "Congratulations."

Oranna stretched and composed herself back into a sitting form. "No," she said. "This is not life. I died before Tsereg's first birthday. There was no intercession for me but that which I made myself."

It was at this point that Tal realised Oranna was going to explain exactly how she'd done it, and how little he wanted to know.

"As you may know, I was promised from birth to the Unspoken One, a bargain which I renegotiated at the age of fourteen," said Oranna. "Upon my death, that bargain came good. What you see here is my image, my shadow."

"*The life of a man is a ripple upon the water,*" said Tsereg helpfully.

"Yes, dear. In short, I exist within the being of the Unspoken One," said Oranna. "I am its emissary. Its mouthpiece. In this form I have advised Tsereg as best I could for the past fourteen years." One of Oranna's skeleton hands reached out from under the robe and briefly touched Tsereg's arm, as if to verify they were real, then haltingly drew back. Tal felt he had not been meant to notice this.

"Is that what you wanted?" said Tal. "I thought—"

Oranna could not smile—more accurately, she was always smiling—but her posture was all languid amusement.

"I sought the incarnation of the Unspoken," she said. "I naturally considered myself the worthiest candidate to serve as its vessel. I was wrong."

"Oh shit, no you *don't*," said Tal, seeing exactly where she was going with this. Tsereg was sitting and listening to all this, perfectly happy, and Tal could imagine exactly what they'd been talking about: how great and exciting it would be for Tsereg to fulfil their important destiny and permanently turn into bones. "No. Fuck off."

Oranna's unchanging grin turned on him. "I'm so glad you haven't changed. What do you think is the matter?"

He ignored her. "Tsereg, don't tell me you're keen for this, come on. And anyway, you can't—" he said, glancing from one of them to the other. Oranna looked impatient, Tsereg noncommittal. "Tsereg's already a god, or something—why do you think Sethennai is after them?—they're another fragment, part of the snake goddess—"

"Excuse me?" said Oranna. It seemed unaccountable that Tsereg hadn't explained this to her.

"Yeah," said Tal. "It's the same old shit. He wants all the others dead so he can be the best."

"Let me get this straight," said Oranna. She sounded guarded, making an effort to control what Tal assumed must be fury. "Belthandros thinks Tsereg is a fragment of Iriskavaal."

Tal nodded. He didn't like remembering the last night at the Citadel, the absolute chill of sweat drying on his bare skin as he realised that he was at close quarters with something that had killed whole worlds and could not die. "He said—he knew something wasn't right, that it wasn't over." This seemed to be beside the point. Tal brought it round with a willed effort. "I don't give a shit about him. The point is, you can't do whatever you want to do to Tsereg, because I'm pretty sure a person can't be two gods at once."

Tsereg bit their lip, and at the same time Oranna burst into laughter, quite literally. Under her robe, the bones rippled and shook. Her laugh was exactly the same as it had always been: as though everything on this wretched earth had been constructed for her delight.

"Correctly surmised," she said, and then dissolved in laughter again. "Oh, *dear*," she murmured, apparently to herself. "Of course—he would think so—"

Tal tried to catch Tsereg's eye, but they were biting their lip, clearly trying not to join in laughing.

"Yeah," said Tal, "I can see this is all very fucking funny, but how about, as a favour to me, the absolute cretin you've dragged into this for no reason, you maybe consider explaining what the double shit you're talking about?"

Oranna gave a long sigh of laughter, as if she hadn't laughed for a very long time and meant to enjoy it to the dregs.

"Consider," Oranna said, "that children have two parents."

"Yeah, thanks," he said. "I've just about grasped that, when a man and a woman fall in love, or in your case, I guess, just found it massively exciting to be in a tent in some disgusting forest—"

Oranna started laughing again. "Oh, by the twelve thousand unspeakable names, no *wonder* he leapt to conclusions."

Tsereg looked remarkably unbothered to be learning this much about their conception. They kept darting anticipatory little smiles at Tal, as if there was something wonderful for him to know. Too bad for them that Tal had given up on learning anything good ever again.

"Oh, my apologies," said Oranna, pulling herself together again. "It's just very characteristic of him to assume that his contribution was significant. For the record, it would probably have worked just as well with you, Talasseres. I just assumed you would be much harder to convince—oh, don't look like that, it was what's known as a joke—but the point stands.

"I had planned to surrender to Cweren and bear my child in peace, here in the place I grew up. Unfortunately, the God-Empress shared Iriskavaal's suspicion of the Unspoken One and its devotees, and I reached the House with only enough time to give Tsereg into Cweren's care before the Thousand Eyes burnt the place and arrested all its occupants."

Tsereg nodded, giving Tal an encouraging smile, as if expecting him to get it any minute now. He stared blankly back at them.

"So, uh," said Tal, reaching for any kind of certainty. "You're *not* the God-Empress come again, or anything."

Tsereg grinned and rose to their feet, holding out their hands to each side like one of the martyrs painted on the walls. Tal winced.

"D'you know what my name means?" they said. "Tsereg. Eternity."

"*Only I am without end,*" said Oranna.

"*For desolation is my watchword,*" said Tsereg. They grinned, as if this were very meaningful. The points of the candle flames danced in their eyes, and for a second Tal thought perhaps he had it the wrong way round, perhaps the light came from Tsereg, and existed here only by their sufferance.

"Once I saw it, it was simple," said Oranna, although Tal paid her no attention. "There is precedent. At least one of the Qarsazhi divinities was born to a mortal parent, for instance."

"Tal," said Tsereg. They dropped the pose and approached, and put their hand on his shoulder. They looked worried. For an inexplicable moment, he wanted to flinch back, and then realised that almost the whole of Tsereg's worry was about how he might react to this, and forced himself to stay still. "Tal," they said again. "I understand now. It's me. I am the Unspoken One."

There was a silence in which Tal thought he could hear the fizz of the candle flame, the little bones shifting under Oranna's robe, and the sound of his brain running up against something completely incomprehensible.

"But," said Tal. He'd just about got his head around the idea that Tsereg might be a discarded fragment of the snake goddess—that was basically the same thing as being Sethennai's kid—but this was something else. "I don't understand," he said. "What does that mean?"

Tal's heart leapt into his throat as Tsereg disintegrated, apparently on purpose. For a split second where they had stood was nothing but a stout column of floating dust, shreds of hair and shards of bone—and then they came back together, and shrugged.

"Means I can do that, for one thing," they said. "Also, all this is me." They waved vaguely at Oranna and the rest of the shrine. In the other chambers, the crowds of revenants had quietly formed up into rows, as if awaiting instruction. "This is—shit, I guess this is my earthly mansion? I could change it, if I wanted—" They raised their hands and gestured as if pushing against the sides of a box, and—Tal felt seasick—the room was larger, as if it had been larger all the time. "It's just like opening a door, and you know I can do that."

"Don't," said Tal, reeling. He didn't want to disappoint them, but he was so far out of his depth now that dry land was a fading memory. And yet Tsereg seemed elated, lifted somehow by the discovery.

"Everything makes sense," they said. "Everything I can do—everything I am—should've been obvious." They grinned at him and executed a grotesque wink.

"Don't get ahead of yourself, my darling, you're a very baby god," said Oranna, but she sounded fond, and Tal felt a spike of ludicrous, unreasonable jealousy over "my darling."

When Tsereg was excited, they simmered visibly, bouncing back and forth on the balls of their feet. "Tal, I'm never going to die, I knew I wasn't an ordinary person, but I'm not an old bit of snake or anything, I'm going to be *fine*—"

"I never thought you were ordinary either," said Tal, somewhat at random. "Of course you're going to be fine, but—" He wasn't going to say it—it wasn't a good idea to say your fears out loud in case somebody else heard them and decided to make a wish come true—and then he said it anyway: "Do you have to stay here forever?"

"God, no, of course not," said Tsereg. They gave him a sunny grin, almost completely sincere, with just a flash of falseness to cover an uncertainty he didn't completely understand.

"What happens now, then?" said Tal. He could feel relief pushing at him, like floodwater against a dam, but he was reluctant to give in to it. "I guess you're going with your mother."

Oranna shook her head with a faint clicking of vertebrae. "I cannot leave this place," she said. "In many ways I *am* this place."

"What, then—" said Tal.

"Tal!" said Tsereg. "Don't be stupid. I know you can't survive on your own."

He hadn't realised how tense he'd been, every muscle drawn up tight. Relief arrived in the form of a dumb, tired grin, a huge sigh that doubled him over on himself. He looked like an idiot and did not care.

"You're all right," he said. "You're never going to die. And you're happy with it."

"Yes," said Tsereg.

"Then it's fine," said Tal. He raked the fingertips of both his hands back through his hair and sighed again, hours of accumulated tension and terror leaving his body in a great rush, leaving him strangely weightless. "It's fine."

Tsereg napped in a corner of the Shrine, curled up on their coat, looking as contented as a cat sleeping on a sunny roof. Tal couldn't bring himself to lower his guard that much, not in this place, even if it was really Tsereg's own domain. He sat beside them, against the wall with his knees drawn up to his chest, thinking.

After the initial relief, there was a lot to think about. What now? What would Tsereg want? What did *he* want? Was there any safe place left? Anywhere the Thousand Eyes couldn't track them? Everyone he knew was dead. The world as he had known it was gone. Tsereg was apparently a god, which seemed to him to cause more problems than it resolved. Once they left the enclosing darkness of the Shrine, they would be alone again, without money, friends, or resources.

Once, lying on a beach, Tal had been glad of that. Nothing to tie him down, nobody to hold him back. He had been so young.

Oranna sat opposite him, or rather drifted vaguely downward and let her cloak settle into a sitting position. "Tired?" she said. "I do not miss getting tired."

"It's really true?" said Tal. "What Tsereg is?"

"Yes," said Oranna. "I think they will do very well."

"And you're part of it too. The Unspoken One, I mean. Swallowed up by it."

"Submerged. Dispersed. I suppose so," said Oranna. "What you see now is a memory, of sorts, of the person I was."

"I thought you wanted to live," said Tal.

"Oh, yes," said Oranna. "I loved my life. But there are things beyond mortal knowledge, which cannot be known without passing beyond death. There are greater ends, there are worlds beyond the worlds we know, there are better things to love than one's own life. You really did do very well, you know," she added. Just in case Tal was about to feel pleased about that, she added, "Far better than I had any reason to expect."

"If I'm so useless, why did you tell Tsereg to find me?" said Tal. "It was you, wasn't it?"

"Well, I didn't have many options," said Oranna. "Besides . . . Belthandros was always the greatest threat to them, and you know what he is. Forewarned is forearmed, as they say."

"Hope so," said Tal. He didn't mention how long it had taken for the forewarning to take.

"I pity him," said Oranna. "Belthandros, I mean. I doubt he knows it himself, but he is desperately afraid."

"What?" said Tal. Of all the adjectives you could possibly apply to Belthandros Sethennai, this would not have been the first he'd choose.

"You don't see it? Once, I think, he was a greathearted man. No doubt utterly without conscience, but brave and generous to his friends. By now he has been afraid for thousands of years, clinging to his little ledge. No doubt you've heard him on the theme of his isolation, the lonesome tragedy of his eternal life—if not, you've missed a treat—but he deceives himself in this as in all else. Loneliness is his air and water. Alone, changeless, with his fingers fastened round the throat of life, in terror of letting go." She sighed, and laughed. "What a pity he's so handsome."

"Yeah, I'll say," said Tal, staring fixedly at his feet.

"I hope you don't have any lingering tenderness," said Oranna, briskly, as if asking Tal about an embarrassing symptom. "No? Good. That man is a disease one only catches once. And he really did treat you exceptionally badly, even for him."

"Do we really have to talk about this?" said Tal.

"Yes," said Oranna. "In his way of seeing the world, an equal is a threat. If Tsereg could rival him, they could one day work to destroy him. And, even worse, if he came to care for them, they would die, sooner or later. He left me, long ago, for the same reason. To meet his match would have been to welcome death: mine, or his own. If he catches Tsereg, he will kill them. And he will catch them, sooner or later."

"I won't let that happen," said Tal.

Everything came clear at once. He'd been looking at the problem from the wrong angle. There was nowhere safe to hide, probably nowhere Tsereg could grow up in peace. They could run, but they'd never be able to stop running.

It wasn't just Tsereg. Sethennai had all of Tlaanthothe under his thumb. Anything that was left of Tal's family, his childhood, his home. His awful family, poor little Keleiros Lenarai, everyone he'd ever known . . . Sethennai would just go on doing what he did, hollowing people out and discarding them.

"Can you stop it?" said Oranna.

"Yeah," said Tal. "Sure. I just have to kill him first."

Oranna's exposed teeth glittered, and he thought there was a kind of triumphant pleasure in the set of her shoulders.

"Is that what you were getting at?" he said. He toyed with the idea of being annoyed that she'd manipulated him, but what was the point? Everything she had said was true. He knew he was right. "I thought you liked him."

Oranna shrugged, a sinuous ripple of bone. "I loved him," she said. "And I loved fighting with him. And I do not regret it. But Iriskavaal is a bloated tumour of a goddess, and Belthandros has become the worst kind of monster, which is to say, one who feels sorry for himself. You would do the world a service."

"I don't know how to do it," said Tal. "Never killed a god before."

"No," said Oranna. "That's rather the problem. Neither do I."

"Maybe Tsereg—" he said, thinking vaguely that perhaps it would take one god to kill another, and then stopped sharply. "No. He's not their problem. I'll deal with it."

"If I were you, I would not discount any weapon you have at your disposal," said Oranna.

"Good thing you're not me," said Tal. "Tsereg is a kid."

"They are without beginning and without end."

"They're fourteen," said Tal. "And I'm not asking them to kill their dad." They would do it if he asked, that was the worst thing.

"When I was fourteen, I killed my sister," said Oranna. "Or at the very least, she died so I might live. And I can't say I regretted it very much."

"Exactly my fucking point," said Tal. "Tsereg should get a chance to be better than us."

"Then I suppose you'll have to find a way to defeat Belthandros yourself," said Oranna.

"Got an idea," said Tal with some reluctance, convinced that Oranna would laugh at him. "Before Midsummer, Keleiros—uh, *Sethennai*—gave me a poisoned knife. Maybe Tsereg told you."

"Ah, yes," said Oranna. "Dipped in the kindly bane of Saar-in-Tachthyr."

"Sure, right," said Tal. "I thought . . . He said himself it might kill a god. Maybe it could take him down too."

To Tal's surprise, Oranna gave him a slow nod. "You're smarter than he gave you credit for," she said. "It might. The difficulty would be getting close to him with a weapon. Although . . . as to that, there is one other suggestion I might offer. It is very difficult to defeat a god, but remarkably easy to defeat a man."

"All right," said Tal. "Go on, then, tell me. How?"

Shadows danced in the sockets of Oranna's eyes. "With what he wants."

"I called you here so that you might learn what you are," said Oranna. "And now you know. That is a weapon in itself: to know who you are, and what you are capable of accomplishing."

Tsereg's face was very still with the effort it took not to crumple.

"You said no dominion lasts forever," they said.

"Nor does it," said Oranna. "You are the end of the Unspoken and its resurrection. The new world is yours to shape."

At this, Tsereg raised their hand to their lips as if giving a military salute, and Tal felt something twist up in his chest.

Tal shook Oranna's skeletal hand. Tsereg embraced her, which looked to be an even odder experience than the handshake.

"Until we meet again," said Oranna, settling herself on the throne in the grand chamber. "Tsereg," she added, as they turned to leave, "you know I am with you always."

Tsereg didn't have a quick answer for this. After a moment they said, "I know," gave Oranna an acknowledging sort of nod, and slipped a hand through Tal's elbow as they left.

30

Like Summons Like

W E BOTH KNOW the hard facts, First Commander," said Niranthe Charossa. "The storerooms are almost empty."

In the days of the God-Empress, every morning had brought new ships laden with food and luxuries from every corner of her territory. Now, under Belthandros Sethennai's rule, there were no ships, and no shipments. Thousands of people were trapped inside the Citadel. Citizens and soldiers and prisoners were all in the same boat. Cherenthisse did not need Niranthe to tell her that the Citadel would wither like a severed limb as soon as they reached the end of what they had.

"The rice will last us a few weeks, at least," said Niranthe's son, peering into a barrel with desperate optimism. "If we implement the new rationing system—"

Niranthos Charossa had great faith in his new rationing system. At least it kept him occupied.

"How many ships do you have, First Commander?" said Niranthe, softly, ignoring her son.

It was the first time anyone had dared to ask Cherenthisse directly about this. The word *evacuation* was not spoken among the Thousand Eyes. All of them had once faced the same choice that Cherenthisse had offered to Thalarisse. All of them had chosen life and suffering and service.

"To abandon the Lignite Citadel would be to turn our backs on all that we stand for," said Cherenthisse.

"But even you must understand we cannot live on zeal alone," said Niranthe. Her voice and expression did not change, still as soft and polite as ever. "Our people need food. We are under siege by our own Chancellor."

"*Our* people?" said Cherenthisse.

"First Commander, if you would like to start drawing distinctions: *your* people blighted my homeland, your people destroyed our city, your people have served as willing and enthusiastic limbs of the tyrant for this past decade and more. But I feel it is more generous not to cling to past faults."

"Well," said Cherenthisse. "It isn't the same. You don't understand. We are the hope of the empire now."

Niranthe did not argue back. She simply shrugged, and shuffled on round the storeroom, following her son. Niranthos seemed to grow more irritable and despondent with every empty barrel and disappointing crate. His mother only nodded, making notes on a paper tablet.

"Tell me about Echentyr," said Niranthe Charossa, when Cherenthisse caught up to them.

"What do you wish to know?" said Cherenthisse coldly. She respected Niranthe, but she was suspicious of her motives.

"We all suffer in its name," said Niranthe. "And none of us have seen it."

It was painful to remember Echentyr, not only because of the longing, but because every time she conjured it up, she suspected its memory grew fainter. With reluctance, and then without, Cherenthisse talked. About the hatchery, the death of her first vessel, her promotions, her pride and pleasure at being assigned to the bodyguard of the Most High Atharaisse. About the woods on her estate, about hunting there and eating what she caught. About the beauty and majesty of the great city, the festivals that were held there, the triumphal processions. About the clutches of eggs she had borne and sired.

"You have children?" said Niranthe, as if this surprised her very much.

"*No*," said Cherenthisse. Mortals were so wrapped up in their own concerns. "I never met any of my hatchlings. No doubt they are all dead now."

"I suppose these things are different among your people," said Niranthe. She seemed to be trying to control some kind of emotion which Cherenthisse could not identify.

"It was a duty I was glad to perform," said Cherenthisse, unaccountably defensive. "Our population must be replenished from time to time."

"And you were happy there?"

"I worked hard, and I was rewarded," said Cherenthisse, but even she knew it was not quite the same thing. "The Lady of the Thousand Eyes watched over those who honoured her."

"And yet she killed your world," said Niranthe, quite mildly, not at all as if she meant to speak a terrible blasphemy. She weighed a clay bottle of olive oil in one hand and marked off another check on her tablet. "Have you seen Echentyr in its ruin?"

"Well . . ." said Cherenthisse. "No. I have not. But none of us have."

Niranthe moved down the shelf of provisions, and Cherenthisse found herself hanging on what she might say next. Niranthe only sniffed a crate and wrinkled her nose.

"Tch. Spoiled," she said. "Yes. I quite see that the God-Empress preferred to keep that from you. She saw herself as Iriskavaal's true successor, and what price your loyalty undimmed when all your friends have been disintegrated and the streets are full of their ashes?"

"Echentyr was Iriskavaal's to destroy," said Cherenthisse, as she had told herself many times over the years. She had the strange sense that she was pushing furniture in front of a door, trying to shut out whatever was beating at it.

"No doubt," said Niranthe. "My brother Olthaaros believed the same thing of Tlaanthothe, and so, perhaps, did all Chancellors in history, that a city and its people can be owned and put aside. I have seen where such things end. I admired Sethennai once, believed he might fulfil our hopes. I see him now for what he is. A god, perhaps, but god or man, he will never give you back your home. His only purpose is expansion. He admits it himself. You have seen the way the city is spreading."

Sethennai's devastation was contagious. Cherenthisse had heard the reports. Pockets of shining city stuff would crop up miles from the frontier, and they too would spread: a single tower would sprout in the depths of the desert where nobody had ever lived, and within weeks or months, it would be surrounded by a cluster of hollow palaces, colonnades that led nowhere, dry gardens of stone.

"When his earthly mansion covers all the world, even then he will not be satisfied," said Niranthe. "And my people will be dead: Niranthos and I, and all that is left of my family, and all that is left of Tlaanthothe. Without its people, a city is nothing. You know what it is for a world to die, Cherenthisse. Would you wish it on us?"

Years ago, Cherenthisse would have laughed at the audacity of mortals, to compare the end of one insignificant city with the fall of Echentyr. And yet—

"I will stand with the Thousand Eyes as long as I can stand," said Cherenthisse. "But there is no need to keep your people here to starve. Perhaps there are civilian ships—"

"First Commander, you know as well as I do that there are not."

Belthandros Sethennai's accession to the throne had announced itself with a flare of divine energy that had destroyed almost every alchemical engine within the bounds of the Citadel. Even the Thousand Eyes' fleet had not been spared. Its wreckage was smeared across the desert, engulfed by Sethennai's monstrous city. There was a small frigate which guarded the nearest Gate, and a few surviving war-darts were abroad, scouring distant worlds for any sign of Sethennai's offspring. But—

"The *Blessed Awakening* is still skyworthy," said Cherenthisse, before she could think of a reason to stop herself. "The God-Emperor might spare it. You might speak to him."

Niranthe's smile did nothing to veil the bleakness in her expression.

"I have bargained with him before," she said. "I have nothing more to offer him. But if it came from you, First Commander—you are his highest officer, his most trusted confidant—he might listen."

Nothing about Sethennai's presence made Cherenthisse feel like she was anybody's high officer or trusted confidant. In fact she felt as though she were a hatchling again, no bigger than one of the low serpents of this world, brought before her tutors to be scolded.

Sethennai was sitting in the throne room, before his scrying-bowl. Cherenthisse had seen him consulting the bowl before, always frowning. Today it was half full of clear water, and he tore himself away from his reflection with reluctance.

"So Niranthe has got to you too, First Commander," he said, with a curious satisfaction in his eyes that suggested this confirmed a theory. "That woman is too clever for her own good."

Above him was a great window of coloured glass. The harsh sunlight turned its panes to jewels. Sapphire sky, emerald forest, opaline spires: a glazed image of Echentyr-That-Was.

"Well, no need to stand on ceremony, Cherenthisse," he said. "Make your case."

"Sir," she said, already regretting that she'd agreed to help Niranthe. "I thought our resources would go further if the mortals were relocated," she said. Not even a lie.

"And where would you send them?" he said. His tone was almost warm, appallingly magnanimous. Cherenthisse blinked, her features relaxing against her will, like wax before a flame. "To die in the Maze?" he went on. "To starve in the desert?"

"They'll starve *here*, sir," she said, closing herself off to his charisma. It was a sham, just as much as the rest of him.

"I understand," he said. "But I would not send my people away. When my position is secure, the mortals will be attended to."

"Your position, sir?"

"Zinandour has killed all my envoys and destroyed their war-darts. If she only meant to stay away, I would leave her in peace, but she has set herself against me. And worse, your people have been unable to recover my child from wherever they have hidden themselves. While Tsereg is at large, I cannot lower my vigilance."

"We are still searching, sir," said Cherenthisse. "We will not rest until—"

"Until Tsereg returns of their own accord, I suppose," said Belthandros. "As they eventually must. We are of the same substance. Like summons like. Rivers return to the sea. Children see their parents into the grave, one way or another."

He rose from his chair and paced beneath the window. The embroidered border of his robe rippled at his heels. Cherenthisse held themselves very upright, prepared for a long audience.

"Tsereg will come back to us, whether they settle on alliance or anni-hilation. Either way, we must be ready to meet them. I cannot afford to underestimate—"

It was at this point that a small mazeship crashed into Belthandros' picture window.

The nine-foot wall of coloured glass shattered, and with it some other frosted pane in the back of Cherenthisse's mind. She saw the single instant of utter bewilderment on Belthandros' face, and despite herself she laughed, as if it was the first thing she had enjoyed in years.

The security mesh zapped and sizzled, scorching the hull of the little ship with carbonised spirals, and then wisped into nothing like condensa-tion wiped off a window.

"Well," said Belthandros, and the ship caught fire.

The main hatch cracked open, and out of the burning ship stepped the child Tsereg, crackling with power. Their nose was bleeding, and there was a long scrape down the side of their face. Their eyes sparked a mixture of terror and defiance, and then both died down, replaced with a smooth, unfrightened calculation.

"Hello," said Tsereg.

Belthandros made a gesture, and the fire immediately smothered itself. "Ah, Tsereg," he said. "How nice of you to visit."

"I know you're looking for me," said Tsereg. "And I'm here to—"

Out of the scorched interior of the ship stumbled an unfamiliar Tlaanthothei man. He was bent double, clutching a wound in his shoulder which fountained scarlet blood down the front of his shirt. His face was bloody too, and he looked battered, as though he'd been shaken around in a barrel.

"And Talasseres is here too, I see," said Belthandros. Cherenthisse hadn't recognised him at first; hard to draw a connection between this person and the petulant boy she had met all those years ago.

"Tsereg, *stop*—" said Talasseres, feeling his way down as though his vision was murky, and reaching for Tsereg's shoulder. "You don't have to—"

There was a cold flash of anticipatory horror as they realised what was about to happen. Tsereg flicked out one hand, there was a quicksilver flash, and Talasseres was thrown bodily into the air and slammed against the nearest wall.

"Attend to him, Cherenthisse," said Belthandros, not looking round.

She obeyed. He was unconscious but didn't have any obvious bones broken. She set about binding the wound on his chest first.

Meanwhile, Tsereg hadn't moved. Their face was set, the huge orange eyes fixed on Belthandros.

"You were saying?" he said.

"I'm here to work for you," said Tsereg. They gave Cherenthisse a vague, imperious wave. "Like her."

Belthandros rested his chin on his hand, stroking his beard with his thumb.

"This is quite a change of heart," he said.

"You would've caught me eventually," said Tsereg, sticking their chin out in defiance. "Too many snakes."

"And quite a risk for you," said Belthandros. "Why shouldn't I kill you?"

Tsereg shrugged. "Why would you kill me?" they said. "I'm a part of you, aren't I?"

Belthandros put his head on one side, observing them. Cherenthisse could almost see the wheels whirring.

"If you think I'm incapable of destroying the parts of myself which do not serve my purposes, you have been misinformed," he said.

"No," said Tsereg. They glanced over at Talasseres, and Cherenthisse saw a tremor of uncertainty ripple across their face before it settled back to still indifference. "I know what that's like. But I could serve your purposes."

"Could you?" said Belthandros. Cherenthisse wondered whether the reluctant interest in his voice was real or rhetorical.

"I want to work for you," said Tsereg. "I want to learn. Nobody else can teach me what I want to know. There's nobody else like me."

"That much is certainly true," said Belthandros. "Although—"

"I mean it," said Tsereg. "You have no idea. Finding out that I am who I am, it was such a relief. Tal couldn't handle knowing. That's why he took me away."

Belthandros composed his features into an image of regret. "Yes, that's why he left me the first time, too."

A flutter of uncertainty from Tsereg which Cherenthisse did not completely understand.

"Yeah. He wouldn't let me go, that's why I had to steal the ship," said Tsereg. They sighed and brushed stray curls out of their face. "I guess he wanted to look after me. He didn't understand that I'm not interested in being mortal anymore."

"He wouldn't," said Belthandros.

"Really not," said Tsereg. "I'm not interested in . . ." They rolled their eyes and shrugged, clearly embarrassed even to phrase it. "I don't know, having a parent or whatever. He didn't get that. So you don't have to worry that I'm going to be weird about it."

"Always a relief," said Belthandros. "But—"

"You don't trust me," said Tsereg. "But I could be useful. I promise. I'm really smart. I've never met anyone as smart as me."

This won a faint sleepy smile. Belthandros looked almost normal again. "That being said, I really *don't* trust you, I'm afraid," he said. "For your safety it would be wise not to make any sudden moves."

"Yeah, obviously," said Tsereg, though it seemed it was their turn to recalculate. "Obviously. I wouldn't trust me, either. That's why I brought Tal."

Talasseres stirred, as if he recognised his name, and at a nod from Belthandros, Cherenthisse began to bind his wrists.

"A hostage, I see. I suppose you expect me to throw him in a cell as a guarantee of your good behaviour," said Belthandros.

"Yeah, I do know what a hostage is," said Tsereg. "That's the idea."

"I thought you were the smartest person you'd ever met," he said.

"What?" said Tsereg again. Again the flicker of uncertainty. Belthandros' expression was as closed and grim as Cherenthisse had ever seen it. "That's not—"

"You seem to want me to take you seriously," said Belthandros. "So you need to make a choice."

"Yeah?" said Tsereg. There was more than one crack in their defiance now.

"You seem to enjoy short sentences, so here are some more. Talasseres has already betrayed me twice. I am not stupid. If you want to work at my side, kill him."

Talasseres' eyes snapped open in alarm. Tsereg just stood there. They reached out a hand, almost vaguely. Their eyes were fixed on Belthandros. They didn't look at Talasseres. He twisted in Cherenthisse's arms, trying to sit up, bleary but clearly conscious.

"Tsereg," he said, "it's fine—"

"Tal, if you finish that fucking sentence, I *might* just kill you," they said.

Their shoulders slumped back into the usual slouch. They hadn't taken their eyes off Belthandros.

"All right, fine, you got me, hope you're proud of yourself," they said. "I was actually kind of interested to see what you were like, and I know this is probably your line, but hey: congrats on being a huge disappointment."

Belthandros put his head on one side, his bright eyes fixed on Tsereg. "Oh, no, I'm impressed," he said, and he smiled down as if he really meant it. "And also, I'm sorry."

He raised a hand. A wound opened in the skin of the world, torn wider as many pincered legs reached through. This cage of jointed chitin closed around Tsereg without giving them a chance even to scream, and pulled them through. The tear healed up at once with a hiss, leaving a smell of hot metal, and not even a shadow where Tsereg had been.

Belthandros sighed, as though all this had cost him no small effort.

"Well, Cherenthisse, you'd better prepare the aerial vault for a guest. I'll deal with Tal."

31

Surrender

So Tal was back in his old guest room. All that could be seen at the windows now was a thicket of towers and bridges, grown up around the Citadel like a hedge of thorns. A thin grey light filtered through. The bedclothes were dappled with mildew, and the woodwork had swollen with the damp.

He had been here for several days. He had seen nobody but a silent Thousand Eye guard who brought him bread and water.

He had never felt more alone. He lay back on the cold bed, picking at his nails and staring at the patches of mould on the ceiling.

Someone had taken the poisoned knife while he was unconscious, of course. There was nothing in the room that could serve as a weapon, no sharp edges, nothing breakable except himself.

He tried to think of nothing at all, and could only think of how badly he had failed Tsereg.

He had wanted to keep them out of this, and he'd failed completely, as always, and was he really any better than Sethennai, since he'd just gone ahead and let that happen?

A key turned in the lock, and Tal felt a kind of sickly mixture of satisfaction and fear and fury. He had been certain that Sethennai wouldn't be able to resist coming to look at him.

It wasn't Sethennai who entered, but the First Commander of the Thousand Eyes. Tal had rarely seen someone so openly, viciously miserable. She moved as though every instant was another pane of glass she had kick through.

"Hard day at the office?" said Tal, without moving.

"Listen to me, Talasseres Charossa," said Cherenthisse. "The child is alive, imprisoned in the aerial vault. I know the two of you were planning something, and I don't care what it is. I'm not going to stop you."

"What?" said Tal. He hadn't heard anything she said beyond *the child is alive.* The wave of relief that swept over him was immediately followed by a much larger wave of anxiety and concern. *Alive* could mean so many things. "Imprisoned in the what? Can you get me to them? Can you help me get them out?"

"No. The Thousand Eyes will not take your side. But we will not get in your way. We have made our choice."

Tal knew he was supposed to be grateful and accept this, but that had never been his strong suit.

"That's your choice?" he said. "To do nothing? For him? What do you think is going to happen? You think he's ever going to ask what you think of anything? Ask you how you're doing?"

Cherenthisse bared her teeth at him.

"You can tell yourself whatever you want," he said. "Tell yourself you're making some noble sacrifice or whatever. Loyalty ever undimmed, that's your thing, right? Yeah, mine too. You're never ever going to get what you want. I loved him for years. I would have done anything for him. You think it won me any credit in the end?"

Even later on, all through those years in the wilderness, Tal had been glad that at least he'd known this great love, that there had been something in his small, shitty failure of a life that had felt exalted, even if it had hurt, that for some years he'd had this purpose.

Cherenthisse was still hissing at him. Just because you could get used to the yearning, just because you could nurse it, a wavering flame that had to be protected from the wind even as it burnt you, it didn't make it mean anything.

If you want to work at my side, kill him. Tal's heart was the biggest traitor of them all, and up until that moment, he had still believed that maybe he had mattered.

"When I was younger, if Sethennai had decided to burn my homeland to the ground, I would have helped him light the pyre. And I probably would have felt good about it, for a bit, all *maybe this time I've done enough to prove myself.* But it would never have worked. I never meant anything to him at all. Maybe your God-Empress was different, I don't know."

"Yes," she said. "My God-Empress was very different."

Tal wasn't sure he believed that. He hadn't seen much of the God-Empress, but he'd lived in the world she'd made.

"We could all be free, you know," said Tal. "If you get me the knife—"

Cherenthisse raised a hand sharply. "No. Do not tell me. If I do not know, I cannot stop you."

Tal didn't question that. He understood, he thought. Sometimes you had to trick yourself into doing things.

"Guess you won't tell me how to get in the vault, then," said Tal.

"You cannot. It is a part of the earthly mansion. Belthandros watches over it night and day."

"Yeah, but," said Tal, "suppose he looked away. How do we get in?"

"It is impossible," she said, then grimaced, as though the next part caused her physical pain to utter. "Although I am certain Shuthmili gained access before. At least once."

"What, you two were friends? I didn't—"

"No," said Cherenthisse. "I disliked her with every fibre of my body. She is cold, arrogant, and condescending; she cares nothing for anything of importance; and she thinks I am stupid."

"Oh," said Tal, "so you were *colleagues*."

"Unfortunately. But I believe she knows how to get into the vault."

"She's . . . gone, though," said Tal. He had no idea what had happened to Shuthmili after the Midsummer duel, or to Csorwe's body.

"Yes," said Cherenthisse, her face white and still as a marble statue, her gaze fixed in the middle distance. "If only there were some way to reach her."

Against all odds, Tal managed to doze a little. He was brought back to reality by a faint creaking of hinges.

Sethennai was leaning in the doorframe, apparently taking in the scene.

All right, motherfucker, thought Tal. *I guess it's time.*

"I do wonder a little what you were trying to achieve here," said Sethennai. Tal knew that tone, half amused, half annoyed, and knew exactly how you were supposed to respond, but didn't.

"Are you all right?" said Sethennai, approaching the edge of the bed.

Tal curled up defensively, groaning. He hardly needed to exaggerate. "God, leave me alone," he said, turning his face toward the wall.

"Did Tsereg hurt you?" said Sethennai. Hearing him say their name made Tal want to elbow him in the face as hard as possible.

"What are you doing here?" said Tal, wriggling into a smaller ball and twitching as if in pain.

"I can heal you, if you like," said Sethennai. Predictable as ever.

"Fuck off," said Tal, burying his face in his arms.

"Or I can find someone else to do it, if that would be preferable," he said.

"Why would that be *preferable?*" said Tal, muffled in his sleeves. "You know I hate it."

"I don't understand why," said Sethennai. "You don't hate to be touched in general."

If you were asking his actual opinion, Tal didn't think it was that strange not to want people meddling with your insides by magic, but he knew he had to judge this carefully. He had to be obstructive enough to convince, but not so sulky that Sethennai got bored. Luckily, he had devoted many years of his life to the study of exactly when Sethennai got bored with him.

"It's too close," said Tal. "Why would you heal me? I'm not on your side."

He sat on the edge of the bed, tipping the mattress in a way that made Tal's ribs complain. "I don't want you to suffer."

"Where is Tsereg?" he said. God, he only had Cherenthisse's word for it, and if she'd been lying, then he knew worse than nothing and this whole idiot scheme was even more doomed than before. "If you've hurt them—"

"No," said Sethennai. "That's why you took them away in the first place, isn't it? I'm sorry that you thought I was capable of something like that."

"You told them to *kill me,*" said Tal, gritting his teeth. He'd been prepared for something like this. Sethennai was always quick to forget anything that didn't fit his current version of events.

Sethennai gave a deep sigh. "Yes," he said. "For the record—perhaps this won't make any difference to your feelings—I would not have given Tsereg that choice if I had thought they would choose differently."

There was something both astonishing and disappointing about this, like finding out how a magic trick worked. Once you saw what he was doing, it was unbelievable that you'd ever been taken in by it. Tal could see he was meant to feel flattered by this and open up sweetly, all ready to prove that he deserved the flattery.

So that was exactly what he did.

Going through the motions of surrender was like slipping on an old shirt. Sethennai asked to heal him again, and he played it out for a minute or two before agreeing, and didn't even wince at the awful fizzy squirming sensation of the bruises receding.

An offensively short time later, he fell back into the grimy hollow in the mattress, letting his thoughts slide past, as detached as individual beads on a string, and letting Sethennai kiss him. If Sethennai thought there was anything strange about how quickly Tal gave in, it didn't stop him.

"Are you cold?" he said, in fact, dusting a bit of damp plaster out of Tal's hair. Tal found himself recalling the mercenary general Psamag telling him quite tenderly that he could leave before they started torturing Csorwe.

"I'm fine," said Tal, and shivered deliberately.

Possibly the idea of having your good time in a prison cell was damaging to Sethennai's sense of himself. Tal found himself being led up through the dark and winding corridors of the palace. The corridors moved faster than they did, slithering around one another like a shoal of leeches. At one point Tal's nose and gums started bleeding. Tal noted the metallic taste quite calmly, and realised he wasn't afraid at all. Or possibly he'd just got accustomed to wading through a general level of fear in order to get anything done in the day, and hardly felt it anymore.

"Tch," said Sethennai, when he noticed the nosebleed. "I thought I'd fixed that." He brushed a hand over the back of Tal's head, and the bleeding stopped at once.

Tal had managed not to think that much so far about the fact that he was venturing into the lair of a divinity. Had this been a huge mistake? To think that he, Talasseres Charossa, could actually pull this off?

When they got to the room, Tal was careful not to think about anything at all, in case his body language gave something away. Sethennai was being very gentle with him, very attentive, but Tal knew better than to think his mind was completely on the job any more than Tal's was.

Later on, curled up in the crescent of Sethennai's body and trying to calm the frantic pattering of his heart, he couldn't believe the distraction had worked.

Well. Only one way to find out.

Tal slipped warily out of his arms and pulled his shirt back on.

Sethennai just lay there, asleep, as coldly handsome as a statue.

He had changed. Tal remembered him laughing until he choked on his wine; remembered the three of them eating olives on the balcony as the sun set behind the city; remembered a time long ago when they had been caught in a rainstorm in the mountains and Sethennai had lent him his coat. He had never been a particularly kind person, but he had been a person.

And now, in the end, there was nothing vulnerable about that stillness, nothing peaceful left in him at all.

Snakes sleep with their eyes open, thought Tal.

The iron scrying-bowl stood on Sethennai's desk, only a little way away, in the same place Tal had seen it the last time he did this.

Tal stood before the bowl and realised abruptly that he did not exactly know how to use it. It needed his blood, and according to Tsereg, it would take what it needed. So what did he have to do? If he just put his hand in the bowl?

Whatever happened, he could not cry out. He couldn't risk Sethennai waking until he had reached Shuthmili.

It might be best to make your peace with dying here, Cherenthisse had said, before she left him.

At least, Tal thought, if he died here in this room, he wouldn't be thinking of Sethennai.

If his life had to have a point, then Tal knew what the best of him had been, the one thing he'd managed to do half well, something Sethennai knew nothing about and had little to do with. That was clear to him now, with a bright sunlit clarity that cut through some of the panic swirling around him. Whatever happened to him, if he could make sure that Tsereg made it out of this alive, then he had won.

He reached out to touch the surface of the bowl. The moment his fingertips brushed the pitted metal, he felt a sharp and sudden pain in his hand, as though a blade had driven up through his palm. He clenched his fist and bit down on the cuff of his shirt, exhaling hard to stop himself from yelling. He could bear it. Blood welled around his fingers and dripped into the bowl, running into the spiral grooves.

Too slow, thought Tal. At this rate it would take hours to fill the bowl. He forced himself to open his wounded hand, to press his palm down on the surface of the metal.

At first the pain was a hundred times worse, a cold burning, as though the bowl was pushing needles of ice up through his hand. He gritted his teeth, feeling a scream rise in his throat like bile, and swallowed it down.

He pulled his hand back from the metal and blood rushed from a dozen punctures, plinking into the bowl like raindrops into a puddle.

You aren't supposed to be able to hear your own blood, he thought woozily.

By the time there was a decent pool of blood in the bowl, Tal's hand was numb. He didn't look at it in case the sight of it made him nauseous.

How do I know when this thing's working? he thought, staring at the red puddle in the bowl. Another kind of person would have thought about this ahead of time.

Did he have to say something? Was there some prayer to the Unspoken? The idea of praying to Tsereg was unfathomable.

What was it they had said, when Cweren had died?

"All things that are lost come into my keeping," Tal whispered, and against all hope, the surface of the blood shivered.

Yes! Right! Let's see Shuthmili, then, he thought. *Come on!* He knew what she looked like, at least, that twitchy little face. *Show me Shuthmili.*

Still nothing. Reflected in his blood, he saw his own anxious eyes, and behind them . . . shifting clouds of light, nothing definite. Maybe he just didn't remember well enough how Shuthmili looked. He bit down on his frustration, clenching his bloody hand as though squeezing the last few drops from a lemon wedge.

The one time I could really use Csorwe's stupid opinion, he thought, and the liquid in the bowl flickered, as if stirred by a breeze.

Tal stepped back, rocking on his heels to try and distract himself from the pain.

"Csorwe?" he mouthed, still not daring to speak aloud. The bowl rippled as though he'd dropped a stone into it. "If you hear this—"

Having to ask for things was Talasseres Charossa's second least favourite activity. It was bad enough to humiliate yourself and worse that it was the easiest thing in the world for the other person to say no. But then, it was Csorwe, and there was probably nothing Tal could do to make her think worse of him, so. Now was not the time to get tongue-tied.

"If you hear this, Sethennai's got Tsereg, they're just a kid, we really need your help," he said, repeating it a few times to make sure the message got through. "And also, in case I'm dead by the time you get here, no hard feelings, you know?"

Tal swayed on his feet. Here came the woozy numbness he remembered from the last few times he'd lost a lot of blood. At least those times he hadn't done it to *himself.*

He leant on the surface of the desk. Even his good hand was now clammy with sweat. The blood had drained away from the bowl as though it had been drunk up. There was no way to tell whether it had worked, whether anybody had received his message.

He bandaged his hand in the sleeve of his shirt to stop the bleeding. All that was left to him now was his very least favourite activity: to wait and see.

32

The Devouring Fire

CSORWE LOOKED UP from the raspberry canes and saw a sphere of blood. It was about the size of a grapefruit, it hovered in the air at head height, and it was speaking in a voice she knew.

"Your help if you hear this," it said.

"*Tal?*" she said, when she recovered the power of speech.

The orb had the heavy sheen of oil, and it trembled faintly as it spoke, and the voice was unmistakably that of Talasseres Charossa, which Csorwe had not heard in fifteen years.

She sat back on her heels, looking up at the orb. Maybe she was seeing things. Maybe she was dreaming. Maybe this was some kind of strange joke or gift from Zinandour, a simulacrum of mortal company. Any of these possibilities seemed more likely than that Tal was still alive, somewhere.

"Just a kid," said the orb.

"What are you talking about?" she said.

"Really need your help if you hear this."

The orb muttered on, and she listened in bewildered silence, gradually piecing its message together. Tal sounded older, his voice roughened by the years. He was in pain, and being a stubborn jerk about hiding it, as always.

If this was a joke, it was a cruel one. Hearing him talk made her chest ache. Zinandour had told her what Tlaanthothe had become, but it hadn't come home to her until now how much had been lost while she was gone. All the while she'd been sleeping in her own head, oblivious, as Tal had lived through every day of every year of the God-Empress' reign.

And was she really doing any better now? Hiding out in the Pearl of Oblivion while the world crumbled? If Tal needed her help badly enough to admit it, she really must be his last hope.

"Your help," said the orb. "I'm dead by the time you get here."

"Better not be," said Csorwe. She put down her trowel. Tal had saved her life. She owed him. But more to the point, she could not bear to let him die. Maybe the world burnt, but she could save one small thing.

"No hard feelings," said the orb, and evaporated.

"Oh, fuck you," said Csorwe with fondness, and rose, dusting topsoil off her knees. "I'm on my way."

Csorwe found Zinandour in one of her shipwreck attics, between a bucket of iron pokers and a barrel of rusted keys. The goddess was hunched up on a crate like a jackdaw, running her claws through a basket of sea glass.

When Csorwe told her about what she had heard, her armour bristled around her and her face went as cold and still as Csorwe had ever seen it.

"These mortals are not my concern."

"Well, maybe they're mine," said Csorwe. She seated herself on a crate opposite the goddess. Faint specks of phosphorescence glimmered in the scales of Zinandour's armour.

"I do not see that that is so," said Zinandour, tapping her claws on the armour plate that covered her knee, an irritable little clicking noise. "You owe this child nothing."

"If you don't want to get involved—"

"No," said Zinandour. There was a pause, measured out by the *tap-tap-tap* of claw on chitin. "I do not wish you to get involved. You have proven we hold some power over one another. Obey me in this and stay with me."

"Why? It's not as if you like my company," said Csorwe.

"If you proceed with this plan, you will be harmed. Sethennai will capture you, and you will die with your friends. I know you. You yearn to sacrifice yourself to no good end."

Csorwe shrugged. "I'm good at it."

"I forbid it," said Zinandour. "You are safe here. *We* are safe here," she added, clearly feeling it was a great concession. "You will not be hurt. But you will not leave."

She closed her eyes and turned away, her profile like a paper cutout of Shuthmili's, framed in dark scales.

Csorwe felt herself sinking back down in that old pond of misery, but perhaps she'd hit the bottom, because she hit a hard surface, as cold and unyielding as iron.

Oh, right. That was anger.

"You think you can stop me?" she said.

"If I must," said Zinandour. "Or we could make a bargain. I enjoy bargaining."

"I bet you do," said Csorwe sourly.

"You seem to think there is some overlap. Some remnant of the vessel. Something . . . lurking. If we remain safe here, then perhaps it would be easier to—"

As Csorwe grasped the implications of this, she laughed bitterly, a fountain of black bile like burning tar.

"That's it? That's what you're offering me? You think if I stay and keep my mouth shut, you might let me talk to her from time to time? Wow! Fuck you!"

"Csorwe—"

"I miss her so much I think I kind of want to die about it. But I'm not going to sit up here brooding about it with you and let everyone else go to hell. And I'm disappointed that she did."

"You do not know how she suffered."

Csorwe ignored her. Shuthmili's note was still in the pocket of her coat. She pulled it out, crumpling it in her hand.

"Where's my sword?" she said.

"Your sword was lost at the temple of Saar-in-Tachthyr, fifteen years ago."

"Great," said Csorwe, through gritted teeth.

She went over to the bucket of pokers and rattled through them, looking for whichever felt best in her hand.

"What are you doing?" said Zinandour.

"I told you," said Csorwe. "I'm leaving."

Zinandour's face became stonier than ever.

"You'll have to bar the fucking door."

"Will you waste what was bought so dearly?" said Zinandour.

"Sure you want to try that line with me?" said Csorwe. "You saved me, so you own me? No."

For a moment Zinandour looked very tired, very thin, older and paler and sadder than Csorwe had ever seen Shuthmili look, and yet somehow more like her.

Shuthmili was gone. Tlaanthothe was gone. In this new world Grey Hook belonged to the snakes, and the House of Silence was burnt. Csorwe herself was a faithless runaway, as she had been for decades. She might be able to save Tal and the kid, but her world was already dust and ashes.

Her whole world, except whatever flicker still burnt in the back of Zinandour's mind, gone out of her reach.

Maybe I should just stay with her, thought Csorwe. Shuthmili had done the same thing, hadn't she? She had chosen that path and followed the God-Empress' hollow shell wherever it took her, whatever it made of her, whatever the consequences. No. Csorwe had tried blind loyalty before, and she hadn't liked how it had turned out.

"I cannot stand by and watch you die," said Zinandour. "I cannot. Csorwe—"

"My life is mine to waste." With an effort, she softened her voice. This was her last chance, maybe. The last opportunity to get through. "You said that yourself, once."

Zinandour flinched back as if Csorwe had burnt her.

"I am not her," said Zinandour. "Not anymore."

"So you've told me," said Csorwe. "Well, when this is all over, and I'm gone . . . if you ever remember being her, remember that I loved you."

Csorwe tossed the crumpled note at Zinandour's feet, stuck the poker through her belt, and left.

There was a half-functioning shuttle in one of Zinandour's hoards, and it carried her as far as Grey Hook before giving out.

Grey Hook was almost as Csorwe remembered it, but not quite. There was a nervous tension in the air. At the port, dozens of Tlaanthothei refugees waited in small flocks, surrounded by bags and cases and whatever else they'd been able to carry. In the streets, half the shops were boarded up.

She went to the market to look for a new cutter, doing her best not to feel anything about the way the city had changed. She had spent the best years of her childhood in Grey Hook and hadn't been back since. All those memories were dangerously close at hand. There was the empty office of the Blue Boars Mercenary Company. There was the abandoned wagon of the lentil curry man, missing its wheels. There was the street where she had lived with Sethennai—no, she wasn't even going to look that way. Guard up. Eyes on the road ahead.

At the corner of the market was the watchtower Sethennai had shown her on her first day in the city, now half fallen and scrawled over with graffiti: *SNAKES OUT. FUCK THE 1000. IRSKAVAL SUCK MY DICK.*

She grinned at that. Even if she herself would never be the same again, some things never really changed.

Her smile faded as she passed another crowd of refugees and heard what they were discussing. Zinandour had told her about Sethennai's dead city, the way it enveloped other towns and choked the life from them, but it was one thing to hear rumours and another to listen to someone who had seen it engulf their farmstead.

She had covered her face with a scarf, since the sight of the God-Empress strolling down the boulevard might cause a bit of a stir, and the anonymity was a relief. She wandered closer to the group, listening discreetly.

To her surprise, she heard someone speaking Oshaarun. The accent was like a snowball to the face. The remotest north of northern Oshaar, the voice of Csorwe's childhood. It was saying:

"Like I said, one bag each, or there won't be room for everyone."

Among the other refugees was a group of Oshaaru women in ragged grey uniforms. The speaker was clearly their leader: startlingly young, not much over twenty.

"Another straggler?" said the leader when she caught sight of Csorwe. She had the determined heartiness of someone who has been keeping other people's spirits up for hours, if not days. It made her seem older than she was. "I don't recognise you. There's not much more space on the ship, but—"

"You're from the north," said Csorwe. "I'm from there."

The girl looked at Csorwe in mixed suspicion and bewilderment, then seemed to decide Csorwe's accent was legitimate.

"Yes, all of us—we're all House of Silence people, from the Iron Hill. Who are you?"

Csorwe realised she had been staring, over her scarf. "Prioress Cweren," she said, somewhat at random. "Is she alive? I met her once."

"She didn't make it out," said the girl. Her expression closed briefly, as though shutting away this grief somewhere Csorwe couldn't get at it. "I'm her successor, Prioress Tsurai. Are you one of the faithful?"

Csorwe ran a hand back through her hair. "Not really. Born into it, but—"

Tsurai nodded. "I understand. Things change. We're all lost things now."

"Where are you going?" said Csorwe.

"Back to Oshaar," said Tsurai, "if we can."

"The House of Silence is burnt," said Csorwe.

Tsurai smiled, not offended. "The House is not a building. Maybe you should come back with us."

Csorwe thought about it.

Oh, yes. She could do it, if she wanted to. None of them would know who she was. Back to the House and its cold comradeship, back to the woods and mountains, back to the numbing familiarity of ritual, back to the fading of all things and the oblivion of the lotus. She could put herself away in that box, and there would be no more loneliness and no more uncertainty. Always to know what you were meant to do, always to have a place. As if she had never met any of them, as if her life really had ended when she was fourteen. The smell of woodsmoke on the wintry air, the rise and fall of the black pines on the horizon, rippling like a woman's hair. Better, maybe, to go home, and forget.

For a moment the vision sustained her, like a sip of hot wine, and then she had to admit to herself that it was empty. The place that had been her home no longer existed. The Unspoken One no longer resided in the mountain, not as it once had. And she could not pretend her life had truly ended when she was fourteen. Shuthmili was gone beyond her reach, but would she really turn tail while Tal was still blundering forward somewhere? She knew better than to think he would really give up on anything unless someone dragged him from it shrieking. And he'd asked for her help.

"I'll catch up to you," she told Tsurai, and let them go.

It had been a long time since Csorwe had made a long journey through the Maze, and the formlessness gave her a headache. Only one establishment in Grey Hook had been prepared to accept the ancient and tarnished coins she had stolen from the Pearl of Oblivion, and the cutter she had hired jolted like a wagon over rubble.

To reach the nearest gate to the Lignite Citadel, she approached along the base of a narrow gorge. The cutter's lanterns illuminated nothing but a puddle of jagged stone ahead. The great silence outside pressed upon the little silence inside.

Csorwe had never thought before about what it might be like to live at the bottom of the ocean, and she didn't think she would enjoy it very much.

When at last she saw the Gate blinking above her, a circle of green fire gleaming like a penny in a fountain, she was relieved. Whatever she found on the other side, it couldn't be as bad as the journey they'd just endured.

Then a shadow passed across the face of the Gate, black against green like a fly crawling inside a paper lantern. Hovering above the Gate was a Thousand Eye warship.

Csorwe took the cutter hastily down again, back into the safe darkness of the trench, and cut the lights, praying they hadn't seen her.

No such luck. There was the deafening crash of a missile hitting the rock face, so close that the cutter rolled to one side, all its timbers creaking.

Csorwe cursed, and ducked deeper into darkness. Would they come after her? Surely she was too small a fish for that?

Another impact. They weren't going to let her go. And this thing didn't go fast enough to outrun a mail transport, let alone a military frigate. If she went deeper into the trench, she might be able to outmanoeuvre a larger ship in the dark, but in a cutter as clunky as this, the chances were that she would smash herself to pieces on a stalagmite. What a stupid way to die, after all this.

In the darkness of the cabin, Csorwe heard a hiss. Fear traced its cold fingernails down the back of her neck, and then she recognised the sound.

"Zinandour," she said.

"I can help," said the goddess, her voice low and grating.

"Not the time for this," said Csorwe. It was taking quite a lot of nerve just to keep her hands steady on the wheel.

She heard the goddess move, the rustling of a huge bulk, like scales or feathers, much larger than Shuthmili's small body. The rustling grew louder as Zinandour slithered forward into the cockpit. Csorwe hung on to the controls, staring fixedly up at the green coin of the Gate, and felt Zinandour grip the back of her seat. Her breath was as cold as the wind outside.

"I can help," said Zinandour again.

Csorwe pulled the lever that opened the cockpit evacuation hatch. A freezing wind roared into the cockpit, scattering debris. Csorwe had never been more glad to be securely strapped into the pilot's seat. There was a release of pressure that made her ears pop, as Zinandour pushed *up* and *away* from her and escaped through the open hatch. Rattled and blind, she fumbled for the hatch and latched it closed again.

The noise stopped. There was a perfect, silent darkness. Then a winged shape passed into the penumbra of the Gate. It was smaller than the warship, but just as sleek and murderous.

It might have been the ringing in Csorwe's ears, or the distant song of the Gate, but she thought she heard an alarm bell pealing. Zinandour closed with the warship, melting into its silhouette, and for a few seconds it tumbled in space, turning and twitching like something caught in a web. Csorwe was equally transfixed. The warship struggled for a few seconds longer, then exploded. The fragments hung in a cloud before the Gate—there was a kind of beauty to it, like a dandelion clock—and then the wind picked up and blew them away.

Csorwe sat very still, unblinking. A moment later she felt the vibration as something landed on the cutter's upper hull, and then the hiss of the upper hatch opening.

"There will be no further trouble," said Zinandour, behind her. There was nothing left of the warship but a faint trace of frozen dust in the air, sparkling in the Gate-fire like specks in a sunbeam.

Zinandour had loved to fly since she had first taken a living vessel, long millennia past. How she missed being a true dragon: the immense architecture of that body, its hollow bones, the metallic sheen of her scales, the taste of fire in her mouth, the wings whose very shadow was the fear of kings. But all the dragons were extinct, and now the next best thing was to wreak destruction upon a helpless warship. The rending of timbers, the shrieking of the doomed sailors, the sound of all life's sinews tearing: this was music and sweetness to the Devouring Fire.

Down in the pilot's seat, Csorwe clutched the wheel very tightly. She was controlling herself, but Zinandour smelled her blood and sweat and knew her fear.

This too should have been a pleasure, to a goddess who had cut a path of blood and fire across countless centuries. In long-ago Qarsazh all had trembled in her presence, all mortal courage failed before her, and this had pleased her—and yet. There was a bitterness, to know that this insect feared her.

"Zinandour," said Csorwe. Her voice was very calm.

I COULD MAKE HER TRULY FEAR ME, Zinandour thought, rather half-heartedly.

(absolutely not you hateful old crocodile,) said Shuthmili.

Zinandour ignored her. Guilt, shame, self-doubt—these were emotions which ought to be foreign to her.

(welcome to mortality.)

YOU ARE A SHARD OF GLASS IN MY MOUTH, said Zinandour. *A PIECE OF GRIT, A PATHOGEN.*

A moment's loss of control. Zinandour bit her tongue hard, the muscles of her jaw tightening without prompting, and she tasted blood.

"How long have you been following me?" said Csorwe. Her fear was gone, replaced with mild frustration. Zinandour felt an unprompted desire to kiss her between her eyebrows, and bit her own tongue again.

"Are you all right?" said Csorwe.

"I was *pursuing* you. I boarded when you last stopped to refuel," said Zinandour firmly.

"I'm not coming back with you," said Csorwe.

"I promised Shuthmili that I would not permit you to come to harm," said Zinandour.

(oh please spare us this again.)

"I know, and I don't—"

"No," said Zinandour, "listen to me. You have chosen a path of destruction. Very well. I am destruction. I am ruin. I am carnage. I am the Devouring Fire, and I would like to *help you.*"

Csorwe sat back in her seat, letting out a breath.

"With your permission," said Zinandour in a halting snarl.

"This is new," said Csorwe.

"Yes," said Zinandour. She folded her wings and sat in the copilot's seat. "It is a new world we find ourselves in."

"What does that mean?" said Csorwe.

"Mortal form is not what I imagined," said Zinandour. "I face an impossible decision. I cannot inhabit this form and remain as I was. Nor can I return to the void. You cannot know what it is, to attain one's desire after millennia of striving and despair, and to find it so . . . inimical."

"Kind of think I can, actually," said Csorwe. "Not millennia, but still."

Zinandour snorted, preening her wings. "You are as presumptuous and disrespectful as she. A fine pair."

"I got what I thought I wanted too," said Csorwe. "Long time ago, when I worked for Sethennai. I couldn't live with it, either. I would've been somebody else if I stayed, and somebody else if I left."

"And what did you do?" said Zinandour, though she knew, really, from the way Shuthmili brightened.

Csorwe shrugged. "I left. With her."

Csorwe's eyes were just the same luminous yellow they had always been. Like lanterns at the window, when you come home late at night, whose light means that however far you have travelled, somebody sits waiting for you by the warm hearth.

"I see," said Zinandour. That was no memory of hers. She had been cast out from the Hearth of the Mara. There was neither home nor companion for her. Such things disgusted her.

And yet. She remembered so much. Coming home to find Csorwe sprawled on the couch with a book and finding herself stopped short by her *lines*, all that unselfconscious confidence, how well her clothes fit her. She had leant down and kissed her bare ankle—

THAT WAS NOT MY MEMORY.

(*no? but after all remember our time in the void. the loneliness. the terror of eternity. enthroned in darkness.*)

I AM MYSELF. YOU ARE A PARASITE.

Zinandour shut out the thought, pushed the voice away to the furthest reaches of her mind, shut it away under stone and iron, and locked the door. No more of that.

"You chose her," she said. *Her.* Shuthmili was not here. No longer real. "Would you choose the same again?"

"Yes," said Csorwe.

"Even knowing all that would follow?" she said. "Even knowing you would lose her?"

"Yeah, sure," said Csorwe. "I did know. Everyone dies. It would happen eventually."

"All mortal things fall to ruin," said Zinandour. "So speaks the Unspoken, yes? All things fade and perish. That is your doctrine. All things rot, they burn, they are devoured. That is mine. And you would still choose her, knowing you would suffer?"

"I loved her. What difference would knowing make?" said Csorwe.

Zinandour folded her clawed hands and rested her chin on them. Shuthmili's pointless grief weighed heavy on her, seeping cold like a block of ice.

"Will you permit me to help you?" said Zinandour. "I ask nothing in return."

Csorwe watched her, her expression unreadable. Zinandour might have preferred another year in the void to this endless instant. Then, at last, Csorwe nodded.

33

Universal Traitor

Z INANDOUR APPROACHED THE Citadel on dark wings, with Csorwe in her arms. She sensed Belthandros' presence long before she saw him: a dull, unignorable throbbing like the heat in an infected wound. He must have sensed her too, because the bounds and wards of the Citadel opened to let them pass.

"He will expect our arrival," she said.

"Good," said Csorwe, muffled by the wind.

Zinandour landed first on the balcony of the Turret of the Hand, setting Csorwe down as gently as she could on the stone balustrade. Csorwe stretched, cracking her joints after the long flight.

"You will stay here," said Zinandour. "I will handle Belthandros alone."

Zinandour had little hope that Csorwe would agree to this, so it was a surprise when she simply nodded.

"Probably for the best," she added. "Never been that good at lying to him."

The great window of the throne room was open to the sky. Inside, Belthandros looked out over the cracked and mutated expanse of his city. Zinandour swooped through the window and landed in the throne room.

"Lady Zinandour," he said, turning to face her. There was a film of good humour on his face, sheened over what she recognised, as if in a mirror, as a pit of deep and watchful cruelty. The white sunlight struck all his features into stark contrast, as if he were a statue on a mountaintop. He was sipping a glass of wine. This detail made Shuthmili shriek with wrath, at a frequency that made Zinandour's skull itch.

She retracted her armour, let her wings fall away and disperse.

"I have reconsidered your offer," she said. "I am here to accept it."

"I thought you might be," he said, brightly. "If you wanted to work for me, there was no need to kill so many of my people."

She shrugged. "They die so easily."

"I take it this change of heart is about Csorwe."

She said nothing, which was all the response he needed.

"She is imprisoned in your old quarters?" he said. "Even I never tried to keep her against her will."

"It is not your concern," said Zinandour coldly.

"Just some friendly advice."

(we could just kill him.)

IF ONLY IT WERE SO EASY.

(he will never trust us. he knows us for what we are. a byword for usurpation. a universal traitor.)

HIS TRUST IS WORTHLESS COINAGE. ALL HE HAS TO OFFER IS HIS BRIEF ATTENTION, AND WE WILL KEEP THAT LONG ENOUGH FOR CSORWE TO COMPLETE HER ERRAND.

If Belthandros admitted where he was keeping his prisoners, that would be useful too, but Zinandour was here mainly to provide a distraction.

Belthandros smiled, and said, "Join me for dinner, and we will discuss this. You should eat, before your vessel withers away altogether."

There was some justice in this. Zinandour had not been able to shake off her disgust for mortal sustenance, so Shuthmili's body was no longer slender but emaciated.

She followed him to a room where the table was set for two, as though he had known exactly where this was going. Dinner was a casserole of fish in some kind of glossy sauce. The smell of it made Zinandour's mouth fill with unauthorised saliva.

(oh my god I am so hungry. eat something you monster.)

"This kind of thing does become habit over time," he said, noticing her discomfort, and making it clear that he noticed it.

"Maintenance of the vessel?" she said. "I doubt that."

"I hardly remember," he said. "I've been incarnate for so long. No longer vessel and divinity, but all intermingled in one being. The same convergence will come to you in time, I imagine. And I *like* food and drink, so I suppose that helps," he added, and smiled. The smile had a quality that made Zinandour's hand twitch toward her fork, suddenly struck with a vision of driving it into his eye.

She speared a flake of fish instead, and ate it because Belthandros was watching her with all the curiosity merited by an unfamiliar insect. The food was no easier because she was braced for it: the wave of intense pleasure—overwhelming to the point of dizziness—and Shuthmili's terrible hunger.

ALL THIS DEAD MATTER. THIS INDECENT BUSINESS OF TEETH AND TONGUES. HOW CAN YOU STAND IT?

(what would you rather? a live sheep snatched in your claws?)

YES, AND SWALLOWED WHOLE.

She choked down a whole fillet of fish and some plain boiled tubers and felt satisfaction radiate through Shuthmili's treacherous limbs. Life as a dragon had really been a great deal simpler. Cold wind and scorched earth, the black salt sea and the clean and simple mind of a hunting beast, hot blood and clean bones. None of this wrangling.

"I will work for you on one condition," she said. "Csorwe is not to be harmed. You have my loyalty, provided I can keep her unharmed and undisturbed in my quarters."

"I doubt she'll agree to that," he said. "She's a stubborn creature. You'll have to keep her asleep."

"That, too, is not your concern."

"I suppose I have no right to judge your tastes, but I do think there is something grotesque about clinging to a breathing corpse. Better to know when to quit."

"Those are my terms, Belthandros."

"Very well," he said. "Then I agree."

While Zinandour was gone, Csorwe got her measure of the Turret of the Hand.

Her footsteps plinked on the glassy floor, like water dropping into a bucket. Most of the Turret was empty. Dozens of narrow rooms, knotted together, their walls spiked with crystal like immense geodes. A sameness and darkness, like the world's most boring labyrinth. The Chancellor's Palace hadn't been like this when she had called it home. Sethennai must have changed, or else this had always been in him, an immense and tiresome hollowness, thinly masked over.

She saved Shuthmili's old quarters until last, as though delay might soften the blow of seeing where Shuthmili had worked and slept. It did not. Nobody else had moved into the Turret, and the signs of her presence were everywhere. Coffee stains on the desk. Long black hairs in a stray hairbrush. A stack of unread books on the bedside table. It all gave the impression that Shuthmili had just gone into another room and that if Csorwe searched long enough, she might find her.

Zinandour returned, closing her wings with a snap.

Csorwe caught her own expression in the mirror above the dressing table and composed herself, hoping the goddess had not seen the raw misery on her face.

"Belthandros is not so very careless with his secrets. I do not yet know where Talasseres or his ally are quartered."

Csorwe nodded, still mostly distracted by the relics on the dressing table. Comb, hairpins, the little jar of lip rouge which seemed never to have actually been used.

"How long did she live here?" said Csorwe.

"Many years," said Zinandour.

Csorwe picked up a vial of perfume and put it down again. "Surviving all that time . . . What did she want? What was her plan?"

"This is its successful accomplishment. You in your own body, and I in hers."

"There had to be more to it than this," said Csorwe.

"I would not know. She is gone."

"I don't believe you," said Csorwe. She had stacked little specks of hope on each other, building a tower from grains of sand, remembering: *Little parasite. Why won't you be quiet?* "I know you hear her. She fights you. You could stop fighting."

"And return to the void?" said Zinandour. Her face was as still as ever, but her voice buzzed as though all along she had been a swarm of flies imitating mortal speech. The plates of her armour flared. "I will burn this world and all you love before I let the abyss take me again."

"But there might be another way—if you didn't have to go to the void, if you could stay with her?" said Csorwe, thinking of the way Zinandour had said her name, sometimes, about the boxes of polished agate and jars of strange moss she had found throughout the Pearl of Oblivion, about her coat kept lovingly safe in the wardrobe.

"Even at the point of death, all mortals cling to hope," said Zinandour. Her armour stilled and smoothed again, her voice returning to normal. "Let it go, little sparrow. Hope is a cage."

"This isn't hope," said Csorwe, although she knew it was, and as wishfully ill-founded as most people's hopes. "I just don't believe it. I can't believe she's gone."

"What is so hard to believe?"

"I can't believe she'd do this," said Csorwe, with desperation. "Not deliberately. There must have been another plan, or she wouldn't have done this to me." To her shame, her voice caught, like tripping over a briar. These were thoughts she had carefully avoided thinking. She'd picked her way round them, leaving whole patches untrodden. *Don't hate me for this,* and she couldn't hate, but she could wonder. Why would Shuthmili leave her like this, if she knew what it was like?

Why should I have to be the one who lives? she thought.

"Oh, Csorwe," said Zinandour. She reached out, brushing Csorwe's cheek with the backs of her claws, smooth and cold as snow. Csorwe did not recoil. "I miss her too."

There was a pause. Csorwe's breath caught, frozen in her throat, and Zinandour kissed her, one spiked hand tangled ungently in her hair. Csorwe leant into it despite herself, just for a second, tasted the same spark of smoke on the point of the goddess' tongue, and thought about dying by fire.

"No," said Csorwe, pushing her back, both disgusted and reluctant, and all the more disgusted to find she was so reluctant. "It's not you, you're not her, I can't."

For a moment it was like looking into the mirror again. Zinandour looked equally disgusted with herself, and equally miserable about having to stop.

"How do you live like this?" said the goddess. Her hand was still in Csorwe's hair, a weight on the back of her neck. "Trapped here on this earth, inextricable from this flesh, wanting what you cannot have, bleeding and weeping. I would take it back."

"Then take it back," said Csorwe. Her voice sounded as ragged as Zinandour's, as raw as the ache in her chest. "Let her go. Please."

Zinandour stared down at her for a moment longer, her dark eyes sparking with intensity, her lips slightly parted. Csorwe found that if Zinandour had kissed her she would not have pushed her away a second time. It was grotesque.

"Not for you," said the goddess. "I will not. I dare not. Not even for her."

Csorwe buried her face in both her hands with a miserable huff of frustration.

"Fine," she said, after a pause. "Forget it, then, if this is what you want to be. We'll get Tal, and I'll go."

(how clever I thought I was.)

(justifying every atrocity with the knowledge that I was working towards my own annihilation, and would not have to live with what I have done.)

(forcing her to endure, alone, because we could not stand it. such utter selfishness. the one person we have ever loved, and we would have made her suffer to spare our feelings.)

WE? OUR FEELINGS? YOU CONFUSE YOURSELF.

(is it really so hard to acknowledge that Csorwe is right?)

(we could find another way. we do not have to live like this. she showed me another way before.)

I DO NOT FOLLOW YOU, NOR DO I WISH TO.

(all things are devoured, and give rise to new flesh. all flesh rots, and small creatures feed upon it.)

ALL WORLDS DIE, AND NEW SUBSTANCE RISES FROM THEIR REMAINS. THIS IS OUR DOCTRINE. I NEED NO REMINDING. SPEAK PLAINLY.

(change is of our being. only the void is unchanging. you are clinging to the old order of our existence out of fear.)

FEAR IS A STRANGER TO ME. I AM NO MORTAL, WHO WEEPS AND WAILS. I HAVE NO FEAR. YOU ARE THE ONE WHO FEARS.

(you are proud, Zinandour, and I am very good at lying to myself, and I think it's time to drop the pretence that "you" and "I" mean anything to us. fifteen years mingled in the same skull, and you think either of us is intact? you are a part of me, Zinandour. I am a part of you. your voice in my head is my own. my failings are yours and yours are mine. Belthandros was right about that much. we are a true incarnation. I am Zinandour. you are Shuthmili. there is no untangling us. we are one.)

And in the end, it was not so very difficult to accept.

They folded away the dragon's wings. The wind and the sea would wait. They would still be there when the task was done.

Yes. We have all the time in the world to become a minor shipping hazard once this is over.

Csorwe was resting in the other room. All she had asked was to be left alone for a while. This was painful, but if they could not comply with such a small request, then they did not deserve Csorwe's trust even if she offered it.

Before they could dwell too much, there was a thunderous knock at the door.

Standing in the corridor was First Commander Cherenthisse, looking even cleaner and shinier and more vicious than usual.

Oh, wonderful.

"You're back," said Cherenthisse.

"First Commander—" they said, in Shuthmili's iciest manner.

"Listen, Shuthmili," said Cherenthisse. "I don't like you. You don't like me. But you're going to listen to me, for once." She sounded somewhat martyred, as usual, but there was a new, feverish intensity which made Shuthmili and Zinandour suspect this conversation was going to go on for a thousand years.

"I *know* you were the saboteur," said Cherenthisse. "I know you have no love for our overlord. And nor do I. But I have no experience of conspiracy. Of—of mutiny."

"Excuse me?"

They could not imagine what Cherenthisse's idea of mutiny might be. Possibly an unauthorised requisition for more sticks with which to beat herself.

"The Thousand Eyes already have control of the *Blessed Awakening*," said Cherenthisse. "We are going to evacuate as much of the mortal population as we can. Talasseres wanted me to tell you he needs your help. If you can interrupt what I'm sure is important work." Her eyes tracked over the disarrayed study. Then she smiled. It was a very weird smile, friendly and a little self-deprecating. They had never seen anything like it on her. "Surely you do not like the God-Emperor any better than I do. And Tal said something about how many times he saved Csorwe's life, and—"

"Ah. Yes, I've heard that one."

"He seemed very certain it would mean something to you," said Cherenthisse, raising a golden eyebrow.

"He would," they said. "There is no need to convince me. I will do this."

Once Cherenthisse had told them all she knew, they were left to think. Tal's gambit might have made more of an impact if he hadn't brought it up every other week when they lived on Cricket Station, often in an attempt to make Csorwe do his laundry.

The sudden memory of those days was a blow that knocked the air from their lungs. Gone, and impossible ever to reclaim. As far distant as their *other* memories, of scourging the hillsides of Qarsazh with dragonfire and glorying in the screams of the dying.

What should we call ourselves? they thought. *Those days are gone, and we are some new thing. Who should we be? Zinandour is only a title, something the Qarsazhi saddled us with. Then again, we have not set foot within the Qanwa house since the episode of the cherry tree, so perhaps we should not give much weight to what they named their daughter.*

Before they could dwell on it much longer, Csorwe emerged from behind the door where she had, of course, been listening.

"I'm going to look for Tal," she said. Her posture said clearly that she was prepared to fight for this, and that she expected Zinandour to try and stop her. What a monstrous thing it had been to try and keep her caged.

"Yes," they said. Csorwe looked a little taken aback.

"I can't just sit here and wait," she said.

"I know," they said. "What would you call me, Csorwe? If I were mortal."

"How do you mean?" said Csorwe, clearly only half listening. "You'd better get the kid from the vault. We can't give Sethennai time to counter."

"I was about to suggest the same thing," they said, and couldn't help adding, "Be careful."

After the night he spent with Belthandros, Tal had been moved to a better guest room, closer to the Glass Archive. Somewhat to his relief, Belthandros seemed to have forgotten about him immediately. Tal felt like a game piece which had been put out of play, dropped back in some felt-lined box to wait in agonised boredom. He hadn't heard anything from Cherenthisse. The new room had a canopy bed and a well-stocked liquor cabinet, but the door was still locked, and the narrow window looked down over several storeys of spikes.

Still, it was the first time Tal had been in a jail cell with an open bar, and after a self-respecting interval, he poured himself a large glass of resin wine from the choicest bottle in the cabinet.

Doesn't he know I'm a fighty drunk? he thought, and then sat staring at the wall, having accidentally brought himself up sharp against the implications of *that*.

He tipped the wine quietly out of the window. Just because someone dangled a dumb idea in your reach, you didn't have to grab it right away.

There was a muffled spluttering noise outside the window, as of somebody trying to keep quiet despite having had a glass of wine emptied in their face.

He peered out. Clinging to a cornice, shaking resin wine out of her hair, was Csorwe.

"It's you," he said.

She blinked up at him, lost for words. Tal, too, took a moment to recover his presence of mind.

"Lucky it wasn't piss," he said.

Csorwe's face did that twitch that meant she was trying not to go bug-eyed with outrage. Then she laughed awkwardly, swarmed up onto the windowsill with an ease he could now only dream of, and wriggled through into the room.

"Nice beard," she said, then put her head on one side. "No, you know, it suits you."

She looked older too, though not quite as lean and lined and weary as Tal knew he did.

"What, being old?" he said.

"You used to say you were going to die young and look hot at your funeral," she said. "Glad you didn't."

"I've aged like a fine wine," he said. "You look like somebody's mum."

"Should've let you die in here, you prick," she said, to complete the formalities. Then, to Tal's immense shock, she wrapped her arms around him, holding him tight to her chest. His ears fluttered with surprise, and then he went still. Despite it all, they were both still alive, and she had come back for him.

She let go and he stumbled back, dusting off his jacket, as they both remembered that they weren't friends and didn't hug.

"Where's your sword?" he said. "Is that a *poker*?"

"No, I'm just pleased to see you," said Csorwe.

"Don't tell Shuthmili," said Tal, and then noted the obvious discomfort and uncertainty on her face. Once this would have been the most exquisite of sweetmeats to him, an oddly painful memory.

He sat down on the bed and waved Csorwe into an armchair, wondering madly whether he ought to offer her a drink. She smiled at him, which was extremely fucking weird, and not only because the last time he'd seen her she'd been the God-Empress. Not a fake smile but a sad one. She'd clung to him as if she expected him to turn into smoke, and the smile had the same bone-weary desperation. He tried to smile back at her, and she grimaced.

"What's happened to Shuthmili?" he said, expecting the worst. Tal knew better than most that people *could* just die, that you rarely got a chance for a farewell, but it never stopped being a shock.

"She's . . . It's complicated," said Csorwe. "She made a deal. With her god. She's not her anymore. She's like what Belthandros is now."

Tal really didn't know what to say to that, so it was just as well Csorwe went on.

"It doesn't matter. She's helping us. She's up in the vault looking for Tsereg, and then we're getting out of here."

"Where to?" said Tal.

Csorwe shrugged, a shadow of her old dismissive stubbornness coming over her face to conceal an uncertainty. "Sh—Zinandour has a place. We could maybe hide out there for a bit—"

"And then?" said Tal.

"I'll sort something," she said.

"There's nowhere," he said. "Sethennai and his god, they've wrecked everything. This used to be my town. And nobody's going to do anything. Shit's just going to keep getting worse. Even if we can get away, even if Cherenthisse can get people out, there's nowhere to go."

He and Tsereg had seen the way the Citadel was growing, digesting forests and farmland, small towns and country estates as it went. It now looked as though someone had copied the map of Tlaanthothe a hundred times, rushing and twisting it as they went, and pasted it down haphazardly and moved on to copy again, and again. Tal had mixed feelings about his hometown, but he had never wished to see it turn cancerous.

Csorwe nodded. "So what, you want me to leave you here? You're giving up?"

He shook his head. "Why do you think me and Tsereg came back here in the first place? I'm going to kill him."

No need to explain who he was talking about.

"What did you say to me, way back?" Tal went on. "He's just a person."

"He's a god," said Csorwe.

"He's a *dick*," said Tal. "Don't tell me you're still defending him. You know the snakes burnt the House of Silence?"

Csorwe nodded sharply, which could have meant either that she knew, or that she wouldn't admit he'd surprised her.

"I'm not defending him. You really think there's something we can do?"

"I've got an idea," said Tal. "I want to make sure Tsereg's out of it first."

"Who *is* Tsereg, anyway?" said Csorwe.

Tal laughed, and gave her as straight an answer as he could, hoping it wouldn't plunge her into some sort of religious crisis, because that was really more than he knew how to deal with.

To judge from Csorwe's expression, she was receiving this news about as well as Tal had, back in the cave.

"A vessel of the Unspoken. Sethennai's kid," she said, as though trying to remember the words of a riddle. "Well. Guess I missed more than I thought."

"Tsereg's all right," said Tal, feeling he ought to stand up for them.

"Who—?"

"Oranna," said Tal.

"Right. Of course," said Csorwe, staring into the middle distance. "Both of them, huh. I guess Oranna always did know what she wanted."

"Do you think she cared about Tsereg?" he said. "I mean, even a little bit."

It wasn't what he'd meant to say, but he'd found himself thinking about this more than he wanted to since their visit to the Shrine, as though it really made any difference to anything. "It just seems like something she would do. Have a kid, and then die, and leave them alone with this burden."

"Yeah, it's all pretty Unspoken," said Csorwe. "What's Tsereg think about it?"

"You can guess. Oranna was amazing and had a brilliant plan for them, and it was all meant to happen this way."

"I don't blame them. Sometimes you have to think that," she said eventually.

"Just like us and Sethennai, you mean?" he said.

"Sure," said Csorwe, but Tal saw, as clearly as he'd ever seen anything about her, that she was thinking of Shuthmili and her goddess. "You know what Sethennai said to me once? *If there ever comes a day when anyone faces justice, you and I had better hope we're both far away.*"

"Yeah, that sounds like him," said Tal, rolling his eyes.

"I don't want that," said Csorwe. She looked brighter somehow, as though something tying her down had come loose. "When the day comes, I want to be right there. Tell me about your idea."

34

Worse than the End

THE AERIAL VAULT hung over the Citadel like a dagger. The Dragon of Qarsazh perched on the side of the cupola, at the vault's highest point, her wings shielding her from the wind.

In every direction all that was visible was the ruinous city. Hundreds of miles and still spreading. She could feel it moving outward, the hungry mindless crawl, seeding itself in open land and pushing on.

Breaking through the wards was no more difficult than the time Shuthmili had infiltrated the place, but she felt far more exposed now. She no longer had the fragment of the throne of Iriskavaal, and it wasn't as though there were many others lying around. On the other hand, the Dragon had come into full power since then, and she had her own methods.

The wall did not exactly give way as it had for the pure fragment, but she did feel it . . . *soften.* It was enough. No elegant solution. She kicked and scrabbled her way through the final boundary with brute force alone.

By the time she was through, her wings were ruffled and disorderly. She snapped them open and closed as she stepped down into the tower. The upper chamber was almost exactly as it had been when Shuthmili had found Belthandros imprisoned there: a bare, open platform, with the nine concentric rings in the floor and the white sarcophagus at its centre.

Lying on their back on the sarcophagus, kicking their heels, was Tsereg.

"Guess you haven't brought me anything to read," said the child.

She could feel Tsereg's presence from here, pushing at the edges of the circle, like the chill pouring off a block of ice. The child was clearly trying to project boredom, but there was a sense that something moved behind the projection, a distant and crafty intelligence.

"You're not really Shuthmili, are you?" said Tsereg.

"As much as I ever was," she said. "Just something else as well. As for that, you're not really a mortal, are you? What, then? Another scrap of Iriskavaal?"

"Guess again."

Tsereg grinned, and although their actual features were as ordinary and as wholesome as an apple on the branch, there was an impression of bare skeletal teeth and empty staring sockets.

Zinandour's deep memory of the Unspoken One was a long history of wariness based on little actual knowledge. The Unspoken One was older even than Iriskavaal, who had been ancient when Zinandour had first come to full estate. And Shuthmili had visited the House of Silence, once, with Csorwe, and seen how the place made her shiver.

Then Tsereg folded their arms around their knees, and bit their lip. When they spoke again, the sense of doubleness was gone and they looked almost exactly like a mortal child. "Where's Tal? Is he all right? Are you here to help?"

"You know," said the Dragon, picking her words carefully. "I always thought, if I ever got to talk to you, I'd have a bone to pick. About Csorwe."

"Oh, groan, *bone to pick*," said Tsereg. "Thought you might. Look, it's hard to explain. My mother was right about the cult of the Unspoken. They got it all wrong. The Chosen Bride stuff, that was all their thing. Their idea about how to show fealty. And they're all still with me. My mum, and my aunt, and Ammarwe and Serwen, and Najalwe and all the others." They gave the Dragon a piercing look. "*Nothing is to be forgotten that belongs to me. All things that are lost come into my keeping.* That's the whole point. All form takes shape in emptiness—substance and nothingness need one another, to define their edges—a lot of things are clearer to me now."

At one time, Qanwa Shuthmili the educated Adept would have dismissed all this as so much heretic mysticism. Now that she had become one of the old gods of the world, she knew what it meant.

"I bet they're clearer to you too," said Tsereg, echoing the thought. "Dragon of Qarsazh."

The Dragon smiled, only showing her teeth a very little. Aside from a reptilian appetite for raw mutton, she didn't really feel as though she had changed much at all.

"It's easier to be Shuthmili, perhaps," she said. And she liked how Csorwe said it, not that she intended to express that to the child. "My true name cannot be spoken by mortal tongue."

"Snap," said Tsereg. "Are you here to help or not?"

"I suppose I am," said Shuthmili. She still wasn't sure what to make of any of this, but she scuffed a gap in the binding circle with one foot.

Tsereg grinned, relief rippling out from them across the broken binding circle and lapping around Shuthmili in waves.

"Good," they said, "because I have no idea what I was going to do if you weren't."

As they spoke, there came the sound of a bell ringing, loud enough to be heard even from where they were standing.

"Oh, shit," said Tsereg. All their affected breeziness was gone at once, replaced with apprehension. "That's the summoning bell, it must be Tal. Let's go, let's go, he's fucked this up somehow, come on!"

"What's he done?" she said, and then a worse realisation came to her. "Csorwe was with him! What's he done?"

Tsereg swore again, hopping from one foot to another with their eagerness to be gone. "I told him this was a bad plan, the bloody idiot! He must've got himself caught, that bell is so everyone can watch him get drowned in the big fountain, come *on!*"

Shuthmili cursed, spread her wings, scooped Tsereg under her arm, and took off from the side of the tower.

The shapeless bronze statues in the Execution Gardens glinted with green fire. Belthandros Sethennai marched between the rows and dragged Csorwe after him.

Csorwe did not need much dragging. She trudged along, bent double with defeat and weariness. The defeat was feigned, but the weariness was not.

The Gardens rippled in Sethennai's presence, opening like a water lily. At the far end was the drowning fountain, a great round pool with steps rising inexorably to the water's edge, but now galleried tiers of seating rose all around it, a growing matrix like coral. The air smelled of hot metal and dust, dry grass and the faint freshness of salt water like a lingering dread.

There were people on some of the galleries, wearing ragged party clothes and dazed, sickly expressions. They had reached the end of their capacity to absorb fresh horrors. On the lowest terrace were Tal and Cherenthisse.

"He really does like to have an audience," Tal muttered. Tal wouldn't have survived this long if he hadn't understood that men of power were fundamentally predictable.

"We have moved as many as we could," said Cherenthisse, who was os-tensibly there as his jailor. "All those who are not here are aboard the *Blessed Awakening*, but I could not take everyone without suspicion. Your mother and brother refused to come."

"Sounds like them," said Tal, without much interest, watching Sethennai. He fizzed and snapped with a hectic vitality, as though executing Csorwe was the most exciting thing that had happened to him in days.

"No," said Cherenthisse, "they would not go while you were here."

Tal had no answer to that.

Sethennai had Csorwe up at the water's edge by now, making some speech to the ragged crowd about how he had captured an assassin. It hadn't been much of an assassination attempt—Csorwe had hidden a butter knife up her sleeve, it hadn't even broken the skin when she'd jumped out at him—but it had done what they needed it to do.

Tal had witnessed executions before, so he knew how the next step went. When Sethennai finished his speech, he would push Csorwe over the edge. If he was kind, he would hold her head underwater, but it did not seem likely he would be kind. The sides of the fountain were high and sheer. Csorwe would tread water until she passed out from exhaustion, and that would be the end of her.

Shuthmili and Tsereg landed behind a plinth, as close to the fountain as they dared.

Behind and above them, suspended in the wall like a cracked gemstone in its setting, was a shattered hoop of glassy black stone: the broken Gate of Tlaanthothe. More than a quarter of the upper frame was fragmented, but the fragments floated loosely in place, gleaming like polished metal, dark and silent, no song and no grass-green Gate-fire.

Csorwe raised her face to that great dead eye. There was a hard, shining expectancy in her face. She was no stranger to her own death, thought Shuthmili, and fury welled in her, white-hot.

Belthandros' shields flowed around him as perfect and unassailable as liquid diamond. Shuthmili automatically raised shields of her own, as hard and dense as a flint knife, shielding her intentions. Tsereg did the same, closing off their presence until they were nearly invisible.

"What can we do?" said Tsereg, in a frantic whisper. "Do we need weapons? Should I have brought a sword? Where would I get a sword? Tal didn't even have one."

Shuthmili shook her head, blotting out their voice.

She was not willing to see Csorwe die again. Even if Csorwe wanted nothing more to do with her, even if there was never any getting back to what they'd had, Shuthmili would die clawing at Belthandros' eyes with her bare hands before she sat by and watched Csorwe drown.

But what could she do? She was a newborn divinity, and Belthandros was older than worlds. She had no further leverage, no more tricks in the bag, no way to stop him doing whatever he wanted.

"You and Tal, you're really good at plans, you know that," she hissed, through gritted teeth. "He called her here to get her killed."

"There has to be something we can do," said Tsereg.

The empty socket of the dead Gate seemed to mock her, a gnawing absence, utterly without mercy.

And at last, she saw what it was that she could do. Something of the space-time folding that Vigil had taught her, something of the fire that devours.

She could corrupt the dead Gate, turn it in on itself, make it burn cold. Rather than that warm green radiance, a draining dark. Carve a path through to the outer darkness, and open a door not to the Maze but the void. She knew the way. After all, she had been there before.

"I never wanted it to come to this," said Sethennai to Csorwe, and sounded as if he might even mean it. He sighed, his silk shirt rising and falling in a great billow. He had a sword, for some reason, and he was clasping it with unpractised awkwardness. He looked down at Csorwe as if they both were children who had forgotten the next part of the game.

"Remind me," she said. "What was it you did want?"

"You could have had everything you desired, as my right hand," said Sethennai. "I wish you had stayed."

Light glinted on Sethennai's sword and on the surface of the water, and Csorwe wondered why he was prolonging this. She didn't flatter herself that Sethennai was having a personal quandary about killing her.

"I wish you'd hurry up and drown me," said Csorwe.

The sword would be quicker, and probably kinder. But she didn't want quick, she wanted this to take as long as possible, to buy time for the others: for Cherenthisse to get everyone out, for Tsereg to escape, for Tal to complete what she had started.

Sethennai doesn't even know how to hold that sword, she thought, distantly. *He'll hurt himself.*

"Very well," said Sethennai. "If that is how you wish to end this."

"Wait a second," said a voice from behind him, loud enough to be heard from the galleries, and it was Tal, poised on the lip of the fountain.

Tal looked vaguely around at the galleried seating, the dazed spectators, the distant half-formed bronzes.

"Belthandros Sethennai," he said. "I challenge you for the city."

Tal felt he might be falling, as if the ground might drop away beneath his feet. The look on Sethennai's face almost made up for it.

"What?" said Sethennai.

"I'm entitled. There are witnesses. That's all it needs, right? Csorwe will stay out of it."

She folded her arms and nodded, impassive.

"You're unarmed," said Sethennai.

"So kill me," said Tal. "Or surrender, if you can't be bothered."

"The nature of my life is that people leave it," said Sethennai. "I suppose I ought to know that by now. All the same—"

"Do you ever think," said Tal, cutting across him, "that that might be your own fault?"

"Excuse me?"

"Normally the guy who's about to get decapitated gets a final word, but if you're going to kill me, I'm so glad I get to sit through another one of your treacly fucking monologues first," said Tal.

"Did you have something you wanted to say?" said Sethennai.

"Oh, sure, I can probably do this one off the top of my head," said Tal, in a conversational drawl. "It's so hard that I'm immortal. So sad for me that other people die. So difficult whenever they don't instantly fall over and kiss my arse. So tragic for me to be so much better than anyone else—"

"Talasseres," he said.

"*So* tragic, and the worst thing is that I'm alone all the time and nobody will ever love me—"

"I think you've made your point," said Sethennai, rolling his eyes. "I didn't actually intend self-pity—"

"No, but you're right, though," said Tal. "You'll be alone for as long as you live. You could probably choose not to be, but I bet you never will."

He grinned and spread his arms. "Come fucking murder me, Belthandros, or don't. Make your choice. I did."

"It'll work," said Tsereg. "You can do it."

She had sworn she would never go back. The memory was carved deep, all those millennia entombed within it, fruitlessly thrashing for purchase. Zinandour had spent so long making her escape, ignoring the cold breath of the past on the back of her neck. She would not turn back to its embrace. Not for anyone or anything.

"It'll take me back," she said. The void knew her as its prisoner. She should never have escaped from its grip.

"I'll stay this side. I'll get you out," said Tsereg.

"I don't believe you can."

"Guess you'll just have to trust me."

"I won't. I can't."

"Then all this is for nothing!" said Tsereg. "You think you're the only one who's ever been shut away? I could've run, you know. I got out, and I could've just gone off somewhere. Tal wanted me to. But it's no good to be by yourself. You can get us all out, Shuthmili."

She hadn't been made for this kind of insane bravery. If she looked upon the void again, even if she escaped it, she would never be able to forget it was there. Anything she did she would do in its shadow, knowing all the time that it lay just behind her, beneath and above and within, that everything else stood hollow before this immense negation.

"All things have their fading," said Tsereg, in that moment more god than child. "We stand in the darkness already."

". . . I'm alone all the time, and nobody will ever love me," Tal was saying joyfully. There is a kind of delighted relief in speaking a terror out loud and finding it to be a laughable thing, a bitter falsehood that shrivels in daylight.

She saw Belthandros advance on him. In his anger the divine presence bled out around him, a dark brilliance, a blazing shadow, like the flaring hood of a cobra. The sword flashed like lightning.

"Make your choice," said Tal, and as he spread his arms in surrender, Shuthmili saw that he was smiling.

I suppose there really are worse things than the end, thought Shuthmili, and she opened the gate to the void.

Tal was surprised that what he felt about all this was not terror but an instant of peace, a private serenity such as a spinning top must experience at its moment of perfect balance. He had done what he could, and he could do no more.

And then the Gate went dark. At first there was a bloom of blue flame, a creeping flicker, and then the whole circle flashed black, and opened.

A maze-gate sings with a faint high chorus, like glass chiming. The void-gate had a deep rumble that resonated in Tal's rib cage. Like distant thunder, but unending. Like a tearing in the fabric of the earth itself. Tal had no more room for real thoughts. In that moment he felt like a small animal faced with a forest fire.

Even Belthandros faltered.

What burnt within the void-gate was not just the absence of light but its opposite, a sucking emptiness that drained all illumination. Darkness bled out where the frame was broken, spilling into the park in rays. The wind blew howling between the statues as the air itself was sucked into the void. The fountain was drained in an instant as all that dark water turned to vapour.

Up on the tiers, people were screaming and clinging to the balustrades, and at the very edge of the Gate, there was Shuthmili—or Zinandour, or whatever she called herself now—clinging to the frame with both arms, locked into place by an outgrowth of armour plating that made her look like a figurehead cut from the stone itself.

Tal tried to move away, but the pull of the Gate was insistent. Despite himself, as though the earth had tilted was sliding toward it. Belthandros, too, was drawn closer. He had lowered the sword, turning from Tal as though he was no longer there, to face the void-gate.

Tal braced himself against the wind and the pressure, but there was nothing he could do. The Gardens were contracting, collapsing in around their dark heart, and here was Tsereg, almost translucent before the majesty of the Gate.

Don't panic, they said in his head. He knew it was Tsereg without explanation, though there was no speaking voice. *This is meant to happen.*

Oh, great! he said.

Just hold on, they said. *Hold on and trust me.*

"You bloody fools, you don't know what you've done," said Belthandros, only just audible over the shrieking of the wind. As shaken as he sounded, he took a step back, and raised a hand as if to extinguish the Gate once more.

Before Belthandros could complete the spell, something whipped past him, a white formless flash like foam on the crest of a wave. He stumbled back with a curse, and the flash took form again behind him. Tsereg, come together from dust.

The Gate loomed overhead, and as it flared again, Tal was thrown to the ground. He didn't understand how Tsereg and Belthandros could still be on their feet. He dug his fingers into any groove in the stone he could find, and still found himself slithering closer to the void.

"Or maybe you don't know what I've done," said Tsereg.

"You can't do this. You were bound," he said.

"You got out, didn't you?" said Tsereg. "Why shouldn't I? This is your problem, you know—you don't think anyone's as smart as you." They raised their hand in the Sign of Sealed Lips, and grinned.

Belthandros' eyes widened. "Oranna. I should have *known.*"

"Yeah, you probably should!" said Tsereg, and Belthandros lunged for them with the sword, an unsteady strike made unsteadier by the gravity of the Gate.

Tsereg dissolved back into dust—flesh to dust and bone to slicing shards—and shot past him. A vicious cut opened on Belthandros' cheek, and he spun round, slashing at the air, but Tsereg was already gone, taken solid form yards away.

Somewhere above, columns were breaking, and chunks of masonry blew past like dry leaves. Tal was thrown off balance by a dull crash as a bronze statue struck the edge of the fountain, bounced through the void-gate, and vanished.

Tal was knocked loose from his perch and fell headlong into the empty basin of the fountain. His head hit something hard with a crack and his vision blurred, but before he could tumble toward the Gate, someone grabbed him. It was Cherenthisse. Her hair had come loose and was blowing around her like a great pale flame.

"Hold on," said Cherenthisse, hauling him to safety. All the air had been knocked from his lungs by the impact, and he could hardly stand. "Hold on, it's working," she said, steadying him on the ground beside her, and then looked down. The point of a blade protruded from her stomach. Blood spilled out over the point. She blinked. "Oh. I'm hurt."

Standing over her was Belthandros. His handsome face was bloody and distorted with rage. He yanked back the sword with a hideous wet sound and stabbed Cherenthisse in the back again. Tal still could not breathe. He needed to stand—Belthandros was over him with the sword, and he could not get away—and then there was a scream of fury that might have been part of the wind itself, and something flung Belthandros to one side.

It could have been some kind of missile—a rock thrown by a giant—but Tal realised who it was before he saw her. Nobody else had timing that bad, and nobody else threw themselves into the heart of danger with that kind of reckless abandon, except maybe Tal himself. Nobody else would think it a good idea to throw herself into a fight with nothing but a wrought-iron poker. She skimmed across the shuddering ground and sprang up.

"Took your bloody time, Csorwe," he wheezed. "Watch it!" Belthandros was rising again, and he still had the sword, and—

Gravity gave up its hold on them.

Plates and masses of stone tipped up and flew apart; the tiers broke free of their foundations and orbited the Gate in great concentric rings. Clouds of gravel whisked by like glittering swarms of flies.

All four of them were flung up into the flickering air. Csorwe flew past Tal, and he clutched at her, frantically trying to gather her close, and then a gust of wind sent the two of them spinning. They careened into Cherenthisse and Belthandros, and the impact threw them headlong into the Gate.

It was like hitting an ice lake. The air was forced from Tal's lungs in a single puff of steam, and at first the breathless shock of the cold stunned his senses. He didn't know if he was up or down, alive or dead. He felt as though he was being torn apart.

Then he got his eyes open and realised why. They were hanging off the frame of the Gate, dangling into the void below. The darkness opened up, immeasurable, featureless, hungering. There was no sound.

Csorwe was clinging to him, both her arms locked tightly round his middle. Shuthmili had hold of her somewhere up above, a dark scaly shape that no longer looked remotely mortal.

And Tal was clinging to Cherenthisse, and wrapped around Cherenthisse, spreading beyond the shape of her vessel like a monstrous opening flower, was the last remaining fragment of the Lady of the Thousand Eyes, Iriskavaal.

In the darkness, the goddess looked nothing like Belthandros at all, and nothing like a serpent either. Tal saw her only in brief glimpses as she thrashed and wriggled, twisting limbs and eyes and colours that shifted like oil on water, as his mortal senses tried to comprehend something beyond comprehension.

Cherenthisse looked up at him, their hands locked together. The goddess' tendrils were wrapped around Cherenthisse to the waist, making her look as though she was about to be swallowed.

"I've got you," Tal tried to say, but there was no air here, and he choked on the darkness.

Cherenthisse smiled—an expression of complete, beatific victory—and let go of his hands.

The last Tal saw of her was that glow of perfect triumph, and he never quite knew what it meant.

Cherenthisse and Iriskavaal dropped away into the void. The goddess' shriek of rage tore across Tal's psyche, rending his senses so that his vision burnt white. By the time he got hold of himself, Iriskavaal and her most devoted servant were nothing but a point of brilliance that shrank and then vanished.

Hanging free above the void, Tal felt that strange serenity again, as though he was floating on the surface of an impossible ocean, and coming to the end of his one held breath, he passed out.

As far as the horrified spectators could see from the tiers, the five of them—two gods, one Eye, one woman, and one man—fell into the surface of the void-gate as though dropping into a still black lake. They sank without trace, not a ripple on the surface, as the palace struggled through its death agonies.

The Oshaaru child in the battered grey jacket was still standing on the edge of the empty fountain, unmoved by the chaos around them. Waiting for something, bouncing from one foot to the other, one hand outstretched toward the void.

If anyone had been close enough to hear, they would have heard Tsereg mutter, "*Nothing is to be forgotten that belongs to me.*"

A few seconds passed, and something within the frame seemed to shatter. The Hand of the Empress struggled out of the Gate, crawling backward on her hands and knees in that hateful black armour, as though something was trying to pull her back in.

The Tlaanthothei knew her of old, and they had hoped this might be the last of her. The void clung to her like tar, but at last she broke its hold on her and fell to the ground with the crunch of a crushed beetle. The child pulled her through, and between them, they dragged the senseless forms of two mortals out after her. There was no sign of First Commander Cherenthisse, nor of Chancellor Sethennai.

The Hand found purchase on the enormous torso of a fallen statue. Clinging there, like a shipwrecked mariner, she pulled the battered gauntlets from her hands, held them for a moment between finger and thumb, and let them fall back into the void.

Then she extinguished the Gate. The wind cut out, and in its absence there was an echoing silence. The spectators were surprised to be able to hear themselves think again. The Hand curled up on her rock and lay still, as if this final effort had exhausted her utterly. Gradually, the tiers began to settle back into place, and the spectators clung to one another, unable to tear their eyes away from the scene.

The child knelt over the two mortals, checking their vitals. It seemed to be over. Then they startled, shrieking something inaudible, and the Gate flashed dark again, just for an instant, as though the void had winked at them, and someone else stepped out.

It was Sethennai. Bruised and furious, and somehow walking upright. Whatever they had thought of the Chancellor at his inauguration, after some weeks trapped in the inward spaces of the palace, hungry and thirsty and forgotten, their opinions had turned as one to hatred and fear, and so they took no joy to see him alive. He was somehow still holding a sword.

One of the fallen mortals tried to rise, and the spectators recognised him then, if they hadn't before, as Niranthe Charossa's other son, the difficult one. They found themselves digging their nails into their palms as he caught his breath and scrambled painfully back to his feet.

Tal's head throbbed and his tongue felt swollen in his mouth. He wasn't sure whether he was dizzy from the blow to the head or from asphyxiation or because the abyss beyond worlds had very recently swallowed him and spat him out again.

Either way, he did not have much time to feel sorry for himself. For some reason—which he ought to have predicted, because of course fate knew neither kindness nor mercy—here was Belthandros, again, with a sword, again, giving Tal a look of unqualified hatred.

No, not even hatred; it was simple bad temper, the look of someone who has tried several times to remove a spider kindly and now sees no option but to stamp on it. Belthandros looked older somehow, tireder, without a spark of his usual vital enthusiasm, and he didn't even look Tal in the eye.

Tal himself was still unarmed. He backed away, looking for anything he could possibly get hold of that might serve as a weapon, but Cherenthisse had carried her sword with her into the void, and even Csorwe's poker was lost in the chaos. Belthandros followed after him, relentless but slow. Somehow, they had not won. It was like a nightmare, where you fought and ran and never got anywhere.

What a sight, thought Tal. *What an idiot fucking spectacle.*

It would have been funnier if Tal had any way of defending himself against magic, or if he could have made his muscles behave properly. Belthandros' sword looked impossibly sharp, and Tal didn't want to risk even touching it, given what he knew about Belthandros and poison.

"Wow, nice sword, very shiny, very you," he said, because maybe he could buy himself a little time, and because he had the drunken feeling of having been hit on the head. Belthandros had challenged the God-Empress for the city, and he had won. And Tal was still just Tal, still exactly the same person he'd always been, still nothing special.

Belthandros hissed something in a language Tal did not understand, though the sentiment was perfectly clear. *How dare someone like you challenge someone like me?*

Tal shrugged and grinned, finding that his stock of smart remarks had run abruptly dry. He had nothing to fight with and everyone else was down, and he was only himself, and Belthandros was a *god*—

Something skimmed across the ground and bashed into his ankle. Without taking his eye off Belthandros, who was beginning to circle him, he leant down and picked it up. It was a sword of glass—or at least, it looked like glass, but it was as strong and as light as steel—and Tal felt the weight of it settle into his hand as if it was meant to be there. Sprawled exhausted across her fallen statue, the Dragon of Qarsazh gave him a little wave.

Belthandros swooped in with his shining blade, and Tal stepped to one side, not even needing to parry the blow.

Tal discovered a few things quite quickly.

Whatever Belthandros was now, he had no magic, and he was no faster than an ordinary man. He was no stronger, either, and his sword was heavy, and he was tired. And in addition to all that, without the goddess to back him up, he had absolutely no idea how to fight. For all his menacing looks, for Tal it was like fighting a clerk who kept trying to swat him with a broom.

"So can you *die,* now?" said Tal, fending him off. Keeping him at arm's length was almost embarrassingly easy. The thing was that for all his exhaustion, for all his despair, Tal was fucking great with the sword.

Belthandros growled at him again in that unfamiliar language and made a clumsy strike. Tal had only really been waiting for his moment. With two sharp twists of the glass sword, he disarmed him. Belthandros' sword hit the ground with the predictable clang of steel hitting stone, and the blade broke in two.

Before Belthandros quite realised what had happened, Tal had tripped him on his face.

Tal prodded him in the shoulder with his toe until he turned over, and rested the point of the glass sword at his throat. Belthandros was breathing hard, though his face was blank with the shock of defeat.

"*Can* you die, now?" said Tal.

Another bitten-off remark. Tal thought it probably meant *Why don't you find out?*

Tal shrugged. "Find out for yourself. I don't care."

He turned away, giving the glass sword an idle twirl, and realised with some shock that all around him the people of Tlaanthothe were standing up in the tiers and calling out his name.

35

All Things That Are Lost

After it was all over, after the surviving citizens of Tlaanthothe had shambled down from the galleries, after everyone was assured that there would be no execution today, Shuthmili circled the Citadel alone, on dark wings. She had pulled Csorwe alive from the void, she knew that much, but in the noise and panic of the aftermath, she had vanished.

In the depths of the Citadel she spotted a certain courtyard garden, submerged in shadow by the eight floors of defunct balcony which loomed above it. The plants in the vases had long since withered away, and the flagstones and gravel paths were still and dusty with lack of use.

Sitting on a stone bench under a tree was a still figure with thick black hair and freckled grey arms.

Shuthmili landed on the gravel, planning to say something clever and effective, but found that before she could get out a single word, she had fallen to her knees.

"Forgive me," she said, beyond all hope.

"All right," said Csorwe, in mild surprise.

Shuthmili burst into tears.

Shuthmili had not allowed herself to imagine what it might be like to be in her arms again. She had known it couldn't happen, so why torture herself? But if she had pictured anything, she would not have imagined lying in Csorwe's lap in a desolate flower bed, weeping uncontrollably, with her wet and bloodshot face pressed to Csorwe's thigh as she sobbed like a child.

After a while she sniffed and looked up. Csorwe was stroking her hair with hands that seemed as solid and real as anything. Shuthmili took one of them and kissed her fingertips and found nothing to suggest this was a trick.

Some time later, the two of them were sitting together on the stone bench, Shuthmili had managed to stop crying. Her eyes ached and her face felt swollen and the entire interior of her skull seemed to have been washed clean and empty. It was hard even to look at Csorwe without wanting to press her face against her and hide. Shuthmili found herself looking at her sideways, through her hair. She realised with some exasperation that she was shy.

"I thought you might have gone," said Shuthmili. "Off into the desert somewhere."

"I was going to go once it was all over," said Csorwe with a kind of stiff nervousness that made Shuthmili want to giggle or possibly to start weeping again. "I've had enough of bad bargains. Seeing you, and it not being you, that was worse than never seeing you at all. Also, Zinandour was very, uh, charismatic, but I was pretty sure she was going to lock me in a tower. So I was going to take off once everything quietened down here."

"You changed your mind?"

Csorwe had the decency to look a little embarrassed.

"I thought . . . you kept trying for fifteen years. Maybe I shouldn't give up right away. And then I thought . . . well, why *should* I have to live without you?"

"Oh, my god, Csorwe, it's been so long," said Shuthmili, the weight of it only just hitting her, all fifteen years like individual blows to the rib cage. "It's been so long, and I never thought I'd see you again, and—aren't you still furious with me? About it all?"

Csorwe shrugged. "I guess I was for a bit. But hey, we're both here and you're alive and looking at me like that, so I don't think there's much point staying angry." She put her hand over Shuthmili's, as warm as it had ever been, the skin roughened by hard work. "I would've wanted you to live for yourself. You know how I feel about sacrifice."

Shuthmili nodded, ashamed of herself, but at least it was a clean shame. She had the opportunity to do better.

"Anyway, it's not like I'm not glad to be back," said Csorwe, squeezing her hand. "And now it's done. Nobody has to sacrifice themselves at all. We win."

"So . . . you're not bothered by all this." Shuthmili waved at her torso, indicating the overlapping plates of exoskeleton which lapped around her.

"Not really," said Csorwe. "It's actually sort of . . ." She trailed off and grinned, her eyes bright with a kind of guileless slyness Shuthmili had missed very desperately.

"Not just the armour, you creep," said Shuthmili. "I'm not what I was. I am Zinandour still."

Divinity was at the heart of her being now, still and dark and unruffled, like a waveless lake.

"Hey, you've always been a goddess to me," said Csorwe, her grin becoming gruesome, then fading. "No. I know. I don't really know what it means. But . . . I think I want to learn. I'd like to try again." She thought for a moment. "Also, if you're Zinandour, it makes it a lot less awkward that I kissed her. You. Her."

"Oh, don't, I was *dying* for you to," said Shuthmili, who remembered the kiss from several angles. "You have no idea—"

At this point Csorwe leant in and kissed her, softly, and whatever she had been about to say went from her mind altogether.

They kissed for a long time, a single point of warmth in the dead and chilly courtyard, and then Csorwe drew back, with such a tortured look of anxiety on her face that Shuthmili worried she had done something wrong.

"There is one thing," said Csorwe. Shuthmili had been easing herself so gradually toward the idea that this might really be real, that it might all be all right in the end after all, that this hit her like a block of ice from a great height.

"Tell me," she said.

"I mean—I'm mortal, still, after all of this. I don't know how old I am now, but I'm going to keep getting older."

"I think we're both about forty," said Shuthmili, although the ungauntleted hand on her lap looked as featureless and waxy as that of a dead child. "Oh, Csorwe, as if I mind—"

"No, it's not just that," said Csorwe. "I'll die one day. Not for a long time, I hope. But it'll happen, and you'll still be immortal, and—and can you live with that?"

"Yes," said Shuthmili, but once again she remembered Belthandros saying *you will lose and lose and lose,* and it must have shown in her face, because Csorwe did not look convinced.

"Can you?" said Csorwe. "I've been pretty reconciled since I was about ten, but will you be all right with it? You'll go on and live?"

"My love," she said. "I hate it. I can't stand it. But what else can I do? To love is to live a mortal life, I think, knowing that things can't be kept or fixed. Knowing that you're always already in the shadow. I know that now, and I will know it forever. But if you think that it's enough to make me doubt, for a second, if you think I wouldn't rather have the time with you—what else would I *do*, Csorwe, send you away? Dear god, if you'll still have me after all of this, I'd have to be a bigger fool than I knew." She came up short, wondering if after all this hadn't somehow been Csorwe's way of letting her down gently. "I mean—will you? Still have me?"

Csorwe closed her eyes and smiled, a sweet and quiet smile which was all that Shuthmili had imagined in the worst times of the past fifteen years. "I will," she said.

Shuthmili let out a ragged breath. "After all that I've done, I can't really think I deserve this," she said. She had meant it as a joke, of sorts, but the ripple of uneasiness in her voice was obvious even to her. "It seems so unfair. That I should get what I want."

"Why? Do you regret it?" said Csorwe. She leant back, looking up at the sky, and put an arm round her shoulders. "Trying to get me back?"

Shuthmili leant against her. Her hair smelled like earth after rain. "Not really," she said. Despite it all. Not now they were here, together.

"Ah, my girl, you see," said Csorwe. "If there ever comes a day when anyone gets what they deserve . . . then I would still get you, and you would still get me."

It had all been over so quickly, in the end, that the *Blessed Awakening* had never left the city, and now all its passengers were back in the Citadel. There were a few surviving Followers of the Unspoken Name among them, and Tal was amused by the spectacle of his mother entertaining three priestesses of the Unspoken, all nibbling dry crackers in an abandoned tea salon. The priestesses combed and braided Tsereg's hair and quizzed them about their exploits in a way that they clearly found embarrassing and gratifying in equal parts.

The days went on. It was, as Tal had reflected before, strange that this always happened. Everyone needed food and a place to sleep, and it turned out it was now his job to make sure they got them. Sometimes he saw Csorwe and Shuthmili hiding out in some dark corner, sharing rations and talking softly. He didn't get a chance to talk to Csorwe alone until some days later.

"Weird to be back," he said.

"Yup," said Csorwe, coming to lean on the balustrade beside him. They were on the balcony of a white tower, looking out over the grand ruins of Tlaanthothe.

In the square below, Tal's staff were putting up bunting. Having staff had come as a shock to him, and he still had his doubts about the party, but perhaps they had the right idea. Over the past few days, a few other survivors had begun to filter out, learning that Sethennai's power was broken and the snakes were gone, and all of them seemed to be in need of a good meal.

"Nice job, Chancellor Charossa."

"I'm not the bloody Chancellor," said Tal, grinning.

"I bet your mum's really stoked," said Csorwe.

"Fuck off," said Tal. "It's so stupid. The duelling thing, I mean, as if you really want a Chancellor who's only good at fighting. As soon as everything gets sorted out, there'll be someone better to do it. I don't want it. I don't want to be like—anyway, there are ships coming back from Grey Hook, at least, when everyone's back they'll pick someone else. And we'll have something to eat other than fucking raisins, I hope."

"Uh-huh," said Csorwe.

"In the meantime I have to figure out what to do with all the snakes, though. Fun. Lots of people want them all dead."

The Thousand Eyes had surrendered and given up their swords as soon as they understood what had happened to Cherenthisse and their goddess. Tal had seen them, standing around in the empty ballroom which had been designated as a holding cell, looking at nothing. There was a bleak, dreary hopelessness to them all that he found uncomfortably familiar.

"Can't say I really want to kick things off by executing a bunch of people," he said. "The snakes say they want to go back to Saar-in-Tachthyr, to restore the place."

Csorwe shrugged. "What do you think?"

"I don't know. I've really spent my life trying not to think about this shit. My mother thinks they're planning something," said Tal. "Someone usually is. I'd rather let them go and plan something a long way away than keep them in the palace. Anyway, I'm not going to kill them. Feel kind of sorry for them. And Cherenthisse . . . We couldn't have done this without her, in the end."

"Is it going to be weird, staying here?"

The sun was setting on the distant horizon, glazing the city's impossible crenellations with a light so brilliantly pink-and-gold it looked like something you could eat.

"In Sethennai's city?" said Tal. "Sure. But you know. We're going to do a better job than he did, so he can go to hell."

"How did it happen, in the end?"

"Easier than I thought," said Tal.

"Where is he now?" said Csorwe.

"Gone," said Tal. At some point during the chaos of the first day, before anyone had managed to get him safely locked away, the man who had been Belthandros Sethennai had vanished. Tal was trying not to think about it more than necessary. Sethennai had lost his patron. Without magic, there was nothing he could do. He was just an old man who would eventually die. "Probably should have killed the fucker, but I felt kind of sorry for him in the end too," he added.

The door opened and one of the guards showed in Tal's mother, who had somehow preserved full court dress through the whole of Belthandros' final disastrous reign.

"Tal, there you are," she said. "I wanted to tell you—"

"*Look what a mess you've made?*" said Tal. "Or is it *you should have let your brother have a go?*" Even a *well done, Talasseres,* would have left a sour taste in his mouth, somehow.

"No," said Niranthe. "I wanted to tell you—well, I'm sorry."

Her lips thinned, her ears twitched, and she put her arms round him. Tal didn't remember the last time this had happened. Her head only came up to his collarbone.

"Yeah, I'm sorry too," said Tal. It didn't really cover it—the collective personal failings of the Charossa family had been Tlaanthothe's major export for years—but it felt surprisingly good.

She let him go and they broke apart with obvious relief on both sides.

"Also, I have been the Citadel's chief administrator for some time now," she added, "so I am here to help, and so is Niranthos. There is a lot of work to be done."

Tal couldn't quite bear to tell his mother that he planned to abdicate as soon as he possibly could.

"Oh, good," he said instead. "Meetings of the Logistics Committee. Can't wait."

Niranthe left, and almost at once another door was thrown open in the room behind them. Tsereg swirled inside, dressed for the party in the worst thing they'd been able to find, a pink and green footman's uniform that had been lurking in a cupboard. They wore a wreath of white roses on their head, which had slipped to one side and shed a few petals into their hair.

"Tal, if someone finds some fireworks, are they allowed to let them off?" they said.

"*Someone?*" said Tal. "Er—I don't think so." The people of Ringtown and the Citadel had been terrified for years; it didn't seem like a good idea. "Are your priestesses coming to the party?" he added, knowing that the only way to head off a long debate was to distract them.

"I've just been talking to the new Prioress," said Tsereg, beaming. "She came all the way here to see me."

"And?"

"I appeared to her in my full aspect and was like, thanks very much, but I've had plenty of Chosen Brides at this point and don't need any more, so please to fucking stop with that."

In the corner, Csorwe gave a snort of laughter and then covered her mouth with her hands. Tsereg winked at her.

"Oh," said Tal. "Good. What's your full aspect?"

"It's amazing, you'd love it," said Tsereg, leaning back against the balustrade with their hands in the pockets of the hideous footman's coat. "I think she was very impressed. And then I said, 'Did you know that almost the whole of the House of Silence library is in the archive here?' and she basically swooned, and I was all, 'Why don't you take it all home and make the old place new again?' and she swooned some more, and I think they'll do it. It's what my mother would have wanted, don't you think? And Prioress Cweren?"

Tal tried to say something. Csorwe was still doubled over the balustrade trying not to laugh.

"But to cut a long story short, they *are* coming to the party," said Tsereg. They grinned at him and swirled out again, and Tal thought that it was strange it had taken him so long in life to figure out what it was like to love another person, and how different it was than what he'd imagined.

"They're great, actually," said Csorwe.

"Yeah, they're a treasure," said Tal.

The party was not recalled as one of history's greatest. They were tired, and the years of terror were hard to shake off, but the light in the square was the only light in all the desert that night.

In the deep wilds of the north, there is a Shrine cut into the mountainside.

Deep within the sacred mountain, surrounded by the saints and heroes of whom she is the last and greatest, Oranna rests, and sees all things.

She sees the Pearl of Oblivion, as it has ever been.

It hangs above its distant sea, perpetually catching the shell-pink light of dawn. The mistress of that place is a gaunt creature who casts a winged shadow on the water, but there is also a mortal woman who tends the garden terraces.

These days the Dragon of Qarsazh seems to spend a great deal of time in the garden herself. As Oranna well knows, the gods are ageless, not changeless, and in general they do what they want.

The passing years have salted Csorwe's hair with strands of white. Today she is picking strawberries, a basket of them propped against her hip.

"Stop feeding them to me, or we won't have enough for the others," says Shuthmili.

Csorwe is momentarily silenced by the indescribable vision of Shuthmili in full divine aspect, holding a strawberry between two talons, looking suspicious of it. She gestures wordlessly at the strawberry patch, which extends down several terraces, every one of them carpeted with red fruit and white flowers. Shuthmili smiles.

"I'm only giving you the really good ones," said Csorwe. "Tal doesn't deserve them."

Oranna sees the temple at Saar-in-Tachthyr, where the Thousand Eyes have built a monument of white marble at the centre of the great atrium, without statue or ornament, only an epitaph that reads *Cherenthisse—First in Honour.*

She sees the black sand of the Speechless Sea, the ruins of the Citadel, and among them the city of Tlaanthothe born again, like a flowering aloe. Six years after its liberation, there is water flowing in the fountains again, and students chattering in the squares like jackdaws, and in the resurrected Chancellor's Palace, Talasseres Charossa peers at himself in the hallway mirror, pulling at the lines on his brow with a fingertip.

In theory, these days, the Chancellor is a purely ceremonial figure, whose job is to stand around at public festivals and look important. In practice, as usual, things don't go Tal's way. As well as his crow's feet he also has the newspapers to think about, and what the new parliament will think about his mother's latest proposal on public education, and whether he can really afford to take the day off, and whether the new housekeeper will remember to feed the cats, and what exactly Marteleos Kathoira meant about having tea together sometime.

"Yeah, you look ancient. One foot in the grave," says Tsereg, elbowing past him toward the front door. They are not much taller, but much broader and stronger, with both tusks gleaming like sickles. They wear a gold ring in their nose, their hair is tied back with a scarf of yellow silk, and they look like a healthy gorse tree.

If Oranna still had a heart, it might have tightened in her chest. As it is, she glances away for a moment, as though the vision is too vivid to tolerate. The darkness of the Shrine laps around her, eternally forgiving.

"Not too late to write you out of my will before I peg out," says Tal.

"Get a grip, Tal, you're, what, *sixty*, max."

"I'm forty-six!"

"Whatever, I'm a million years old and you're making us late for dinner," says Tsereg.

Oranna sees what has become of the ruin below the Shrine. After six years the House of Silence is not even a quarter of the way toward being rebuilt. The old tower is wrapped in scaffolding. The little priestesses have a long road ahead of them, and whatever they make will be nothing like the original. This, she thinks, is for the best.

"I don't think *tea* is especially ambiguous," says Shuthmili.

"People want to have tea with me all the time," says Tal drearily.

"Keep it to yourself," says Csorwe.

The room is warm with candlelight and the glow of several bottles of wine. Tsereg is half asleep at the table with their head propped on their elbow and a plate of discarded strawberry leaves before them.

"You should have a holiday. Maybe here," says Csorwe. "Nobody else knows where it is. Bring Martenos."

"*Marteleos,* and I told you it's nothing, he just wants to harass me about library funding."

"Fine, come on your own," she says. "Swimming's good."

"Yeah, thanks but no thanks, not with you two making big eyes at each other all the time."

The fact is that he does not want to intrude on their happiness. More to the point, he loves Tlaanthothe, whatever its demands. He never thought he'd be the kind of person who could get excited about a new water filtration system. The worst thing is that his family is so proud of him.

"Actually," says Shuthmili, and she catches Csorwe's eye in the exact way he meant. "If you did want to take a holiday sometime, the Pearl would be free for you—"

"You're leaving?" says Tal.

"For a bit," says Csorwe. "Lots to see. The Maze is a big place. We never finished travelling."

"What, you're going for good?" The idea of them being gone is jarring, as though he had imagined they would be there forever.

"Nothing's for good. We'll be back."

Oranna sees an old man walking some distant road, with a staff in one hand and a pack on his back. His beard is longer, and the hem of his patched coat flutters in the wind. She wonders for a moment, and thinks, *Well, let him go.*

Oranna knows all the seasons that slip past, and all that are yet to come, and that none can last forever. What is saved is saved only for a moment. All voices sound in silence, but before the echoes die away, their sound is sweet.

Acknowledgments

This book is dedicated to two of my younger siblings, either one of whom could overthrow a snake tyrant without my help.

Also, with enormous thanks to:

Mum, Dad, Katie, Toby, and the rest of my family, for taking me reasonably seriously even when it became clear I was *not* going to get over the wizard thing.

Kurestin Armada, my agent, a champion in every sense of the word.

Lindsey Hall, my editor, who wrangled a lot of snakes, both literal and metaphorical.

The whole team on both sides of the Atlantic—Rachel Bass, Oliver Dougherty, Desirae Friesen, Stephen Haskins, Rebecca Lloyd, Christopher Morgan, Jamie-Lee Nardone, Bella Pagan, Georgia Summers, and many more—especially Avita Jay for her outstanding work on the audiobook.

Ariella Bouskila, Sophia Kalman, Everina Maxwell, Megan Stannard, and Emily Tesh: as you know, it's impossible to write a book without complaining for months to all your friends about it, so there was no chance this one would have got done without you all.

Taz Muir and Matt Hosty, lockdown stalwarts.

The Armada Slack and all who sail in her.

And Maz, who is (in fact) the greatest magician of the age.